①

9-9,   12-29
9-15   1-10
9-21   1-19
10-12   1-28
10-19   2-2
10-30   2-8
11-8   2-24
11-15   3-1
12-3
12-10
12-29

Getting
Away with It

Getting Away with It

LESLIE GLASS

DOUBLEDAY & COMPANY, INC.
GARDEN CITY, NEW YORK 1976

All of the characters in this book
are fictitious, and any resemblance
to actual persons, living or dead,
is purely coincidental.

Library of Congress Cataloging in Publication Data

Glass, Leslie.
    Getting away with it.

    I. Title.
PZ4.G5522Ge [PS3557.L34] 813'.5'4
ISBN: 0-385-12113-x
Library of Congress Catalog Card Number 76-2774

For Edmund

Acknowledgments

I would like to thank all the fine people at Doubleday for their good work on my behalf and especially: Janice Friedman for all the details and for letting me have my way with the spelling of "good-bye"; Carolyn Blakemore for her encouragement and good sense; and most of all my editor, Lisa Drew, who did all the things an editor should do and none of the things an editor shouldn't.

LG

CHAPTER 1

Every once in a while there is a day so sparkling and wholesome in New York that the city seems to have a glory unmatched anywhere else in the world. It is not that the city is colorless on all other days, but during those rare times when the air is really clean and the sky so sharply blue it seems unreal, the richness of the city is suddenly apparent everywhere. Days like that get written up in the *Times* as though they were planned events. All the six o'clock news programs devote precious chunks of time to showing people biking to work, walking around outside, eating outside, holding hands outside and, when possible, kissing outside. All of them, of course, smiling. It is one of the truest indications of what New York is like that a day on which people smile is news. The news is that New York is safe, clean, and above all beautiful. Like much of the news offered, only the smallest part is true. The rest is pure hype, as pure as advertising and promotion, for most of the media these days are very little more. Each magazine, paper, or news program just has something a little different to sell.

Wholesome America is the one thing that can't be sold any more (except on truly exceptional days). After the unwholesome events of the last dozen or so years, no one is buying. That's why, of course, magazines like *Inside Track* made such a hit every week in grocery stores and on newsstands all over the country. The editors, who all got started at cheerful upbeat publications that no longer exist, knew they could report now only those things that shocked, pleased, or horrified. The trick was to generate both hope and despair in each issue. Americans aren't so dumb any more and won't be taken in by anything average, middle, simple, or merely pleasant. Truth comes only in extremes these days, and if there is a good day it can't be just a good day, it has to hold all

1

the promise of a new world to come, as bad days—like the day the CIA admitted it had plans to blow up all of Russia—must always forecast the absolute End. New movie stars must be the most talented ever seen, new singers the most something ever heard. A bathing suit story could only be told if the bathing suits shown were the smallest ever made. And any story on any creative person had to be accompanied by several pages on how that person made more money with that talent, product, or job than any other person in history.

Inside Track, the most successful magazine produced in magazine city, read like the *Guinness Book of World Records*. There was hardly a city or small town in the country that didn't have the magazine somewhere. It was read and talked about, and the maker and breaker of countless careers. Yet the magazine had its quarters not in a towering giant of a building on one of the fancy stretches of Third, Park, or Sixth avenues, but rather in a crummy five-story building between Fifth and Sixth avenues in the forties. The magazine was on the third and fourth floors. Below them was a milliner and a coffee shop. Above them a gym. It was not a prestige section of town, or a building with even the minimum of creature comforts. There was rarely very much heat or air conditioning, and even the elevator worked only intermittently. But on the beautiful days when the whole city seemed like a shining jewel, those who created the influential, widely read *Inside Track* magazine felt that they were on the spot closer to heaven than any other on earth. Such is the effect of promotion on the promoters themselves.

After a rainy weekend followed by two steamy days of fog, it was the last day of May and one of those crystalline days that cause New Yorkers, in a fit of exuberance, to buy things they ordinarily never would buy; go to restaurants for lunch far more expensive than their expense accounts allow; and plan elaborate summer activities they can't afford. It was the kind of day that made people even more aware of what other people were wearing, of the glamor of Madison Avenue. The day itself seemed to call for money, made the ever present sunshine on glossy pages of magazines appear true and available for sale along with clothes, beauty, and furnishings for the home.

Usually a day like that made Barrett Martin, the executive editor of *Inside Track* magazine, call for an emergency editorial meeting to plan special issues in which New York could be sold— a photographer would be sent out to take pictures of roof gardens, restaurants suitable for secret trysts, people kissing (for an issue called "Kissing Is Not Dead"), jewels seen at lunch, clothes to show you're alive, furniture capable of running your life. Don't make the mistake of thinking Barrett was illiterate, he knew that kissing was never alive nor furniture capable of running. The point was to catch one's eye at the newsstand.

It was Barrett's habit to point out such a day to his wife Sidney as though the insight were his alone. He believed that there were days on which things could be done that could never happen on ordinary days, and he pointed out the good ones so Sidney could accomplish accordingly. Sidney wrote a column for *IT*; Barrett said without bias that it was the best in the magazine and Garth Carter, the editor/publisher, along with much of the public agreed.

On this particular morning, however, Barrett was not speaking to Sidney and because of this he didn't at first notice the morning. He went through his morning ritual of sitting at the dining-room table, eating one tiny, very fresh croissant crumb by crumb along with coffee as bitter as it could be made, while reading the *Times*. He did not look up, for looking up where the window was would necessarily require acknowledging Sidney, and he wanted to leave without saying one word to her. He would have to admit this to Terry later on and it would cause him some pain to do so; but as he was sitting there with a chilled expression on his face and when he left without saying good-bye, he thought his behavior was perfectly fitting, given the situation.

Since Barrett had taught Sidney how to write, think, act, and dress, he felt she should do as he thought best in all the remaining areas as well. They had been arguing all weekend and when Sidney hadn't given in by Monday morning he decided to treat her with silence until she changed her mind. Monday and Tuesday they had hardly exchanged a word and now it was Wednesday. Barrett felt he couldn't give in even though it was Wednesday, especially since he knew how upset she was. She was fiddling with the silver, muttering to herself, and not eating anything. He

3

could feel her uncertainty as surely as he could feel his own conviction.

In spite of his conviction, however, Barrett left the apartment slightly unnerved. It was not like Sidney to wait so long before breaking down and begging his forgiveness. It was Wesnesday. He always took her manuscript with him on Wednesday. It was one of the last columns to be processed and if he didn't have it set by three there would be a hole in the magazine.

Once out on the street, though, Barrett was no longer worried. What a fantastic day it was, he thought. Why had he worn such a shabby suit. What a splendid day. He walked down Third Avenue thinking how beautiful the day was, how beautiful his city was, and how stupid Sidney was for fighting with him over something as petty as money. He turned once and looked back at their building. They lived on the twenty-first floor of the Phoenix. So pleased was he at the sight of his building, the only one to tower over the avenue for miles downtown (thus catching sunlight no matter what time of day), and the freshness of the air, that he was certain Sidney would present herself manuscript in hand in no more than an hour's time. He knew her that well.

And he was right about one thing. The day before Sidney had thrown herself into her work to avoid making a decision. She had finished the column and was even satisfied with it for once. It was a particularly scathing life-style story on a dress designer (a four-time winner of the "coveted Coty Award") whose clothes and life style she loathed. His clothes were designed for an anomaly, not the female figure as it most often occurred. They were for an undeveloped woman of five foot fourteen, in other words a drag queen; and he billed himself as one of the five most organized people in New York. "It's how I get things *done*, sweetie." Sidney was five foot three and not overly developed herself. The story was sitting in her top drawer and she had meant to give it to Barrett as he left.

As she sat at the table watching him at breakfast, however, she decided not to give him the story to see what he would do. She had, without seeing him, known that his chin stuck out farther than usual, that his eyes were narrowed, and the edges of his mouth twitched every few minutes the way old women's do ceaselessly without their being aware of it. It was a sign of tension

4

and fury ill contained; and when it happened at the office, people ran out for small presents with which to appease him. Barrett's rage when it surfaced was a terrible thing to experience. Even the smallest sign of his disapproval was enough to make people want to rend their flesh. He had assimilated the technique of making people feel unworthy of life from his mentor and boss, Garth Carter, without even knowing it and now, as with Garth, it was part of him.

Sidney had not counted on his leaving without the story. With that move he had made the issue a matter of her responsibility. He had left without the story. Now she was faced with the problem of getting it to him. One could never get around Barrett; once more Sidney felt her own foolishness for trying. In every question that had faced them in the eight years of their marriage, Barrett's point of view had won over hers. And each time he made her back down she felt like a gnome, small and witless. It was as though he had to make himself superior to her in every way; he wouldn't even accept her commas and periods. He was always putting dashes in her stories (dashes denote wit and immediacy, Barrett thought) and starting sentences with the word "plus."

She sat on at the table for a few minutes listing old grievances and regarding the crumbs left over from his croissant. He must have been upset, she thought, since he left so many crumbs littering his place. Then she got up. After eight years of holding out on him, she was going to have to give him the money. She knew that now.

Sometimes when she was very angry at Barrett, Sidney imagined him dying on the way to work. Occasionally he had a heart attack and though a crowd gathered no one called for an ambulance until it was too late. But usually he was hit by a bus or taxi. Sidney sat at her desk on those mornings—or those evenings when he went out with their best friend Terry Hammer and left her home to work—and pictured herself cleaning his possessions out of the apartment. By the time she got halfway through his clothes she generally regretted his death. Now, as she got dressed, Sidney saw herself arriving at the office in time to find Barrett's dead body still at his desk. Every part of her rebelled at the idea of giving him the money. For eight years she had struggled to be a writer, to make money for Barrett so he wouldn't need her in-

heritance. She made eight hundred dollars a week for her column
—twice that if she wrote something else. She had published two
books in the last four years. The first earned them thirty thousand
dollars and the second more than twice that and there was still
the paperback sale on the second book to be made. They had
done all the right things, been seen at the right places, gone to
the right parties, given the right parties. They had even rented,
and finally bought the summer before, a house on Martha's Vineyard so they could have weekend guests. Barrett wouldn't pay for
the house outright even though they could have because all his
life he had wanted a mortgage. Now he wanted a magazine of his
own.

Sidney went through her wardrobe looking for something appropriate to wear for giving away fifty thousand dollars. That, Barrett told her, was the amount he needed to make the first payment. She had a lot of clothes, several choices for every
conceivable weather and social eventuality. It looked sunny outside for once, probably about sixty-five. Sidney chose a rust-
colored jersey dress with long sleeves and a turban to match. She
also wore three yards of gold chains that Barrett had bought, she
was almost certain, with one of her own pay checks. Since she
never saw them, it was difficult to know exactly where they went.
She stuffed the manuscript into a handbag too small for it and
left the apartment about forty-five minutes after Barrett.

But she didn't head for the magazine right away. She was
struck by the extraordinary brilliance of the day. And as it was
doing to people all over the city, the day cheered Sidney up. She
would have a walk, look in a few windows, breathe a little air, and
then give away fifty thousand dollars. She walked over to Lexing-
ton Avenue and then across Fifty-seventh Street. She pretended
that she wasn't going anywhere special, but it was a walk she had
taken often that spring. She stopped and looked in at the Cour-
règes Boutique to see if the spring coats had gone down from
$595 yet. They hadn't. She looked in the window at David Webb,
then crossed the street to look in at Tiffany, at Bonwit Teller.
Not even the Via Condotti or the Rue St. Honoré was a better
walk than this, she thought as she did each time she took the
walk. She crossed Fifth Avenue to see what Bergdorf Goodman
had to sell, then crossed Fifty-seventh Street again for the win-

dows at Henri Bendel. Slowly she walked down to the corner where I. Miller was and looked at shoes, pretending even then that Doubleday next door was not where she had been heading all along.

Finally she was in front of Doubleday and there it was, still in the window, her second book, called (though not by her) *Portraits II*. She wasn't fond of the title, or cover I. Cover I, the front, had what appeared to be a stack of glossy photographs spilling out of a portfolio, revealing parts of famous faces. It looked as if they were tumbling to the ground or being otherwise disposed of. A very tacky visual, Sidney thought for the fortieth time. The type face was all too similar to that used in the logo of *Inside Track*. Cover IV, the back, which was also displayed in Doubleday's window, showed Sidney sitting alone at a table set for two at the Palm Court. Her hair had been done and her face made up by an expert just for this picture and she was wearing a copy of a Chanel suit and earrings borrowed from Van Cleef & Arpels. Sidney looked surprised in the photograph, as though the photographer had caught her off guard. In fact they had worked for hours to make her look natural and at ease in the setting. It was all Barrett's idea of how a columnist should look, and in fact revealed more about him than about columnists. Sidney had wanted a small picture (or preferably no picture at all) on the back inside flap of her sitting at her IBM wearing her real uniform, a red T-shirt with her name on it that Terry had given her and an old pair of jeans the color of wheat. She was appalled by the cover of her book and was drawn to it again and again as though it exposed something about her that she should but didn't understand. Each time she went there she stood outside of Doubleday staring first at the front cover and then at the picture of herself. Her hair had been layered then, cut short so that her somewhat narrow face looked, to her eye, too small to be that of an adult; "piquant" was the word the hairdresser used. Touching, *Vogue* called it. The color was ash because no one who did color at Elizabeth Arden believed she meant gold when she said blond. Ash was the color she already was, and it was a dead color. Lightening it just made it look deader, Sidney thought. Her eyes were brown, the lids for the picture had been painted blue with something that later did not wash off easily.

7

Sidney had several copies of the book at home, of course, and she could have spent any amount of time studying the picture there. But she never did. Only in front of Doubleday's window did she ever try to analyze what it was that upset her so much about it. Barrett said it was a fine picture and her editor, an earnest balding man called Wynn Elliot, said that no author was ever pleased with a book cover or satisfied with his or her picture. He was careful to say his or her. It was in the very nature of an author to disapprove, he said when he was sure she had noticed that he had not forgotten to add "or her." It was the sort of thing one had to be careful about, he knew, having been attacked on the point before.

In all the times that spring when the book came out and Sidney went to Doubleday to see it, no one ever recognized her. Not even when she went inside, bought another book, and casually asked how her book was doing did anyone ever recognize her. The most the booksellers had to say was that they had no complaints. She never quite knew whether that meant the sales of the book were good or that the salespeople merely had no complaints.

Sidney passed Doubleday without going in. Today, and probably forever after, it didn't matter how the book was selling. It didn't matter how the cover looked or whether she resembled her picture or not. Fourteen years before when her parents died in an automobile accident, she had put off making a decision about what to do with the money she would get from the sale of her father's small company that made costume jewelry. She wouldn't talk about it, didn't want the company sold. She told the lawyers (a group of people she would forever after consider a slimy lot) that when a person devotes a lifetime to making something, even though it's only paste diamonds and fake pearls, you don't just sell it away and make the effort stand for nothing. Her father really loved his creations, had worked hard to make them look more real every year. Sidney had spent her whole youth with her front covered with too white pearls the size of marbles. She didn't want to see that silly company go.

Afterward the lawyers explained very carefully to her and her sister Nicky that they could not just take the money away since it was now In Trust (like God). They could, however, have the income on the money. How did she want it: every three months, every six months, or once a year? Sidney told them to put it back In Trust while she thought about it. They told her there was nothing to think about since income existed to be spent. Sidney had been thinking about it for fourteen years nonetheless, because not all people react to inheritance the same way. Some people want to spend it right away to get it out of the way so there won't be any reason for guilt, on that score anyway. Some people are careful to make it last as long as possible, and sometimes a person doesn't want to touch it at all.

Sidney left Providence, settled in New York, and got a job at *Time*. She did not feel poor enough to require an income. Then she felt that her income was not large enough to change her life in any big way. And then when she married Barrett she decided to keep it for her child. But basically she simply didn't want to touch it. They had just disappeared one day, had been smashed to nothing in one instant. Within the next two months the house was sold, the company was sold; and without the solid things, she had no faith in her memory. Aside from the box of photographs, report cards, old letters, diamond pins and pearls, all Sidney felt she had was In Trust.

From time to time Barrett asked her what kinds of things had been in the house and why she had given everything away to Nicky. "All you kept was this rubble," he said when once a year he oversaw the cleaning of the closets. He kicked at the box and suggested she leave it out. Barrett also tried to explain to her that what had started at just over five thousand dollars a year was now much more since the interest had compounded every year. Barrett always had much more interest in her trust than she felt he should; but when she told him that he became very angry. He said she didn't have confidence in him and told her she wouldn't ever have a child anyway. "It'll all be wasted in the end." One thing Barrett couldn't stand was wasted money.

Sidney walked downtown on Fifth Avenue. She had to get to the magazine within the hour, but she was not in the mood to hurry. The sun was on the other side of the street; she crossed over. A really swell day it was. Soon the photographers would be out to record it. Barrett had really made it clear to her for the first time that weekend. No, he had said it before. It was only this weekend that it became clear. It was the money or him. After all

9

those years of fighting about it, Sidney felt it was no longer just the money, it was the principle of the thing. She swung her handbag as she walked. It was a Gucci. She passed Gucci without looking in the window. She asked herself what the money mattered anyway. It wasn't even all that much money. If they lost it she could make it back again in a few years. She even wondered why she had fought so hard to hang onto it. Just money. Just because her father had said over and over never to let any man, especially any husband, manage her money didn't make it right. They couldn't all squander money on cars and failing businesses. Anyway Barrett said it wasn't a failing business. It was a respected magazine. Not failing. As she thought about it Sidney was almost relieved that they wouldn't have to fight about it any more. Yet it irked her that her columns would appear in a magazine printed on newsprint, not the shiny pages *IT* used.

A hundred times her father told her. A hundred times a lifetime ago. Yet he had been right in a way. Her columns would appear on newsprint just because of Barrett's whim. She didn't want her columns on newsprint in a magazine that looked no more classy than *Screw*. Why did Barrett's whims always have to win out. Hell, Barrett was a bastard. On a day like this you could really see it.

Sidney swung her handbag, it pulled her around. She kept turning with it until she was facing the direction of home. Right at that minute Barrett was washing his face in preparation for her arrival at the magazine. In her head she was packing her suitcase. It wasn't fear of Barrett that made her decide to leave town; it just seemed the safest thing to do. If she stayed and told him her decision, he would just begin to harass her all over again. When she got home she called for a messenger to deliver the manuscript and included a note. When Barrett got it, he read it over and over all afternoon, then destroyed it before Terry could see it.

CHAPTER 2

Terry Hammer moved around the city that day quite unmoved by the weather. He had to go to California again the next day about that pipe deal, and there were a lot of things he had to finish up before he could leave. So far he had been out there about this deal twice, and the thought of having to go again dejected him. One of his clients, an actor who now had more money than was good for him, had gotten visions of a gold-plated Alaska pipeline so firmly embedded in his greedy mind that he simply would not be content without participating in it. Terry was a lawyer for actors and writers. He looked after their contracts, made sure that the government never got more than its fair share of their earnings, and helped them find good homes for their money. He started corporations, negotiated the acquisition of small profitable companies, and traveled back and forth to California a lot.

One of his finders had found him this pipe company. It was small, California based, and had a few contracts to supply a certain kind of fitting for a certain kind of pipe needed along about ten percent of the Alaska pipeline route. The owner of Ensko Vibro Piping Co. had decided after getting the contracts that he'd rather take the money and run. A wise decision, Terry thought. Since the company was a small one, and the weather in Alaska iffy at best, the risks were great. The present owner of Ensko Vibro was asking for a million and a half for his company. If all the terms of the pipeline contracts were met over the next five years the company would make about fifteen million dollars. The catch was that the company had to be expanded to be able to make delivery of the fittings and if the weather wasn't just right that first year they would be wiped out. All the actor could see was the zeros in the fifteen million even though Terry had inspected the plant and told him fifteen times there wasn't much there. Now Mr. Vibro wanted to close the deal in a hurry and

11

Terry had to go out there and talk to both of them one more time. The lawyers in California had already drawn up the papers; the bank loan had come though. All that was hanging them up was Terry. He wanted to make sure, really sure, that Vince wanted to risk that much of his own money for such a risky thing. Vince kept saying that it couldn't be such a bad thing if the bank was putting up twice as much as he was. Terry couldn't quite make him see that if they went under the bank would get its money back; but he wouldn't.

Terry went to several meetings that day, all the while trying to convince himself that it would all work out all right; and anyway if Vince lost his shirt it would be Vince's fault. Terry didn't believe that, though. He thought it would be his fault. Usually his clients did what Terry suggested. He had a serenity about him that seemed to border on the religious. He never got angry or displayed his disappointment at setbacks. He told people that he would just keep working until it came right, and he did. Money is always such an emotional subject. Clients found it comforting to have someone around with such a tranquil approach. Terry had a way of making them think they were only dealing with beans. Barrett called Terry "The Rock," and the name annoyed him. He knew someday he was going to make a really bad mistake. At times like this he wished he could be hysterical and yell at Vince, "You're going to be poor, poor, poor, you asshole."

Because he was out so much that day it took hours for Terry to get Barrett's message. After he saw it he felt that prickle of anger he sometimes got at having to be a nanny even to his best friend. The word came into his mind because an English actress had used it once. She had called him her best nanny, and he never forgot it. The message read, and it was the dramatic tone more than anything else that irritated him: "A disaster concerning Sidney. Meet me at home, seven." Then scrawled at the bottom as though his secretary had asked and Barrett been forced to answer, "She's still alive of course."

He spent the rest of the afternoon wondering alternately if there was anything he could do to prevent Vince from signing the papers and what disaster could possibly involve Sidney. He called the apartment several times to ask her, but she didn't seem to be at home. He did not call Barrett because, although disaster in the

12

news always means hurricanes, earthquakes, and fires, in telephone messages it meant a threat to wealth, not health. He was as certain as anyone could be that Sidney herself was fine.

He didn't know what announcement he expected to hear, but he would have rated her leaving about the most unlikely. Barrett didn't even wait until Terry was properly in the door to say it. And he didn't say it, he croaked it, "Sidney's gone."

"Oh, Christ," was Terry's first reaction, not said out loud of course. Oh, Christ, couldn't anybody make it any more. Later Terry would go back to his apartment, which was two floors below their apartment (they had both moved in when the building first opened five years before), and think about how the breakup, if permanent, would affect his own life. But right then he got down to business. It was a habit he couldn't seem to break, fixing up messes as they occurred and then later worrying about what they meant.

"Well," he said. Barrett was blocking the entrance to the living room. And because he didn't move aside to let him in, Terry said, "How about a drink?"

"Yeah, sure." Barrett went and lay down on the tufted leather sofa. "Scotch, two medium cubes, and a twist."

A twist of what, Terry was tempted to ask. Instead, while assembling Barrett's drink and his own, he asked what happened.

"She left." Barrett lay flat on his back on the sofa, his feet up on one of the arms.

"So you said."

Barrett repeated that a few more times lying in that same position that made him look as if he had been boned. He wanted to talk about her having left but not about her leaving. It made sense to him but Terry kept asking why, as though the why of it were more important than the fact of it.

"If you found a dead body would it make any difference at all why it was dead?" Barrett asked. "It's just because you want to make a value judgment about whose fault it is that you're asking why."

"Oh, Christ." This time Terry did say it out loud. He had been called to the scene of many breakups before, but this was the first time he had been attacked on arrival for asking what happened. He looked around quickly and noticed that neither the leaving person nor the left person had destroyed any of the furniture or crockery. This particular breakup looked too quiet to be a lasting one. "I don't care whose fault it is," he said. In fact he actively didn't want to know. All those intimate things people always tell when they think It's Over hang on in the memory long after the couple has gotten back together and themselves forgotten the incident. Terry had a whole file of them he wished he could forget.

"It's her fault," Barrett said.

"Well, now that we've settled that, where did she go?"

"How should I know? She sent me this note and she left." Barrett was being very snappish. Sometimes he thought Terry was a waste of his friendship. "I feel sick," he said.

"I guess it happens to everybody about a dozen times. What do you want, aspirin or Alka-Seltzer?"

"Do you think her sending over the manuscript is a good sign or a bad sign?"

"What manuscript?"

"Didn't I tell you? She didn't give me the manuscript this morning because she was sulking. But she knew she had to get it to me. So finally she sent it by messenger and the note was with it. Honestly, I don't know what to think. What do you think?"

"I still don't know what you're talking about. And I'm not sure I want to. Whatever it is, it will pass. I'd rather not have any part of it."

"But you've got to help me make her reasonable." Barrett sat up. "You really do. It's all your friend what's-it's fault for telling me about New Journal. It's your fault. You sent him to me."

"I didn't send him to you. I just mentioned your name. I know Garth is looking for new properties and I thought he might be interested. It wouldn't have hurt you any to show him the deal. I never thought you'd be crazy enough to want to buy it yourself."

"I'm not crazy," Barrett said, suddenly angry enough to strike. If Terry hadn't been so big he would have hit him. "It's a great deal, I tell you."

"I don't know whether it is or not." Terry sat first in one of the Mies van der Rohes and then the other. One was on one side of the sofa on which Barrett was once again lying, and one was on the other. He found that he was uncomfortable with both the back of Barrett's head and his feet. "Is that why Sidney left?"

"She didn't want me to buy the magazine. She doesn't trust me. She said if she stayed I'd only harass her. When have I ever been known to harass anyone? I don't know where she'd get such an idea."

"You couldn't run it anyway. It's going down the drain in a toboggan."

"I could turn it around. I know I could."

The leather sofa was hard as a park bench and slippery. Barrett kept changing his position as though it were possible to find one he could stay in. He had bought the sofa because he thought it was handsome, also because he didn't want anyone to be overly comfortable or relaxed in his presence. The only way to stay on the sofa at all was to sit absolutely still, which no one else and not even he, at this moment anyway, could do.

"Come on," Terry said. "Sidney's right. Even if everything went perfectly: if there were no typesetters' or printers' contracts coming up to be renegotiated, and if you got a new art director and the subscriptions and advertising doubled in the next two years (which would mean sending out a million flyers and hiring some decent space salesmen), *and* if you put out a hundred and two irresistible issues, you *still* wouldn't break even for three or four years and you haven't got two years' worth of losses to put into it."

"So you have been studying the deal," Barrett said. The news cheered him so much that he got up and refilled their glasses. "Would you like some nuts?" He poked around in the highly lacquered Danish modern bar that stood in the entrance hall between two trees that shed in spring and fall. "I'm sure there are some in here somewhere."

"I don't know a thing about it except that you have to be both rich and crazy to want to buy a magazine. And you're not rich. And the magazine is losing money. That's why they want to get rid of it. Forget it. Call Sidney and tell her it's safe to come home."

"I'm not going to do that."

"Why the hell not, Barrett? I don't blame Sidney. She doesn't want to risk the book money—you haven't even paid for the house . . . oh, I'm sure Sidney has said it all."

"Neither of you has any sense of adventure. You just plod,

plod, plod. That's all you ever do, making pots of money for other people. You're just slaves, that's all. Don't you know you have to go out on your own to get rich?"

"And unless you're already rich, you have to risk your life for it. Where did you say Sidney went?"

"She didn't say, but I'm sure she went to the Vineyard. She doesn't have any place else to go."

Terry dialed the number; no answer.

"For Christ's sake she just got there. It'll take her a week to figure out how to get the phone turned on. Without a phone she's lost. Hell, she'll be back tomorrow."

"What if she isn't back tomorrow?"

"Then she'll be back on Friday."

"Call her tomorrow morning, will you?" Terry said. "In fact call her tonight. If you wait till tomorrow it may make her mad."

"Hell no. She left, it's up to her to come back begging."

"Barrett, I'm telling you, even if Sidney weren't your wife, it would be the thing to do. Use your head, you don't push around your best writer like that. And since it *is* Sidney and you know she's afraid to be alone up there and probably sorry she left, the *least* you could do is call her up and let her come home gracefully."

"I can't."

"Why not?"

"It would ruin our relationship."

For the next several hours in a neighborhood restaurant and two neighborhood bars, Barrett explained to Terry that if one once gave in to a woman like Sidney there would never be peace again.

"I have to go home and get some sleep," Terry said four or five times. Twice at the Sign of the Dove, an expensive restaurant and bar across the street from their building where they never ate but often drank, he left Barrett at the bar and went to telephone Sidney on the Vineyard. He thought she might not accept a collect call from Barrett, but she would certainly talk to him. He hung up each time after about a dozen rings. He decided it was time to go home.

"Shit, Terry, do you have to go to California tomorrow? Can't you go next week instead?" Barrett's speech was a bit slurred but that was only the result of intemperance. When concerned he became twitchy and birdlike, his words came out like corks from a champagne bottle. Now he was merely whining.

"No, I can't go next week."

"I don't think she's coming back tomorrow." Barrett tried to prevent Terry from picking up the check. "How about another?"

"No."

"Please, Terry. Will you talk to her? Tell her *New Journal* is a *great* magazine. It would change our lives, really it would. There's a place for you too. You could be publisher. Would you like that, Ter? Can you see the three of us—"

"Come on, Barrett." Terry paid the check and turned to leave.

"Will you talk to her? Just tell me you'll talk to her."

"I can't talk to her, she hasn't turned on the phone."

"Will you go up there tomorrow on the way?" Barrett was following Terry, talking to his back.

"Come on, Barrett. Don't be an ass. It would take me all day. I'd have to leave from Boston. And we don't even know she's there."

"She's there. I'm sure she's there. How about on your way home, tomorrow?" They had crossed the street, gone into the building, and now Barrett was getting off the elevator at Terry's floor. In another second he would have him. He knew it. "What do you say, Terry?"

"I'm not coming home tomorrow."

"Friday then."

"I'm not asking you in, dear. I had a swell time but—"

"Oh, fuck off. That's not funny."

"I won't be back until Saturday." He still had his key in the door. "She'll probably be back by Saturday."

"Saturday then, on your way home. Leave Friday night. You can go to Boston and take the earliest flight from there."

"Shit, Barrett, you should go yourself."

"I can't. I told you—"

"All right. But only if you promise you'll forget about *New Journal*."

Barrett nodded solemnly. "Okay, I will. Just don't come back without her. She's got an interview with an albino on Monday." He slammed Terry on the back as he turned to leave and felt the

17

impact of a thousand needly prickles on his palm. A solid bastard was old Terry. Christ, it felt like he was wearing a leaded vest. Well, it all went to prove that you could take a farmer out of the country, but he'd always have the body of a hayseed. Barrett came from Brooklyn, which was the reason he gave himself for never having grown a chest. Terry was all right, though, Barrett thought. He didn't even ask who the albino was. It was the sort of thing he knew.

CHAPTER 3

Thursdays were always very bad days at the magazine. Garth usually came in at eleven and then returned after lunch. Whenever he was there the place turned into chaos anyway, but on Thursdays the magazine closed. There's always a special tension at a magazine on closing day. Everybody always goes over things one last time in the hope of catching the one terrible something wrong they didn't catch the first fifteen times.

Garth's arriving at the magazine always intensified the general fear that something was about to or had already gone wrong. He was like the general at inspection time whose business it was to find fault. At first he strode into the office like a ship in full sail. He was a stout man, not tall, with small, slightly bulging eyes, heavy eyebrows, a very thin mouth that he sucked inward when angry, and more black hair than it seemed he should have. It was the sort of hair that looked unreal, like a bad toupee. It was, however, his own, albeit dyed. He looked neither to the right nor the left as he made his way to his office, which was at the very back of the one huge floor that served as editorial department, art department, and production department. During his walk, the phones would ring but not be answered; his staff would be taking Garth in. They tried to gauge his mood by his walk, by the fixedness of his stare. The higher-ups on the masthead called out good morning. Sometimes Garth muttered good morning back and sometimes he didn't. He did not even glance at the queue of people standing outside his office waiting to see him. He knew they were outsiders because staff members never lined up until he arrived. Garth never looked at them because they were others; as far as he was concerned they lived there always, an unhappy condition like mold, that one noticed from time to time but did not bother about.

His first words were, "Where are the blues?" On those rare Mondays when he came in to see the new issue, it was, "Where the fuck is my copy?"

When the elevator was working, people arrived at the magazine in the middle of the production department. The stairs and the editorial department were in front. Editors had tiny roomlets across the front of the building and down one side in an L shape. The roomlets had no doors and the walls only went to the shoulder height of a medium-sized person. The art department was in the back, along one side. In the middle of what was technically the art department was a long table that they used for standing around when planning an issue. Under the table was the library —bookshelves with the New York Times Index, maps, dictionaries, Who's Who, books of grammar, reference books of all sorts.

Garth was the only one at the magazine with a door to call his own. His walls, though they did not go as high as the ceiling and did not serve to keep his conversations private, did close him off from public view. He was so far at the back because he liked people having to come all that way from editorial to him. Barrett's desk was right outside Garth's door. Barrett was second-in-command, or first mate as he liked to call himself. He was entitled to the best cubicle in the front, the one with the window. But he didn't want it. He wanted to be as close to Garth as possible so he wouldn't miss anything. Editorial was far too far away.

Barrett had his desk wedged in front of Garth's two secretaries. Opposite, almost in the aisle leading to Garth's door, were the desks of Muriel the copy editor and Lespedeza the number one researcher. These two people Barrett couldn't stand having there. They didn't belong there, and he had been unsuccessfully trying to move them back into editorial for the last five years. They made the flow of copy almost impossible, since everything had to go from editorial through them and back to production.

As uncomfortable as it was, Barrett liked his desk there. He was always the first one to meet Garth's needs as he did now. "Here are the blues," he said, pushing aside a free-lance writer of some reputation for whom Garth's social secretary, a beautiful girl called Anne, had made a ten o'clock appointment knowing full well Garth never arrived before eleven.

"Good morning, Garth. I think it looks very good this week. We've got—"

"I know what we've got," Garth snapped. He sat down and put his feet up on his desk, which was so cluttered with magazines, manuscripts, galleys, old mail, records, books, and reports that it was actually round. He flipped through the blues, so called because the magazine, put together as it would appear on Monday, was photographed on blue paper. There were holes, of course, where the artwork would be, and in places where the final page proofs were not ready yet. Sidney's column wasn't there, neither was the gossip page.

Garth turned the pages looking at headlines and subheads. Barrett stood at his side watching him. Garth would look at the magazine this way on Monday, too, the way he instructed his staff to look at each issue. As though they were totally disinterested possible buyers at a newsstand. The contents page wasn't there, but on Monday he would look at that first, then check the masthead for his name at the top, Editor and Publisher. Then he would look at the ads and the pictures accompanying the lead articles. Now, as he was turning the pages, something seemed to catch his eye. He turned back to the page. It was a collection of photographs lined up in two rows with a key at the bottom to indicate which caption belonged with which picture. Garth threw the magazine across his cubicle, causing the dust to rise in a cloud.

"God damn it," he yelled.

Anne tiptoed into the room. "Jim Hadley is here," she whispered. "Sorry to bother you about it."

"S'okay." Garth didn't look up. "Tell him to wait."

Anne went out without telling him that Hadley already had been waiting and had asked twice if he should go away and come back some other time.

"Who the fuck is responsible for this?" He looked at Barrett for the first time that day. He noticed that Barrett's face, which was naturally rather long and thin and woebegone, was even more indented than usual. His chin always looked larger when he was miserable, and in that state he always seemed determined and rather dogmatic.

"Don't look at me that way," Garth said.

"What way?" Barrett looked alarmed.

"Never mind what way. Who did this?"

"What, Garth?"

Garth raised his voice in fury. "You *know* we put captions under every picture. We've gone through this before, god *damn* it. A caption under every picture. We're not the *Times*. We don't make people decipher lists. How many times do I have to tell you?" Garth paused for breath. His face was distorted and looked unhealthily red.

"I don't remember any pictures without captions," Barrett said calmly, wracking his memory for a picture without a caption.

"Here, damn it." Garth discovered that he had tossed the blues behind his couch. There was an awkward moment while Barrett went to retrieve them.

"Here," he said when he had them once again in hand. Garth pointed to the page he didn't like.

"Why, that's our newest house ad," Barrett said. "The whole idea of it was the list. Don't_ you remember? Photos from our most successful articles of the year—"

"I hate it," Garth shouted. "Get Dan in here. Get Dan. Get me Sidney, too, damn it. I want to talk to her."

"Sidney? Sidney didn't have anything to do with this."

"I also want an editorial meeting at lunch. Ask Anne to get some sandwiches in. Call Sidney and tell her to come for the meeting—I want to talk to her after." Garth turned his attention to his mail folder.

"Today's *Thursday*, Garth, nobody has *time* for a meeting today."

"Pastrami, I think," Garth said. "I'm sick to death of those stuffed grape leaves Anne's always getting. Tell Anne *sandwiches*, nothing fancy."

"Sidney's not around today," Barrett said quietly. Sometimes Garth turned off so completely he seemed to have gone deaf. He hoped that Garth didn't hear him now. He added, "Do you want me to pull that ad or what? I could put in the poster competition announcement a week early."

21

"I really hate it," Garth said peevishly, looking up at Barrett once again. "When did you change the layout?"

"It looked too chunky the other way. The pictures were small, so the captions took up four lines each. It looked awful, I'm telling you, like islands."

"You didn't tell me."

"You weren't *here*, Garth."

"I call you twice a day, don't I? . . . Well, I suppose we could lay it out again."

"Sure we can, but it's already eleven-thirty; if you want a meeting I have to go tell everyone to break their lunch dates."

Garth debated for a minute. "All right," he said. He turned back to his mail folder again. When Jim Hadley appeared in front of him, he looked at him blankly. He had forgotten who he was and what he was doing there, even though it was he who had summoned him. "Sit down," he said, and, "What can I do for you?"

There was not enough space for an editorial meeting on the fourth floor. Garth believed a magazine should look like the newsroom of a newspaper. He wanted that feeling of immediacy about the place—too many desks in one place, all the phones ringing at the same time, the clutter, the noise of a lot of people doing their jobs out in the open. He liked to go from desk to desk picking things over, checking people out. But it was no place for a meeting. The meetings were held downstairs in a room with a door and walls that went to the ceiling. Downstairs all the staff below the rank of editor on the masthead could be kept out. Even Jenny, Anne's counterpart who did Garth's typing, notes, and ordered the food, was not allowed to come.

Six editors, two contributing editors, a regular writer, Anne, Garth, Barrett, and Dan the art director were there. Garth looked around. "Where's Sidney?"

"I told you," Barrett said, "she's not around today." He went over and helped himself to a sandwich from the tray. Then the others, who until then had been milling around, took their sandwiches and a chair and sat down.

"Shit," Garth said.

For a few minutes everyone sat around the very small cluttered room and chewed. There were two very old swivel chairs that Garth and Barrett always used. Everyone else sat on folding wooden chairs that were folded up and stacked against the wall when not in use. They sat around a large undistinguished table. The walls were covered with posters and artwork from old issues, and the corners were piled with those things that were neither usable nor disposable like the various papier-mâché models that had once been photographed (with people, of course) for the cover.

Garth began by telling about a party he had attended the night before. He told a story about one of the guests and then Blake and Seth, two senior editors of opposite styles and sensibilities, began to argue about what the person's true character was. Blake was a political and crime expert. He was Southern and blond and liked to tease and provoke Seth, who was an extremely sloppy, bearded, and heavily accented Jewish person from Queens, with exploded capillaries in his nose. His expertise was the scamier side of life.

Since he had not intended for them to take the attention from him, Garth suffered their quibbling with ill grace. He usually let them banter back and forth for sixty-two seconds and then he said, "Shut the fuck up." But today he was in a hurry; he wanted to tell them what was happening.

For years Garth had walked around with something growing in him, that was how he put it. First it had been *Inside Track*. He nurtured it, thought about nothing else. There were many complaints about Garth from his staff about what they considered his neglect. He never allowed an issue to come out without his approval on each tiny detail. But for days at a time he didn't come into the office. Barrett, Blake, and Seth usually decided on a line-up and prepared the articles, even the cover; and Garth would arrive at the last minute—on Wednesday—and tell them that what they had done was shit. Some members of the staff thought that Garth was a tyrant who appeared at the magazine irregularly for the sole purpose of making them miserable. He changed his rules often, frequently without any reason one could see. Even stories he had approved himself on Monday he threw out on Wednesday. Garth didn't tell them why he wanted to replace one thing with another; he was too preoccupied. And when he did tell the editors what headlines to use and what line for the cover, the editors were appalled and begged him to read the article. They thought he spent too much time having a good time and not enough time paying attention to them and their needs. When they complained that a headline or title didn't correspond to the contents of the article, he walked away. They thought he was brainless and successful only because of the dumbest of dumb luck.

They were wrong. Everything Garth did he did with a purpose, and although he spent a lot of time away from the magazine, he never thought about anything else. He merely worked according to his own theory of how things should be done. He didn't sit at the magazine shuffling manuscripts in an attempt to decide what should go with what when. He was out on the street where things were happening. At parties, screenings, lunches; meets and eats, he called them. Or he was in Washington, L.A., or anywhere something was breaking. Thursday afternoon to Wednesday he was vague and available only infrequently. He was thinking, mulling over the events of the week. It didn't occur to him that his staff might have been working for days, even weeks, on a project when he killed it. He couldn't afford to think that way. That was what a staff was for, after all.

"I think it's time we started talking seriously about this new magazine," Garth said.

Everyone leaned forward the better to listen except Barrett. Barrett swiveled out of Garth's view while he tried to control his fury. Thursday afternoon, five pieces that hadn't yet closed, the printer shutting down at three, and here Garth was holding a meeting about a magazine that wouldn't come out until September. The shit.

CHAPTER 4

Barrett had no word from Terry. He had been worrying about it since Garth said, the last thing on Friday, that he had something he wanted to see Sidney about.

"What?" Barrett had asked. "Don't you want her to do that albino rock star interview on Monday? I agree. I hated that idea."

"I want her to try a few Washington stories." Garth didn't want to tell Barrett and it showed. "He's not an albino."

"Washington?"

"Yes. You know that senator with the wife who says he's incompetent? She's running for the junior senatorship of the same state. That would be a really great life-style story. Tell Sidney. I've already had Anne call about an interview. Tell Sidney."

Sidney hadn't called. Twice Barrett had called the house on the Vineyard. He hadn't prepared anything to say to her yet, so if she answered he thought he would just hang up. But there was no answer. He didn't know what to think about that. There had been no plane crashes, no floods or hurricanes or earthquakes. Barrett asked himself how he could be so worried. Sidney had a job to do and she never missed a deadline.

Barrett went in on Saturday to see if he had something to run in Sidney's column if, heaven forbid, Sidney failed to return by Monday. He also went in because going in on Saturday was a ritual with him. Sometimes he had a thing or two to clean up, or he realized he had left behind something he wanted to read. Sometimes he didn't have anything else to do. And more times than he wanted to admit, Barrett went to the office for no other reason than to see who else was there and what they were doing. Barrett wasn't exactly paranoiac, but he felt that people were poking around in his papers when he wasn't there (which happened to be true). He also had some strong suspicions that there was some kind of indefinable spy system that kept track of who was the most devoted, who did the most work, and who kept the longest hours. This also was true. Most of the magazine's staff, none of whom were exactly paranoiac either, did feel that it was a wise policy to drop in at the office during non-working hours just to let themselves be seen. The result was that there were usually quite a few people around no matter when one was feeling insecure enough to go and investigate.

That Saturday Barrett did not get to the office until afternoon. And for some reason, perhaps the change in weather, for it was particularly warm and sunny that day, there was no one there. Some offices have a calm and satisfied air when deserted, but at *Inside Track* there was the feeling that a war was in progress. The place was in such an appalling mess it seemed almost as though

25

there had to be some kind of national crisis to explain it. When no one was there the jumble of papers, piles of books, piles of material, personal possessions—old socks, rubber boots, sweaters, coffee cups—seemed to say, "They've just gone for the air raid, they'll be right back when it's over."

Barrett's desk was one of the neat ones. He checked to see if any of his papers had been tampered with and found that indeed some things were in a different order than they had been the day before. He fumed for a minute before sitting down and then sat down, adjusting his reading light. After a minute he discovered that he couldn't even think about working because he was too concerned about who had been there earlier and why they had left before he got there. He felt like putting his head down on the desk and having a good cry because it was true the quality of aloneness was different since Sidney had specifically said it was forever.

"Hi." Lespedeza Liveright came in swinging some kind of saddlebag thing that hung so low it slapped her knees when she walked. "What are you doing here all alone?"

Good question. "Hello, I must have dozed off." Barrett snapped himself to attention. He rustled some papers around on the desk to prove his busyness. He picked up a pencil and began making some short margin notes on a page he hadn't even read.

Lespedeza swung around behind him and leaned over his shoulder. "Whatcha reading?" she asked.

He quickly turned the page lest she see that what he was writing was nonsense. "Oh, it's an article on . . ." Barrett realized he didn't know what it was on. He tapped his forehead.

Lespedeza laughed and turned away. "I guess it wasn't very compelling a subject." She went to her desk which was not very far from Barrett's desk—sort of cater-corner to him so that, if he wanted to, he could see up her skirt. He swiveled his chair and looked up her skirt. In the nine years they had been sitting in that office, in that position, it was the first time he had made that particular swivel and taken in that particular view. Lespedeza wore very short skirts; she leaned over to get something from under her desk.

"It was a good party last night," she said, straightening up. "You didn't go."

"No, I had some work to do." He eyed her speculatively, the very reason he had not allowed himself to look up her skirt all those years. He believed that if a man slipped in his mind it was a command to slip in real life. He didn't know why he looked.

Lespedeza came back and sat on the corner of Barrett's desk. She put the wine bottle between her knees. Of course she had noticed Barrett's look. It made her snap her hair back with amusement, and smile. It was a rather crafty smile. Lespedeza thought it was a foxy smile. She hadn't changed it since she was eighteen and practiced such things in front of the mirror. Nice Barrett, and how are *you?* It was a smile half a lifetime old, for Lespedeza was no longer a young girl.

Barrett shifted uncomfortably in his chair.

"Have you come up with a name yet?" she asked.

"I haven't really thought about it."

"Do you really think he'll come through with the five hundred dollars?" Lespedeza swung her legs back and forth.

"Do you doubt his integrity?"

"It had crossed my mind to. I think if someone came up with a name he liked he would choose it and say it was his idea."

It would be just like him, Barrett thought as he watched Lespedeza's knees. Garth had called the editorial meeting to tell those of his staff who had been able to make it that his new magazine was brewing in him like yeast. Those were the words he used. Barrett had wanted to tell him that yeast didn't brew. But what would have been the point. The new magazine as they all knew would be a monthly. It would be a sort of how-to magazine as opposed to the how-it-is approach of *IT*. *IT* was more a news magazine. This new one would emphasize sexual adjustment. It would tell people how to cope with coupling—a sort of sexual *Psychology Today*. Garth was thinking of calling it *Pairs*, but since his first issue would ask the question "Is Three a Crowd?" he felt *Pairs* would set limits. At the meeting it was decided that they would have a competition to name the magazine. The winner would get five hundred dollars and his or her name on the masthead. That was supposed to be a joke because the staff was going to produce the new magazine in their spare time. They would all be on the masthead anyway.

"I think it should be called *Lovelife*. What do you think of that?" Lespedeza said. "I could use the five hundred."

"Actually, that isn't bad. Not at all bad. A magazine has to have a name that tells the reader what it's about. *Lovelife* really does it, you know. *Lovelife*. Not bad."

"How's yours?" Lespedeza reached over and picked up the manuscript he was still clutching, and squeezed his hand as she took it away. "Oh, hair replacement, ugh." She threw it back.

"Is that what you came in for?" Barrett jerked his head to indicate the bottle.

"Well, I had hoped to find someone to drink it with me." Lespedeza tossed her hair back again. It was very long hair, very pale. She looked around at the rows of empty desks.

"I wouldn't want to be your court of last resort," Barrett said, smiling woefully, watching the bottle as it bobbed up and down. A cheap New York State. What the hell.

"Where's Sidney?"

"She's out of town."

"I thought so. You have the look. Well, do you want to come over for a while?"

"No," Barrett said quickly. He realized that he didn't want any glimpses into Lespedeza's life. He didn't want to see the famous brownstone apartment she had somewhere in the neighborhood where people often dropped over for lunch. He had a feeling that his image would be imprinted on its walls, his name added to its list, that he would be somehow involved.

"Why don't you come uptown?" he said. He congratulated himself for the idea. Lespedeza had already been to his apartment many times. In the early days of *IT* when the magazine was still a risky venture most likely to fail, they had readings there. And they had dinners when everyone who came had to create a new gourmet dish. Barrett's apartment already had the memory of Lespedeza in it. One more couldn't do any harm—would in fact be quickly merged with Barrett/Sidney memories.

Barrett didn't say a word on the way home in the cab, not one word. Eight years he had been married to Sidney and he'd never done anything like this before. But then she'd never left him before. Lespedeza was telling him the story of her life.

"I was born in Florida, you see," she was saying as though that

28

explained everything. "And my mother said she would name me after the first thing she saw after she woke up. Boy or girl, it didn't matter." It was a story she told often and the words came out with cheerful indifference.

"It was a long labor, you see, and she was mad. So, I guess the first thing she saw was the parking lot outside her window. She was pretty close to choosing between Chevvy and Caddy when she realized that the first thing she really saw when she opened her eyes was some green grassy-looking stuff growing up between the cracks in the cement. So she called for the nurse and asked her what it was, and she said, 'Why, that there's lespedeza.'"

Afterward they fell asleep. When Barrett woke up it was dark outside. He turned on the light and looked at the naked body lying face up on his wife's side of the bed that was not his wife. The fact that it wasn't his wife was very exciting. She was still asleep even now with the light in her face. Barrett took a rather scholarly interest in bodies, and regarded this one for some time. He employed a characteristic discipline to restrain himself from touching it until he was finished taking an inventory of its parts. Before he had been too eager to take the time. He had also been afraid that if he did he might change his mind. Lespedeza had a body that held a somewhat ambivalent appeal for him, being about the same above as below. Also in between. It was a body without a waist. In fact Lespedeza's body seemed like a female version of Barrett's body. They were both thin, breastless, thighless, bony about the joints, straight up and down with no indentation to indicate waistlines, and muscular about the shoulders and buttocks. Her muscles derived from something she called contrology that she practiced all the time and was most eager to demonstrate at dinner parties and on other social occasions. His came from the fifty sit-ups and twenty-five chin-ups (he had a chinning bar in his bathroom) that he did religiously every night before going to bed.

Barrett, however, had liked the sex he had with Lespedeza. Sparks hadn't flown and he hadn't exactly been transported, but it was interesting in its way and he was looking forward to having some more. As he looked her over—he was relieved that she had no moles or scars or black and blue marks—he bemoaned what seemed to be his unalterable fate. Never. Never, *never* had he

29

ended up with a girl who had any tits to speak of. Shit. A small bland smile covered his wolfish face. It was a long thin beaky face that usually had a rather wry, somewhat woebegone expression. Nice squishy breasts, he was thinking, big and plump that one could really sink into and roll around with and suck-and-fondle. Not little pointy things, mere excuses for the real thing that, supine, disappeared completely.

Lespedeza, or Clover, as she was sometimes called, watched Barrett's face as he looked her over. After a few minutes she wiggled her finger around in his navel. He jumped.

He adjusted them so that they were both on top of the blanket and not touching any part of the sheets or pillow. He didn't know if Sidney was the kind of person who, coming home from a few days of running away, would smell or otherwise examine the sheets. But in case she did, or there was any leakage, he preferred to have it on the blanket. It did not occur to him that changing the sheets might be an even more effective deterrent to discovery, or that she might not come home in the three-day period before the maid would come and change the sheets.

Lespedeza had a smooth and hairless body and fine baby hair that she artfully spread out above her head. She seemed about twelve at most. Barrett, unable to contain himself any longer, rolled over on top of her. She seemed so young, he thought, like that terrible cheerleader with the blond hair. Funny, Lespedeza had never reminded him of her before. He screwed his eyes tightly shut and tried not to remember her. She came back all the same. Linda, her name was. She took it out in a telephone booth one night, and rubbed it between her hands, daring him to do it. He had been thrilled and ashamed, and then devastated when she pulled up her sweater, pushing her breasts against him and calling him a baby as he withered in her hand. Baby, baby good for no one but his mama. She had shoved his hand into her pants.

Barrett's hands stopped moving on her thighs. His heart was pounding as if he had run all the way home. Baby, baby. He could see Lespedeza's crafty smile as she sat on his desk in the office. Why did he do it, why oh why. This slut, this terrible slut, who had everyone filed in her memory like money in the bank. Barrett willed calm into his heart. Nothing could happen to him now. Nothing, he was the boss. He could fire her, ban her from the industry altogether. There was nothing she could do, no one to tell who would believe her.

With Sidney, Barrett liked to pretend they were children fooling around wrestling, who didn't know what was coming next. And to whom the final violence would come as a surprise. He liked to be surprised by it, as though he had lived forever on a desert island and didn't know what pressing flesh could lead to. Now, as he kept his eyes closed, he tried to recover. He thought of Sidney, who had cried the first time; he never forgot it. This twenty-five-year-old girl lying on the sagging couch in his studio apartment with her bra still hanging from one arm and tears leaking out of her eyes as though such a thing had never happened to her before. No girl had ever produced in him such intense feelings of longing as Sidney had that day. Even now as he thought about it with another girl on Sidney's side of the bed, he began to feel excited again, was aware of that sense of suprise he got when aroused beyond constraint.

Lespedeza flipped him over with one quick twist of her knee. He was still trying to get over the blow of landing stunned and rather powerless flat on his back when Lespedeza launched into a merciless attack on him that was both appalling and overwhelming in its force. She was very limber, and probably double-jointed, and she later called what she did the Oriental Squat. Barrett was so wrung out by it that he continued to lie there after Lespedeza had finished and was dressing to go. She didn't look at him as she collected her things. She wanted to look in Sidney's closet, but didn't.

Barrett was weird, she thought, really weird. Not your usual at all. He might not like her looking around. "Hey, you know. Garth's hired Amelia Norton to do a Women column in *Lovelife*," she said in her most offhand manner. "*Lovelife*," she said again, savoring the sound. Her back was to Barrett, she was looking for a boot. She didn't see Barrett sit up as though electrified.

"You're kidding, really?" Amelia was an even bigger name than Sidney.

"Yep." She had found the boot and was putting it on.

"I didn't know he knew her." Garth hadn't told him. Was that a sign?

31

"Didn't until last weekend. They spent Saturday night together in Sag Harbor. I guess it was all right."

"Shit," Barrett said. "Come back here." Was Garth shoving him? Sidney?

"I gotta go. No, no. Stay where you are. I know the way out."

"Wait—" Barrett got out of bed. "Shit." He couldn't find his shorts, couldn't find his shirt. And then it didn't matter, he heard her call out, "Bye now," just before the front door slammed.

Barrett put on his pants and went into the living room. He got the bottle of scotch and sat down in one of the chairs that faced Third Avenue going downtown. He sat like that in the dark for what seemed like hours watching the lights change. For the first time in a long, long time he didn't know what was going on, what he was supposed to do, or even if the experience he had just had was generally a good one or not.

CHAPTER 5

The house was on a nice strip of private beach. It hadn't been a fancy house, just one of those shingled Vineyard shacks with six unimpressive rooms and holes for the mice to get in. Before Barrett bought the house, he and Terry got three contractors to put in bids for the work they wanted done. Contractors on the Vineyard are unreliable about finishing anything; getting a new room put on a house might take two years, three if they didn't like you. Barrett and Terry said the work had to be done in six weeks or they wouldn't buy the house. If they didn't finish in that time they wouldn't pay them for the work done. Terry put it in the contract.

So they finished it in eight weeks. All the walls on the beach side of the house were replaced with huge sliding glass and screen doors. The walls were taken down between the small living room and small dining room and small kitchen so that there was just one big room with a new, very modern kitchen on one end, separated from the rest of the room by waist-high wooden counters. The house was furnished with very spare modern furniture: the living room, two bedrooms, and a tiny room not much bigger than a walk-in closet where they kept the books, a desk, a typewriter, and a small television. Outside each bedroom was a small screened porch big enough for two chairs and a table in between. The front of the house was kept the same except for a coat of bright blue paint on the shutters.

For three days Sidney stayed there in terror waiting for someone to come and get her. Every night she sat in front of the fire feeling every noise, every creak in the house. Moths and other flying things that were attracted by the light charged the windows, making soft eerie thumps. Not as loud or as human as the city sirens, the early morning truck rumblings on Third Avenue, the odd backfiring, building creak, or explosion, the country noises seemed ominous and unreal. The quiet was almost unbearably menacing. It felt all night long like the peace before the storm, the moment of safety before the sniper pulled the trigger, the time when the Russians or Nazis, or whoever, surrounded the house and closed in for the kill. Each night Sidney took a long time to get to bed and then lay there on her and Barrett's king-size, extra-hard mattress, rigid, and on a diagonal, as though taking up more space would make her less vulnerable. She listened. For hours she caught every shift in the lapping water sounds, every creak in the wood.

She calculated her escape up the beach, or on the road, depending on where the attackers were. Several times she had her awake dream of paralysis at the most crucial time of the chase when her legs cramped and she couldn't run. At that point in the dream there were always others making it across the mine field, or the stretch of shark-infested waters, or the gap from one building top to another. But she was behind, the last one, inching along, dragging her crippled limbs while the enemy got closer and closer. Death stalked on all sides, and there was no one to help her, no one to neutralize the terror or bring back reality. Each night she was convinced she would die. Those bastards. Those crummy bastards, leaving her like that. Those bastards. Sidney started many times in the night, sure there was someone in the house. It was too far away to get help, more than a mile down the road to the next occupied house. Yes, that was a human creak. It was. She put the covers over her head. If she was lucky there would be one shot in the head and she wouldn't even know she died. Oh, God. She wanted to go home. Couldn't go home. Couldn't go back no matter what. Those bastards.

"That's the silliest thing I ever heard," Sidney said cheerfully when (after she had the phone turned on) Terry finally reached her. He had called collect from California at noon on Friday to tell her he was coming there on the way home. "That's crazy," she said. "You'd have to fly to Boston first. And I don't want you to come anyway." God *damn* that bastard. It was Friday. Sidney felt tears collecting and her throat clenching up. Friday, damn it. And it was Terry, only Terry.

"I'll be there tomorrow morning first thing."

"What time is it there?" Sidney asked. She had to work hard not to yell.

"Ten o'clock. I'm taking the ten-thirty. I'm so glad I reached you."

"That's really silly," Sidney said, counting on her fingers. She figured he would be in Boston by no later than five. God damn it. He was going to spend the night in *Boston*. Was going to leave her all alone while he—

"Sidney, are you there?"

"What are you coming here for? I don't even want to see you," she said sullenly.

"I want to assure myself of your continued existence."

"This is the real me. This is not a tape recording. I'm fine." Pompous ass, she thought.

"I'll see you tomorrow then. The first flight gets in at about nine-thirty, will you meet me?"

"Terry."

"I've got to go now. The flight's been called. I'll take a taxi if you're not there."

"Teerreee," Sidney wailed. "What are you doing tonight?"

"All right," he said wearily. "I'll come tonight."

At eight-thirty she was outside at the airport waiting for him. The fog was coming in, and already it was dark. Twice the plane had circled the airport and not found the runway in time to land

34

on it. It went away to try Nantucket, which didn't have the equipment for instrument landings either.

She blew on her hands and pulled her old Mexican bathrobe sweater more tightly around her. She decided to get rid of it this year. Even though the bulky sweaters were in fashion again, Sidney didn't like hers. The wool had bits of wood in it and still smelled of dirty sheep even thought it had just come out of moth flakes three days ago. And it was oily. If it began to rain right then, the drops would roll off the sweater. The only good thing about it was it kept out the cold. In spite of this last quality, however, she had never seen a Mexican wearing one. She wore hers faithfully every summer because Barrett had given it to her the year they went to Puerto Vallarta to do Elizabeth Taylor.

Barrett had wandered around buying things. He bought silver bracelets for Muriel the copy editor and for Lespedeza. Emily (fat Em) got earrings. If he hadn't married her six months before and advanced her to Staff Writer to get her out of the Assistant category in spite of her apparent lack of talent in that direction, Barrett would probably have bought Sidney a silver bracelet too. But he bought her the sweater instead.

Sidney went and sat in the car. She didn't notice how the fog was rising and falling several feet in a kind of teasing dance over the runway. She was playing with the car keys, debating whether or not she should go home. The crummy old DC-3 would never make it. It would land in Hyannis or New Bedford and Terry would have to spent the night in a damp motel. It was too late for him to make the last ferry now.

But it was one of those rare times when the fog rose just enough at just the right minute for the pilot to see the runway, aim for it, and land on it. The DC-3 thundered down the runway and parked at the gate, looking in the fog like the last stirring frames of *Casablanca* run backward.

Terry was the first one off. No matter where he sat he always managed to be the first one to breathe real air. He always stood on the top step for a minute as though in silent thanks for making it yet another time. Although he admitted it to no one, Sidney knew that he was really afraid of flying. She could see it in his face every time she went to meet them at the airport when they came for the weekend on a later plane than she (she always came early to sweep out the house and do the shopping).

Now in the fog she couldn't tell how pale his face was, only that he was very rumpled. He had with him his battered briefcase that was big enough for a shirt and a razor but not another suit. "Oh, hullo, Sidney," he said. He came forward to brush his lips against her cheekbone as usual, but she backed away from him at the last minute, too mad to kiss him. The creep.

There was an awkward moment while he recovered his balance and tried to think of a smart remark. When he couldn't think of one, he merely turned and walked toward the no parking spot where Sidney always parked the car.

"Are you tired?" she asked.

"No, have you had dinner?"

Lawyers who traveled around a lot never admitted that they were tired. They tried to pretend that they were awake and alert at all times and had not been equipped at birth with a biological clock. Sidney had seen Terry fall asleep on the couch while explaining just how tired he wasn't.

"Swordfish with mustard sauce, beets the size of acorns, red salad, potato, and blueberry pudding," she muttered.

"You had all that without me?"

"Who did you miss seeing in Boston?" Sidney drove faster than was good for the ten-year-old Volkswagen, but Terry didn't complain as Barrett would have.

"No one, why?"

"Ha, you preferred a night at the Ritz-Carlton to me?"

"You're mad."

"No, I'm not." She regretted saying anything, didn't even know why she had let him come. Actually she rather resented Terry, there at every important and unimportant moment of their life. Hardly ever a Sunday brunch without him. Barrett thought of him as the brother neither of them had ever had. "It's important to love more than one person," he said frequently in a tone Sidney could kick him in the balls for. Why not love a child, Sidney asked. Hell, a child's not a person. Barrett always got the last word.

"I didn't have it without you. It's waiting." Sidney knew she was being terrible not to ask him about his trip or why he had inconvenienced himself so much to see her (Barrett asked him to, that's why). But he didn't notice how wretched she was, the rotten creep. So she wasn't going to notice how awful he looked.

Sidney had a crummy dime-store bandanna tied around her head to hide her hair and make her look even more ugly, the black circles under her eyes even more pouchy, her skin deader. She had on blue jeans with holes in the knees, an ancient baggy sweater of Barrett's, and the Mexican sweater she despised. Sidney was not a person overly satisfied with her looks and even less so now that Barrett had spent years and pots of money trying to make her look better. He called her the little brown mouse and had her made up every six months or so, so that it seemed to her every time she looked in the mirror a different person stared back. Her hair was frizzed or straightened, cropped or shagged or shingled—darkened or lightened. It was like paying one's debts to society, Barrett said of his efforts to beautify her. The problem with beautifying, though, is not that it's painful to come out looking better (or anyway interesting), but rather that one's flaws are pointed out along the way. The make-up man explains the maroon strips he has applied along the jaw by saying they're to bring out one's receding chin. Until that moment one hadn't known one had a receding chin. Sidney had decided to leave Barrett the way one leaves a psychiatrist: when the make-over is complete and the patient returns home to carry on exactly as before. But Terry didn't look at Sidney long enough to see that the princess was again a sneakered frog.

"I'm so relieved," he said, referring to his dinner.

When they got to the house he commented on how good it looked. He put together a fire in the fireplace. He got a drink. He didn't mention the cause of his being there. He didn't say, "Sidney, I was so worried."

"I love swordfish," he said.

Sidney put a forkful to her mouth, imagining the gobs of shining silver mercury that would soon be coursing through her body. Reflected in the window, she saw herself small and shabby, with the narrow venomous face of a woman trudging toward middle age having missed her prime.

"I love blueberry pudding," he said.

What a jerk she thought he was.

37

"Good. Are you tired?" Sidney watched him eat. She knew he was. She knew he would say he wasn't. Why did she ask.

"Not at all. Would you like some brandy?" he asked even though he knew she always said no.

She shook her head. "You look awful, what happened?"

"Vince Garden is going to lose his shirt."

"Oh, he signed." They had been discussing it for weeks.

Terry shrugged. "He wanted to. It's like getting married, I guess. When they want to there's not a thing in the world that can stop them." He put the dishes in the dishwasher. Sidney blew out the candles. Coming up was the time she liked least with Terry.

He would give her a glass of port. Why, she didn't know. Then on those rare occasions when they were together alone at home, they would fumble around finding a place to sit. Usually Sidney could manage all right with him. She thought of him as an old wart that she wouldn't have chosen to have but after a number of years was so familiar life would be strange without it. It was only when they were alone that she felt uneasy.

Terry was that kind of hulking presence, so quiet sometimes one forgot he was there. He was the son and grandson of New York State dairy farmers. He had been to Harvard, Yale Law School, and was a partner in a medium-sized Wall Street law firm until he found out that law as it's practiced downtown has less to do with law than politics. He moved uptown into a more people-oriented practice. Like Barrett, he was thirty-eight and hadn't lived at home since he was seventeen; but, unlike Barrett, he still had that fresh, slightly vacant look of a hick. He looked dumb, had that kind of bushy hair that stuck straight up in places no matter how carefully it was cut. He moved slowly as though something inside might break. In social situations he was silent unless specifically provoked. He had never married, was never seen with the same girl more than two or three times. Most of the time he went around alone, and was totally unashamed of being the odd man at a dinner party. Sidney thought he was homosexual.

Or if not active, then latent. Although most of the time she didn't think about it, or didn't think about it consciously, certain times—like when the three of them were on the beach together, or when she and he were alone someplace—she thought about it and it bothered her. She felt a man who didn't like women intimately couldn't like her even casually. She knew from the way they talked that homosexuals looked more critically at the cosmetic aspect of women; they noticed flaws more. She was afraid of seeming sexy or provocative. She was afraid of touching him in case he thought he was being challenged or she a whore. They always think of women as voracious, "hoorish." If he had looked at her with that look or hugged her with his hands around her waist as some of their friends did from time to time just to see what she felt like, she wouldn't have been uneasy about him. She would have taken some pleasure in wearing a negligee to breakfast or her shirt open, or being caught in a towel. But even less than interested, Terry seemed positively disapproving, as though her femininity itself was the barrier to an unstrained friendship.

Terry settled in Barrett's chair by the fire. He was thinking, "Poor Sidney." Usually in that situation women put on their best face for him, not their worst. They looked at him with new interest; it didn't matter whose side he was on. If he had a meeting with the wife, before it was over, more often than not there were tears shed against his chest and determined, still-married hands working their way up his back. Such were the benefits of divorce. Although it was not a favorite situation of his, Terry felt somewhat sorry for Sidney that she could not do it. She wouldn't even look to see what else was around. She wouldn't even cry.

"Well, Sidney," he said in one of his more businesslike tones.

She stood around trying to decide where to sit, finally sat on the square Design Research sofa opposite him. Her knees showed through the holes in her pants.

"It was nice of you to come, of course, but I don't want to talk to you about it," she announced. She felt tears coming again. Barrett really didn't love her, that was the truth. The *Wall Street Journal* said that was the reason women left their husbands. Waah, I don't have a mommy. I don't have a daddy. No one to love me. Hiccup, hiccup. Sidney could see it all, even splotches on her cheeks. A small shabby wail—no one loves meee. She wasn't going to let *him* see her like that, nod to himself how right the *Journal* always is about everything. Not that nelly.

"Okay, but I happen to think you're right about *New Journal*," Terry was saying.

"You do? Did he tell you about that?" Sidney blinked away her tears in surprise.

"I guessed."

"I think he's crazy." I could kill him. Give me a knife, I could kill you too.

"I do too, but is that a reason to leave him?"

"That's not the reason," Sidney said sullenly, reluctant to pay attention.

"Are you afraid he'll fall on his face, or lose your book money?"

"It's not the book money he wants to use. He wants to use George's money."

"Who's George?"

"Never mind, you wouldn't understand." She turned away so she wouldn't have to look at his wholesome earnest face.

"Try me."

"Terry, I like you, really I do. I don't want to hurt your feelings"—Sidney pulled the bandanna off her head as though without it she would seem more sincere—"but there are a few things you just don't know about. Things that can happen in a marriage." Sidney took a few breaths of air and a sip of port. "Barrett's your friend—I don't know what he told you—but he's your friend. I'm not going to tell you how I feel about him. . . . And he just couldn't run that paper, you know that."

"We could talk him out of it."

"No, we couldn't. Barrett never stops until he gets what he wants. You know how he'd say we didn't care about his needs, didn't trust him. He'd tell us we wanted to ruin his life. It's not that I haven't heard it all before. You know, when Barrett decided it was time to get married he took me out to meet his parents in Brooklyn. We went to some delicatessen they liked for pastrami. It was Sunday night. After the pastrami sandwiches, Barrett said, 'Sidney and I are going to get married.' He hadn't even asked me."

Terry laughed.

"I thought, terrific, a man who knows what he wants. I was so flattered it was me—"

"Sidney."

"I mean it. There was Lespedeza sitting right next to me with no shirt on practically and underpants only once a week and everybody hanging over my desk to get a look at her as though I weren't there. She was so used to my being ignored that when Barrett asked me out to lunch that first time *she* said yes."

Terry laughed again. "I know it's not funny, but what did Barrett say?"

"He said, 'Hey, you, want to go to lunch?'" Sidney, too, was laughing now. "It never occurred to either of us he meant me, so he said, 'Not you, *her*,' pointing to me. I was flattered."

"Are you going to come back?" Terry asked abruptly.

Sidney shook her head, although she was still sort of undecided about it. Maybe if Barrett really loved her . . .

"We had a lot of good times together," he said sadly.

"The two of you will. You'll have plenty of good times."

"It won't be the same," he muttered. He had forgotten that he had promised Barrett he was going to bring her back no matter what, even handcuffed if necessary.

"I'm going to bed," Sidney said. "Should I lock up or will you?"

"We have to talk about the magazine," Terry said. "Your column—"

"Tomorrow." She had gotten up before he could finish, walked across the room without looking back. The creep. What did he know about anything.

A few minutes later Sidney lay in bed and wondered which were the times Terry considered the good ones. She thought of the Christmas party they went to last winter. Barrett complained all the way there. It was snowing and he hated snow. It was Christmas and he hated Christmas—the party was late and the food was cold. They were required to sing Christmas carols and dress up a tree. Barrett was rude.

When they left there were three inches of snow on the ground and they couldn't get a taxi. The four of them walked down Madison Avenue, a free-lance writer called Caroline hanging onto Terry's arm. "Let's walk," she said. "Ummm, isn't it beautiful," and a few minutes later, coyly, "I want to come inside your coat."

"Caroline's an asshole," Barrett said. He called her the hennaed tart.

She and Terry were plunging ahead while Barrett trudged miserably along with his head down. He had announced that he would rather go blind than take a subway.

41

Sidney watched Terry and Caroline stop to look at a display in a bookstore window. They seemed just a blur in the snow until Sidney got closer, when she saw that Caroline had indeed made her way inside Terry's coat and they weren't looking at books at all. It seemed as though they were kissing. Barrett dragged her across the street.

"Terry's going to catch cold," Sidney said. She had tried to link arms with him going across the street, but he brushed her off demanding irritably whether she wanted him to fall down in the middle of the street.

"What?"

"Didn't you see what she was doing?"

"If I didn't know you better, I'd think you were jealous." Barrett laughed.

She hadn't really seen anything, just the two of them standing so still they could have been statues. It made Sidney's throat ache at the time. "I'm getting sick," she told Barrett. She wanted him to give her a hug.

"Don't get sick, I hate it when you're sick," was his reply.

They stopped at the Carlyle for a drink, sat together for an hour with no one talking much except Caroline, who felt no sense of menace. Was that one of the good times. She never saw Terry with her again, had decided that they hadn't been kissing. Later Caroline called twice to ask if she knew where Terry was. Others had called her the same way. Now, as then, she didn't know what these women saw in him. She heard him padding around in the living room without his shoes. Idly she put one hand to her breast and wondered if he had any clothes on.

CHAPTER 6

"Barrett." Garth came out of his office putting on his seersucker jacket, ready for lunch. It was Monday. "What's this I hear about Sidney canceling out on what's-his-name today?" Garth spoke loudly in a voice that threatened to get a good deal worse.

Barrett stood up. All weekend he had felt as if he were in a decompression chamber. He moved in slow motion, had that kind of half nausea he used to feel when the results of exams came in. I can't fail, I just can't (he never had, but the fear was more terrible for never happening than it would have been if failing were common). All weekend he had been saying to himself that Sidney couldn't leave him. She just couldn't. And if she did, he'd kill her. Now he stood in front of Garth faced with Sidney's leaving. Barrett was very thin and sometimes when he was confronted by Garth's yearly enlarging stomach and his full flushes, as Sidney called his tantrums, he felt as though he were in the jaws of a Cadillac crusher. He felt that now.

"She's out of town," he said. "She planned to come back, but she got the flu and she doesn't like to fly with the flu. You can go deaf, you know."

"I want that story, damn it. You know that." Garth was the sort of man who liked to stamp his foot but knew it was the one thing that could compromise him.

Barrett could see him controlling the stamp. He was furious at whoever had told Garth about the cancellation. *IT* was definitely becoming a vipers' nest. It didn't used to be this way. Garth was turning red again, and Barrett tried to read from him what had happened over the weekend. He didn't usually start so scrappily. "Well, we'll do it later on," Barrett said with more confidence than he felt. "We have a lot of copy we can run."

He thought he might weasel the conversation around to some of the stories they had in the house, but Garth was firmly focused on Sidney.

"I was counting on that story."

"Maybe we could send Blake. I think Blake could do a good job on it if you want it done right away."

"Blake has the insight of a mole. He's a bore," Garth shouted. "He can't do this kind of thing. He can hardly make rape and murder interesting."

Barrett looked around guiltily, hoping that Blake wasn't in that morning. He didn't see Blake and turned reluctantly back to Garth.

"Where the hell is she anyway? I want to talk to her. I've never known Sidney to miss an interview," Garth said.

"Oh, she's probably on her way back by now."

"Well, you reschedule that interview for tomorrow." Garth began to walk away. "I want it this week."

"She can't do it in one day," Barrett called after him. "It'll have to be next week." But Garth was already five desks and fifteen ringing telephones away. He wasn't listening.

It didn't matter how long a person had been with Garth, he always gave the impression that, if he were mad enough or someone had done something stupid enough, he would fire anyone instantly. Occasionally, just to prove he meant what he said, he did fire someone, and for the next six months to a year everyone else worried that he or she was going to be personally singled out, disgraced, fired, and exiled from the industry altogether. It never occurred to anyone that there was the possibility of working somewhere else, and consequently no one ever left *IT* willingly.

Barrett was worried that he was being kicked out. What better time could there be than when a new magazine was being founded. Garth would be reorganizing. He would be shuffling names around on the masthead. No matter how optimistic he was about having the same staff doing the work for two magazines, Garth would have to get some more people in. The volume of copy would be too much. No, they simply couldn't handle it.

Barrett watched everyone file out for lunch. Then he made a few phone calls to people who were out to lunch. To the loan man at Bankers Trust where they had their accounts. And to Stewart Adams, the owner of *New Journal*. Shit, they would call him back in the afternoon and everyone would know. He dialed Terry's number for advice. But Terry was out to lunch too.

Terry and he had spent Sunday afternoon trying to work out what Barrett should do.

"Is Sidney going to come back?" he kept asking, then, "When do you think Sidney will be back?" because he couldn't face the idea of her not coming back.

"I don't know," Terry said.

"Well, what the hell did you talk about if not that?"

"We talked about old times."

"Which ones?" Barrett wanted to know. He also asked what Sidney had fed him, how she looked, and was she coming back.

44

"Do you think she's having a nervous breakdown?" he asked. A nervous breakdown was a no-fault illness and curable in time. He was furious at Terry for not bringing her back.

"She didn't want to come. What was I supposed to do, drag her by the hair?"

"But I *told* you I have to have a story for her column. What am I supposed to do about that?"

"She did have a suggestion to make about that, but I won't repeat it."

"But it's *her* career at stake, not mine. Didn't you tell her what would happen? Garth has already hired Amelia Norton, that squirrely dyke—"

"She is not."

"How the hell do you know? . . . Can you imagine what he'll do when he finds out she's gone? She's crazy. She ought to be committed, that's what."

Ultimately Barrett decided, tiresome as it would be, that he would have to write Sidney's column for that week himself. He went home on Monday night without having reached any of the people he wanted to reach, not even Terry to have dinner with him. Instead of dinner, he sat down at Sidney's desk to write her piece. For a while he sat there chewing on the end of his pencil, examining the yellow legal pad in front of him. He tried to clear his head of all worries. He sharpened the pencil and contemplated the pad.

How come the background is so muted, he asked himself. Why are the lines pale blue instead of navy blue. Why is the margin so wide on the left side and non-existent on the right side. Barrett wrote "Ode to a Legal Pad" on the top of the page. He looked at it for some time and then tore off the page, ripped it in neat little squares, and threw it in the wastebasket.

Soon he had gone through one whole legal pad and several pencils this way. He would write a title at the top, look at it for ten or fifteen seconds, and then curse himself and his wife and Garth Carter vehemently as he tore the page into bits. He drank down the rest of his glass of Pepsi and then crushed one of the ice cubes with his teeth. It gave him great pleasure to do this because Sidney could not bear the sound of ice crushed between teeth—"You

45

sound like a beaver." And his dentist repeatedly warned him that chewing ice and chicken bones was lethal to teeth.

"My trip to the dentist," Barrett wrote. Paragraph one: My dentist wears a monocle and has a thick mane of whitening hair (it didn't seem quite strong enough as a lead). He tore off the page and cursed. He had five empty glasses lined up on the desk in front of him. One of the reasons he was cursing was that the glasses had never at any time contained scotch. He wanted his mind clear, so he drank Pepsi and coffee and the wastebasket slowly filled up.

Sidney's desk was perfectly clean and neat and had nothing on top of it but a tray of new unsharpened pencils and a leather-framed picture of Garth in a bathing suit. Sidney said she had it there to inspire her. Over the desk was a shelf that contained an English dictionary, a French one, a dictionary of biography, a *Roget's Thesaurus, Elements of Style,* and a battered copy of Bartlett's *Familiar Quotations* that dated from Barrett's high school days. There were three drawers in the desk. Barrett went through each one carefully. All they contained were neat stacks of supplies and her and his joint checkbook and some old notebooks. Barrett took the top one out and turned a few pages. Nothing.

There was no old manuscript file. That was what bothered him. He knew that somewhere she had a few general pieces that she kept in case she got stuck for an idea or wanted to take a vacation. But except for the note pads, it was as though no one ever worked there.

Whenever he felt he could no longer cope, Barrett went downstairs to Terry's apartment. The first time Terry wasn't there. Barrett prowled around as much as he thought would be appropriate in Terry's eyes if Terry returned suddenly and caught him. Terry had the same apartment as Sidney and Barrett. In the dining area, he had his pool table. The rest of the apartment had been decorated by a decorator who thought Terry's image required a macho approach, so the apartment was done in high hunting lodge. The frames of the two side chairs were made entirely of antlers. There was a leering moosehead on one of the walls, a zebra skin on the living-room floor, a few African chieftain stools and a mask or two scattered around the place. The two dying plants—Terry replaced them every few months with new ones—lived in hollowed-out elephant feet. The decorator wanted to put a mosquito net over Terry's large bed to round out and "authenticate" the look, but Terry refused to have it on the ground that he wanted to keep things simple. On his first visit, Barrett discovered that Terry kept all of his papers, even the grocery bills, at the office. But he found half of a cold chicken in the icebox and ate it along with a small jar of sweet pickles that caught his eye. Afterward he played pool for an hour, while watching Terry's television because he didn't want to go home.

Then he went home to do some more work. On the second visit, at around eleven, when Barrett was in a state of greater upset, Terry was there. He had a Pepsi to prove to Terry that he wasn't dependent on alcohol and told him about Sidney's missing old manuscript file.

"That's really the clincher," he said. "Really malicious of her."

"I guess it is significant, isn't it?" Terry had a scotch in one hand. "Sure you don't want any?" he asked Barrett.

"What am I going to do?" Barrett wailed. He paced back and forth across the zebra rug.

"Tell Garth the truth," Terry advised for the fourteenth time. He did not mention the missing chicken.

Barrett ignored him. "You see, it's the story that really counts right now. Sidney can't make it by herself. Can you see her trying to manage on her own? I mean really. Can you see her single?" Barrett snorted. "She's such a prude, she even screams when someone *looks* at her funny. She's very dependent. And you know she can't stand quiet."

Terry made no comment on this although he thought some of it, anyway, was true.

"If I can just get a story in, everything else will work out fine." He didn't mention the *Journal* just then. He watched Terry set up a few difficult shots and resin his cue.

"Well, did she say anything to you about her old manuscript file?"

"No." Terry got two balls in with one shot and put the cue down. He had been thinking of walling up the dining area and making it a squash court.

47

"Listen," he said finally. "What Sidney should do is a nice woodsy piece about the Vineyard. A city-person-in-the-country piece like one of those terrible seasonal editorials the *Times* always runs about the flowers in Central Park bursting like confetti. That's what Sidney should do. Sort of get everybody all excited about summer coming up. Something naturish and easy."

"Sidney doesn't know anything about nature. If she had an assignment like that, she'd try to interview a goose," Barrett said.

"I wasn't suggesting that she do anything that required any knowledge or expertise."

"You know, I like that idea. You're right. I'll do it." Barrett began to chew on an ice cube.

"What do you mean you'll do it?" Terry said.

"I'm going to write it."

"But he wants a manuscript from Sidney."

"Sidney, in case you haven't noticed, isn't here. He'll get a Sidney-sounding manuscript." Barrett had been sprawled out, almost lying down in his chair. Now he sat up. He had his subject, all, or nearly all, was right with the world again. "I'm going home. Might as well get started right now."

Barrett went back upstairs with a new bounce in his step and then sat down at Sidney's desk once again. This time he sat down with the finality of the pianist at a concert who knows that after the tails are arranged there's no turning back. He sharpened a pencil. Once again he confronted the gaping yellow legal pad. He counted the number of lines on the page. He figured how many lines of legal it would take to fill a magazine page. It depended on the size of the art. It was better to write too much. He stared at the page, willing it to be covered with his tiny illegible scrawl. He closed his eyes. It was better to think about the Vineyard. Barrett thought about the ferry which he loved but rarely rode because in midsummer when he went the planes managed to land on the island most of the time. He would lead with the ferry, he thought, then decided it was too corny.

Twice in the course of his preparatory thinking Barrett called Lespedeza to ask her out. She never seemed to be at home. He got himself a glass of Pepsi and a cigar. Perhaps it was better to talk about the fog. The fog was really what made the island so special. Otherwise it would be like Connecticut or upstate New

York. He decided to make a list of Vineyard qualities and then when he had the uniqueness of the place right out in front of him he could just write some clever thought around each facet of Vineyard life and have a stirring nostalgic piece. "Ferry," he wrote. "Fog." He erased "Fog" and wrote "FOG."

"Sometimes the island is fogbound. That is what I like best about it. I like to watch the ferry coming across from Woods Hole, but I like it even better when the fog is so thick that I can't see the ferry, or even the old wooden pier out in front of our house. That's when the foghorns go all the time and being in the house is like being in a cocoon. When the fog closes in, one feels as if there's no way out, that one has to stay there forever. It's a sort of modern wilderness."

Barrett read what he had written. It had Sidney's tone all right, but it didn't read quite like Sidney's best, so he wrote "preliminary notes" across the top of the page, and "revise necessary." Continuing the list, he wrote, "Digging for clams in Lake Tashmoo." "Sailing." He wondered if Sidney had taken their small sailboat out of the Vineyard boatyard, but concluded that it was unlikely since she couldn't sail. "Horseshoe crabs," he wrote. "Famous writers." "Private planes." "Menemsha." He made an insert caret and added "Wife (husband) swapping." Then, "Exemptions—us." Garth would want that made clear. Then Barrett wrote, "Movie houses, lousy," "Nothing to do at night but give and go to parties." "Sweet corn at the end of the summer." Ummmm. He had another glass of Pepsi.

What a boring job writing was. Barrett wrote "Fogbound," realized that he had already written it, and erased it carefully. He put a page of medium-weight bond in Sidney's IBM and typed up what he had so far. It didn't seem like quite enough to go on. He turned the picture of Garth in a bathing suit around. He tapped his pencil against the desk. Finally he dialed Terry's number. Four rings and he answered.

"What are you doing?" Barrett asked.

"Readng a dirty book."

"Can you come up here?"

"What for?"

"I want whatever thoughts you have on the Vineyard. I need a few ideas."

"Forget it."

"Come on, Terry old buddy."

"You know I'd do just about anything, but I won't go along with fraud." Terry hung up.

"Cocksucker. Motherfucker. Fink."

Barrett had forgotten to turn off the typewriter. It hummed. He said the other two dirty words that he knew and turned off the typewriter. Sidney did not seem to have this kind of trouble, he thought. Barrett concluded that he had writer's block.

After two more hours of alternating between the humming of the typewriter and the quiet of the legal pads, he decided that maybe he wasn't a writer. That was not a pleasant thought. He decided to break down and have some scotch. He got out a bottle of Chivas Regal and brought the bottle back with him. Alcohol really did make a difference; he had been telling Sidney that for years. A few drinks and nothing ever seemed quite so bad. Barrett sipped the scotch. He could not understand how he could have taught Sidney everything she knew about writing (piquing the reader's interest: lead, bulk, sparkling finish) and not be able to re-create her style.

All these years the thought that he had taught Sidney to write had given him a warm secure feeling. It was like being a writer himself without having to do any of the work. It was Barrett who made Sidney a star, who gave her style and a format for her life. But for him she would have been a dull girl forever, a slightly plain, humorless, overly serious, fact-checking comma pusher like Muriel. Every time she came out with another story he had the pride of authorship. I did this, he thought. I talked it out with her, edited it, whacked it into final shape, and gave it a title. It was inconceivable to him that now he couldn't do it himself. It was a nightmare; worse than a nightmare, it was true. How could he create a style and not copy it. Barrett didn't know which was the greater blow, the fact that Sidney could leave him after everything he had done for her, or that he couldn't do what she did. Even the best editor is nothing without a stable of writers making work for him. Barrett dialed the phone again.

"Listen, Terry," he said when Terry finally answered yawning. "We've got to get working on *New Journal* tomorrow."

CHAPTER 7

"You can't make a deal like this without a lawyer," Terry said the next day when they met in a coffee shop for breakfast. "Look, you'd have to meet with the guy again to see if he really wants to sell and what kind of a deal he wants if he does intend to sell. Then you have to have someone go over there and see if he has everything he says he has."

"What do you mean?" Barrett asked.

"Well, sometimes they say they have a half a million in cash and all the labor is fixed for the next five years and then you find out they have two hundred and eighty-five and the contracts are up in six months' time and the unions have been agitating for a year for bigger salaries. So what you thought was going to be a great deal turns out to smell pretty bad."

"That's misrepresentation," Barrett said, indignant.

Terry shrugged.

"But why would someone lie like that?"

"Why do you think?" Terry was attacking his ham and eggs with some relish. "So then if you agree on terms and everything at the ranch looks okay, you sign a letter of intent. I take it Adams wants fifty thousand dollars with his letter of intent."

Garth thought it was cheaper to begin a new magazine than buy an old, falling-down one. In any case, one magazine, no matter how successful, does not an empire make. For several years he had been looking around for another magazine to buy—all over the country and even abroad. But none had come along that was exactly what he wanted. The more he thought about it, the more he realized that it would be much cheaper to start his own. He was already paying all those salaries, had a typesetter and a printer, production department. He had everything he needed. He figured it would cost him about thirty to forty thousand dollars to get the first issue out.

Barrett was pleased by Garth's thinking for two reasons. First, he knew there was one thing missing in this equation that Garth wasn't mentioning. Circulation. People don't pick up a new magazine on the newsstand just for fun. Unless it's something really special. But even if it were something really special, it would sit there month after month while people watched to see if it would last. Nobody wants to buy a product without staying power. Also there was the question of identification. *Lovelife* was a good name for the magazine—Garth wouldn't use it because he hadn't thought of it—but even with a name like that people wouldn't know for ages whether or not it was for them. The second reason Barrett was glad Garth planned to start his own magazine was that he was going to be so preoccupied trying to solve the first problem, *Inside Track* was going to have to suffer for it. And with *IT* suffering for it and the two stars of the magazine— himself and Sidney—gone, there would be all sorts of interest in the overhaul of *New Journal*.

In spite of all Terry's warnings, Barrett met with Stewart Adams. He was a tall, thin, scruffy person with a beard just around his jawline, from ear to ear. He was a youngish person, hippyesque, who bounded nervously around his loftlike premises in aged sneakers and a holey sweatshirt. Barrett had carefully dressed in his best summer suit.

Quite the opposite of *IT*, *New Journal* had closed-off little places for everyone to sit. It was like a rabbit warren, or a maze. But, like *IT*, the *Journal* was dusty and the furniture grim. There wasn't a bit of color anywhere, except in the art department, which was miles from the editorial department. It was a place where one could have a lot of secrets. Barrett went to the men's room and flushed the toilet. He opened and closed the window and turned on the hot water. At *IT* there was no hot water and the window had been sealed shut for as long as he had been there, nine years. There was hot water. I'll take it, he decided. A little paint, some modern furniture, a rug.

New Journal had begun in the early fifties. It was an exuberant little paper that told local news, printed short stories, needled the Eisenhower administration, the City Council, and anything else with an establishment label. It reflected the easygoing bohemian life of that part of town now known as SoHo. Over the years the paper built up quite a following. In the sixties it added a big music section and a section called "Washington." The owner ran for Congress and made it. He sold his then very successful paper to Stewart Adams, a rock enthusiast. His first official action was to add a column called "Gay Today."

Looking at him now, Barrett could see why the paper had declined in the last few years. Adams was unhinged. He was in motion all the time. A very nervous fellow he was. He either had a concussion or was taking something, Barrett concluded from the size of his pupils. He had the uneasy feeling that he was going to be offered a pill. He refused the cup of coffee he was offered in case it had something in it.

"Far out," Stewart said from time to time as though in response to something Barrett had said. He bobbed his head and tapped his foot.

"We don't need any lawyers," he had said. "You can have everything."

That's very generous of you, Barrett thought. He may look crazed, but the guy is very shrewd. Very shrewd. When Barrett asked him why he was selling just now, Stewart said, "Man, I just can't handle all the debts." He wanted to go out to California and do a straight music rag. That's why he was giving it away, he said. He wouldn't be getting a thing really.

Barrett felt a thrill of anger. This jerk had run the paper into the ground and now wanted to get rid of it; he should give it away for nothing for what he had done. Barrett thought that a magazine was like a person. It lived and breathed and functioned, just like a person, in exact proportion to its care and feeding.

Adams wanted fifty thousand dollars up front as an act of good faith and proof that Barrett could assume the hundred and fifty thousand dollars' worth of debts the magazine had accrued in the last two years. Then he wanted another fifty thousand when the deal closed. He wanted an agreement and his first payment in no more than three weeks' time. "If you want it, you'll have to take it now," he said when Barrett protested that three weeks was not enough time for him to get the money. He didn't show Barrett any papers about the magazine's earnings and newsstand sales or anything and Barrett didn't think to ask. He liked the look of the place.

He did remember to ask Adams to keep their meeting confidential and Stewart said, "Yeah, sure. Don't worry about a thing." He was eating a cashew nut butter sandwich with sprouts on it as Barrett left. He had the feeling buyers often have about the people selling something they want. Yech, what a creepy guy.

Barrett went back to the office with a really brain-splitting headache. What if Adams told Garth. Maybe he should forget the whole thing. It was such a lot of money, and not a sure thing at all, no matter how clever he and Sidney were. But then it would be theirs, it would be his. The *Journal* was a good paper, basically sound. He'd have to get rid of "Gay Today," though. He put his hand on and took his hand off the phone several times, worrying the question back and forth. How was it arranged when debts were paid off over a three-year period. Could he get them to accept five years. There was no question, it was going to be complicated.

"Hi," said Muriel. She sat down in his guest chair uninvited.

"Uh, I'm busy right now, Mur," Barrett said. He couldn't stand Muriel. Muriel had come to the magazine after working for years at the Christian Science Reading Room on Madison Avenue. She had come there in the hopes of finding a man but so far had not succeeded. Most of her concentration was taken up with punctuation and spelling. She claimed her talent for seeing typographical errors at a hundred yards came directly from God whence she expected her man to come as well. She was somewhere around thirty-four (maybe thirty-eight), had a mousy-brown page boy, copied from Sidney's when she had her hair that way. And was somewhat emaciated from her ritual fasts. She lived in Brooklyn Heights near the headquarters of the Jehovah's Witnesses, to which she had converted some years before. She gloried in the neon sign on the Brooklyn Heights side of the river that flashed sayings like "Jesus Saves" and "Read Your Bible" across to Wall Street. Muriel spent many of her lunch hours handing out, or trying to hand out, copies of the *Watchtower* on Third Avenue.

"It'll only take a second, Barrett," Muriel said. She held out a red pen.

Barrett groaned. Not again.

Muriel had brought this up before. She wanted everyone in the office to have a different-color marking pen so when mistakes were made during the processing of copy she could trace them back to the perpetrator by the color the mistake was made in. She had found, and gnashed her teeth over the fact, that people were not good at initialing their corrections.

When she complained to Barrett about the failure to initial, Barrett said sometimes people don't *like* to be so individualized. He said no to the marking pens. He didn't like Muriel; he just felt like saying no. He had been angry because he wanted to be black and Muriel insisted that Garth be black.

"Red," Muriel said firmly. "We're going to try it. . . . Please, Barrett. Pretty please, with sugar." Muriel had a pointy unfulfilled librarian-looking face which she turned to him in appeal. "Red is the chieftain's color," she said.

"Okay," Barrett said to get rid of her. He held out his hand for the pen.

"I made Garth the color of evil," she whispered even though Garth wasn't there at the moment. "Lespedeza is purple—for you know what—and I'm yellow because yellow is the color of calm."

"Yellow is the color of urine," Emily said. She stopped on her way to the bathroom. She was holding a ketone stick with which she was going to test her urine for ketosis—which, if she had it, would mean she was losing weight.

"Get out of here," Barrett snapped. "Both of you. Can't you see I'm trying to get some work done?" He pulled out the manuscript he had prepared for Sidney's column that week. The column was called "IT's Eye." The story was one Blake had written about solving the dog elimination problem in our cities. Barrett loved the story. He knew Garth would hate it. Tough shit. "Here, send this out." He handed her the manuscript. "Mark it 'Eye' 5/14."

"Where's Sidney?" Muriel screeched upon seeing Blake's name at the top where the author usually was, next to Barrett Martin, editor. "Is something the matter with Sidney?"

"Just the flu, Muriel," Barrett said ominously. He had turned livid with rage, for half the office turned to look at Muriel when she screeched. She backed away now, seeing that she had made Barrett angry. At lunch she would buy him a bunch of violets to cheer him up.

As soon as things quieted down again, he reached for the phone. This time the loan man was there.

CHAPTER 8

Wasn't it funny, Garth was thinking, that the beautiful ones never turned out to be the best writers. Amelia Norton had her back to him. She was looking through some of the bound copies he had of early issues of the magazine. He was examining her. Unbelievable how these women got fat and then walked around displaying it as though they were on stage at Atlantic City. Amelia was clearly proud of her waist—not that it was small, merely considerably smaller than what came below it. The lady was fat. She wore a clinging black jersey dress that hugged her waist and hugged her broad hips, and cupped at that place where her fanny ended. It was that indentation of fabric that interested Garth. He watched it with some disgust and irritation as she leaned forward, shifted her weight from one foot to the other as she turned the pages. The shiny black fabric rippled against her buttocks. It looked like leather.

Amelia was waiting for him to make up his mind. She was prepared to wait all day if necessary. Garth said he had a few things to clear up and then they would go to lunch and talk about it some more. She didn't hear any rustling papers, but didn't turn around lest she catch him thinking. Several times Anne came in apologizing profusely for bothering him, but so-and-so or such-and-such matter had come to her attention and did he mind *very* much giving her a yes or no answer. She apologized in such an abject manner that Amelia sensed it was an act. When Anne was not there perched on Garth's desk with her skirt brushing his crossed shoes, Amelia wondered if he thought her beautiful.

56

"The thing is, Garth," she had said, arriving at eleven-thirty (their appointment was for ten, but Amelia had not for nothing spent the last ten years free-lancing for every major magazine in the country), "if Sidney is away somewhere cracking up, which is what I hear, then what you really need around here is someone to do 'Eye,' not for the new magazine—by the way, do you have a name for it yet?"

"Where did you hear that?" Garth demanded. Already his face was beginning to redden. How dare she come in there and suggest taking Sidney's place. It was outrageous. He began to see her as a moose he should shoot for his wall.

"Oh, I couldn't tell you that. Oh no," Amelia said, shaking her finger at him in what she thought was an appealing manner. "Certainly not. I always protect my sources. That's why people trust me."

"Well, your sources are wrong this time. Sidney happens to be on vacation this week," Garth said. "Now about your column in the new magazine."

"Well, Garth," Amelia said. "Oh, *no* coffee. Thank you so much, I never have a *thing* before one." She was sitting on his green plastic sofa. Anne was serving coffee in plastic cups. Amelia waited for Anne to go before continuing.

"The thing is, you want me to sign up to do a lead column for a back-of-the-book salary and not write for anyone else. I'm not sure that's a very good deal for me."

"I want to make life easier for *you*, Amelia. You'd only have to deal with me. A regular column would be a cinch for you."

"But it's a monthly, Garth. That means only twelve stories a year. There's no way I could do it. Even if you doubled your offer, I still couldn't do it. And what would I do with my energies, money aside?"

Garth smiled nastily. An editor was like a father to his children, had to look out for their every want and need. No, he thought, an editor was a lover. He had to keep those little bodies busy in order to get the product supplied.

"Listen, Amelia, I have a few things I've got to clear up here, and then we'll go out for a bite and settle this thing. You've got to trust me, honey. I want to make you happy. That's what I'm here for."

57

So Amelia unwisely turned her back. She didn't have too bad a face. It didn't look much under forty, though. She ate too much, drank too much, and it showed in the creases around her mouth, the thickening of her neck and chins. A damn good writer, though. Garth answered a few phone calls. But from the back she was, well, not his favorite sight.

Garth liked the people on his staff thin. Really thin, so that when they went out for the baseball games in spring and summer against the other magazines in the league—*Esquire*, *The New Yorker*, *Harper's*, et cetera—his staff of girls would be the best-looking. He also liked the way they looked moving around the office. He wouldn't tolerate anyone's obesity but his own. Garth left the office several times just to wander around and see what was happening. He wanted to see if Amelia would get annoyed. He wondered if she would follow him or do anything rash. The second time he left his office after sitting and chatting with Seth about his doing another women-and-violent-crimes story, he found Amelia sitting talking animatedly to Blake.

"Hi, Blake, how are you?" Garth strode over and shook his hand as though he hadn't seen him in months. He did this with all of his staff members about once every eight or nine months. When he approached them that way, some were so terrified they couldn't speak.

"Hiya, Garth," Blake said heartily. Naw, he wasn't going to be fired right then, was he?

"I thought you were out poopy scooping. Ha-ha," Garth laughed. Then he said, "By the way, where's that story you were going to do on—"

"It's right here. I've just finished it," Blake said eagerly. "Want to see it?"

"Yeah, yeah. Give it to me. I'll get on it right after lunch." Garth turned to Amelia while Blake hesitated. If he gave him the manuscript, which he said he wouldn't read until after lunch, he might put it down somewhere and forget it. If he didn't give it to him Garth might be annoyed. Finally he said, "I'll have it on your desk right after lunch, Barrett said he wanted to see it now."

"Fine, fine." Garth took Amelia away by the elbow. "Now you sit right here. I'll only be a second."

Things began to quiet down a bit as a few people started going out to lunch. Once again Amelia turned her back on him. A very foolish thing to do. Garth put his feet up on the desk. What was he going to do about Sidney. He didn't even know where she was to talk about her next week's column. Dog shit. That's what they had to run this week. Sooner or later it all came down to this. They started having tantrums and carrying on, and it was just too much. Was Sidney going to price herself out of the market. Was this one worth the trouble. He could always have the column written by a staff member and have no by-line on it the way they did in the beginning before Sidney had to have a by-line. Hell.

Garth watched Amelia's buttocks. The fabric soit of shimmered. It cupped her ass, pulling tight at the bottom where it should have hung free. Why did it do that, pull in that way. She didn't seem to be wearing any underwear. With a dress that tight, he'd be able to see some lines, he thought. Amelia put the book down on the table and bent over it as though she couldn't read it from that far away.

She was fat; Garth didn't like fat. A fat woman made him feel like a whale. But now, Amelia merely looked lush. Her black dress shone in the half-light (one of the overhead fluorescent lights in his office had burned out months ago and Garth had never had it replaced). Her large bottom beckoned. He sat at his desk with his feet up. Was she wearing underpants or wasn't she. No stockings. Sandals and smooth legs, egg white, for she hadn't been in the sun yet. Garth knew that because they had discussed it once before. On Saturday night in fact.

Anne poked her head in and said she was going to lunch. Garth nodded. "Fine, fine." Her appearance didn't affect his erection. "Close the door, will you."

He got up and went behind Amelia. "Beautiful," he whispered as a statement, not a term of endearment to which she should reply. He rubbed his protrusion back and forth against her. Against that place where the silky material went in. He squeezed her big loose breasts. The dress was cut so low in front he could put his hand right in and feel the whole thing, first one and then the other. As he rubbed back and forth, he clutched at her hips.

Outside there was the low murmur of voices, the clacking of typewriters, but Garth was aware only of the big ass with a dent

59

in the middle that made a bump (like a car going over a pothole in a highway) as he rocked back and forth over her. With one hand he gathered up the dress, pulling it up her thigh and squeezing her smooth white flesh as his hand traveled up. When his hand was on her breasts Amelia squirmed with pleasure. He thought she was beautiful. She wiggled against him. A friendly rub before eggs Benedict and white wine. But when his hand traveled up her leg, up her thigh and burrowed into her panties, that was too much.

"Not *here*, Garth," she whispered, not wanting to make him mad, but wanting to make him stop. "Later." She tried to turn around to give him a fondle and a pat and steer him toward the door. But Garth had a firm grip on her under her very small bikini underpants. He was working on her with his whole hand.

"Stay that way. You're so beautiful," he said to her back. "Don't move."

"No, Garth. Stop it." Her twisting around only made her awkward. It didn't stop his progress. Two fingers. Three fingers, and she was beginning to perspire, both with anxiety and the persistence of his erection. She wiggled to get away, tried to wrench out of his grasp. Horrified and humiliated. What if someone came in. He was pulling at her pants. "Come on, Garth, we can go home if you want to. Right now," she hissed, not wanting to talk in a normal tone. She clutched at her underpants on one side while he pulled at them on the other.

He wasn't listening to her. He was pulling at his zipper, holding her with one hand, the big fish that wasn't going to get away. Right here he was going to do it. He got his zipper undone was working at freeing himself. It was no easy task in that position and the friction he made trying aroused him even more.

All the while she was talking to him, trying to pry his hand out of her underpants. To her horror, she was damp. Damp all over. "Come on, Garth, *no*." She spoke as though he were a reasonable person who could be stopped. It wasn't until he wrenched her skirt up from between them and thrust it wildly against her bare bottom that she realized what he really had in mind.

He meant to do it *standing up*, her bent over like that like a defenseless animal. "No. Absolutely not." Why hadn't someone come in all this time. Where was everybody. What was going on here anyway?

"Take them off," Garth commanded.

Amelia was whimpering like a little girl. It turned him on. She was damp; she really wanted it, he thought. He thrust against her again and she squeaked, a tiny sound for such a big girl. But he couldn't do it with those things on. "Take them off," he urged. "I won't let you go until you do."

But she wouldn't. They were thin little things, made of some kind of stretchy lace. He pulled at them and they ripped. That turned him on too. How could she protest, she was as ready as the Holland Tunnel.

He plunged into her, holding hard onto her hips. He didn't feel at all fat that way. He felt like a charging bull, huge and powerful. She gasped and whimpered while he kneaded the insides of her thighs, felt himself through her and then forgot about her entirely as he heaved himself at her over and over. Heavy stomach beating against heavy ass. Garth felt the impact everywhere. It was solid and satisfying.

He didn't hear the sounds she made or even look at her when he finished. He turned his back, zipping himself away as though he had just had a particularly good visit to the men's room. The tremendous feeling of elation, of being completely lost in sensation, was gone now. He didn't need a thing. He was almost surprised when he turned around again and realized that Amelia was still there. She had pulled her dress down and combed her hennaed shag back into shape. There was a mean look in the corner of her eye, but she managed to smile halfheartedly.

"Well," she said. "That was something all right."

"You can come and see me any time," Garth said in what he thought was his most agreeable tone.

"Now about that column."

"Do it," he said. He looked at his watch. Twelve forty-five.

"I mean 'Eye,'" she said firmly. That's what she'd come for and she wasn't going to let it go now. Not now.

"All right," Garth said as though it didn't interest him at all. "Get an idea and we'll see how it looks. Only this once, though," he said.

"Oh, that's really *terrific,* Garth. You won't regret it. I promise you that. Shall we go?" She held out her hand to him.

He looked at his watch again, this time as though he'd never seen it before. He slapped his forehead. "Oh *no*. It's too late now, honey. I have a meeting at one."

CHAPTER 9

Where was Garth was what Sidney wanted to know. The closing day of her column passed and no one called but Terry. Terry called every night at nine o'clock. "Hello, how are you? Are you all right? Not frightened, are you? Anyone up there you know?" He always ended with, "Are you ready to come home yet?" and "You can call me any time, you know, if you want to talk."

Terry's calling her made it easier to stay. If he hadn't kept asking her if she was frightened, she might not have had to prove she wasn't. If he hadn't kept asking when she was going to come back, she wouldn't have had to prove she wasn't coming back. "So, he's not going to give in, huh?" she said.

"He's not very happy."

"It's one thing not to give in when the other person is still there. But when the other person isn't there and he still isn't going to give—well, that's quite a statement."

"He's just dumb, Sidney. It isn't any indication of his true feelings."

But Garth had no political reason to boycott her. What the hell was going on anyway. Every day Sidney drove slowly into Vineyard Haven and then lingered over the grocery and paper buying as long as she could. She didn't want to go home and be alone. But then she didn't want to call anyone either. If she started seeing people, they'd ask her all sorts of questions about Barrett. And she didn't want to say she'd left him. She hadn't wanted to make such a big commitment. More than anything she really wanted him to understand how strongly she felt, and to realize by her absence that he cared more about her than her money. So much for the writer's understanding of people. Even after eight days, she still nursed the hope that he might see his foolishness and relent. Even though, as the days passed and she got used to the quiet, she started thinking that maybe she didn't want to go home.

On Thursday, the closing day of the first week in about five years that Sidney had not contributed to her own column, she finally met someone she knew. As she came out of the grocery store struggling with the bag, she saw the notorious bore Henry Meadows coming toward her with a big grin. In spite of her resolve to stay in town until she found someone she knew with whom she could exchange a few words and thereby reaffirm her persona, such as it was, Sidney raised the bag so that it covered her face.

"Hey ho, Sidney," Hank called. He ran up and grabbed at the bag. "How are you?"

"Hank, what a surprise. How did you ever leave the weather?" Sidney relinquished the bag, but reluctantly.

"I'm on vacation," he announced gleefully. "Someone else, I don't even know who, is reading the weather. Of course the usual people are doing the actual charting, but they thought it would be provocative to have a surprise guest read the figures. It did make me the tiniest bit upset, I must say, to have the weather treated like 'Hollywood Squares,' but then who am I to protest? The promotion aspects of news are not my responsibility, you know."

As he talked, Hank looked up and down the street to see if there was anyone else around to recognize him, and then he scanned the sky. "However, I don't even care what's happening in the city. The blues are running and that's all that counts. Have you gotten any from your pier yet?"

"No, I haven't tried. I love to catch them, but I'm not good at organizing."

"Doesn't Barrett take care of the essentials, like throwing your line out and reeling it in? Ha-ha."

"He does. But he isn't here right now." Sidney didn't laugh.

"How splendid," Hank said. "That's splendid. Emma isn't here either. We're trying out separate vacations to see if that brings us together. Nothing else has." He smiled crookedly, which was his television trademark.

"And here's the weather," someone would say. Cut to Henry Meadows with crooked smile. Hank always looked very tall on television. His tallness was caused by the weather map's being hung on a level with his waist, or lower. He looked something like Woody Allen would if he had any flesh. He seemed like the sort of person who should be pigeon-toed and wall-eyed. The fact that he was neither did nothing to alter the effect. On screen, Hank did the weather with Woody Allen-like woefulness. But off screen, he was cheerful and talky and not always discreet. "Where's Barrett?" he asked.

"Working in New York," Sidney said. It was true.

"Well, that's splendid," Hank repeated.

Sidney started walking toward her car.

"Listen, I'm the odd man out at the Winklers' tonight—you know the Winklers," he said, and went on without looking for Sidney's nod of recognition. "Why don't you come along too?"

"Is she having a big party?" Sidney asked.

"No, just four or five intimates. I'll call her and tell her you're here."

Sidney pictured large Laney Winkler with her enormous caftans and buffets for thirty-six. "I don't know. I'm working on something." Her voice trailed off.

"Well, I'll call you later and see how you're doing. Maybe we could go fishing." Hank smiled and turned away. "Bye now."

Sidney watched him walk back up the street and park himself in front of the post office. He wasn't pigeon-toed at all. But he was bowlegged, and there was a thin fluff of hair at the front of his head where last summer it had been as smooth and shiny as a polished marble egg.

She got in the car and drove all the way up the Lambert's Cove road and back looking to see which houses were open. Even though it was early, there were already several airing houses and station wagons—two were so heavily loaded that it looked as if they shouldn't be able to move. Sidney's driving was a ploy for not going home. When she got back to the dirt road that led to her and her neighbors' houses, she stayed on the main road, went past Tashmoo Farm, glanced quickly at the fields of horses, and

64

nearly hit a bunch of wild turkeys that were unwisely trying to cross the road at that moment. She slowed down to watch them and then turned onto the up-island road and drove all the way to Menemsha on the other end of the island.

It took thirty minutes to get there. Menemsha was really only a dock with two fish markets and a gas station, a rocky beach and harbor for fishing boats and, in summer, yachts. No yachts yet. Also nestled in the curve in the pond was the Coast Guard station, a lousy restaurant where they sometimes bought lobster sandwiches, a general store, and some summer souvenir shops optimistically called "galleries"—all fairly authentically tatty. Perched on the hill above it were a lot of summer houses with nice views of the harbor. Many of them had telescopes trained on the bight at the mouth of the harbor at all times so people knew who was on the beach and who was going boating with whom and when. So much for Menemsha. Sidney didn't even park and walk along the dock as she usually did. She made one quick circle of the place and headed back to the down-island road.

Sidney didn't want to go home and hear from Hank Meadows, who would no doubt turn out to be a bore and a pest. And she was afraid about going to a party, even a small one. She didn't exactly consider herself to be shy. When she was on an assignment she could barge in anywhere to get a story. But at unofficial lunches with Garth and some of the other editors, she lost her sense of herself. She continued to feel like a college girl with the professors even after her promotions. Once in a restaurant with mirrored panels, she caught sight of herself. Her hair was newly done and the jacket of her expensive Dior suit was thrown casually over her shoulders. Sidney had a moment of panic when she thought she was a photograph. All she could recognize of herself was her frightened eyes showing through what felt like a disguise. At least when one posed for a photograph behind a funny faked front, the face was usually real. But her face that day was not the same as it had been the day before.

Several times Garth had taken Sidney to parties when Barrett was away or doing something else. Garth always led her in like a pet bear on a chain, and then let her go before the introductions began. He forgot to identify her or give her people to talk to. Once the party consisted of Garth, three very famous male writers, two male actors, a talk show host, and the wife of one of the writers. The wife scurried in and out with trays of food and said nothing. Sidney was neither introduced nor approached by anyone except the wife for the whole evening, which consisted of much drinking and one long discussion about celebrity and how difficult it was.

Each famous person had a great deal to say about his experiences with fame. Sidney kept saying to herself, I'm a tape recorder short and stout, which she hummed under her breath to the tune of "I'm a little teapot." I'm nothing but a tape recorder. They probably think I'm a mistress. Sidney listened and later wanted to write an article on fame. But Garth wouldn't let her. She thought she could do a funny piece about how the big problem with fame was the telephone calls and invitations to parties given by strangers, and being recognized in the street, pointed at and talked to at the most inopportune times—at the urinal in men's rooms, while talking at pay phones. Sidney had noticed, though, that whenever she did an interview with a famous person in a restaurant the person looked around the room many times to gauge the effect of his presence. Once she had to do an interview over again because the famous person was so depressed that he hadn't been recognized, he wasn't able to talk about himself at all.

Sidney wrote a favorable story about him. It was something she understood. At the publishing party for *Portraits I,* her first book, Sidney had been so depressed at the flamboyant way Garth and Barrett were holding court as thought she were merely a front for them (well, they thought so) that she hid in the ladies' room for an hour and a half. She read the paperback she always kept in her handbag for emergencies, and no one knew she was gone. It was Terry, finally, who came and retrieved her and then went to get Barrett when she said she had to go home.

The phone was ringing when she got in the door. She was sure it was Garth calling to ask about her next column.

"It's Laney, darling. Why didn't you tell me you were up here all alone, pet?"

"I didn't know you were here," Sidney said. She didn't like being called either darling or pet, particularly by people she only saw about three times a year, or less often if she could manage it.

"Quickly, tell me all the news. I've read every word you've written and what a fascinating winter you must have had. We've had a pretty good winter too. Davey, you know, has been made head of the department. Maybe you could do an article on him . . . I know he's not the kind of celebrity you usually write about, but he certainly has been doing some interesting things in linguistics, and he does have a word or two to say about that new journalism you're always practicing." Laney Winkler took a breath; it sounded like a vacuum cleaner zupping up a piece of a plastic bag.

"Well," she said, "anyway, we're having a few people in for dinner, and you're coming. Hanky said he's going to pick you up." Mercifully, she did not mention Barrett. "Well, see you later," she said, then, "Anything between you and Hank?"

CHAPTER 10

Sidney reeled in her line slowly, and then cast it out again.

"I have a feeling you two are separated," Hank said.

They were out on the pier fishing, had been quiet for a long time.

"What makes you say that?" Sidney had perceived that Hank was not such a buffoon after all. He was a rather thoughtful person who had taken her to Laney Winkler's and brought her a plate of shrimp curry, and did not get tanked up or force himself on her on the way home. In fact she had had a pretty good time. She wondered if the general improvement in Hank's personality was not due to the absence of his wife Emma, who spent all of her time talking about how much she hated weather and wished he could be in news instead. Which made him devote the same amount of time defending weather and giving reasons why in fact weather was superior to news. It did not occur to her that, without Barrett to do all the talking, people made more of a fuss of her.

"I've never seen you without Barrett before."

"I've gone halfway around the world to do articles without him."

"But neither of you has ever been up here without the other." Hank got a bite and began working at his reel. After a minute he said as though he had just thought of it, "Would you like this one?" offering her his fishing rod.

"No, it's yours." So far they had caught three large blues. One was hers and two his. "What are we going to do with all this fish?" she asked.

He reeled in the fourth and got down with the net to hoist it onto the dock. "We could eat one and freeze three, or I could take one. We could give one to Laney."

"We couldn't eat a whole one," Sidney said. She realized that she had just agreed to have dinner with him.

"We can try." He smiled.

Sidney thought he was nice when he smiled. But who wasn't. She looked at him in his checkered shirt and khaki fishing jacket and thought it might be nice to squeeze a chubby person for once. Nah, she shook her head as she watched him work the hook out of the fish's mouth. Ever since she had married, Sidney had been unaccountably afraid of other men. She backed away when one came near her, was constantly nervous that someone might approach her in a friendly way and then suddenly force her into lip contact. She was afraid she might throw up. She was afraid she might kiss back.

As they gathered up the gear and walked back toward the house, Sidney wondered if she should say something. Like, "Hands off, Hank, or I'll shoot you with my .22." She had one in the attic. It was in pieces, but she figured if she really needed it she could figure out how to get it together and how to shoot. Shooting, she was sure, would be quite easy.

Hank cleaned the fish with his Abercrombie & Fitch jacket still on because Sidney could not bring herself to tell him he could take it off. She stood at his elbow and asked him if he consulted the *I Ching* every day about the weather.

He laughed, which gratified her, since she knew she hadn't been funny and was in fact being rather cruel.

"Frankly I think the weather is a very boring subject when out of the office," he said.

It was uncanny how much he looked like Woody Allen.

"Has anybody ever told you you look like Woody Allen?"

"Nearly everyone, but I looked this way before he did," he said, looking just like him. "Emma hates him," he said, sounding just like him. "Do you think that means Emma hates me?"

"It depends," Sidney said. "Are you separated?"

"Well, she thinks we are. She's living with someone else."

"That's too bad. I'm sorry," Sidney said; "or are you glad it's over?"

"I really don't know. I change my mind every day. When you've been living with a person as noisy as Emma for twelve years, the silence after she's gone is unnerving. I'm sure she planned it that way. Emma and I weren't very happy together." He shrugged. "But then I'm not very happy without her either." He sighed. "Well, I guess it's kind of a relief not to be the object of so much displeasure. Could I have a drink, do you suppose?"

"Oh, I'm sorry." Sidney was very distressed at her reaction to this pitiful confession of Hank's. She wanted to make him feel better. Specifically, she wanted to cross the carpet, throw motherly arms around him, and tell him that Emma was a bitch and he was better off without her, also give him a hug and a kiss. All of this instead of the scotch and soda he had asked for.

She went to get him the scotch and soda wondering if perhaps he said all that to break down her defenses by making her feel sympathetic and motherly. Since there's nothing like a comforting cuddle to lead one directly into lip contact and the sack.

Sidney had never even particularly liked Hank. He was short and rather chunky, had wispy hair and features that were more alarming than endearing. He wasn't any gorgeous hunk of man bursting with sexual energy—but even more provocative than that, Hank was a man in need. And there's nothing like a man in need to get a woman's hormones going.

Sidney sat across the square of rug and glared at him, for Barrett, regardless of how active he was feeling, was never a man in need.

"I seem to be making you angry," Hank said. "I'm sorry to be talking about myself so much."

"It's not you. I'm just so tired of the sexes." She laughed suddenly. "All this rotten angst year after year, and changing partners and not getting along. Wondering what to do and where to go, and if anybody will ever do. It's so awful." Sidney muttered on, incoherently, she thought. "And the whole point seems to be to have someone to rub genitals with on good days."

Sidney was aware that she was not being very attractive, and this too made her angry. She was not supposed to care what Hank Meadows, whom she didn't even want, would think. And all along she had the uncomfortable feeling that he would get her in the end because she couldn't look at her watch any more and announce, "Golly, how time flies. Barrett must be just about here by now. I'll just save him some time and go get the .22."

"That's one way to look at it, of course," Hank was saying so earnestly one could almost overlook his comic resemblance. "I don't like to look at it that way, though. I think companionship and understanding are very important. . . . There's a lot to be said for company, enjoying being with someone and doing things together. It's terrible to eat alone."

"What's the point, though, without, ah, the other?"

"Well, sex of course is important, too. Obviously companionship isn't everything. But in the human being the inflammation seems to die down after a while."

"Oh, God."

"Well, it can't be the same after years, you know."

"Oh, God."

"You are separated, aren't you?" Hank said after a long pause.

"How did you know?" Sidney was surprised.

"Well, you sound so bitter."

"I do?" Sidney walked around the living room restlessly. She straightened the books on the coffee table, plumped the pillows on the sofa. "I don't mean to sound bitter. I was just thinking of you. The way you were talking made me feel so sad.

"You're the kind of person who really wants to be happily married. I've always noticed that about you. She always did everything she could to annoy you and you tried so hard not to be angry and now you're upset because she isn't here to make you angry any more. It's absurd." Sidney finished her tidying and plumping job and looked around. When she saw that there was nothing more to do, she said she would start dinner.

She was thinking about Barrett. When Barrett first married her, he had tried to break Sidney of her fits of feeling; emotional

70

outbursts, he called them. She would get onto some subject like prison reform or the sexual problems of the Chinese pandas in the Washington zoo, or puppies, anything, and suddenly she would be unreasonably fervent. She would get hot, be close to tears. Barrett was not pleased with any display of emotion. He didn't like to be touched in public. He was upset when he first discovered this tendency of hers to be overwhelmed with feeling at the oddest times and for no reason that he could see. He told her that reporters had to be like doctors even at home. "Girl writers always become involved with their subjects," Barrett said. "You must work hard not to think about making anything better. That's not your job. Don't get disgusted or upset. Don't fall in love." He always told her to toughen herself up and stop thinking so much. It was her job to draw little conclusions, not big ones.

There had been other men in Sidney's life who told Sidney she was cold because she shed tears over poodles in pet stores, could hardly be consoled during Mustang commercials when the foal first tried his legs for the camera, but showed little emotional interest when it came to a man between her legs.

"I'm sorry," Hank said again. He followed her behind the counter into the kitchen. "I didn't mean you sounded bitter bitter. I just meant that if you take such a pessimistic attitude it will be harder to start over again." He did not ask her about Barrett again.

They finished off three quarters of the fish. Sidney worried throughout the meal about what she would do if he made a pass at her. Mostly she worried about giving in. Giving in was the sort of thing she would have done before she married. Not so much because she wanted to in those days, but it seemed to matter to them so much, and it was so difficult to say no. She continued to give in to Barrett in much the same way. She allowed him to manage their orgasms the way he managed the money. He did what he wanted and took it for granted she was satisfied. Now it caused Sidney a good deal of anguish that she thought she would give in. She didn't know why she thought she would, she didn't want to. Or did she. It was difficult to tell.

They carried the cups of coffee into the living room and drank them sitting on opposite sofas. They had placed themselves that way because that was where they had been sitting before dinner, now smiled and yawned at each other vaguely. In spite of Sidney's anxiety over the matter, it was not a sexually charged atmosphere. The conversation was about news, how different it was in print from what it was on the air. Hank said he liked air news because it was simpler and shorter and more difficult to slant. Air news, he contended between yawns, was less biased. It was the sort of argument that Sidney usually hated. How could anyone say that TV news wasn't biased because fewer words were used. No wonder he was in weather. You couldn't slant fair and warm. Although partly cloudy could present problems.

At around nine o'clock Hank said thank you and good night. He gathered up his fishing tackle while Sidney stood awkwardly at the door. She thought she was glad he was going without a scene, but she also wondered if she were ugly, emotional, or otherwise frightening. Wasn't he supposed to jump on her and make her give in. She had heard from various friends that separated males were even worse about jumping on one than single males were, since separated ones had something to prove as well as their nerves to soothe.

Sidney didn't think she wanted sex—not with him anyway, who was probably flabby and maybe even grotesque. But she was sort of sorry he didn't put his arms around her and give her a reassuring we're-all-in-this-together sort of hug. All she wanted was to roll around with him on the sofa a little just to feel human for a minute. But she knew she couldn't touch him. There wasn't much touching going around any more, no such thing as friendly fondling between adults. Hardly any friendship at all in fact.

"It was a good dinner," he said. He clutched his tackle box, his fishing rod, and a net.

She leaned against the door, thinking that maybe she should have washed her hair when he said he was coming over to fish. Maybe she should have put on some make-up. She nodded. "It was."

"It was fun," he said. "You're a good person to fish with."

Oh, he shouldn't have said that. A tear sprouted in Sidney's eye. Cold hands, warm heart. Good to fish with, lousy to love. "Thanks," she said stiffly. She turned on the outside light so he wouldn't trip on his way to the car.

Well, should he or shouldn't he. Hank stood there unable to

make up his mind. He had always sort of liked Sidney. She was cute in a muted sort of way. But mad. Mad he didn't need. "Well, I guess I'll go on home. Thanks again."

"Are you all alone in the house?" Sidney asked idly.

"Yeah, kind of creepy, isn't it?"

"Do you really think so?" Sidney brightened. "I thought I was the only one."

"Yeah, I hate it."

"Why don't you stay a little while longer then? We could have a brandy."

"Do you mean it?" Hank asked, looking at her carefully. She was really quite pretty now that he thought about it. "I'm not boring you, am I?"

Sidney shook her head. When he dropped all the fishing gear on the floor, she gave him a small hug to see what he felt like. He looked so grateful she offered him her mouth. He kissed with loose lips, his mouth opening and closing the way a fish's does when it eats. That was enough of that. Sidney backed away just as his hands caught her around the waist. He pulled her lips against him.

"Oh, Sidney," he moaned. He didn't want to let her go even long enough to get across the room to the sofa.

Oh, Christ. It was the same thing even in middle age. When he moaned, "Oh, Sidney," like a high school boy who would die if he didn't get it, Sidney was appalled. Hadn't anybody learned anything since then. He certainly hadn't. He was pawing her breasts, this brokenhearted man with the spongy stomach.

"Which is your room?" he muttered. He was so eager to be everywhere at once he was shaking.

Sidney was aghast. This mild little person. She hardly knew him, thought they'd neck a little to check each other out, yet he was pulling at her clothes and whimpering at her.

"Please, Sidney, it's been so long." He squeezed her waist where he managed to pull her sweater up, made a sort of strangled noise, "Agggh," when he touched her skin, as though he had just touched fire.

Maybe he really hadn't had anybody in a long time, Sidney thought. He was eating her neck, trying to get his hand inside the waistband of her blue jeans, and he was panting with the effort of it all. Sidney thought he was going to have a heart attack and die in her living room. Barrett wouldn't come for anything else, but a man dead from desire for his wife—that would get him up there.

"Hey." Sidney tried to calm him down, but he had already lost himself. Even if he had the will, he couldn't retreat with honor now.

It was easier to do it than not do it. She didn't want to see the shocked expression on his face that she would get if she backed away and told him to go home. She didn't want an argument, didn't feel up to self-righteous anger. It was easier to lead him into the bedroom and lie down on the patchwork quilt she'd made just for that room. She helped him take off her shirt and her blue jeans.

He was so emotional, as though he couldn't believe his luck, almost wept at the sight of Sidney in her underwear. She took it off, gratified at his reaction, and he grabbed her like a cannibal at a picnic. Fresh girl.

She felt sorry for him. He was so inept. He was so excited, so enraptured by her nakedness he seemed hardly able to breathe. He also acted like sex was something he had to get fast; he had to get on top of her and stick it in before she knew what was happening, or else he'd lose his chance. He held onto her, didn't even try to take his clothes off, as though if he let her go even for an instant, even with her already undressed she'd get away.

He tried to roll her over and pin her down so he could get between her legs. But she wasn't trying to get away. It was her bed and her room. His desperation only made her feel wanted, his plumpness made her feel thin and his awkwardness made her feel competent. She unbuttoned his red checkered fishing shirt and offered her breasts to his stomach. She tickled him with her nipples, with her tongue; let him squeeze and chew on her, and petted him back as though he were her favorite kind of man. Which was true at that moment. She felt so slim, so sleek and useful. She rubbed what Barrett called her mousy little body against Henry Meadows, who still had his shirt and trousers half on. He had stopped trying to force her onto her back and was begging her to let him, please, before he couldn't stand it any more. She had been pressing his penis between her two hands, as though it were a new thing to her. She thought it over for a split second and then

74

did something Barrett never let her do. She took it into her mouth.

"Oh, God, Sidney." He was certainly well over forty, but groaned and sighed and shivered like a virgin of fifteen.

Sidney knew she didn't have to do anything else. That would be enough. But she wanted to. After a few seconds she pulled away from him, helped him out of his clothes, and then slid under him, opening her thighs.

CHAPTER 11

The man's name was Grey. It took days for Barrett to get in to see him. He spent the waiting time alternately trying to write Sidney's next column and trying to make a date with Lespedeza. Lespedeza kept telling him she'd see in a day or two when her calendar cleared up. But she didn't. She acted surprised when he asked and always started whispering when he called her at home. "Oh, gotta go now, Barrett, see you," she'd say as soon as she heard his voice. Barrett couldn't understand her reticence, her unwillingness even to speak to him. He thought she was embarrassed and wanted to make her feel at ease. But sometimes it occurred to him that what had happened between them didn't mean anything to her. She didn't want to have dinner with him because she didn't like him.

Mr. Grey had gray eyes, a gray Brooks Brothers suit that looked ten years old but was probably new. He had a silver-gray crew cut and wore a white shirt and red and blue striped tie. Barrett disliked him immediately. His sculpted features looked unbending and rather unintelligent, Barrett thought. He looked anti-Semitic, and Barrett could tell right away he had no imagination.

"Great little paper," he had said when Barrett told him days before that he wanted to buy *New Journal*. Now he said, "Where did they get that story about the bank robber? Shouldn't they have turned him in?"

"I, ah, don't know anything about the paper yet. Except what I read in it." Barrett smiled. "I wasn't there when the story came in."

"But he is a felon, isn't he?"

"Yes, I guess he is, if what's in the article is true," Barrett said cautiously. He thought it was time to leave.

"And he did hold a hostage for several hours. That makes him a kidnaper, doesn't it?" Mr. Grey stabbed the air with a pencil. Clearly this was a subject to which he had been devoting a good deal of thought.

"Well, yes, I guess, one could look at it that way."

"It was a poorly written article and it should have ended with 'J' whoever it is being put away for life."

"That may be the case. I can't argue one way or the other the moral implications of either protecting or revealing one's source."

"I'd like to hear your views, though," Mr. Grey said.

"Mr. Grey, I intend to buy a weekly magazine. I plan to run it better than it's being run at the moment." Barrett tried to control his irritation. "It's going to make money, and I will pay back the loan with as much interest, I'm sure, as the law allows."

"Oh, I'm so sorry," Mr. Grey said. He took some glasses out of his desk and began to play with them. "It's just that I so rarely get to talk about anything that isn't bank business. I'm just curious really. What *would* you do about an article like that?"

"I'm sure I'd run it," Barrett said.

"Would you? And not turn the guy in?" Mr. Grey persisted.

"I'm a magazine editor, not a policeman. Mr. Grey, I'm sure Stewart Adams doesn't know who he is to turn him in. It would be a deal between the writer and the robber. The editor wouldn't have anything to do with it."

"Hmmm . . ." Mr. Grey tapped with his pencil. "Are you planning on making any changes at all?"

Barrett hesitated. He didn't know whether Mr. Grey habitually read *New Journal* or just read one issue because of this loan. He didn't know how much information one was supposed to give a loan man. This one had all his bank records on the desk in front of him. He and Sidney banked there. He could see the records in the folder. He knew their salaries by the check deposits, knew the savings account figures. Was he required to give this person his views on editorial policy as well. Was he supposed to get approval for the new layouts he planned for features, the new cover he had in mind, the addition of color on pages with lead articles. Also that he would accept four-color ads and do a center fold with lots of little-known national news items. He looked at Mr. Grey warily, not knowing at all what he should do. Finally he said, "I'm going to drop 'Gay Today' and add a big book section."

He knew the book section was a dangerous thing to add, but he didn't think Grey would know that. Book publishers were not a good source of advertising revenue. They were very conservative and tended to advertise only in a handful of well-established papers and magazines. But Barrett felt very strongly about books. He didn't think very much of publications that didn't run reviews, even though he knew that adding book reviews was not likely to increase readership. Barrett tapped his fingers against the arm of his chair. How long was a loan supposed to take anyway. His chair was very hard, was that supposed to mean it shouldn't take long. Barrett was very annoyed at Terry. Terry would have known what to say. In fact Terry should be here at this very moment doing this job for him. This kind of thing was not in his province at all. But Terry said he wouldn't even discuss the deal until Sidney came back and gave her approval. Although Barrett argued with him, there wasn't very much he could do.

"What a mistake," Mr. Grey was saying.

Barrett snapped to attention. He had been staring at the carpet, visualizing wringing Terry's neck.

"I think it's an extremely interesting and timely column. Very important in today's society."

Uh-oh. Barrett hunched down in his chair. The one thing he thought was sure to please Grey, and he'd misjudged.

An hour and a half Mr. Grey kept him sitting there. After an hour Barrett wondered if he was waiting to hear a promise that Barrett would singlehandedly apprehend the bank robber. Then he wondered if he was meant to offer his body for the money. Finally Mr. Grey said they would be delighted to lend him some of the money, if Barrett would put up some of his own.

"In some cases, we will put up all the money in an acquisition

Lespedeza. He saw her smile at Alden, their sports expert. Alden didn't do much but work out at a nearby gym. Once in a while he wrote a story that Barrett rewrote word by word. Alden was tall, had lots of straight black hair and a strong jaw. He wore plaid sports jackets and loafers. Garth had given Alden his job because Alden's father was a governor. Catching Lespedeza's smile, Alden came over and sat on the corner of her desk. She squeezed his elbow, then stroked his knee as though it were an old friend.

Barrett was so incensed at this betrayal of hers that his plan came to him in one piece. He would call Peter Marshall, tell him he wanted to talk over his summer reading piece, and get invited to Fire Island for the weekend. That way he would have Lespedeza where she couldn't get away, a place to write Sidney's column, and he would be able to sound Peter out about starting a book section for *New Journal*. Immediately he began to brighten up. Maybe he would get away with it after all. Maybe he would, he thought.

But now he couldn't bring himself to tell Terry what he had done. He was afraid that Terry wouldn't approve, and he cared what Terry thought.

"Well, listen," Terry said after a long silence into which he did not offer one encouraging word, "I'll talk to you later. I have some work to do right now."

After having a closing-day-editorial drink with Seth, Alden, and Blake at a nearby bar, Barrett went to Bloomingdale's to pick up the things he had ordered from the gourmet shop: a whole ham, a whole side of Nova Scotia salmon, two loaves of black bread, and a pot of French mustard. He charged these things to the magazine. What the hell. Then he bought some socks and hung around in the cosmetics department to see if anybody interesting would turn up for a make-over. When no one did, he went home.

Terry didn't get home until ten o'clock. Barrett was furious that he had gone out to dinner without him.

"Where the hell have you been?" Barrett demanded when he finally reached him.

"Not even my mother has ever dared to ask me that question," Terry said. "What do you think? You think that, with Sidney gone, I have to be with you every minute? I have my own affairs to look after, you know."

loan," he said, "but then we participate in the deal ourselves. In this case, however, we are not willing to participate in the deal. I wonder why you are not advancing any of your own capital."

Barrett couldn't say he didn't want to risk it since it had been so hard to come by, and it had been so long in coming. It was as simple as that. Barrett's father was the owner of a small, perpetually failing dry cleaning establishment. The fact that there had never been any money was a constant source of recrimination and bad feeling in his family and, Barrett felt, accounted for, more than anything else, the miseries he suffered in childhood. He didn't want to ask Mr. Grey if he had ever been poor. So he told him he was going to use his own money to redecorate and pay some of the bills, and generally improve the place.

Mr. Grey said that was indeed fine, but the bank needed some indication of *his* confidence in the money-making potential of *New Journal* in order for them to have confidence in the loan. Barrett said he would guarantee the loan, and wasn't that good enough. No, Mr. Grey said. They would give thirty thousand dollars if he would put up twenty thousand. In fact they would give him sixty thousand altogether if Barrett would put in the forty thousand Mr. Grey knew perfectly well Barrett had.

"Why isn't a guarantee good enough?" Barrett demanded in spite of Mr. Grey's increasing impatience. Barrett suspected Mr. Grey was just being arbitrary. He was being absurd. What was the difference anyway between a guaranteed loan and Barrett's putting up the money in the first place. Barrett told Mr. Grey that if he put his own money in at this point and the magazine failed, he would not be able to pay back the loan. He would in fact be bankrupt. But if he *guaranteed* the loan and the magazine went under, he would still be able to pay the bank back. "That's logic," Barrett said. He wasn't going to offer his body. He wasn't going to promise to catch a bank robber, or even leave in "Gay Today."

"That's our position," Mr. Grey said, leading him to the door of his office. "I'm sure if you think about it you'll see it our way." Barrett did not tell the man he thought he was an idiot. How could they run a bank that way. It was absurd.

Barrett called Lespedeza again that night. He hated the risk of asking her anything personal at the office. "What are you doing Friday?" he asked when she finally answered.

"Oh, hi, George," she said.

"What do you mean, George? This is Barrett."

"I know, George, but you can't come over now. I have some friends here from the office."

"I don't want to come over now. I want to know if we can go out on Friday." There was a plaintive quality in his voice that Barrett knew was there but couldn't quite control. If one more thing went wrong he didn't know what he'd do.

"Now, let's see, Friday. Hmmmm. I just don't know right now, George. You see, I promised Peter and Majorie that I would go out to Fire Island with them this weekend and I haven't decided whether I should go on Friday or Saturday."

"Well, when are you going to decide?"

"I haven't decided."

"Terrific," Barrett muttered. He tried to control his irritation. "All right, call me when they've gone." He hung up.

Barrett called Terry. "What are you doing this weekend?" he asked.

"I haven't decided."

"We can't just sit around here," Barrett said. "Christ, did you know it's summer? Have you come to realize that, and I am being deprived of my summer house. Did you consider that, when you left Sidney up there, that she was depriving me of my house?"

"Why don't you go and see Sidney? Remember Sidney, she's there with the house. Why don't you go see both of them?"

"You know perfectly well why I can't. She has to come back on her own. Even if it takes another week," Barrett said.

"Look, I have people here," Terry said. "I'll have to call you later."

Barrett called Lespedeza back at ten-fifteen. "Well, what have you decided about Fire Island?" he demanded.

"I'm going on Friday after work."

"You're avoiding me. Why are you avoiding me?"

"I'm not avoiding you."

"All week you said you would see me, then you said you were busy—you can't be busy all the time—and now out of the blue you're telling me you're going to Fire Island."

"Well, I told you. This was a very hectic week for me. I had Danny and Ellen over to lunch to celebrate *National Geo-*

graphic's buying his bird series. And then Mother's cousin Mamie was here—"

"Lespedeza," Barrett whined.

"Well, I just *have* to go see Peter and Marjorie. After all that work I did typing up his book and everything, he'd just be crushed if I didn't come out."

"Lespedeza, you always sound as though everybody and his brother's well-being depends on your presence."

"That's a cruel thing to say, Barrett."

"I'm just trying to determine why my well-being is so unimportant to you in contrast to that of so many other supremely unimportant people whose well-being you seem to take very seriously."

"You're married to Sidney."

"What the hell difference does that make?"

"I like Sidney."

"Christ, I like Sidney too. Only Sidney isn't here right now and can't be damaged by what she's not around to see." All this Barrett said very patiently, but he was getting very annoyed. Since when was she so particular about marriage.

"I thought you and Sidney were so straight with each other. I thought you had a policy of faithfulness. That's what Sidney told me."

Barrett cleared his throat. "Things change after you've been married for a while. Why do you think Sidney isn't here? We're going through a kind of change of life. Maybe things will stabilize back to what they were and maybe they won't." This was the first time Barrett had even thought such a thing.

"Barrett, I think you're wonderful. I really do," Lespedeza said. "If someone told me I had to get married or else, I would marry you. I really would."

"Does that mean you're staying Friday night?"

"No, but maybe we can work something out next week, okay?"

CHAPTER 12

Barrett had been watching his secretary water her many shelves of plants. He watched her apply yet another layer of maroon to her nails. His mail folder was in front of him untouched. Finally he opened it and read the first letter. "Dear Mr. Martin: I love your magazine. I read it every week. I was thinking about a subject that I think would be very good for you to do. It's a sort of general interest story. My wife is a plumber and I think . . ." Barrett looked up from the letter. He swiveled in his chair and looked directly at Lespedeza. She was wearing a purple leotard on top and a green corduroy skirt that very nearly disappeared while she was sitting. She was talking on the phone.

"I'm sorry you didn't like that article—yes, we did try to present an unbiased view—no, the editor is in a meeting right now—no, I'm sorry the writer isn't here either. Why don't you write a letter to the editor? Well, I understand how you feel. Yes, I know you think it's an insult to your ethnicity, but a letter to the editor is the best approach." Lespedeza said all of this in the most drawn-out Southern drawl she could conjure, sugar sweet and super reasonable. She looked up and saw Barrett staring at her purple legs. She flashed him a smile that was pure Miss Florida.

"I'm sorry you see it that way. No, I can't personally cancel your subscription. You'll have to talk to the subscription department. No, I'm afraid I can't transfer the call. You're being very rude." Lespedeza held the phone away from her head. "Frankly I don't know the number of the subscription department. I think it's in Colorado somewhere—you No'theners, Ah declare." She hung up.

Throughout this conversation, something terrible was happening to Barrett. Various parts of his anatomy were lurching about dangerously. Blood had risen to his cheeks and his breathing became labored. He was just about to call Muriel to bring him

Merck's quickly before he started hyperventilating when he realized that Lespedeza was the cause. It was something about her purple legs and the way she said, "you No'theners, Ah declare."

Barrett turned back to the letter folder. "Firm no thanks," he wrote across the query from the plumber's husband. He underlined "firm." Sometimes they didn't believe you the first time. Barrett looked up as Garth strode into the office looking neither to the right nor the left. "Barrett," he called when he was halfway across the room but nowhere near Barrett's desk.

"Barrett, I want you in my office right away." He went into his office and slammed the door before Barrett could follow.

Barrett had just been dialing the phone that minute. He was trying to reach Terry, was irritated because Terry hadn't called him back the night before and hadn't picked him up when he went out to breakfast that morning. He hung up before the phone could ring, looked around to see if anyone had that keen excitement the staff always displayed when someone was in trouble. All worked stopped, no one answered the phones. They just stood outside Garth's office and listened to the screams. It was a dangerous thing to do, though, because Garth couldn't stand still when he was angry. Sometimes in the middle of a scream he came storming out of his office and carried on with the tirade in the art department. If there was a crowd gathered there, he screamed at them.

No one had any particular look of anticipation. All heads were carefully bent over mail folders and manuscripts, the slimy hypocritical bastards, Barrett thought. If he could just keep Garth's voice down.

"Well, good morning, Barrett, m'boy," Garth said, waving his hand toward the green plastic sofa. "Come sit down."

"Morning, Garth." It was a bad sign when Garth started the day calling him "m'boy."

"Would you like some coffee? I haven't had anything yet—Annnnee—" Garth yelled.

Anne came in. "Good morning, Garth."

"Anne, honey, will you get us some Danish and coffee?"

Barrett knew better than to say no. Garth had his eyes narrowed in challenge. "So you think I shouldn't be having a Danish. Is that what you think, huh? Well, I'll have two," is what his face clearly said. No, Barrett knew he was going to have to keep Garth company in his sin, he would have to wolf down one of those inedible, indigestible Danish from the corner deli that were made without the benefit of one single natural ingredient.

"Don't look at me like that," Garth demanded.

"Like what?" Barrett was alarmed. He hadn't even been thinking of him.

"I'm beginning my diet at lunch."

Barrett sighed. He didn't say he didn't give a flying fuck about Garth's stomach. He was relieved. This was just going to be a meeting about the new magazine. The competition was over next week—it wasn't a large enough staff to require a very long entry period. He and Garth were the judges, and he had already decided on *Lovelife*.

"Barrett, have you heard anything about *New Journal* lately?" Garth asked.

Barrett jumped. "It certainly is getting worse, isn't it?" he said after a pause he thought was an hour long. He pulled on a hangnail and it began to bleed. Shit.

"Adams is trying to sell it," Garth announced. He slapped his thigh. "*What* do you think of that?"

"Really," Barrett said musingly. "*Really*, how interesting." He sucked on his finger. Shit, this wasn't funny at all. He wondered who the viper was.

"Ha-ha." Garth laughed. "What kind of fool would want to take on that tired old thing?"

"Really, you think that, Garth?"

"Well, it's been losing money for a long time now. What a mess it's in."

"It doesn't appeal to you at all?" Barrett didn't believe it.

"Nah. Does it appeal to you? That little local paper? What kind of circulation does it have—a hundred, hundred ten thousand? Nothing."

Barrett shrugged. "A loyal following nonetheless."

"Now listen to me, Barrett. We've got a lot of work to do around here. You're my head man. Right? I can't do a thing around here without you. Now don't go mooning around about this *New Journal* thing. We don't want it, I don't think anyway, unless we could make it national. Weell, even so, I'm not so sure about it. You know—ah, thanks, Annie. That looks good. Here, Barrett."

Barrett took the paper plate offered him. It had a cherry Danish on it. The cherries were made of a petroleum by-product. No doubt about it.

"You see, Barrett, there's room for just so many *Rolling Stones*, and *Rolling Stone* has all of it. We can't find another hidden audience for that kind of material. Everyone who wants it gets it from that. Now what the country is really hankering for is a raunchier *Playboy*, a *Oui* or a *Penthouse* for the family. Dirty but clean, if you know what I mean. No dirty pictures, of course, no fucking-on-motorcycle fantasies or anything like that. But copy that *means* something to them. You know, strikes *home*."

Barrett nodded. It was all that was expected of him.

"Now keep your mind on that, okay? You're the one. I trust you and rely on you. I want you to be there with me, you know that. We're going to be big. Don't you forget it."

Barrett nodded again. He was touched. How could he be so disloyal to a man who had done so much for him, who thought of him even now when he was being betrayed. He managed a weak smile with his nod.

"You know, it's funny." Garth bit into his pineapple Danish. "I hear that Adams has a serious bidder. I wonder who it is—well, never mind. Whoever it is, we won't give him any help, will we?" All this he said chewing.

Barrett took a sip of coffee to avoid looking at him. What a bastard he was, threatening him with his mouth full. Stupid Anne. There was a whole quart of milk out there and she had filled his coffee with Coffeemate.

"Barrett, what's going on with Sidney? It's been a long time since we've had a chat about it. Are you two in trouble or something?"

"No, of course not." He carefully put the coffee cup down and examined the hangnail, which now had a colorless liquid seeping out of it. "Sidney wanted to take a few days off, and I could hardly deny her."

Barrett made an effort and faced Garth's chewing. "She works very hard as you well know. Very hard, and she wanted a few days off. I thought it was only fair. Everyone needs a retreat from time to time."

Garth's eyes narrowed with suspicion again. "Where the fuck is she? I want to talk to her." His voice rose menacingly as he remembered how irresponsible she was being, how insulting to him, her editor. "God damn it, what does she think this is, an optional course?" he yelled.

"Now, Garth," Barrett said soothingly. "Don't get excited. She didn't mean anything by it. You know Sidney. If she were any more stable she'd be dead. This is the first time in years she's needed a rest. Don't get exercised about it."

"What does she want, Barrett?" Garth's mouth twitched in fury. "These *women*."

"She wants a rest, that's all. You can't get mad at that."

"I'm telling you, Barrett, if I don't get a column from her next Monday or Tuesday, I don't know what I'm going to do. You tell her that."

Barrett nodded.

"No, I'll tell her myself. Where is she, the Vineyard?"

"NO. She went to Hawaii." Barrett didn't know why he said that. What a peculiar thing to say. He had perspiration on his top lip, no handkerchief. Oh, that guy, the one from *Time* or *Newsweek*. He went to Pago Pago, that's why he thought of it. Hell.

"Hawaii? Oh, come on, Barrett. . . . Don't worry. I'll be very gentle with her. I know what to say."

"I'm telling you, Garth, Sidney's not on the Vineyard."

"Okay, okay. I just want you to understand me. If you can't handle your wife, I will." Garth went over to his mail folder and picked up the first letter. As soon as Barrett was gone he was going to call Sidney.

Barrett knew he had been dismissed. He got up and walked to the door. When he got to it, it looked unfamiliar. There was a dartboard on it. Barrett stared at the darts and dartboard. The door was so badly scarred from the darts, it would soon have to be replaced. Barrett wasn't sure how he got there. You see, Sidney, he was thinking. You *see* what happens when you start fooling around. You *see*. Now we don't have any choice. Somehow he got back to his desk and dialed the phone. But Terry still wasn't in.

CHAPTER 13

Garth finished what Barrett had left of his Danish, then sat back in his chair and looked at the ceiling. He sat that way for some minutes. Several nights before he had met Eagleton Redpath at a dinner party. Not a *very* good dinner party, but there were a number of people Garth had been happy to meet. Eagleton among them. He was a young business person from CBS. Garth didn't exactly get what he did, but then Eagleton probably didn't know either.

Over the years, as they disagreed with him, Garth had forced out the various business partners who had helped him reorganize *Inside Track*. There had been three of them. One was the scion of a rich investment company, and two were merely young geniuses. The son of the investment company stayed on the longest. He had gotten them the money they needed, and Garth was reluctant to quarrel with him even years later in case he might need him again sometime in the future. From the beginning the other two advised branching out from the magazine. If they had another company inside the corporation that was a guaranteed money-maker, they felt, they could amortize the losses *IT* would have over the first four or five years. They explained to Garth at the beginning that, since they didn't start with a limitless supply of capital, after a few years they would be so deeply in the hole that even if *IT* eventually began to make money they wouldn't make anything. Now if they had a nice little company minting money, they could work out all kinds of tax breaks. The magazine itself could be a shelter. When they needed—or if they needed—more money, they could go public and quickly get a lot of ready cash, buy something else. Garth, of course, had seen the wisdom in this approach, and they had purchased a nice little greeting card business that did the kinds of things that Hallmark didn't do. For several years everything happened exactly the way his partners said it would.

There was only one problem with the setup. Garth had made a reasonable amount of money, lived in a nine-room cooperative apartment at Sixty-first and Fifth Avenue—not in the Pierre, but right next door in a new, very exclusive building. He got a tax write-off for most of the apartment because he used it for business purposes a lot of the time. The problem with the setup was two-fold, and Garth worried over it for several years before he acted. First, he was not in control. He was not the undisputed boss of the corporation. He was not even publisher of his own magazine. The scion was publisher and he was editor. Although he did not at first care about being publisher, in fact knew very little about that side of the business, publisher was still first on the masthead. Since Garth had always been both the head and the body of the magazine, not being first on the masthead irked him. The second part of the problem was the greeting cards and the partners. One did not build an empire in communications through mildly por-nographic greeting cards. Or any kind of greeting cards. Garth wanted to get rid of the greeting cards as soon as the magazine got into the black. The partners argued that they were doing too well to make that kind of a change. They had in mind buying another company. But the company was not a magazine, it was another greeting card company. Garth could see very well that his goals were no longer the same as those of his partners, and if they continued on together, before too long his would be the weakest part of the corporation in their eyes. One by one the friendships broke up as Garth drove wedges of suspicion between them. Now Garth was editor and publisher and, though not as rich, thought himself doing very well nonetheless without benefit of greeting cards or partners.

However, Garth felt that he needed some business genius of a broader base than his own now that he was expanding himself. As he sat at his desk the crumbs of his Danish and Barrett's still dust-ing his lap, he weighed the advantages and disadvantages of Eagle-ton Redpath—a rather peculiar name for someone not of the In-dian persuasion, he had thought upon meeting him. Now he thought, what better place to raid of talent than CBS. Garth smiled. And who better to advise him than someone who before him had advised the best. He did not waste any of his time worrying about Barrett. Barrett had his hint and would make no further moves. Though he was concerned about Sidney.

Garth shook himself as he remembered Sidney. For a minute he debated calling Anne to get Sidney on the line for him. He even opened his mouth toward that end. Then he shut his mouth and reached for the phone. He had a good head for numbers and knew Sidney's on the Vineyard without having to look it up. The roar of Thursday had risen just enough by that hour of morning for him to have a private talk. If he called Anne and told her to get him Sidney, the whole office would quiet down so they could listen. Two rings. Three rings. Garth was not accustomed to waiting. He was just about to hang up when Sidney answered.

"Hello?" she said cautiously, as though expecting an obscene caller. It was a very reluctant hello.

"Precious?" Garth said.

"Garth," Sidney shrieked.

He had to hold the phone away from his ear, such a piercing noise she made. He was nonetheless gratified at the response.

"Why did you leave me?" he complained. "I miss you. What happened?" He pitched his tone at grievous hurt. No one to date had ever resisted grievous hurt.

"Why didn't you call? I thought you didn't care about me," Sidney said. She was calculating on her fingers how many days it had taken him to call. Was torn between fury and relief.

"I didn't know until this minute where you were. You didn't say anything to me. Not a word."

Sidney had no reply to this. It was true, she had let him down. She meant to hurt Barrett by her departure, not Garth, who had always been more than fair with her.

"Are you over your flu?" Garth asked. "Barrett said you had the flu. Also that you were in Hawaii."

Sidney didn't say anything.

"You know I don't like to pry," Garth said. He was drumming his fingernails on the desk. If Sidney didn't say something in two seconds, he was going to tell her to get her ass back there or she was fired.

"Garth—" Sidney said.

"Yes, my love."

88

"Did Barrett tell you to call me?"

Garth hesitated a minute. What was the right answer, yes or no? Finally he settled on, "No. He told me you were in Hawaii as I mentioned before. Sidney, you know I don't like to pry. But this is a magazine, my sweet, not a marriage counselor. Now why don't you get on a plane this morning and get back here. We'll have a little dinner tonight—any place you want—and talk about it."

"Garth—ah, I can't."

"Why not, my love?" Garth was trying to be reasonable, he was doing everything he could, but a muscle in his eyelid was beginning to twitch and when that happened he was angry.

"I want to, I really do," Sidney said, "but I can't."

"Sidney, did I tell you, you are too valuable to me for this. Now what the fuck is the matter?"

"Don't make me cry, Garth. That tone always makes me cry."

"I asked you to dinner, for Christ's sake. Now what's the matter? Don't you want to go home? Is that it? Well, you know you're always welcome at my place. Move in there for a while."

"Don't be mad at me, Garth."

"Oh, for Christ's sake, Sidney, stop whining and get in here. I can't play any more games."

"This is my life. It isn't a game."

Oh shit. What did she want. More money. Her picture on the cover each and every week. A good fuck.

"I know it isn't. But I'm a busy man, honey. I can't solve your problems and run a magazine at the same time."

"I'm sorry, Garth, I really am. I hate to be so much trouble—"

That was it. That was what she wanted. "All right. Okay," Garth said before she could finish. "I'll come to you. I'm coming to Nantucket for the weekend anyway. I'll come to you tomorrow. Don't cook—we'll go out for dinner." Garth smiled at that touch. They always liked that.

"Oh, Garth, really?"

"Yeah, but I have to leave early on Saturday."

"Oh," Sidney said, her tone dropping. Saturday meant all Friday night. "Oh dear," she said.

What did she mean, Oh dear. He was coming, wasn't he. It really annoyed him the way women always thought they owned him after the first feel. Sidney was really something. He hadn't even arrived yet and already she was upset at the thought of his leaving. For a moment the muscle in his eyelid had relaxed, but now it was beginning to twitch again. "I'll make it up to you, sweetheart," he said. Then he reminded her once again what a busy man he was, what a sacrifice his coming all the way to Martha's Vineyard was, especially since he didn't even like the island much, and by the way he really had some terrific news about the turn her career was about to take.

"What is it, Garth?" Sidney said suspiciously. Ever since the first hello she had been feeling worse and worse, now she wondered if there was any way to tell him not to come. "Listen, maybe you're right," she said before he could tell her what turn her career was about to take. "I've got a lot of things to do. I think I will get on a plane and meet you there for dinner."

"I gotta go now, honey. Annie will call you and let you know what plane I'll be on. Meet me at the airport, will you, sweetie."

Garth hung up as Sidney was saying, "Garth, wait—"

As he often did at news he didn't want to hear, he had turned off. He was thinking about something completely different, Sidney's thighs. There was something very nice about Sidney's thighs, but Garth couldn't remember what.

CHAPTER 14

Terry was negotiating the terms of a contract between a writer who felt he deserved at least half the earth for his next book and his publisher, who was inclined to agree only if he could see some of the book. Terry had been arguing about this with the writer for some weeks now without success. M. Peters Gate said he was getting an attack of writer's block and could not continue work on the book unless he got a lot of money. He had finished no more than a hundred and fifty pages of the book in the last two years and during this time had presented in the way of an outline only two unacceptable scraps of paper that he claimed were all the publisher needed.

"They don't trust me," M. Peters Gate yelled over the phone from his house in Vermont. "Me, the greatest living novelist in America." He produced a remarkably accurate list of the advances paid several other writers of much smaller talent, he felt, than his. An outline is an outrage, he insisted.

Terry thought then as he often did that the more successful writers became the less the work itself mattered to them. What mattered, of course, was getting more money than anybody else. That was after all the way success was really measured. M. Peters Gate, who had been poor and a failure until well into his forties, who still lived in a wooden farmhouse with twelve animals, usually an unkempt female of indeterminate age and only an unreliable ancient Ford pickup truck to get him around, wanted $250,000 for a book he was terrified to show anyone. Terry wasn't even quite convinced it existed at all. It was not beyond the realm of possibility that M. Peters, with his whimsical Kentucky perceptions of how the world worked, was trying to sell nothing at all. If he really did have a chunk of the book, Terry reasoned, and he really did want to make a deal, he'd show the book and they'd get some sort of contract. Terry debated going up to Vermont for the weekend to have it out with M. Peters. Better known to his friends as Morvan. Terry was hesitating because he always had to clean the farm up when he got there and Morvan always offered him whatever unkempt female he had in residence as payment.

But Morvan had been only a part of Terry's concern that week. He was also worried about what Barrett and Sidney were doing. Everything about their behavior in the last two weeks belied the kind of marriage he thought they had—and even the kind of people he thought they were. And because he had an orderly mind, he was upset.

He always thought they would go on looking after each other as they had. Forever. And if not forever, at least for the foreseeable future. Of all the people Terry knew, Barrett and Sidney were the only ones he loved. He didn't even know why he loved them instead of somebody else, or some other couple. He just did. And he thought that since he loved them in spite of their defects—and they had quite a few between them—they had to feel that way about each other, too. Especially since, unlike members of a family, they were not required to tolerate each other. For him, the small irritations he suffered on their behalf only strengthened his sense of loyalty. Until now anyway, it never would have occurred to him to leave Barrett simply because he was difficult. In fact he had felt a sort of bond with Sidney all these years, as though they had a special responsibility for being sensible and loving in the face of Barrett's unreason.

"Who the hell is George?" Terry had asked Barrett after failing to work out just whose money it was that Barrett was trying to take.

"Damned if I know," Barrett lied.

These past weeks had been so upsetting to Terry not only because after so many years of such rapport, such solidarity, there was a break. But rather that Barrett was too absorbed with himself to care. All he could talk about was his magazine, the trouble that Sidney was causing at *IT*, the threat of Garth's revenge. He did not talk about Sidney. It was as though Sidney herself were merely a vehicle for his bad luck. He simply refused to go and see her; he seemed to consider her a recalcitrant child to whom catering would mean spoiling forever.

And Terry was very irritated at Sidney for testing a man whose faults she knew well enough would not allow him to react as she wanted. Barrett had certainly been childish many times before and she had been wise enough not to challenge him. Why now. Feeling as he did angry at both of them, Terry had resolved to leave them alone. In spite of this decision, however, he found himself returning to the problem over and over. It interfered with his plan to go to Vermont for the weekend to see Morvan, and his work in general. He felt he should be doing something specific to save their marriage, particularly since he was beginning to discover that without Sidney, Barrett was intolerable.

Terry tried to convince Barrett several times that they should go up to the Vineyard that weekend. But Barrett was forming another plan.

"I've got to get out of town. I can't stand it here alone," Barrett said pitifully when he reached Terry on Thursday afternoon.

"I agree," Terry said.

"I've got to get the next column written, and the atmosphere isn't right here." He wanted to, but could not bring himself to tell Terry about his interview with Garth. Terry would not be kind. He had not been kind about Mr. Grey. Altogether Terry was not being as comforting as one would wish. He called him because he wanted help. He had had trouble with the day even before Garth and the cherry Danish. Even Lespedeza wouldn't talk to him. But now that he had Terry on the phone, he couldn't tell him how miserable he was, how he felt his life was being drained away by the bad will of his wife and friends. No use to say that to Terry. His mind ran in only one direction. Once Terry gave his point of view he never offered alternatives. It wasn't fair that Terry had turned against him; he should have turned against Sidney, made her give in. Barrett tried to think of a way to phrase his plan for the weekend. He didn't want to seem frivolous, even thought he didn't have to tell Terry at all. But of course, it was he who had called Terry. He had to think of something to tell him.

After his talk with Garth that morning, Barrett had gone back to his desk. He felt a certain agitation in his body, as though all of his cells together were vibrating slightly in different directions. It was the kind of feeling one has before losing control and smashing things. Barrett didn't usually smash things when his cells started to vibrate. When at home, he went into the bathroom and choked into a towel. He made noises that sounded like death. He clawed at the towels on the towel rack. And as he did this he was aware that such reactions—even having such rage at all—were not quite normal. Not really appropriate, as psychiatrists would say. But sometimes he felt that he was not in control of his environment, not even the tiniest things were certain, and his cells would shake in and under his skin and he would suffer an anguish he couldn't even describe in a calm state. That morning he had his attack while sitting at his desk, staring down at his aged scarred blotter. Everything was going wrong. This Barrett blamed on the great unnamable authority that watched over him, making sure that he alone would be punished for things almost everybody else got away with. Garth always got away with it no matter what he did, and Garth was not a great man. He was not even a good man. Barrett made a few gurgling sounds in his throat but knew he could not have a real attack here.

He looked up to see if anyone was looking at him, then over at

"That's a very ungrateful attitude to take," Barrett said bitterly, "after all the times we made sure you weren't alone."

"I'm sorry," Terry said, "but your aggrieved tone is very irritating. What's on your mind?" Now that Terry was feeling the full weight of Barrett's peevishness, it occurred to him that Sidney never talked back, never told him to shut up or stick it in his ear as he said so often to her. He remembered a time when Sidney had called them to lunch. He came, but Barrett wanted to finish an article he was reading. Sidney brought in a perfect cheese soufflé and the two of them sat there watching it sink into itself because Sidney wouldn't dare cut into it until Barrett came. When Barrett finally arrived at the table he said, "I thought we were having soufflé, not a cheese pancake."

"I'm going away," Barrett said. "For the weekend," he added.

"Good for you." Terry was relieved. Now he had one less thing to worry about. "What plane are you going on?" If he felt the slightest disappointment at not being included, he did not admit to it.

"What? I'm not going there. I'm going to see Peter and Marjorie on Fire Island . . . and I can't be responsible for anyone else who might be there."

"What do you mean by that?" Terry asked.

"Nothing. I didn't mean anything." Barrett felt stupid for saying anything. "I'll see you when I get back, all right?"

"Fine," Terry said.

Barrett hung up and immediately a powerful sense of guilt rose in him. He had hung up too fast, he thought. He shouldn't have said where he was going. He got a drink and stared out at the view. Maybe Terry would start getting suspicious and tell Sidney something. Maybe Muriel was spying on him so she could report to Sidney. Who had told Garth about *New Journal?* Barrett stopped the thoughts right there. If he went any further with them, he would have to jump. He dialed Terry's number.

"Listen, Terry. You sound like you need a weekend away yourself. Why don't you come along? I know that Peter and Marjorie will be delighted. In fact they were just talking about you the other day and complaining that they never get to see you. I think it would be fun, don't you?"

"I don't know. I was planning to . . ."

"Don't be ridiculous," Barrett said, his tone hardening with anticipatory fury. "You're coming and that's settled." He held his breath while he waited for Terry to answer.

"Ah," Terry said.

"Come on, Terry."

"Weellll, I better call Peter and ask him if it's all right."

"Tell him I'm bringing a lot of food, will you?"

CHAPTER 15

Back and forth from two rooms away Barrett and Terry argued about taking the train versus renting a car. Terry was sitting in the living room and had already opened one of the two bottles of scotch he had bought for the Marshalls. He had gotten a glass and a small fingerbowl that he filled with ice and taken them into the living room where he opened one of his two gift bottles and poured himself a stiff drink. Terry thought that it was spoiled to go out and rent a car just so it could sit in a parking lot for two days in Bay Shore because Barrett thought trains were dirty and germ-filled and took too long and often crashed.

"You're thinking of Amtrak. The Long Island Railroad never has crashes, just long waits—and mostly in winter," Terry said. He tried to point out the advantages of taking a nice ride with a nice book and having a nice drink on the way. He was trying not to feel guilty about Morvan. Morvan had put it off so long, how could he feel neglected now. Maybe next weekend he would go up there.

Barrett was wandering restlessly around the bedroom. He had a small canvas suitcase open on the bed, but so far it was empty. Along one wall of the bedroom he had built a huge closet with chests of drawers and hangers on two levels that went around in circles on a track when one pushed a button. One side of it was Barrett's and the other Sidney's. Barrett was very fond of clothes and had a great variety of what he called wearables, that were arranged according to season. Those out of season were meticulously plastic-bagged. He couldn't decide what to take with him.

He whipped out the shirt drawers one after another. The Marshalls were two different types. Peter was the baggy madras and seersucker jacket type. He liked crew-neck sweaters and button-down shirts. Loafers from Brooks Brothers a hundred years old. For him Barrett chose his alligator polo shirts and his double-breasted Bill Blass blazer suit. He put these things on the bed and examined them. Marjorie, on the other hand, was the long-flowered-skirt type. She was quite a well-known photographer.

Barrett put the blazer suit back and pushed the button. The suits and jackets whirled around. Perhaps for Marjorie his old white Mao suit from several years before would be appropriate— ah, or his French military jacket with all the buttons. He let summer go around once again. Finally he decided the best thing for Majorie was his plantation suit and the El Exigente straw hat. He might even take his grandfather's pocket watch with the Hebrew numerals on it for an extra kick. Barrett reached for the straw hat perched on a stand high on the shelf. He always thought he made the perfect El Exigente double, and sometimes imagined himself quitting magazines altogether and going into the coffee business. Steaming jungles and cheering villagers were just the thing to soothe an overintellectualized existence. Refried beans and rotten rum. He'd make a wonderful drunk.

But then there was Lespedeza. Lespedeza would go for fishnet undershirts and raggy blue jeans with an unbuttoned blue-jean jacket over it. He opened a drawer and flipped through the pile of silk shirts regretfully. He did have a recycled blue-jean jacket with the star of Texas embroidered on it, but he had to be in just the right mood for that.

Terry yelled from the living room, "The last ferry will leave and we'll be stranded in Bay Shore. We'll have to rent a boat to get over."

Barrett called Weather for the third time just to be certain that the fair and warm forecast hadn't changed in the last twenty minutes. He went into the bathroom and threw together his toilet articles. He had to shave anyway. Terry and Peter were always closely shaved. Peter, particularly, never had the slightest shadow. He either shaved twice a day or had no hair. Barrett always

97

secretly thought that Wasps had less hair, along with thinner blood and sexual problems. He took along his mouthwash, his guaranteed effective 48-hour anti-perspirant, his Monsieur Givenchy cologne, his Pearl Drops toothpaste, and his albumen keep-your-hair shampoo. Allergy pills he threw in at the last moment.

Dressing was such a difficult thing on Fire Island. The prerequisites of appropriate dressing changed from house to house. Barrett riffled his shirts again and because his temples were beginning to throb he quickly chose in favor of Lespedeza. Ha, he said to himself, snapping the suitcase closed. He reminded himself not to forget the Bloomingdale's shopping bag that he had crammed into the refrigerator.

"Well, that took you long enough," Terry said.

"Did you call up about the car?"

"Yes, but I was hoping you'd see how senseless it is."

"Look at all this stuff, Terry. How can we schlep all this stuff into a taxi, then into the train, then into another taxi, then onto the ferry? I refuse to schlep," he said.

Instead they carried the two shopping bags and two suitcases over to the rent-a-car row on First Avenue and Sixty-fourth Street and waited for twenty minutes to be assigned a shit-brown car (so Barrett called it) with a deep dent on the right front.

"It's all we have," said the illiterate-looking person with a heavy Spanish-in-origin accent at the desk about whom Barrett had a number of racially slurring things to say for the next half hour until they were well into Queens.

Terry always thought Barrett was a joy to drive with because he became so voluble. He leaned out of the window and called menacing truck drivers who one could tell right away were three times his size "Cunt." He cursed out the road, the lack of direction-giving signs, the stupidity of Long Island in general. If he hadn't had several drinks himself, Terry would have insisted that he drive. He never got lost and in the other seat Barrett usually forgot to be irritated and fell asleep.

The Marshalls did not have one of those Fire Island houses made of glass with three levels and several sun decks. It was one of the old houses, entirely unrenovated, the kind that leaks slightly when it rains and remains so waterlogged the rest of the time that even in hottest summer the mold never quite disappears. It was the kind of house Barrett hated. All the furniture was distinctly Salvation Army in nature. Overstuffed sofas that had not been dusted in a century were only slightly improved by lengths of bright fabric tucked around here and there to suggest slipcovers. There were a lot of unclean needlepoint pillows and aged tea cozies, and lamps with fringed lampshades that had a gritty gray coating that came off on one's fingers. It was altogether a coy house with too many things inside, rag rugs and sand on the floor—sagging beds upstairs. In the first five minutes there, Barrett could feel his nose start to run.

They had scrambled eggs and Nova Scotia salmon and the black bread Barrett had brought. Terry and Barrett hadn't had dinner; they never found out if Peter and Marjorie and Lespedeza had or not. Terry handed around the bottle of scotch. Barrett vowed that on this visit he would not venture into the kitchen even for a glass of water. The last time it had been fatal to his appetite. He had since discovered that, as with pain, he had no memory for disgust.

Lespedeza was wearing some sort of plastic skirt that was very short. Every time she moved, it made embarrassing noises like bare skin being detached from plastic car seats in summer.

"Ah declare," she said glibly enough when they shook hands all around, and, "As I live and breathe," several times. But she was clearly shaken. She even looked a bit afraid, Barrett thought with some satisfaction. She disappeared into the bathroom for what seemed to be a long time, and Barrett had to work hard not to go rap on the door to see if she was still there. He thought she might get out through the window and run away.

CHAPTER 16

Lespedeza wondered how long she could stay here. She sat on the closed toilet seat thinking about men. She had always prided herself on her way with men. Like many Southern girls, her whole upbringing had centered around pleasing them. Now transported up north, she was the most hospitable, least afraid girl in the whole city, equally happy with a hairy-chested pizza maker or the president of a corporation. Lespedeza had had both and knew that a man was just a man no matter how he looked on the outside. That was the reason she had so many: to cut them all down to size, to properly finish off her mother's teachings of reverence and humility. Billi Hooper, whose daddy owned a towel- and sheet-making mill in Georgia, had been all set to marry her when she was eighteen—just in time, her mother thought, because Lespedeza had a bit too much natural curiosity and not enough respect to know fear. Lespedeza ran away to Paris the day before the wedding because the one thing she knew was that, nice as Billi Hooper's shoulders were, he was just a boy really. Never since then had she gotten as close to matrimony, though she was continually experimenting with living in sin.

In the course of her travels, as she called them, she had had flings of varying intensity with many of the men who hung around the magazine. She was as comforting as fudge, perfectly satisfying in small quantities. Of those men available only Garth had never taken her on. Like a hungry fish, Garth was usually interested in anything that flashed silver in the darkness. But Lespedeza for some reason did not appeal. She had no ambition whatever. Unlike the others on the assistant level, she had no hankerings for advancement, no yearning for fame. She was happy checking facts, looking things up in the dictionary, calling reference libraries, fighting in her Southern accent with people about whom a story was breaking. Lespedeza loved to go to writers' apartments even when it wasn't necessary and go over a story word by word, looking for facts to check. "And where did you get this?" she would say. She pored over people's notes, studied documents, shed her clothes. She knew everyone but never took advantage. She never asked for anything.

Lespedeza was the only person who ever dared to goose Garth when he passed her desk. She called him "Horsecart" and sometimes "Girth." But she wasn't concerned about fame, and Garth preferred women who wanted to get somewhere beyond his bed. Bed was his lure to the beyond. He must have known that Lespedeza would not have asked to go further, would do anything he wanted and then go away totally untouched by him.

Lespedeza never thought she would have a fling with Barrett. Never. For Sidney's sake—because she thought men were weak lumps of flesh—she bit the smile off her lips when she and Barrett had what she called contact at the office. She pulled her dress down and tried to look ethereal. She always told herself that Barrett was too thin or too serious to merit any real sexual speculation. And besides he was Sidney's, so she told herself. She also told herself that Barrett's quite obvious lack of interest over the years did not really goad her since it was certainly a proven fact that she could have just about anyone else she wanted. In spite of these honorable intentions on his behalf, however, Lespedeza did catch herself studying him from time to time, did wonder what he was like in bed, and did feel the smallest tinge of resentment at Sidney's marrying well and marrying out of her circle. Oh, Sidney said it was the same for a while. She said it didn't make any difference. But it wasn't the same. It didn't take more than a few weeks after the sacred ceremony. Almost immediately she had begun to look different, to sound different, and to stop hanging around with her old friends below decks on the masthead. It was funny how they could all work in the same room and yet the differences between them be so very clear.

Lespedeza told herself it wasn't Barrett who was the goad in her side. It was Sidney. On the days when she felt discouraged or disgusted with her lack of moral fiber, Lespedeza thought a great deal about Sidney in her "writing" room with the big window that overlooked Third Avenue going downtown where the office was. She thought about how Sidney used to wear ragged tweed skirts from her college days and sit at the slightly sticky desk next to hers. Sidney didn't have to work any more, didn't have to pay for rent or worry about the bill when she needed to have a cavity filled. She had become a lady, as Lespedeza's mother called properly dressed and married women. As opposed to herself who was still a girl, though the same age as Sidney. It was marriage that worked the change, Lespedeza felt, not the accomplishment of being a writer. Marriage was what forced a person to have an apartment with a powder room and a complete set of dishes. In Sidney's case, two.

On her good days, Lespedeza loved the challenge of a new man. In most cases married or unmarried made no difference. Men were so involved in their sexual images that the merest hint of a possible conquest was enough to bring them down. Lespedeza hardly knew a man who could resist her leotards, her grins, and the little pats she was always offering. It was partly her, she knew, but mostly it was their own vanity. Still, she had what she called flutters when even a marginally attractive man gave her the right kind of look, and she was nearly always pleased with what followed. Being unmarried meant to Lespedeza that every day there was the possibility of a new adventure, and the absolutely right person appearing. Being married meant that she would have to live out her life with a man who wasn't absolutely right, for flutters nearly always ceased after the second or third month if someone did manage to survive in her good opinion that long. It meant that she would be the one to suffer when her husband began fooling around with little girls at the office as all married men eventually do. The idea of being stuck with a jerk seemed worse than dying alone.

The certain bitterness with which she regarded Sidney and her position stemmed in part from the fact that Barrett treated all women apart from Sidney with absolute indifference. Sidney had committed the unpardonable sin of marrying a man who was faithful. Barrett was one of those men who got himself together in an extremely provocative way and then refused to deliver what he advertised. He wore tight pants, then looked severe if anyone noticed. When he said he was working at the office, he really worked. Except, of course, those times when he was out drinking. This prudishness Lespedeza found angering. She thought, but only occasionally, that Barrett needed taking down. But when she thought it, it was a thought without a plan behind it. Therefore, when she had actually done it, she was more surprised than pleased. She had hoped that the little flingette would be her secret, that she would have just this one slip (this chink in the armor of what she had heretofore judged as the perfect husband) to cherish on days when she was depressed with her lot.

In the last two weeks, however, Lespedeza had grown somewhat uneasy. Sidney did not come back to claim her role, and Barrett called her frequently and breathed heavily over the phone. It was like seeing one's daddy with an erection. Lespedeza wasn't happy with him this way. She had thought that the weekend away with Peter and Marjorie would bring some resolution to the problem— a resolution in the form of Sidney's return was actually what she hoped for.

Lespedeza sat on the closed toilet examining her hands. From the living room she could hear Barrett talking about his shit-brown car. She heard him say he hated the train and what a relief it was to be in the country. With the door between them, she could almost imagine Sidney out there, too, sitting in the corner of the couch as she always did, watching everybody and thinking her own thoughts, whatever they were. God, she never got over missing Sidney as she had been. Sidney always made her feel there was hope for herself. And now look what happened. Sidney was away somewhere losing her job and her husband. And it was she, Lespedeza, who was turning his head. She laughed suddenly to herself; at least she couldn't take Sidney's job. Lespedeza couldn't bring herself to open the bathroom door. If she didn't soon, he'd make a fuss. She knew he would. And if she didn't sleep with him, he might even find a way to fire her.

But if she did sleep with him, Terry and Peter and Marjorie would know. And if they did know, it wouldn't be Barrett they would think badly of. Lespedeza couldn't bear the thought of Marjorie thinking badly of her. She knew what they all thought of her anyway. As she sat there, Lespedeza even considered calling Sidney and telling her the truth about what had happened—not the whole truth of course, but enough about Amelia and Barrett to make her know she had to come back. You couldn't leave the magazine for more than a week or two without being replaced. Nobody cared really who was there and who wasn't. But Lespedeza cared. Amelia was loud and domineering and, unlike Sidney, thought she was genuinely more deserving and worth-while than everyone else. Sidney wouldn't like it if she thought Amelia was taking her place.

But even if she did tell Sidney, Lespedeza knew it would not help her now. Finally she decided she would go out and tell every-one she had the *worst* cramps—and was bleeding like a stuck pig. Did anyone have any Tampax? Marjorie would give her a few aspirin, and then she could limp up to bed clutching her stomach. Barrett wouldn't dare touch her then.

Fifteen minutes later she lay in her bed, safe. Her room was between Terry's and Barrett's. Peter and Marjorie slept across the hall next to the other bedroom that Marjorie had made into a darkroom. She listened. In a little while she heard them go out. They were going over to have a drink with somebody or other. Well, too bad about that. She closed her eyes, thinking that sometimes getting some sleep wasn't the worst thing that could happen. She wouldn't be drunk in the morning. That was her last thought before she was aware, some time later, of a hand fumbling with the sheets on her bed. For a minute, before she remembered where she was, her heart started beating at a terrifying rate. When she knew where she was, though, she wasn't afraid. Such a thing had happened to her more than once in other people's summer houses. The first thing she thought was that it might be Terry. And Terry would be nice. But then the hand found her. It was Barrett's.

"Very clever of you, Clover," he said as he slid in beside her.

She groaned, but he didn't care.

CHAPTER 17

Sometime in the early morning, long before the others appeared, Barrett was up and jogging on the beach. He was trying to dispel the thick fog of last night's indulgences. It was not a hangover he had, for Barrett did not have hangovers. What he had was more in the line of depression. Fire Island was not his favorite place and, without Sidney, it seemed to be a taste of what life in future summers could possibly have in store for him. Climbing in and out of someone's bed in the middle of the night, hiding in the hall in his Knize dressing gown—making washing noises that someone or everyone could hear.

And sometime in the night while he was feeling drained and

displaced, Barrett remembered the small typewriter he had left on the night table at home. He had planned to write his pastoral piece while sitting on the beach. He had seen himself with the typewriter balanced on his knees above the sand. All morning before the others got up, he tried to justify the leaving of the typewriter. He couldn't carry it to the rent-a-car place along with all the rest of his equipment anyway; just because he had the vision of himself doing good work with the typewriter didn't mean he couldn't do it without the typewriter. He was still on the sand, wasn't he? He could give himself another vision—himself with a legal pad—couldn't he?

Barrett had worked all his life to restrain, and banish when possible, all emotions that smacked of desperation. In his childhood he had been defeated by the bullies on his block, the terror his father had felt of going bankrupt any moment, even by his mother's leaden matzo ball soup. He left all that desperation behind him with his parents in their stuffy Brooklyn apartment above their barely surviving dry cleaning shop. So he told himself. Depression, Barrett thought, was reserved for women and failures. You didn't see Garth wasting any time on depression. When upset, he attacked. And secondary editors like himself, Barrett had discovered, always found a way out. They did not have the same kind of failures that businessmen had, or doctors or lawyers. Editors couldn't be held responsible for an issue that didn't sell, or a lack of advertising. If a magazine failed, it was due to a change in the times. A failure of the subscription department, the space salesmen, the price of postage. A mere editor was never in control—he had to do what his boss told him to do. He had to work with the material at hand; if it wasn't any good, it wasn't up to him to slit his wrists. Just change the headlines on the cover to make it seem as if the articles inside were better than they were.

The only suffering an editor was subject to was that of chronic passivity. An editor couldn't control the whole structure and more often than not didn't write. There was a wearing away of the sensibilities after a while. Alden, who was only twenty-seven, though the son of a governor, often said that "your nuts get ground down." Since he was an editor who wrote, he advocated the policy of having all editors write at least one major story a year. "That way you feel more a part of the magazine and closer to yourself," he said from time to time at editorial meetings

"Rat crap," Barrett muttered. For years his being only one editor and not the editor had made him feel not passive but safe. He was a contributor who could not be blamed for any ultimate failure. When an issue was good, he was the reason. When several were not good, it was Garth's neglect. It was, in part, Sidney's increasing success that made his position more difficult. Her book that spring, the invitations to appear at seminars, to appear on television. He felt he was being pushed more and more into the background. But also what Alden said was true. His nuts were being ground down. Garth had made him what he was, but now that Barrett knew so much about the business, now that he virtually ran the magazine himself, being Garth's second-in-command was becoming terribly irksome. Especially now that Garth himself nursed greater dreams of glory. At every party he went to, Garth sounded out bigger and bigger names for his masthead.

Lespedeza was ignoring him. She sat on the sand some feet away from him dribbling sand on her knees. Her head was bent forward and her long pale hair hid her face. Barrett felt insulted, and pained as well, by the extreme delicacy and thinness of her hair. He wondered if hair wasn't meant to thicken when a person matured. His had. It would take about five strands of her hair to make one of his. Did that make him more stable than she? Sidney also had thick hair.

"You think I don't have any morals," Lespedeza said just at that moment. She didn't look up as she said it. "But you'd be surprised how many morals I really have."

"I know you have thousands of morals," Barrett said, startled. He added, "But it's not really your morals that interest me."

"What's that supposed to mean?"

"I'm interested in you as a person." Barrett said this with some intensity, and it succeeded in making Lespedeza look at him.

"I'm interested in you as a person, too, Barrett. But I don't want to make a conquest of you. Do you know what I mean?"

"I'm not altogether stupid. What makes you think you can make a conquest of me, anyway?" Inadvertently, he had accepted her terms. Later, he realized that it was a mistake. It institutionalized what he meant merely as an adventure. ·

"Oh, I usually can," Lespedeza said. But she didn't seem to be boasting. She hitched up the bra part of her bikini, freeing a nipple for a moment before she tied the cloth tight. Barrett thought, how ungainly, how thoroughly unladylike she was. Still, he felt the thrill of the nipple, and felt it for several seconds. Remembered it later.

"Well, don't worry about it," Barrett said. "We'll agree that I'm not a conquest. I'm a friend. How's that?"

Lespedeza tossed her hair back. It was so long that when she sat straight up it almost touched the sand. She looked at him somewhat mistrustfully. "Do you really mean that?"

"Of course I do."

Lespedeza smiled either wistfully or with relief. Barrett couldn't tell which. She leaned over and put her arms around him and quickly, like a snake, flicked her tongue into his ear. Sodden is the primary sensation left by most people French-kissing in ears, but Lespedeza had a long pointy tongue that felt to Barrett's ear the way he had always imagined a French tickler would to a woman's insides. He swooned.

It felt like an hour inside his head before his ear came back to normal. But actually it was only the merest second before he opened his eyes. He saw Peter standing there with Marjorie's Leica pointed at him. Barrett thought it was a paranoid fantasy until Peter spoke.

"Hello, children," he said.

Barrett turned to Lespedeza, who was once again dribbling sand on her legs.

"Hello, Peter," he said. "How's the old summer reading piece coming along?"

"Just fine. Point your chin a little that way, Barrett." Peter motioned to his right. "You have a very prominent chin. Anybody ever tell you that?"

Peter had a round cherubic face and small round rimless glasses. He was pink and had lank fading hair the color of Wheatena. Garth had hired him at a cocktail party without even having a book review column for him to write. Barrett always thought the reason was that he was so literary-looking. Literary critics were supposed to be unlined—thoroughly untouched on the outside, like hangmen. Slightly squinty and with small discreet paunches.

Garth had been euphoric because he had managed to get Peter away from another publication whose editor Garth didn't like. The column he began almost as an afterthought.

With him, Peter had two cameras and a great many lenses and different kinds of film. He liked to experiment, but for some reason fed only black and white film into the Leica. The Nikon hung around his neck. "No, Barrett, that was toward Lespedeza. Put your knee down. That's right." Peter hunched this way and that, angling the camera.

Peter had posed him almost lying in Lespedeza's lap. Maybe he's trying to arrange for my divorce, Barrett thought. My destruction even. In the more rational part of his mind, he remembered that this was the way Peter passed his weekends, pretending that he could be his wife if he wanted. Peter said one had to have more resources in life than just one's job. Barrett noticed, however, that he never urged Marjorie to take up writing. Peter took a few more pictures and then wandered away. Lespedeza wandered after him. Barrett cursed her for going.

He put his head back on the sand and tried to think Vineyard. Sand was sand, wasn't it. Just as inspiring wherever it was. Sea air was sea air. Except that on Fire Island the houses were piled one on top of the next, and the brush, for that was all the greenery amounted to, crept along the ground in a cringing sort of way as though even the sky here were taken. And Barrett could swear that there wasn't a single beach plum bush on the whole island. People with volley balls began to swarm onto the beach. I love Fire Island, he thought. He turned his head and noticed that some hulking sixteen-year-old-looking hood was talking to Lespedeza. He could see that she was laughing.

He wondered what Sidney was doing. In moments of anger or misery he often wondered what she was doing. He remembered how calm and orderly their life had been, how utterly untortured. Barrett had not thought it was possible that two people could live together in such peace. For the first years of their marriage, he waited for Sidney's transformation into a haggard, middle-aged shrew like his mother. Though he didn't know it, he yearned for this to happen. But they seemed to grow them different in Providence. Sidney was an inward sort of person who was willing to listen and learn. She didn't complain no matter what he did, did not find fault even in those areas where Barrett knew there were faults to be found. Quite unconsciously, he was bitterly disappointed. He had grown up with fighting. He expected fighting. His mother often made disparaging comments about his father's sexual equipment, and about his lack of ability in bed. "He's not in the land of the giants," she liked to say.

Barrett told Sidney her tits were like raisins in the sun. She covered them up; she did not reply. As he sat on the beach he felt there were things swimming under the surface of their relationship that he should have known about. There were perhaps things he should not have done. But there's something in the nature of man that prevents him from admitting—sometimes even knowing anywhere in his conscious—that he has done wrong, has hurt, punished, tormented without reason. And that all people do not respond to torture in the same way.

He almost never saw Sidney working. She always seemed to be reading a book or a magazine. He thought of her as an idle sort of person. She never seemed to be taken up with anything even when she clearly was. It enraged him that she had no emotion. Compared with Lespedeza, she was a closed-in sort of person. He could see her lying on the beach with all of her clothes on. Sidney didn't like to take her clothes off. In winter she was cold. She took baths with the door closed. In summer she wore long terry cloth robes over her bathing suit. If anyone looked at her, she buried her feet in the sand. If she could have buried her head, she would have done that too. Barrett ached for her even with Lespedeza's nipple in the corner of his mind. It was funny how bland Sidney seemed now.

Oh well, once again he tried to concentrate on Vineyard properties. And once again his eye slid over to where Lespedeza was now tossing the volley ball to the young hulk who had thrown it to her. As her lover, Barrett supposed, he could object. But as her friend, he couldn't. Terry and Marjorie strolled back in his direction. Peter was following them, taking pictures of their backs, the waves lapping at their feet, the clouds above and the seaweed below.

Barrett made himself go immobile. He tried to bring on a state of comfort and repose. He succeeded. Then a few old complaints came creeping back to mind. Whenever he was supposed to be in repose, Barrett worried about what had happened to the great old days. He liked this worry and conjured it now because he felt it was best to diffuse one's specific agonies with as many general misery-making thoughts as possible.

Here they were, Barrett thought, a literary critic, a famous photographer, the editor of a successful magazine, a lawyer of formidable talent—Lespedeza counted as the courtesan. In any other age, there would be something magical about them. Why did he have to be born too late for Bloomsbury, too late to be a part of the movable feast. Why did they, lolling about on the beach, have to be so very unremarkable. No one looked at them. No one cared. Barrett cursed the junk society in which he had unjustly been placed. The whole point of now was to be as thoroughly low and insignificant as possible. To be gone tomorrow, in fact.

"What are you mooning about?" Terry asked. He sat down on the sand next to Barrett. "You look particularly sour."

"I was thinking about Peter's summer reading piece."

Peter stood in front of them with the Nikon now. "Marjorie, you sit down next to Barrett now. Ah, that's lovely."

Lespedeza came and knelt behind Barrett. She made the sign of the goat above his head, but he was scowling and didn't know she was there.

"For Christ's sake, smile, Barrett. You're ruining the picture."

"Please, will you sit down for a minute. You're making me dizzy," Barrett snapped.

The picture broke up and Peter reluctantly sat down. Barrett suddenly felt better. He had been obeyed. "Now, I want you to tell me what you're doing about that summer reading piece."

"I've done fifteen short reviews and was going to write an introduction of some sort." Peter shrugged. "You know, the same thing we do every year."

"Oh," Barrett said. He knew that was what Peter was doing. He hated what Peter was doing. He wondered if now was the time to tell him.

One night at a party Barrett had been particularly loath to attend, a man came up to him and said he was a doctor—a very good doctor—and wanted to be famous. What else. "How can I get some publicity?" he asked. Maybe publicity wasn't exactly the word he used, but it was something like that. Barrett said, "What do you do?" He wasn't appalled. People asked him this all the time; sometimes he helped, and sometimes he didn't.

"I'm an orthopedist," the doctor said.

Barrett heard "orthodontist," and asked the man to do an article on straightening teeth. The doctor was stunned and walked away with glazed eyes. But oddly enough there had been an orthodontist at the party as well who heard the name of his specialty said aloud. He took the opportunity to call Barrett the next day. The orthodontist wrote a piece about straightening teeth and became an instant celebrity. He went on television. The orthopedist, following his lead, wrote an article on lower back pain and also became something of a *grand homme* in his field. He, too, went on television.

What Barrett wanted to bring back with his book section in *New Journal* was the great days of the literati. There had to be something wrong, after all, with a society that embraced the dental surgeon and sexual therapist, and ignored the thinkers, those in charge of the printed word.

"I think it is the how-to book that has ruined publishing and journalism," Barrett said. He had been quiet for some time, thinking.

"How do you mean?" Peter said.

"I mean that the whole idea of service reporting and service books have made people stop thinking. Do you know what I mean?"

"Not yet," Peter said. He looked bored. Lespedeza got up and trotted down the beach.

"I mean that instead of writing literary criticism you're writing quickies telling people what to read. It's a service piece, not an intellectual exercise. People have gotten so used to being told how to be mentally stable, how to be beautiful, how to be thin, how to be a great knittist in ten easy-as-pie lessons, how to be your own best lover. Do you want me to go on or do you know what I mean?"

"Go on, go on," Majorie said. "How do I be my own best lover? Tell."

"Do you see what I mean?" Barrett snapped. "Masturbation has been advanced over thinking. Unless something is presented in easy lessons or leads to a better, happier, sexier, more fulfilling life, it has no value. I think individual narcissism has to be stopped. What do you think?"

"What?" Peter looked at him in surprise.

"Really. Don't you ever find yourself yearning to review a thin volume of philosophy? Don't you ever want to stop summarizing how-to books and prove that junk isn't the bulwark of our society? Did you review Perkman's new book?"

"You know I didn't."

"Why not? It's the most important book to come out this season."

"Garth hates him."

"Did you review Spender Stevens' book, that novel?"

"Of course I did."

"Why?"

"Garth hates him."

"You *see*, and I bet you said a few things about his drinking problem and his gimpy leg and his wife the prostitute."

"I didn't say she was a prostitute. What's the matter with you anyway? I thought you loved feuds. I thought you were the greatest promoter of readership identification, and the service principle."

"Well, I am. But it's time for the common man to be common again and for thinkers to start thinking again—take you for instance." Uh-oh, he must have gone too far. Peter was looking at him with definite distaste.

"Do you really mean all this?" Peter said. "I mean really?"

"I do mean it, of course I do." Barrett didn't know whether he meant it or not. That is, he meant it in a theoretical sense. Societies had their high points and their low points, and Barrett hated the idea of living in a low point. Rome's decline, Britain's, America's were all equally bad. America's just seemed worse, maybe, because he was contributing to America's decline. He was promoting the dental surgeon. People wouldn't turn to the dental surgeon for someone to idolize on their own, after all. They might have been bracing up their kids' teeth for the last thirty years, but it took people like Barrett to get them to think of wiring up their own teeth.

"You haven't forgotten how to do real criticism, have you?" Barrett asked slyly. "Since coming to *IT*, I mean. I thought you'd be aching for the old verbal pyrotechnics, criticism more fiery than any prose between the hard covers. Or is simple summarizing just a lot easier?" Barrett sat back and pretended to read a review. "In April Springhaven's new book *Merry Is the Month*, you will find a read equal to her last book *Dawn Comes*—Margret Webber sits by the bedside of her dying uncle for five hundred and fifty-four pages. During that time, approximately five years, she relives their lives; hers and his, the lives of their three illegitimate children, and her lesbian relationship with the housekeeper. A neat story, deftly told with an ending so surprising you'll remember it for hours." Barrett chuckled. "I have really hated criticism ever since 'read' ceased being a verb."

"You know," Peter said, "I know what you mean."

Barrett sighed. Maybe it really was possible to bring integrity back to journalism, to tell the truth about books, and other things.

CHAPTER 18

Barrett wondered what he could do to Mr. Grey. Could he go to a higher-up at the bank and tell the truth about him. Or should he go to someone else for the money. The bank couldn't have only one person giving away money. But Barrett didn't really like the idea of a loan anyway. They were robbers really. He thought of the mortgage on their house. Seventy-five thousand dollars the house cost. At the end of twenty years they would have paid the bank more than a hundred and fifty thousand dollars. Could that be morally right. One hundred and fifty thousand dollars for what had been worth no more than twenty-five thousand at the outside, a collection of aged shingles, leaky pipes, and a cesspool. Barrett snorted at the thought that what he should do was to sell the house right now while Sidney was still in it. She wouldn't know what happened to her, wouldn't have any place to go but home.

Barrett had this thought while sitting up in his room with the door locked.

Downstairs there was an after-lunch party going on. Barrett hated the people. Two writers from the *Times*. One of Marjorie's photographer friends who somehow got away with shooting nudes for a fashion magazine, Barrett couldn't remember whether it was *Vogue* or *Harper's Bazaar*. When assigned the clothes to shoot, he laid them elaborately over chairs, on beds; he hung them from pipes in basements and then took pictures of the girls clothesless. He posed them standing with arms around each other, sprawled across a bed reading a magazine (not his own), washing each other's flat breasts at an old-fashioned sink. He was all the rage and Barrett loathed him. Even with the door closed, he could hear the *Times* men arguing about which of the fifteen editorial writers should be canned. Fifteen and the page was a disgrace. Barrett would not go down there until they left. He hated the *Times*. The *Times* hated him. He wondered how they could be arguing like that in front of each other when each knew the other was a potential spy. Nowhere was there greater perfidy and repression than at the *Times*. It was like Russia, everyone knew that. And whenever they had a chance to do a story on *IT*, such lies they told. Barrett was breaking the rules by not going down there. He knew they would all talk about him later, say he was strange. But he was busy worrying about getting the money for *New Journal*. They'd see when he had the best weekly magazine in the country.

Once again Barrett thought about the house in the country, and as he thought about it, the solution to his problem came to him. Once he knew it, he wondered why he hadn't thought of it before. So perfect it was, so infallible he was dumbstruck. All he had to do was write to the Providence bank on Sidney's stationery, request the money, and sign her name. When the check came he would write on it "For Deposit Only SM" as he did with all of Sidney's checks. And then when he wanted it, all he had to do was withdraw the money in his own name. Sidney had received statements for fourteen years and put them away without looking at them. She had never once taken any money out. The bank would not question the withdrawal. That was, in fact, the beauty of banks. They were not there to ask questions, they were there to send one the money whenever one wanted it. All they had to do was sell off a few of those highway bonds.

Barrett was so excited by this idea, he didn't hear the others go out. He was busy writing a letter to the bank. He was cashing the check and building up the best little weekly in the country. Sidney would thank him in the end. She'd never complained at his management of the money before, and she wouldn't now, once it was done. He'd tell her and she'd thank him in the end. He put on another bathing suit and went down the stairs two at a time. Maybe he would find Lespedeza and persuade her to go back to the city that night.

To his surprise, Barrett found Lespedeza alone in the living room. Barrett threw himself down beside her on the sofa and yawned elaborately. She was reading a magazine and didn't say anything so he took a strand of her hair and played with it. He wrapped it around his finger, tickled her cheek with the end of it, and weighed it. The hair had gotten no heavier since the last time he weighed it. It was still very light hair. Its texture absorbed him for a while.

Finally he said, "They go out?"

She nodded.

"Want to take a nap?" Barrett asked.

Lespedeza didn't answer right away. He took the silence to examine her thighs. They were nice round thighs without dents or puckers or hair to mar them. He reached out and squeezed one. It was lovely and rubbery. The excitement of it traveled around in him like the little balls in a pinball machine. "We've never had a nap before," he said. "I'm very good at naps."

Lespedeza squirmed out of his reach. He thought this was her idea of a good time and followed her down the sofa.

"I promised to go over and see Manny this afternoon," she said without turning to look at him.

"Who the hell's Manny?" Barrett said, edging closer and closer until his front was pressed against her side.

"He's the guy I was playing volleyball with on the beach this morning." She clutched the magazine with both hands. She wasn't going to let him get her again. She'd already told him so this morning and he had agreed.

"You're kidding. He isn't a day over fourteen." Barrett was shocked.

"You're wrong. He's twenty-six."

"Twenty-six," Barrett repeated. He started gnawing on her shoulder, was gratified that she didn't move away.

"Yeah, he says he's in marketing research at McCann-Erickson, but I think he's really in the mailroom." Lespedeza bent her head closer to the magazine as though there were a detail she wanted to examine more carefully.

Barrett was becoming annoyed. He had one arm around her shoulder and his hand clamped onto her breast inside the bikini she still had on from that morning. One good thing about girls with flat chests, Barrett noted, was that there was always a pretty good gap between bathing suit and skin. But Lespedeza, surrounded on all sides by Barrett's increasingly octopus-like progress, was not paying any attention to him.

"Let's go upstairs," he said nervously. He was chewing on her earlobe and had one eye on the door. He was afraid that Terry might come back. Sitting on the beach always made Terry thirsty. Maybe he had some contracts or something he wanted to look over.

"You won't be sorry," he said, thinking of nothing else he might add but please.

"I told Manny I was going over there," she said. "We were going to have a joint and then go jogging. Have you ever gone jogging after a joint?" Lespedeza turned to him for the first time. The sudden movement arrested Barrett's activity since she had to move away from him to face him.

"No, I've never jogged after a joint, but I'm willing to try just about anything," Barrett said, hoping that she meant a different kind of joint than the one he usually referred to. He draped himself across her front and began kissing her neck, her ear, her mouth, aware the whole time that he was in mortal danger, and that it was she who was putting him in this wretched position.

At first he had to give her short kisses on the mouth because she wasn't pressing back and her lack of enthusiasm was not encouraging. But once she sort of kissed him back a little and he was so delighted at the breakthrough that he engaged all of his energy into whipping together all the oral charm he had. Before he knew it, he had given up the idea of going upstairs in the hope that he could carry it off on the grimy, but that was no longer of any consequence, couch downstairs. Endangered passion has it points, Barrett sort of thought. He was thoroughly thrilled with the way Lespedeza seemed to have changed her mind (he did not ask himself why). She was wiggling the important part of herself out from inside her strings.

Barrett was sprawled half on and half off the couch, but he hardly knew that since he was all the way on and nearly in Lespedeza. The pitch of his excitement was beyond anything he had felt since he was around eighteen when he spent nearly all his time trying to get himself into just this sort of position. He didn't have time for chivalry or the fine points until he had his own establishment years later, by which time he was rather bored with frenzy.

Now, however, the bit of desperation and fear made him realize through the steady throb of his blood how much he had been missing since he had gotten old. So, there he was, spread as though for a proctoscopic examination with hardly any of Lespedeza showing at all, when Terry walked in the door.

Barrett knew that Terry was there although he had his back to him. But he never saw his expression, if there was one. Terry did not hesitate or even skip a step as he made his way through the living room and back to the kitchen where Barrett, after rearranging himself, found him some minutes later, pouring a double.

The bastard, was what Terry was thinking. The fucking bastard. He had never particularly liked Lespedeza, and right now he didn't like Barrett at all. All he could think of was poor little insecure Sidney alone in that house waiting for Barrett to come to her. Christ, it made him angry.

"Hi, old buddy," Barrett said. He examined Terry for signs of disapproval or any touch of the traitor. But Terry had a look of bland summer weekend on his face. It was the look that he had when people were most convinced of his general stupidity. Barrett knew that look well. He had to say something. He turned, "We were just looking at the pictures," over in his mind, but decided against it. He thought, by Terry's silence, he was saying it was all right, or maybe that he hadn't seen anything. Maybe it was just his guilt that worried him, Barrett thought. Terry wasn't particularly visually oriented. Maybe he was so intent on getting that drink that he didn't look right as he walked in. But then Lespedeza was making that humming noise, he would have had to look right. Then he would have seen Barrett in that undignified position. But on the other hand there was no way for Terry to know for sure whether Barrett was just fooling around or he was in fact *in flagrante*, which he hadn't been able to accomplish. On the other hand, in that position it didn't really matter whether he was *in flagrante* or not since he was discovered with the deed clearly in his head.

Terry didn't say a word to help him. So Barrett made much of getting himself a drink. He concluded by the time the drink was ready that it wasn't any of Terry's damn business. And where did he get off disapproving of him anyway. God damn it. Still, Barrett hung around the kitchen waiting for Terry to say something. "Please, Terry don't be mad," he felt like saying, he didn't know why.

He knew what Barrett was waiting for, but Terry couldn't say anything. The injury to Sidney prevented him from speaking. It was almost as though he had been betrayed himself, so intense was his anger. Poor Sidney. Poor little Sidney. She didn't even know how hurt to be. Terry took a sip of his drink. He had his back to Barrett, refused to turn around. Maybe he would go up there and see how Sidney was, he thought. He was angry that Barrett had to inflict even this upon him. He couldn't even be bothered to find some place else to do it. Oh, he knew that Barrett and Sidney would get back together again, would behave like all reunited couples did, as though they had just invented love. And, as always, he would be left with the bad memories. This time it would be of Barrett so desperate to fuck Lespedeza it didn't matter to him who saw it.

And Sidney, who would care as he did, would never even know. She wouldn't ever know. Terry felt a tightness in his breast and realized that he really hurt for her. She was one of those women who seem to have no defenses against cruelty at all. Maybe he really would go up there. He could take her out somewhere for dinner and cheer her up.

CHAPTER 19

As most of Garth's employees, Sidney did not like him. But she admired him. They all admired him. There was a stubbornness about him that made those around him think that, come what may, Garth would always be the winner. He did things no one else dared to do. He loved to get even with his enemies—sometimes the slight was so small they didn't know they were enemies until they got hit with his revenge. He had been known to wait as long as five years for a chance to get even. When Sidney's first book came out two years before, it had gotten a bad review from one of the most important national news magazines.

Instead of reviewing the book, the reviewer reviewed Sidney. Actually he reviewed *Inside Track*, a not uncommon practice. Reviewers hate to review books and will do authors instead every chance they get. Sidney was an easy target because her name was never linked with any other publication. Usually magazines release articles or whole sections early for advertising purposes. An advance copy of Sidney's review came to the magazine on the Friday before it was due to be out on the newsstands. Since it was a special week for Sidney, Garth had told them he would come to the Vineyard for the round of parties. They hadn't planned any round of parties until he mentioned it, but Barrett got on the phone right away. On Friday when they were all packed and ready to leave, someone came in shouting and waving the review. Garth snatched it away before Sidney could see it. She didn't see it until Monday. He read only the first line of the review, then handed it to Barrett and rushed back to his office shrieking as he went, "Get fucking El Allwit on the line."

Anne, calm as always, her red 1940s fingernail polish unchipped, and all hairs in place, a serene smile curving her lips, picked up an *IT* pencil and dialed the number without looking it up. "Mr. Allwit, please," she said.

"Garth Carter for Mr. Allwit. Is he there, Gracie?"

Anne always remembered a secretary's name even if she only called once a year. She remembered Gracie's name and they had very little to do with this particular magazine. "Good." She motioned Garth into his office.

By this time a number of the staff had seen at least a few lines of the review and, although Sidney herself was so mortified she was nearly out of the door, the rest of the staff was inching nearer and nearer to Garth's office. What would he say. What could he say considering the things they printed about other people's books, other people's magazines, other people's sex lives, even. What chutzpah. What arrogance. What ecstasy. They crowded closer, sorry only that they could not hear the other editor's responses.

"Hi, El. How are ya?

"That's fine, El. Listen, I see you're running a little review here on Sidney Martin's book.

"Uh-huh. Well, let me tell you this. Sidney is a fine and distinguished writer. One of the *best*, El. I want you to know that, and if you hurt Sidney, you're hurting me."

There was a pause while El made some sort of reply. Garth, who had his head thrown back and was talking to the ceiling, now turned away so that the staff could no longer see him.

"Are you telling me you don't know what's in your own fucking magazine? You're telling me that pimply little beast has autonomy in his department? What? Distinguished my ass. He's a fecalphile if I ever saw one. Even if he *could* learn to read, he wouldn't know a good book if he saw one. . . . All right, never mind about that, I want to know what you're going to do for Sidney—she's in here crying her eyes out."

And Garth went on at some length before the conversation was over. No one ever did find out what El promised to do for Sidney, there certainly was no retraction the following week. The staff, of course, was transported by the word "fecalphile," which was new. Shitlicker had been a favorite for some time but was now rather tired. El got his later, of course.

How could Sidney like a man who embarrassed her so badly she felt at the time nothing but her death could restore her honor. In the early days of *IT*, though, Garth had been just as happy making his writers as he was hiring already established ones. It was much cheaper making them. And when you take someone like Sidney was, raw, not completely trained, goggle-eyed, you have her for life. After being at the clip desk at *Time* or deeply buried somewhere in *The New Yorker* where even middle-range editors and writers would rather lose all ten typing fingers than talk to a commoner who was less than beautiful (a small female person could go for years there without ever hearing the words "good morning") being at *IT* was heaven. Although nobody took special notice of Sidney at first, Garth certainly never made overtures, she was spoken to every day. She never had to have lunch alone. At *Time*, she had often eaten lunch alone. Like the rest of the staff at *IT*, because she could hear everything, see how the articles were edited, hear how the decisions were made (arbitrarily), she felt it was her magazine. Once a person feels that kind of identification, even a brute at the helm cannot lessen the pleasure. A person always remembers what elsewhere is like and makes excuses for the man.

Sidney had spent the twenty-four hours before Garth's arrival alternately worrying about what he might do to her physically and making excuses for the flaws in his character. It was a tough one all right. She wanted to stay at *IT*. Quite rationally, she could think of all the things that were wrong with the place, wrong with the magazine, wrong with the way she was treated even. But she hadn't ever been successful anywhere else. She had an uneasy feeling that if she were no longer at *IT* no one else would want her. She would be a copy person again, or worse. That's what happens when you stay too long with the person who made you: you think that the success is his, not yours. You think there is no real world out there—that the magazine is the world and the rest of the world only there to serve as source material for the magazine. Sidney wasn't crazy. Everyone thought that way. Garth thought that way and passed the opinion on as fact. Everyone thought of his press card as the respirator that kept him alive. Only sons of governors didn't think so. And they always fared the better for it.

Sidney waited at the airport. Once again she had dressed in the worst combination of old sweaters and pants that she could find. She thought if she looked terrible he would take pity on her and not make her service editor or otherwise demote her. She thought if she looked terrible he might not make advances. But when he got off the plane she thought the negative feelings she had about him were unjustified. Quite unexpectedly, she felt a rush of affection for him. He was carrying a shopping bag with Godiva on the side—chocolates, how nice. He was as tiny as ever; his stomach separated the left and right sides of his shirt and curly black tummy hairs showed in the gaps. But he was smiling, and waved when he saw her. Wasn't he nice after all.

Seeing him that way, striding with short quick steps in from the runway, he didn't seem mysterious in the least. Not the figure of political intrigue at all that certain people thought he was. There were two schools of thought about Garth's past and the money he always seemed to have and couldn't, or wouldn't, explain. One school persistently claimed that he had been recruited in the early sixties—maybe even earlier, in the fifties—by the CIA when the CIA was busy recruiting college kids and writers and CBS people and magazine editors. People like that. The CIA gave Garth not all the money of course because everybody knew that Garth had impeccable Wall Street connections, but rather extra money, the money that kept him going when he broke off from his partners. It was rumored by those people that the reason Garth knew ahead of time so many things that were happening (Garth absolutely refused to watch the evening news programs) was that he was being briefed by the CIA all the time. He was working for them; that was the reason he didn't come into the magazine from ten to seven-thirty every day like everybody else. It was the CIA that paid for the lavish parties he gave and his brown suede apartment on Fifth Avenue. What he gave in return in addition to valuable information, they said, was an occasional article—a cover story—totally out of character with the touted political beliefs of the magazine. IT wasn't supposed to be a political magazine, but every month or so there would be a very political article. After the election of Governor Brown of California, IT gave Brown a lot of bad press not because he was a bad guy, but so that Reagan could emerge, split the conservative wing of the Republican Party, and let Rockefeller win the presidency by default. Toward this end, Rockefeller got good press no matter what he did. Never did the articles have the liberal point of view their headlines proclaimed.

Those who believed in the CIA theory believed that Garth was a political power directed by the forces of evil. The flaw in this theory, of course, was the unanswerable question of how the CIA could possibly profit from a Rockefeller presidency. When one examined Garth's connections, one did find a number of political figures of one sort or another, some none too savory, he counted among his two thousand closest friends.

But those who belonged to the other school of opinion on his recent background and wealth and goals believed that all three were sociosexual in origin. Garth had come from a small town in Pennsylvania where his father was the owner of the general store. Quite simply, not unlike a great many other people, Garth loved the rich. The sociosexual school of thought knew that Garth as a younger man—slender and with lots of black hair, a mouth as thin and sharp as a razor, an aristocratic nose and other equipment—had enormous energy, wit, and a legendary sexual appetite that endeared him to the group he wanted to join. His money came, like Nixon's, from his friends. It was no more complicated than that. The articles he sometimes ran on Wall Street doings, Arab oil, Detroit, California, Washington politics were hardly subversive or reactionary. They were merely kindness to his friends, payment for past and future support, the very least he could do. The facts that he sometimes stayed out of politics altogether for months at a time, that he never ran a thing about foreign policy, foreign aid, or food, all proved to the sociosexual school that Garth had nothing whatever to do with the CIA.

"Dearest," Garth said. He embraced Sidney warmly, then held her slightly away from him so that he could examine her face. "My poor sweet," he said. "You look so tired."

A tubby little man who dyed his hair—nah, this was no CIA agent, Sidney thought. But she had worked for him for years without giving the subject a single thought. She wondered why she was even wondering it, knew that she was thinking the thought— the dirty secret if it were true—because this might be the last time she ever saw Garth this way. She knew that a friend of hers who was the editor of another magazine had been convinced for perhaps a month before she was fired that her publisher was a member of the Mafia. He was absolutely rolling in money, and his four magazines were certainly not making it for him. The question was asked about him too. Where did he get his money? Sidney thought she was still a part of *Inside Track*, that the magazine was where she wanted to be, really.

Garth was holding her shoulders with his two hands and looking at her carefully, but Sidney couldn't respond. She was still thinking, trying to make up her mind about what she was really doing. Sometimes just speaking out about quitting a job or leaving a husband makes the doing of it an impossiblity. That's why people talk so much about dieting and losing weight. Once they've said it, it's already done. They can do it over and over without doing a thing. But when a person's really ready to lose the five hundred pounds, he doesn't even tell himself. He begins. The fact that Sidney had begun her interview with Garth thinking not of her career but rather of him as a CIA agent was a sure sign that she was divorcing him in her heart. When you're happy with your job, you never think of your boss as a CIA agent, even if he is.

CHAPTER 20

"Now what's all this about?" Garth said. They had driven back to the house where Sidney was presented with one of the two boxes of Godiva chocolates that Garth had in the shopping bag. Sidney was gratified to see that hers was the same size as the other, but did not ask him with whom he was staying on Nantucket. They were sitting in the living room having a drink before going out to the Seagull, a restaurant in Vineyard Haven, for dinner.

He sat in Barrett's favorite chair taking up more than twice the space that Barrett did, and had a glass of straight gin in his hand. Sidney had thought that she was leaving New York to make a point to Barrett, also to protect her job and Barrett from Garth's revenge. She could not tell Garth now that Barrett wanted to buy *New Journal* and she wanted to stay at *Inside Track*.

"I made a mistake," Sidney said simply. "Did you read that article in the *Wall Street Journal* about why wives run away?"

"What?" Garth looked startled. He had had four and the last one, the one he liked best, ran away. He did not like the subject and specifically had not read the article. He thought she was talking about him and frowned to turn her off.

But Sidney didn't notice. "It said that wives run away because they don't feel loved enough—not because they're worked too hard or don't have enough rights. They just want attention, that's all." The phone rang just then, but Sidney did not move to answer it. It was the attention she got for running away. Hank Meadows would let it ring five times and then try again in two hours.

"Aren't you going to answer it?" Garth asked.

Sidney shook her head. "You don't mind, do you? You let yours ring sometimes yourself."

"Come on, let's go out. I don't know what you're talking about, and I'm hungry." He got up, swallowing down the inch of gin that was left in his glass.

The phone was still ringing as Sidney grabbed the bottle of red wine she had taken out since Vineyard Haven was a dry town and Garth would complain if she forgot.

"Better take a white too," said Garth, who never missed a thing.

In the restaurant he squeezed her knee twice. She had put him in a good mood by her choice. It was a small dining room and their table was on the porch that overlooked the harbor. They watched the ferry come in.

"Are you going to have lobster?" he asked.

"Ah." Sidney looked at the menu. She had lobster at home every other night to convince herself that she was not an orphan. Here, it was three times the price. It was the sort of thing she considered in restaurants, although the time had long since passed when it was necessary. Garth clearly wanted her to have the lobster. So he would not look undignified alone? Have to suffer a bib and butter spots on his front while she picked at a steak?

"I was thinking about roast beef," Sidney said to justify the bottle of red wine.

"Have the lobster," he said. He ordered two.

Sidney shrugged to herself. Lobster it would be. "Tell me about the new magazine. What's happening with it?"

He settled back and began telling her about it. Such plans he had for showing the two sex barons of the magazine industry a thing or two about the subject. Sidney hardly had to say a thing all through the salad, lobsters, and blueberry pie. She asked him once about the name it would have, and he frowned over the claw he was struggling with.

"Here, you do this for me," he said, handing it over. Then, "What do you think of *Pairs?*"

Sidney got the claw meat out intact and he made a comment about her competence. That was the second time he saw fit to squeeze her knee. Garth still wasn't ready to give up his own choice of name. He told her about the competition and some of the other suggestions. He did not tell her which name was his favorite.

"It sounds like socks to me."

"What does?"

"*Pairs.*"

Garth laughed. "I hadn't thought of that . . . you mean matrimonial?"

"Well, you do mean inside and outside of the institution, don't you?"

"Of course."

"Well," Sidney said again, and hesitated because it was always a dangerous thing to give Garth opinions that were not his own. "It doesn't really tell you what the subject is, if you know what I mean."

Garth had asked for ice cream on his pie and was now hesitating over ordering a second piece. He looked at Sidney for any signs of disapproval, refilled her wineglass.

"Hmmm," he said. "It wasn't bad pie. Would you like another piece?"

"My God, Garth. I can't even finish this one."

"That's why you're so thin, Sidney. We ought to talk about that." He ordered another piece of pie. "Stockings are certainly evocative, though, aren't they?"

"But nobody wears them any more," Sidney said, watching him with horror as he put away a second piece of pie.

"Exactly. All the fun went out of life when panty hose came in."

After coffee, they walked around the town for a few minutes. Garth told her how much better he liked Nantucket. "If you want this sort of thing, Nantucket is more wild and natural." He added, however, that the Vineyard had a nice little paper he wouldn't mind owning. "I hear Scottie is a bit disenchanted with it, after all the money he put into the new printing process. What do you think, should we buy it?"

"Too small," she said.

He smiled. It was the right answer.

Sidney drove them home and put the car away. She was calculating the number of drinks he had. What would it take, two more, to make him unaware it was night, time to come out of his coffin.

She gave him a large brandy and put the bottle by his glass, went and sat on the other side of the room. He narrowed his eyes in mock displeasure at the arrangement she made. But nonetheless sat in the seat she had assigned him. He took two swallows, then said, "It's time to talk about you, my sweet. Shall we fuck first or talk first?"

Sidney flushed to the roots of her hair. "If you were trying to shock me," she said very softly, "you succeeded." Barrett for all his faults only said fuck when he was angry.

"My little pigeon, you really are," Garth laughed. "How sweet. You know, I've had a very good time with you." He took his glass and his drink and came to sit on the sofa with her. "I think we could do very well together."

"Garth, I'm very full. And I have a headache. Let's just talk for a while, okay?" Well, should she or shouldn't she?

"Okay." He spread out his hands, as though to prove he had no weapons hidden there. "Whatever you want. I'm here to make *you* happy, my love. Not for me. You just unburden your heart to me. That's what I'm here for." He turned slightly away from her.

The problem with Garth, Sidney was thinking, was that he made up his mind about what he planned to do and then neglected to tell anyone. You could never really get anything settled with him. He got that poor boy look on his face and all anyone wanted to do was make him happy and trust him. Right now, he looked so dejected sitting there swilling down Barrett's brandy. He pulled at a strand of hair, poor me.

"Well," he said, as though making an effort to pull himself together, "what's all this about Barrett? Just tell me. If he's making you unhappy, he's making me unhappy. You mean the world to me, Sidney. You know that. I'd do anything to make you happy."

He looked at her with the saddest eyes he could muster. He had suddenly remembered what it was about her thighs. They were very slender and had spaces between them. He remembered that from when she wore short skirts. Spaces, for him. He reached out and patted her knee, then raised his hand again in feigned—but effective—innocence, as though he didn't mean a thing by the pat.

"Look, I just want to come back and do my column. That's all. This other thing, with Barrett, well. I just don't know." He was all right, wasn't he? What was one more or less. What difference could it possibly make, now. One fat man, another fat man. A thin man, who cared if it made them happy. Sidney was thinking this like a condemned person. (Well, one-to-five was better than life.) This was life. Everyone else did it, why not she.

"Of course you are going to come back and do your column. I couldn't do without you."

"Really?" Sidney got up to get herself some port. If she had a few glasses of something herself, maybe she wouldn't feel so bad. She might even like it. Who knew. She came back and sat in the same place, willing herself to be calm. She didn't want him to think she was a prude, or that she was afraid of him. Besides, other than crushing her to death, what harm could he possibly do. Then again, maybe if she handled herself just right, she could get away without having to do it at all. "I thought," she said, rearranging her knees away from him, "you said you had something new in mind for me."

He smiled. "You're going to have to start eating a lot more, Sidney, fill out a bit." She was a sweet little thing. Not too aggressive. Garth liked that. He liked the way she blushed, the way she turned her head away when he touched her.

"I mean, on the phone yesterday you said—"

"I was trying to make adjustments," Garth said. "I haven't decided yet. First I thought you might like to go down to Washington for a while. We really need someone first rate down there."

"For my column?" Sidney said. She still wasn't sure he meant to let her keep it. The column was not called "Sidney's Eye," after all, but "*IT*'s Eye." And Garth was *IT*.

"I thought if you were having problems with Barrett, that might be a good way to make you both more comfortable. But I'm not so sure about Barrett."

"What do you mean?" Sidney didn't like this bit about Barrett. She knew he meant to give her a hard time, but he didn't have to go this far.

"Well, you know, you mean more to me than he does—if he's made you unhappy we could find something else for him to do somewhere else."

"Garth, don't say that. You know Barrett is indispensable."

"No one is indispensable, my chicken." Garth enjoyed her shock. It turned him on. Prim little Sidney was as vulnerable as anybody. He leaned closer to her and sniffed at her neck. "You're beautiful," he said. "You smell like—what *do* you smell like?"

"Ivory soap." Sidney looked at her drink. It was almost gone. Should she get up and get another one, just as he was greeting her left breast. Or should she . . . uh, take something off.

"No. It's *Norell*," he said triumphantly. He was right. He was sure. Norell.

"Can I freshen your drink, Garth?"

See, she hadn't shrugged him off. "It is Norell, isn't it?" Garth asked.

Yes, was the right answer. Sidney said yes.

"The French say a perfect breast just fills a champagne glass. Take off your shirt, Sidney, I think you're perfect."

"I'm not perfect, Garth." Barrett said her tits were like raisins in the sun. He was an authority on tits, so he should know. Even if Garth thought they were perfect, Sidney decided, she wasn't going to take off her shirt. She muttered something about being small.

"I like them small," Garth said. "I like everything small. Are you small down there?"

After shifting around a lot, Sidney was now sitting with her knees together and her feet flat on the floor. While she was trying

129

to think of an answer, he put his hand on the crotch of her pants and squeezed.

"I like a tight little cunt."

Once again Sidney flushed, only this time in fury, not shame. It was the words. She had been squeezed like that before—hadn't everybody—and not died from it. But there was a threat behind the words he chose. A hostility that, even now as he leaned over her, breathing down the neck of her T-shirt and calling her beautiful, was unmistakable.

"Let me put my hand right there. I want to feel you."

"No."

"Just inside your pants, just there. See, you're like a little bird. Let me put my hand there. I won't do anything. I promise. I want to—Please, Sidney. Don't make me cross."

Sidney moved away very firmly and he sat up.

"You're so suspicious," he said peevishly. "Christ, you'd think I were a rapist or something."

She smiled when he said that, but with her back to him, on her way to get some more port. For some reason, now that he had grabbed her, she felt more in control and not less—as usually happened.

"I'm not going to sit next to you, Garth. Because you don't talk when you say you're going to."

"Sidney, you're very cute. Did I tell you that?"

Maybe she could get away with it. Maybe if she said just the right things she could. She took a cushion and sat on the floor, the one place where she knew he wouldn't follow.

"And, Garth, you're very precious to me too. But I'm worth more to you unfucked."

"Oh no, don't say that," Garth said. He thought she really was cute.

"How can you say you care about me when you threaten to fire my husband. I'm telling you there are right fucks in the world and there are wrong ones And I am unquestionably a wrong one."

"I didn't say—"

"I'm not through. You know perfectly well that you have a million girls dying for you—and don't get me wrong, it's not that I'm not tempted—but I'm a writer, not a fucker. You know what I mean? I mean the others are better, believe me."

"Sidney, come back here, you're driving me crazy with this right fuck, wrong fuck shit. What the fuck is a wrong fuck?"

"I am. I've got this puny little body and this really bad emotional streak. You know Barrett says—"

"Sidney, I want to tell you something, sweetheart. I want whatever it is you're trying to hide in there. To me it's beautiful, and if fucking makes you cry that's okay too. I don't mind a few tears. Come up here, baby. I'll take care of you."

Sidney shook her head. "I don't want to disappoint you, Garth."

"I'm never disappointed—and you couldn't. Really. You're my favorite. You always have been. Why, last week Amelia Norton came to my office and said, 'Garth, I want to do "Eye."' And I said, 'Not even you could replace my Sidney.' Come to me, precious. I want to be with you. Doesn't that mean anything to you?"

Sidney shook her head. "It's not that I don't want you, I'm flattered, really I am. But I just want to write my column—contribute the way I know how. I'm not one of your better lays. Think of me that way as an okay writer but not a great lay."

"But I am."

"What?" Sidney said.

"A great lay. You may think I'm overweight, but I'm still the best. Don't think of what you can't do for me. Think of what I can do for you. Do you want to see it, Sidney? I'll show it to you."

"Garth. No."

"You're being unnecessarily stubborn."

"And you're making too much of it."

"But I'm trying to offer you pleasure."

By now both of them were yelling.

"I don't want it, though. If I don't want pleasure, I shouldn't have to have it."

"Sidney," Garth shrieked, on his feet now because she was. "If your job depended on it, would you still feel the same way?"

"Do you have to put it that way?" Sidney had calmed down very suddenly and asked this question in a tiny voice.

"I don't mean it like that, you know that. I just—I really want you, Sidney."

"Well, Garth, I'm sorry. But I don't think you do. I think you feel I'm not qualified to write my column any more because I don't want to sleep with you." She wondered if anyone had ever said this to him before.

"Why don't you want to? I could make you so happy."

"There's something wrong with your hearing. I said you're going to have to fire me."

"I don't want to fire you."

"I'm going to bed. In my room. Good night, Garth."

Sidney backed out of the living room. She was afraid for a minute that he might come after her and beat her. His face was unhealthily red. He was so angry he couldn't speak.

After she was gone, he sat down on the couch and imagined Sidney getting undressed. She wouldn't get away with this, he thought. As soon as she turned the lights off, he would go in there and fuck her because he wanted to and because, in spite of everything she said, she wanted it too. It was an hour before the light under the door went off. As he waited, Garth pictured Sidney's bare thighs. He wondered what kind of nightgowns she wore. He waited five minutes longer before he went to the door. He tiptoed up to it, then turned the doorknob very quietly. The door was locked. Garth wanted more than anything in the world to kick that door right then, but he restrained himself.

"Sidney," he said through the door. "I won't take your name off the masthead. Now will you take some aspirin for that headache, my love."

CHAPTER 21

Barrett was in the office very early on Monday morning. The very first thing he perceived when he looked around, to make sure it was the same place he had left on Friday night, was the new desk squeezed in between those of Alden's and Blake's secretaries. In a room where there were already at least five more desks than the floor space could handle, this new addition looked like the final insult. Barrett turned on the air conditioner to cool the room off before everyone arrived and heated it up again. Because of the ancient wiring in the building, the air conditioner only worked when the lights were off. In summer, sometimes they had lights and sometimes they had air conditioning. Garth refused to pay to have the place rewired because he nursed a half-formed plan to move one day and in the meantime didn't want to waste the money on luxuries they would have to leave behind.

Barrett took off his jacket and sat down at his desk. It was nine o'clock. No one would arrive until ten. He had a whole hour in which to fume alone. Who the fuck had Garth hired this time? After a few minutes during which he sat perfectly still with his fingers in the praying position—he was putting a severe stupidity curse on the new person, and asking please that he not be an executive type from the *Times* or CBS—the telephone man arrived to install the new person's phone. What a vipers' nest this place is, Barrett thought. He took out every paper he had in his active and inactive files and buried himself under what he hoped would look like a mound of magazine management. Someone had to arrange for the delivery of that desk. Though small, it was newer than his. Someone had had to put considerable pressure on Ma Bell to have that phone man there at exactly nine o'clock on Monday so that no one would have the weekend in which to brood and sulk.

Barrett brooded and sulked. The mailroom boy brought up the new issue of the magazine and dumped three copies on his desk. Grumpily, Barrett flipped through the glossy pages of the magazine. Just out of the box and brand new, it smelled wonderful. Without warning a sudden pride welled up in his throat. His name was still second from the top on the masthead. No one else had yet been added. When the new person's name was added, Barrett could always have it misspelled. He could instruct everyone to snub him—though that he wouldn't have to do. No one ever talked to a new person of rank until he had stuck it out for a full eighteen months.

He was planning to leave. In fact, after his interview with Garth on Thursday (Garth hadn't come in on Friday and Anne wouldn't tell him where he was), Barrett knew he had to leave. Yet here was his magazine. Started up again by his own hand after it had been so badly handled, there was hardly any life in it and no money at all. Under his hand, it had flourished. His magazine, and his name was still there, right under Garth's.

Barrett felt much renewed. By the time the staff began to arrive he had calmed down enough not to begin administering to the girls one at a time the-burning-splint-under-the-fingernail torture to find out who had known about the newcomer and gotten him a desk without telling Father Barrett. It had to be the same person who had told Garth that Sidney wasn't going to be around to do the albino rock star. Now, of course, everyone else had done his profile, and it was too late.

Barrett realized he was listening to Lespedeza to soothe his nerves. She was trying to reason with a distressed subscriber.

"The best way to make your complaints known to everyone here is to write a letter to the editor," she said. It was how she usually began. The approach either fired up the complainer to new heights of hysteria and indignation or abruptly calmed the person down. The world of irate callers could be divided into two distinct types. There were the yellers who wanted to "speak" to the editor; these couldn't write and would immediately cancel their subscriptions if it were suggested that they write. They wanted oral satisfaction. The other kind of irate caller was the historian, the expert. He wanted corrections made—the bias of the story adjusted, credit for having written a letter four years before suggesting the topic, the spelling of some obscure name changed. This kind of irate caller was thrilled at the idea of having his name in print and would respond immediately with a three-page, typewritten analysis of the article in question: "Dear Letters-to-the-Editor Editor:"

Lespedeza held the phone several inches away from her ear. She was on the phone with a yeller. "How did you say we're unfair to Lithuanians? . . . Oh, I really think you must have misinterpreted the article. I read it myself and didn't find a slur of that nature at all. . . . I assure you we have no prejudice against Lithuanians or anyone else . . . what is the ethnic breakdown of the staff?" No matter what was asked of her, Lespedeza never sounded harsh or impatient. She was like a good nurse with a querulous patient.

Barrett listened to her from behind his mound of papers. Sometimes when he heard those people out there abusing his girls, he went into a rage. It seemed that their readers thought they had nothing to do all day but answer their complaints and do errands for them. People would ask if the lady on the far lower right of the Central Park concert photo on page 73 of an issue six months old was their cousin Alice who disappeared from Racine, Wisconsin, in 1954. They would call the magazine to ask for the telephone numbers of people who wrote articles, people who appeared in articles, race tracks in Tiajuana, the Bronx Zoo. People would want information regarding just about anything whether it had anything to do with IT or not. How to get in touch with Raquel Welch. How to get a part in Neil Simon's latest. Medical information was a favorite. Who did the neatest mastectomies? was a common one these days. Today, however, Barrett took some pleasure in hearing her voice and did not go over to Lespedeza's desk, wrench the phone out of her hand, and yell obscenities into the ear of the caller as he had been known to do when seriously irked.

"What do you mean what's my name and position?" Lespedeza said gently, then, "No, I'm not required to tell you." Lespedeza held the phone out, offering it around to the other assistants, who had all dropped their work and were devoting full attention to the entertainment. "I really don't care who you are. I'm sorry the editor isn't here right now. My superior, hold on one moment, please." Lespedeza pushed her hold button. "Who wants to be my superior?"

"I will," Muriel said.

Lespedeza transferred the call to Muriel's phone.

"Hello, may I help you?" Muriel said in her sweetest Seventh-Day Adventist manner.

Barrett stopped listening when Muriel started running the argument through. Muriel didn't have his favorite style.

When the morning was nearly over, Garth appeared with a muffin-faced person in tow. At one point earlier in the morning, someone had suggested that the whole editorial floor hide in the bathroom so that when Garth arrived it would look as if no one was there. Several cheers accompanied the suggestion and a few people said why didn't they just go and make it more realistic. But no one was interested in that idea. They all knew well enough that nothing would ever stop IT from coming out. Once they had had a flood and worked with their feet in six inches of water. Once they had been taken over for a day by a little-known gang of black activists who were unhappy about the reporting in an article on Latin dance halls. Everyone continued to mark up copy in spite of the angry faces and six-foot chains around the necks of eight-foot well-muscled potential rapists and kidnapers. Blake, Seth, and Alden hid in the conference room on another floor. Barrett alone stayed upstairs to protect the women. It was often said that, if their firetrap of a building burned down with the entire staff inside, there would be a note in the *Times* the following day saying that the next issue would be a day late that week because of a small fire in the magazine's building. "Relatives need not inquire."

The idea of hiding in the bathroom was turned down because it had been done before. Garth, therefore, billowed forth with the muffin-faced man, who indeed turned out to be from CBS, trotting along behind.

"Hello, my beautiful babies," he said and headed toward his office. He did not introduce the muffin-faced man, who could have been, as far as anyone knew, a Bible salesman. Garth never introduced anyone to the staff. New people had to fend for themselves.

Barrett did an instant analysis of Muffin. He decided that Muffin would henceforth be called Muffin in private by the entire staff—and if they really detested him, maybe Muffin in public, too. He was around thirty-three, with suetish flesh, a gold Rolex, a red, white, and blue plaid suit, blond curly hair, piglet eyes, and very pink moist lips. He was another Wasp complete with bulging stomach that separated his shirt between the buttons and revealed patches of tummy hairs. He was exactly in Garth's mold but blond where Garth was dark and soft-looking where Garth was solid as a kettledrum.

As Garth approached, Barrett whipped together an expression of pleasure and approval and put out his hand. "Welcome, Caesar," he said.

Garth also greeted him in a semi-friendly fashion and the three men went into Garth's office and shut the door. He introduced Muffin to Barrett as Eagleton Redpath, and Muffin said, "The Third." Garth, who was a third himself but never mentioned it, said, "the third," in case Barrett had not heard Muffin say it.

"From now on, Eagleton will be our new acquisitions man. In

his spare time, he will edit whatever catches his fancy." This last bit he rather muttered. Garth then waved Muffin away without another word or look in his direction. Muffin, Barrett was gratified to see, was shocked at the dismissal. Garth told him to shut the door as he left. Barrett smiled. He had been allowed to stay.

"Well," Garth said without looking at Barrett, "what do you think of him?"

"Who?" Barrett said. He could not bring himself to dignify Muffin by knowing who he was.

"Eagleton, of course."

"Oh. He looks pleasant enough," Barrett said. "What is he going to do for us?"

"He'll give me ideas," Garth said. "We need a little new blood, someone new to play with." He leaned back in his chair and pursed his lips pensively.

"I thought I'd make him executive editor and publisher."

CHAPTER 22

Sidney bought a bikini in Edgartown. It was black and shimmery. For the first time that she could remember, she sat in the sun without a beach robe on. During her years with Barrett, Sidney had been convinced that she was not a pretty person. Barrett pinched the skin over her ribs as though she were a skinny chicken in the meat department at Gristede's. He said that her shoulder bones stood out on her back like wings. If she unbuttoned the top buttons of her blouse he buttoned them up again, stood by her side at parties and arranged her dresses so that no more of her neck showed than was absolutely necessary. He liked long nightgowns that got twisted around her legs, and stopped her with his hand if she tried to take them off.

"What would you do without me?" he was always asking her. "What kind of life would you have?"

It wasn't a question she would, unprompted, have asked herself,

137

for it was true that, before Barrett, there hadn't seemed to be many men available, and of those, few who were interested in her. In the years that she worked at *Time*, she had read the dictionary at night to fall asleep. In those days she couldn't help feeling that all love had left her when her parents died, for there was no home to go to on Christmas and no mother to care if she was taking her vitamins. When she was in college, it always annoyed her the way her mother called every Sunday morning and asked if she was keeping herself warm and taking her vitamins. Her mother, the custodian, seemed to have a list of essential questions that she felt revealed the quality of Sidney's life. They covered a range of subjects that included the contents of her stomach, the newness and cleanliness of the clothes on her back, and the background of the person who took her out on Saturday night. Whether or not Sidney had indeed gone out on Saturday night was a question of such deep significance that she could not even ask it. She had to assume that Sidney had gone out, and if Sidney admitted—even implied obliquely—that she had in fact not gone out, her mother was so upset she sat in her completely renovated kitchen in Providence and thought of ways she could make it up to Sidney. Usually reparations came in the form of cashmere sweater sets and fourteen-carat gold chains with hearts on them.

For years afterward she had gone around in the same tattered clothes to prove she had no one to care for her. The brief affairs she had in what she called her shabby days were poisoned by her own hopelessness. Men seemed so grabby and joyless. Their ambitions so small. They weren't like one's mother at all. There was a poster in the subway then that showed a face fading away to nothing. The message was that a person without an education was a person without a face. That was how Sidney saw her roommates when they married. Even with their educations, their faces faded away, as they became as dull as their husbands' fulfilled dreams.

But Barrett, unlike the other men she knew, wanted something different from Sidney. He wanted her as part of his own career. He didn't at first care that she was shabby. He praised her for her ability to work for hours at a time without a break. He said she had splendid concentration. She had promise. And although he was not attentive in the classically romantic fashion, he lavished a good deal of time and attention on her. After they were married he took her shopping. He stood in the kitchen overseeing her cooking. He was fascinated with all aspects of housekeeping. It seemed like love.

Sidney sat in the sun in her black bikini and wondered what Barrett was doing. Once when he asked what would happen to her if he weren't there, he had gone so far as to set up her life alone. In the conversation he had them separate. Sidney felt the clutch of fear as he divided their possessions, set her up in a studio apartment. The conversation started when she asked him why he hated children and he told her she was full of the silly suburban teachings of an unfulfilled mother. "She said you had to have one because it was the only way to justify her own awful life."

"How do you know?" Sidney asked.

"Babies are only useful for people who can't do anything else."

Sidney tried his own argument about needing more than one person to love and Barrett said if he wasn't enough for her she could try and find someone else. To make the threat sound more menacing he divided the furniture and made her move out. Then he went through the list of men they knew to see if, once deprived of him, there was someone else for her to go out with. He concluded, and she with him, that there wasn't anyone. Sidney knew he was only teasing, but she had been terrified nonetheless.

When she bought the bikini sometime after Garth left, she asked herself why having someone else mattered so much in their conversations. What would happen seemed so important that they hardly focused on what was happening. Barrett was always telling her he was more of a feminist than she was. But the truth was that it didn't matter how much a man claimed to be a feminist if he didn't have a woman's capacity for love. Sidney felt fairly certain now that, although it was a substantial part of a woman's nature, loving was not within the range of man's potential.

Why she chose a bikini to celebrate her liberation, she didn't know. But now that the threat that had been hanging over her head for nine years—of losing her job, of being alone without Barrett to oversee her, of not having anyone to want her at night—was the reality, she felt better. Now that she had failed at everything she considered important, there was the possibility of reappraisal. Sidney thought it particularly ironic that, although Henry Meadows was not a good lover, Barrett was not much better. Also, Garth had begged her forgiveness all through breakfast and all the way to the airport. He told her if she came back she could live in his apartment. If she was afraid of him, he would move out. He wouldn't take her name off the masthead no matter what she said. And she said she wouldn't fuck him if her very life depended on it.

Sidney realized now that on all those Saturdays when she had sat in Central Park watching the babies with the old people and the mothers and the nannies, while Barrett was in the office, she had grieved for her lost self as surely as she had once grieved for her lost mother. Perhaps not so surprisingly, she found she couldn't grieve for Barrett at all. What she did after buying her bikini and eating her tuna fish sandwich at the beginning of her third week away was sit on the sand and think about what she would do next. After a while she got a glass of iced tea and went out to the porch off her bedroom with it. Then she went back inside for a pad and pencil. It hadn't taken her any time at all to make the decision. She was going to be a free-lance writer.

There were at least six major magazines—not counting the special-interest ones and fashion/women—that would be glad to have an article of hers. Why, in fifteen minutes without even thinking she could come up with six ideas suitable for each magazine. Then she could choose the best two for each magazine (editors could never cope with more than two ideas at a time) and type up six query letters. If she spent a month on each article and got an average of a thousand dollars an article (some would be much more) she would make at least twelve thousand dollars the first year and have her by-line everywhere. Also she would meet a lot more nice magazine people and have something to keep her busy during the cold winter that would soon be upon her.

Sidney propped up the pad and tried not to remember just who it was who wrote that article for the *Times Magazine* section at their suggestion, did two rewrites using all their suggestions, and then had the piece rejected because the subject was "tired." Was it the *Times* that was well known for that, or was it some other publication. Never mind, she was a speedy writer and could cope with keeping a subject fresh. All she had to remember was not to be the slightest bit humorous. They had a top person over there who rejected everything with a giggle in it. They didn't like profiles. Nothing to do with sex. Education was out. So was art, architecture, food, theater, movies, restaurants, and television. Books. Well, cancer was always good. Science a favorite. What else? The Middle East, war in. Population. Starvation. She was not an expert in any of these subjects.

Well, since she didn't mind being rewritten, there was always *Cosmo*. That *would* be fun! How to help your lover find his penis. The surprising new facts about how masturbation can help your love life your disposition. *Cosmo* was good because one never needed to use any facts. In fact if one used a fact, *Cosmo* would quickly cut it out. The editors were well known for doing that. All they wanted were basics organized in a thousand different ways. New facts on how to overcome your lover's fear of failure. How to overcome your lover. How to get paid for having a good time.

Who was it who called Terry in hysterics just this spring because *Cosmo* had changed the slant of her article from "The Pitfalls of Being Promiscuous" to "How Antibiotics Cured My Fears about Free Love." Terry advised her to take the money and use a pseudonym—like everyone else who had pride and wrote for the magazine.

Sidney's pen remained poised over the empty pad. It was depressing being a free-lance writer. Instead of having only Garth and Barrett to please—whose requirements she knew well—there would be an army of Garths and Barretts. Each time she wrote an article she would have to copy the magazine's style exactly. With research, each article would take a month; she would have to wait a month while everybody read it and made comments. Then she would have to rewrite it incorporating everyone's ideas, which would take more time—and do it quickly because they would need it immediately (for an issue that had already closed). Then the article would sit around for three months while the editors, who said that the piece was now perfect and would run immediately, waited for just the right issue to put it in. Then they would have to hold it up longer because some other magazine had already run a similar story and they would demand a rewrite with a new slant. Meanwhile, she would not be paid because most magazines pay on publication so they won't have to pay for articles they decide, after several months, they never wanted in the first place.

If she worked six magazines and had twelve ideas, it would take approximately six months of back and forth with each article. If she wrote anything at all timely, the odds on getting the piece run would be worse. That was the way it was at *IT* anyway. Editors assigned pieces other editors had already assigned. When the pieces came in, they would run one; or they would decide they didn't like the way either article was handled. Or, by the time the story came in, they just didn't like the idea any more. If they assigned a skiing piece, by the time the copy was "right" the season would be over. They promised to run it next year. If they assigned a piece on America's Coney Islands, by the time everyone read it and corrections were made, it would be August. They promised to run it next year. Sometimes they did. After the author's spending another month on an update of the material.

Often a piece had to be rewritten after it was already in galleys. And getting something in galleys was no guarantee of getting the piece run either. Galleys turned yellow with age while they waited for the proper issue to live in. There simply was no end to the number of complications that could arise from being a free-lance writer. And, of course, Sidney didn't want to meet any more nice magazine people.

Maybe she should write a book. Of course publishers were cutting back their lists, and each one had a lot of editors who had very strong ideas about what they liked.

And there was a pub board that decided on salability. But what the hell. Anyway, she was famous, wasn't she. That should help. Sidney was about to hit upon the perfect subject for a book when the phone rang. She let it ring three times and then picked it up.

"Hello," she said.

"What are you doing?"

"Terry, son of a gun. I'm writing a book. What are you doing?"

"That's terrific Sidney. That's really terrific. What on?"

"Loneliness." Shit, why did she say that. Sidney grimaced at her stupidity. Although now that she thought of it . . . Loneliness was a great subject for a book. *How to Overcome Loneliness*. As a title, it had a real ring. It was a subject she could really get her teeth into. A subject that mattered. Think of the people who would want to know.

"Oh, Sidney, I'm sorry," Terry said. His voice dropped with chagrin.

"Don't be silly. It's a great idea. Don't you think so?" She wasn't going to let him know she was upset that he hadn't called in days. Certainly not. "How are you anyway, old buddy?"

"I'm all right," Terry said, not feeling all right at all. This didn't sound good, didn't sound like the Sidney he knew at all.

"Have a good weekend? I had Garth. Who did you have?"

For a minute there was silence. Terry was too surprised to say anything. He had a sort of sinking feeling that he attributed to general disappointment in the human condition.

"Terry?"

"I heard you."

"Are you upset?" Sidney said. She was rather pleased at the sensation she was making.

"I wouldn't say upset exactly," Terry said slowly. "I'm sort of surprised."

"So, who did *you* have?"

"I didn't *have* anybody," Terry muttered.

"You don't have to get all prickly about it. It's not my fault."

"I mean, I didn't want anybody."

"Oh, Terry, I'm sorry. Isn't there anything you can take for it?"

"Sidney. Christ. What's gotten into you?"

"Well—"

"That good, huh?"

"You dirty old man," Sidney said indignantly. "You really thought I did, didn't you?"

"You said you did. I believe you. Besides, I hear—"

"Terry, you've really done me an injustice. You really have. I don't want to talk to you any more."

"Oh, come on, Sidney, how could I do you an injustice by believing what you tell me?"

"I don't want to talk to you."

"I'm sorry I didn't call. But you could have told me, you know. You could have called *me*. You know I would have come. Why didn't you tell me?"

"I wouldn't tell you anything. You would have told Barrett."

"Oh, Christ," Terry said. "What happened? Was it awful?"

"Yes, it was awful."

"Why didn't you tell me, Sidney?" Terry said again.

"I don't need *you* hovering over me. I can look after myself. Actually, he was kind of cute. He loves me."

"Oh, Sidney."

"That's what he said. Don't get snippy. He said that. He said I was beautiful."

"Well, you are beautiful."

"I am not."

"Sidney, what can I do? You sound kind of awful. Do you want to come home? You can come home, you know. Do you want me to come up?"

"I don't want anything. I'm perfectly self-sufficient. He says he'll do anything for me, Terry. What do you think of that?"

"I think he probably says it to everyone," Terry said without thinking.

"You just put me down, you know that? That was mean of you. What do you know about my desirability anyway?"

"Do you want to come home, love? I'll help you."

"Don't call *me* love," Sidney snapped. Love, he called her. Love, huh.

"Would you like to go out for dinner? I'll come up. We'll go out for dinner, would you like that?"

"Terry, you're talking to me as though I were a mental defective. Is that what you think is on my mind? Dinner? I've just lost my husband and my job. I'm not interested in dinner. If you come over, I'll give you a drink. . . . Fuck dinner," she added.

"You haven't *lost* anything," Terry said quickly. "You know you haven't."

"You're right. They've lost me. When are you coming?"

CHAPTER 23

Barrett walked out of Garth's office determined to leave the magazine right then and never come back. Third on the masthead. Third. He sat down at his desk without even looking at the pile of pink telephone messages that had built up while he was talking to Garth. Right then he would leave. He looked over at Betty and saw her buffing her nails. On her desk beside his unopened morning mail and the stack of letters she was supposed to have typed on Friday were a bottle of nail polish remover, nail polish, nail scissors, and emery boards. It was a sight not unfamiliar to him, Betty doing nothing when there was so much to do. Lespedeza was on the phone. Muriel was reading the *Watchtower*. Two secretaries were showing each other underwear that they pulled piece by piece out of a Bloomingdale's bag. No wonder there was always a panic on Wednesdays. Nobody did a damn thing around there but him. At the far end of the room, Barrett saw Muffin sitting at his empty desk ignored by Seth and Alden, who were reading their mail.

He would leave right then, get up and walk the length of the room to the door. He would open the door and walk three flights down to the street, and then he would flee. He saw himself getting up, putting on the jacket he had just taken off. It was his summer blazer. Blue linen. Barrett saw it hanging on the hanger above his head. He would leave. He wondered what was in his mail. He wondered how Garth could hire a man to edit who had never edited a word before in his life. When he thought of the years he had worked. He was thirty-eight, nearly thirty-nine now, and he had been in magazines for seventeen years. And here was this asshole with blond curly hair that would fall out before the year was over, this creep with the piggy eyes, who had probably never seen a word before. It made him sick.

Barrett sat there too depressed to move. Maybe he should go

and see Sidney. Maybe they should discuss what to do next. It was the first time he had let such a thought stay in his mind for longer than the time it took him to think it. He mulled it over, pursued the feeling of going out to the airport, getting on the plane, calling Sidney from the airport. He could imagine what the house looked like with the sun streaming in and Sidney sprawled out on one of the deck chairs reading something and drinking iced tea. The image brought a stab of pain because he was left out of it, and then a powerful wave of fury. How could Sidney be sitting in the sun drinking iced tea at a time like this. The selfish bitch. Not a letter, not a note. Not a word in all this time. What kind of viperous person could do such a thing? Barrett thought that Sidney must have been nursing her mean streak for some time. She had been going along pretending that she was a safe person, hardly ever saying a word or making even a gesture of discontent, and suddenly she just leaves. Just like that without any warning.

Betty got out of her chair with Barrett's mail folder and dropped it on his desk. She didn't even look, just dropped it so it hit one of his hands. Tthe pile of pink message slips fluttered with the breeze the folder made. Barrett caught the name on the top message: Stewart Adams.

"Barrett." Seth came over and sat in Barrett's guest chair.

Barrett jumped, crumpled the slip in his hand. That girl was going to be gone before the day was over. She didn't deserve to live, much less work in a civilized place. "How are you, Seth?"

"What do you think?" Seth jerked his head over in Muffin's direction.

"You mean about Muffin? Don't give it a thought, m'boy. Don't waste a single thought on him."

"Who is he?"

"No one."

"Oh. . . . Well, Garth said he wanted to go over the line-up."

Garth came out of his office and clapped his hands as though he were a maître d' in a French restaurant at opening time. "What's going on here this morning? Nothing. Eagleton," he shouted. "Come and see how we put a magazine together."

Muffin looked up eagerly. He jumped up from his desk, rushed across the room, tripping only once on a telephone book that hit the floor with a huge bang only seconds before he came to it. "Oh, sorry," Eagleton said to no one in particular.

"Where the fuck is Blake?" Garth snapped. "I want you to meet Blake, Eagleton." He looked from one to the other. "Alden, where's Blake?"

Alden shrugged. Seth shrugged. No one looked at Barrett. They think I've been fired, Barrett thought.

Garth threw out the bathroom story. "Brushing their teeth, I said," Garth muttered. "We've already done them in the tub. I'm sick of tubs. Teeth, I said. I wanted to show different devices for cleaning teeth."

"No one would do it, Garth," Barrett said. He spoke as though to a child he didn't want to hit. "Only Joyce Brothers would do it, no one else."

"She have a nice bathroom?" Garth asked.

"We never sent anyone over, since she was the only one."

Garth threw out for the third time the Coney Island story. Everyone knew he would. He had done the two Disneylands twice, but he couldn't do Coney Island. He threw out the story on Cher, the story on Bella Abzug, the story on George Bush, the story on summer camps for adults. He threw out everything they had planned for that week.

"I think we'll put hair in this week. This is a good week for hair. We have the ten pages, and the cover. We'll do it this week."

"The cover isn't ready. We planned it for later."

"I know the picture is ready because I've seen it."

"What?" said Dan, the art director. "I'm sure it hasn't come in yet."

"Annie, get me the hair picture, will you," Garth yelled, though Anne was standing at his elbow.

"I thought we decided ten pages was too much for hair?" Seth said. "What does hair matter?"

Garth gave him a nut-grinding look. "When are you going to get rid of yours?"

Anne handed him the picture; it was a composite of various members of the staff *au naturel*. Stuck in between and around them were people like Phyllis Diller bald and Yul Brynner wigged. The issue would contain a story on hair removal tech-

147

niques, for those who wanted hair off; a hair transplant story complete with some gruesome pictures of the process for those who wanted hair on. A service story on how to choose a wig. And an article with five pages of famous people who wig themselves: why they do it and what they think it does for them. The pictures, which were tossed on the table, showed them before and after. There was a scramble to see them and then much hooting and pointing as they tried to choose who would be in and who thrown out.

Dan scratched his head. "I was sure that cover picture hadn't come in yet."

They stood around arguing about the cover line. "Flipping Your Wig for Summer," someone wanted.

Garth said he had to have the words "hair" and "summer" in it. "Not wig."

"How about 'Hide and Hair'?" Eagleton said eagerly. This wasn't so hard, he thought.

" 'Hide and Hair,' " Barrett said. "Haw, haw, haw."

"I think that cover picture should show a beautiful bald girl in a bikini with hairy legs," Seth said.

"How about Seth bald in a bikini?" Alden said.

"Who asked you?" Seth said.

"Will you two shut up. We need a Jewish princess hair story," Garth muttered. "For 'Eye.' "

Barrett's stomach lurched. What a great story for Sidney.

" 'Beauty Knows No Pain,' that's what we'll call it. Any suggestions on who should do it?"

"It's Monday. We need someone fast," Anne said softly. Then she remembered and pulled on Garth's sleeve to get his attention. "I thought Amelia was doing something this week."

Garth ignored her.

"How about Goldie?" Seth said. Goldie was his present girl friend. "She could do a great 'Beauty Knows No Pain.' "

"That's because she's so ugly," Alden said.

"It has to be someone who hangs out in a beauty parlor a lot," Garth said. "Goldie's never been."

Everyone laughed, shifted from one foot to the other.

"How about Bella?"

"How about Gloria?"

"All right," Garth said. "Call Amelia."

"She's not Jewish," several people said at once.

"Well, who goes to the beauty parlor a lot and isn't very pretty but tries real hard? You come up with someone."

After much arguing back and forth, they finally settled on the regular free-lance writer they always chose for this kind of story, and to whom they had all known in the beginning they would have to resort. Only to a regular could they turn to do a story in a day and a half. They broke up and Garth clapped Eagleton on the back.

"See how it's done, Eagleton?" He turned and walked away before Eagleton had a chance to say anything.

What was he supposed to do now? Eagleton stood there for a minute as the crowd that had been huddled around the table dispersed. As far as he could tell, they hadn't accomplished anything. There were no cover lines decided on, no headlines for the stories. In fact where were the stories. He only saw pictures. Were the stories finished, in the house, in galleys. What? He riffled through the pictures on the table, as though the stories might be attached. He looked at the line up. The pages were numbered and there were a lot of arrows drawn between boxes. But he couldn't make out what was scrawled in the boxes. Garth had said he wanted him to work on the new magazine. Where was it. No one had even mentioned it. He walked slowly back to his desk, considered going out for a drink, to the men's room. Anything. As he approached his desk, he saw two new things on it. An out basket that was empty and an in basket that was filled with galleys. He sighed with relief and quickly sat down. It didn't take him ten minutes to settle into the favorite time waster of editors at *IT* magazine, reading and marking up other editors' galleys.

Before the meeting was completely broken up, Muriel had already rushed back to her desk and begun typing up headlines and subheads. Since she knew what stories they would use, she started with titles. But she would also do captions for all the pictures even though the final ones wouldn't be chosen for a day or two. This time she was sure they would use some of her ideas, they had to.

Barrett went to the men's room. He was glad he had worked on that hair transplant story the week before even though he thought it was the stupidest piece of shit he'd ever seen. Every time he went in there, he turned on the hot water and every time when it came out cold he was surprised. For all the years they had been in this building there had never once been hot water on the fourth floor and he was still surprised. This time the cold water trickling out on his hands reminded him of *New Journal*. He felt better. In fact he felt well enough to get back to work on it. If he got the money, he was sure Terry would help him look over the assets and everything, and do the papers. He was sure of it. He dried his hands on his handkerchief because there were no more towels and went back to his desk. He began composing a letter to Mr. Poupont, the man who handled Sidney's account. For a minute he thought of how strangely Terry had acted when he suggested that the three of them go out to dinner when they got back from Fire Island, and then he put it out of his mind.

CHAPTER 24

Since Barrett was familiar with Sidney's bank statements even if she wasn't, he knew exactly what instructions to give to Mr. Poupont. The terms of her father's will stated that Sidney could never have outright the capital, which had amounted to just under $150,000. He wanted to be sure that Sidney would always have something no matter how the economy changed. But he had given her the right to leave the money to anyone she wanted. This had always been a source of interest to Barrett because receiving a large sum of money was something that held great appeal to him. Usually such wills stipulated that the money would go to the children of the children, but Barrett thought that Sidney's father had just not thought of that since Sidney was so young at the time he made the will. It was not exactly the reason that Barrett didn't want to have children, but Sidney had never made a will herself. If she died intestate with children all the money would not go to him. It was the kind of thing that Barrett thought about. Rationally he knew it was unlikely that Sidney would die either before or without him. But he thought about it anyway, and he watched her statements. Sidney's yearly income—for which she paid no taxes because it came from tax-exempt bonds—went to purchase more tax-exempt bonds that yielded a greater income every year. Now the original $142,000 had swelled to nearly $300,000. Barrett figured that they could risk half of it and still not touch the original bequest. He could not understand why Sidney didn't want to do it.

He wrote to Mr. Poupont in Providence very carefully. It took him all of Monday lunch and half of Monday afternoon to do it. He sat with a file shielding the pad of paper on which he was trying out different ways of phrasing the letter. He didn't want to sound too girlish, for Mr. Poupont followed Sidney's career and knew well enough that she was no ordinary female. On the other hand, too businesslike an approach might cause suspicion. He might want Sidney to come up there and talk to him about it. He might want to be sure she wasn't being influenced. No, he would have to write a frank Sidney-sounding letter about changing times and change of heart. How she might want a substantial part of her income in the next six or so months, but fifty thousand dollars would do nicely for the minute. The salutation caused no problems, but at the bottom he wondered if he ought to add something more personal to Mr. Poupont, who wrote such nice little letters at Christmas every year, than "Thanks for your attention in this matter." In the end, he decided not.

Barrett typed up the letter himself and addressed the envelope, then stamped it and put it in his out box. He felt much better, sat back in his chair, and looked around. Lespedeza had her head bent over some galleys. He stepped across the aisle to her desk and tugged at a strand of hair.

"Want to go out for dinner tonight?" he whispered into her neck.

"No," she said without looking up.

"Why not?"

Lespedeza continued marking up the galley.

"Hey," Barrett said.

"I heard you, Barrett, I said no."

"What are you talking about?" Muriel demanded.

"Nothing that would interest you," Barrett snapped. He went back to his desk. Muriel had a weak bladder. She would have to go to the bathroom soon, and then he'd try again. Lespedeza was a pain; she had turned slightly in her swivel chair and had her back directly to him. This was something she would not have dared to do three weeks ago.

Barrett noticed the letter in his out box. Only a minute ago he had put it there address down. Now the address was facing up. Barrett snatched up the letter in fury. Without even stopping for his blazer, he left the office. It was an outrage. He did not wait for the elevator. He marched down the three flights of stairs and out onto the street. Outside the air was hot and smelled as it always did in summer, of rotting garbage and dog manure. But Barrett did not take note of the odor or grumble about it even to himself. He went to the post office and mailed the letter. On his way back, he debated whether or not to go back. It was Monday. No one would care if he didn't. All the way back he said he wasn't. Even as he climbed the stairs again, but of course he had to go back for his jacket.

Lespedeza was alone, still working on the same set of galleys. Muriel wasn't in the room anywhere.

"Are you working on that or just decorating it?" Barrett snapped. Usually when he got to the top floor, he waited outside the door for a minute until he stopped panting and his heart slowed down. Sometimes he took the stairs slowly so that he wouldn't pant at all. But now, after the four blocks to the post office and the four blocks back and the stairs, his chest was heaving and his breathing ragged. He should have taken the elevator.

"Barrett, are you all right?" Lespedeza said. Her hard look suddenly softened in concern, for Barrett's armpits were uncharacteristically stained and his face constricted. He looked in pain.

"I'm all right," he hissed, leaning over her desk so that no one else could hear, "except that you upset me."

"How many times do I have to tell you?" She turned her head so her hair fell over her face.

"Since when have you been so concerned with other people's marriages, anyway?"

"She's coming back," Lespedeza said, the "she" referring to Muriel.

"I don't care. We have to get to the bottom of this thing." This last he said in his official office voice, cold and unrelenting, Sidney called it. "Would you step over here a minute so we can discuss it."

"Barrett," Muriel interrupted, "have you looked at my headlines?"

"What headlines?" He started even though he had known she was coming.

"I told you this morning I was going to do some of the headlines for this issue and you said to go ahead.

"I don't remember any such thing."

"They're on your desk. The first ones anyway. If you don't like those, I'll work on some others." Muriel stood between him and Lespedeza. "I think you should look at them."

Barrett didn't move.

Muriel started to snivel, her eyes watered. "I know you don't think I'm good for anything but correcting typos." Her voice rose. "But that's because you never give me a chance to do anything else. I could be an editor, you know I could."

"Muriel, for God's sake, don't make a scene."

"Well, you don't give me a chance. You don't. Remember that time I wrote the copy for that ethnic accessory story, you didn't even give me a by-line. And once I—"

"All right, all right." Barrett said, but he wasn't sure what he was saying all right to. He turned to Lespedeza for support, but she wouldn't meet his eye.

People had begun to look up with that expectant look they got. Barrett could see them preparing to come over and take sides. "Okay, you win. I'll take a look at them. Now you sit down and stop that, do you hear me." Barrett turned away.

He went back to his desk and sat down. He could feel Muriel's eyes on him. Christ, morning seemed a long time ago. He had to get away from here. Barrett hadn't been out of the office for more than fifteen minutes, but already a number of things had piled up. He sat there for a minute staring at the cork board beside his desk on the wall that had covers of the magazine all over it. He pulled the cover off of the issue that had just come in and tacked it up along with the others. Then he shoved everything that was on his desk into a drawer and reached for his jacket. He decided to go home and return Stewart Adams' call.

"He didn't even look. Did you notice that?" Muriel said to Lespedeza as soon as he was gone. "He didn't even stop for two seconds to see what I'd done."

Lespedeza didn't answer. Barrett had become such a painful problem in her life she didn't even want to think about him. He seemed to feel all of a sudden that she was his property, that he could do anything he wanted, never mind what she said. On Saturday night she had locked the door to her room. How much clearer could she make it to him than that. People in summer houses have some pretty peculiar ideas about security, though. The lock was merely a hook and eye. Barrett opened it with a spoon or a knife blade or something.

"Clover, if you scream, I don't know what I'll do," he had said.

"I'm not going to scream. You're going to go away," she told him. But he didn't. He had seemed so desperate and crazy. He said he just wanted her company and she believed him . . . besides, what could she do.

"I won't do anything. I promise I won't," he said again, as though that was what was really bothering her. He sat on the edge of the bed. "Do you ever feel that things are getting away from you, and you can't get back in control no matter what you do?" he asked.

Yes, she had felt that way. She felt that way more often than she wanted to admit, felt it just then as a matter of fact.

"I don't know. I just feel so—" Barrett didn't have the word for it.

But Lespedeza did, and they talked about it for a while. Then Barrett got into bed with her and they fell asleep. It almost made up for everything.

"Lespedeza, you're not listening," Muriel said.

"Yes, I am." For years Lespedeza had sat next to Muriel and listened to her complain. She felt she was badly treated. She felt guilty for working where the language was so bad. She felt wretched and unloved. For years Lespedeza had tolerated her, encouraged her, and taken her out for lunch and dinner when she seemed unusually distraught. Many times Lespedeza had been exasperated and annoyed because it was stupid, that belief Muriel had that she was doomed. Nobody was doomed. But Muriel believed she was destined never to have anyone look after her or save her from a lonely old age. What bullshit it was. Yet never before had Lespedeza felt like slapping her whiny mouth shut. "For Christ's sake, Muriel," she said now.

"Don't swear, Clover."

"That wasn't swearing."

"Bad-mouthing the Lord, that's what it is. And he didn't talk very nicely to you either. Barrett's a mean pig. He wouldn't even look at my headlines."

"Muriel, you're so selfish you can't think of a thing beside yourself."

"Lespedeza, don't talk to me that way."

"Did you ever think that Barrett may have a few other things on his mind than your stupid headlines?"

"You're a bitch, Clover. You really are." Muriel sniffed, grabbed up some corrected galleys, and marched down to the production department where she deposited them in the box marked with the typesetter's name. When she came back she added, "Since when do you care so much about the state of Barrett's mind?"

"Oh, God, anybody but you could see that he's miserable."

"I know what I see."

"Oh, shut up."

"Don't tell me to shut up." Muriel sat down, making an elaborate arrangement of her skirt. "I think there are a few things around here some people ought to know about."

"Oh, Muriel."

"Like Sidney, for instance . . ." When she got no reaction to this Muriel added, "How dare you tell me I'm selfish when you go and do a thing like that to poor Sidney?"

"A thing like what?" Lespedeza said.

"You know what."

"I haven't done anything to anybody. And don't start on that."

"Well, it happens to be true that you whoremonger every man you see. And I can see perfectly well what's happening. I heard him ask you to dinner."

"Then you must have heard me say no."

"Well, you better stay away from him."

"You're crazy, you know that. Just plain crazy," Lespedeza said.
"And where were you this weekend?"

"You're crazy."

"I thought you were my friend, Lespedeza. But I can see what you're interested in. What do you think he's going to do for you anyway?"

Lespedeza looked around quickly and then back at Muriel. "Muriel, will you please shut up. You're all wrong about this."

"Oh yeah, well, we'll see how crazy I am."

Lespedeza leaned over and put her hand on Muriel's arm. "I'm sorry I said you were crazy."

"It's too late for that." She shrugged off the hand and turned her back as much as it's possible to turn one's back on someone sitting at the next desk.

Lespedeza sat there for some time regarding Muriel's skinny shoulders. Muriel was always telling Lespedeza that she wouldn't go to heaven if she didn't mend her ways and accept the Lord. She was always talking about God's creatures and tolerance for the afflicted. But as long as she had known her, Lespedeza had never heard a word of tolerance for the afflictions of Garth, Sidney, Barrett, or any other human being except Richard Nixon. After a long time Lespedeza went downstairs to find another telephone from which to call Barrett in private.

CHAPTER 25

The week after Fire Island was a terrible one for Terry. He had promised to spend the next weekend with Morvan. He had put off calling Sidney. Then, after he had spoken with Sidney, he promised to come to her on Friday night, after spending only the day in Vermont with Morvan. By Friday, though, it was not easy to focus on the subject of Morvan's book. Terry kept worrying about Morvan's drinking too much and not getting him to the airport on time. He was afraid the truck would break down on the way. Already he was calculating the nearest place he could rent a car. He was trying to figure out how long it would take him to get to Woods Hole from here. He wondered if it might be better to drive after all. Suppose the plane was late getting to Boston. If the fog closed in, he'd have to drive down to Woods Hole anyway. Christ, it was difficult getting from one small place to the other.

Morvan had gutted the first floor of his old wooden farmhouse so that practically the whole of it was one room. The front door was in the middle. On one side of the room was a large table behind which was the kitchen, still fitted out with ancient equipment. On the other side were several old rocking chairs, one upholstered armchair which had very little upholstery left on it, and a very modern bed hung from the beams in the ceiling by chains so that it swung back and forth. Morvan had been reclining on this bed for the two and a half hours since lunch, drinking something he called comfort, that Terry would not touch.

Terry had flown up early in the morning before Morvan was awake; so his present mistress, a sturdy-looking girl of hardly more than twenty, had to meet him at the tiny airport forty minutes away. Tina, Morvan called her, though she told Terry her real name was Rosalind. While they waited for Morvan to arise, they walked around the shabby farmyard and inspected the barn. Terry asked her but Tina didn't seem to know anything about a book. She knew, of course, that he went into his tiny study every day for an hour or so, but she didn't know what he did there. He locked the door from the inside when he was in it and from the outside when he wasn't. She had been there for six months and never seen the room.

All through lunch, which consisted of comfort, plover-sized eggs from the scrawny chickens in the yard, sausages from a farm down the road, Vermont cheese, and California fruit—Morvan told this to Terry because he was interested in origins—Terry was thinking, leave at four, five o'clock plane to Boston, arrive Martha's Vineyard at six forty-five. Would he make it.

Morvan was concerned with origins. That's what his book was about. There was simply no way to explain the mess the country was in without getting down to origins first. He said he had this grand plan for a book on America that would tell everything. He was a big man, with legs like whole hams and a wide soft belly.

"Why do you want to go away so fast? You just got here."

Terry said the person he had to see was in greater need than himself and, though he would like to stay, he couldn't.

"Uh-huh," Morvan said. "Have some comfort. That's what you need, Terrence." Morvan swung back and forth on his big bed, which was new since Terry had last been there. He was the only one who called Terry Terrence. "You have a soul like a steel rivet."

Terry wanted to talk, but Morvan wouldn't talk before lunch. After lunch, he wanted to go out and clean the barn.

"You haven't been in that barn for six months," Terry said.

"That's what I'm telling you, boy. Now is the moment. You got to dirty yourself up a little, unbend that mū-seum of a soul you got."

Morvan was always talking that way, pretending he was a hick and telling people to dirty themselves up. He had spent ten years in New York and five years on Long Island perfecting his style. Now he seemed just like the classic backwoodsman who would hit you on the head and bury you out back just for the ten bucks in your wallet. Terry knew, however, that the worst he would do was pretend he was too drunk to get him to the airport.

"I got a nice room for you upstairs, and Tina out there, well, she's not unwilling."

"I'm sure," Terry said.

"What, you already do something while I was up there sleeping? Haw, haw, haw." Morvan sat up for a minute to slap his thigh.

"Morvan, I've got exactly an hour and a half. Why don't we talk about this book of yours?"

"Terry, did you touch that young innocent girl out there?"

"No. Now listen. You've been calling me almost every day for a month. You want to talk about this or not?"

"I've got this great book I'm doing," Morvan said. "All about the origins of America. It's a classic already. So what's the problem?"

The problem, Terry told him, knowing he already knew it, was that an idea was not a salable commodity unless there was some sort of outline to go with it, no matter how great a novelist was.

Morvan began to sputter with rage. "It's a violation of my integrity."

This argument they had been through before. His publisher had already said the idea as presented was not a novel. Morvan had told Terry to go to another one. Terry had told him to finish the book. Now it took some time and much drinking of comfort for Morvan to admit that he didn't have a form for the book yet —though he had several short bits he thought belonged at the end—and couldn't know what he was going to do until he did it. And he couldn't do it without making the sale.

"Don't those fuckers know I'll do it? Ter-rence, I want you to stay here with me awhile," Morvan said finally. "I need to talk it out."

"Can I have what you've done?" Terry asked. "Let me take what you have. Maybe I can make a magazine sale, would that help?"

A little while later, Terry left Morvan snoring on his swinging bed. He had a tattered manuscript in his briefcase, the original, for as Morvan quickly pointed out there was no "zeerox" machine out there. He didn't say good-bye, just collapsed on the bed after giving over the manuscript. Terry knew he wasn't drunk. He was merely sick over his work, so desperately afraid he wouldn't be able to do it again that he had to leave his friends for a barren farm he didn't even know symbolized himself. He sat there talking about the origins of fruit and the origins of America because he didn't know where his own talent came from, or where to look to find it again.

Once again Tina drove to the airport. She was a girl who didn't have a lot to say. Terry thought she wasn't helping Morvan through his drought, could even be a part of it. Oh well, nothing was simple. He decided to call Sidney from the airport and tell her not to come get him until he got there. He didn't like the thought of her sitting out at the airport waiting if he missed the plane. He rang but there was no answer at the house.

Terry was the first one off the plane at the Vineyard. It was Friday night and there was a great crowd at the airport as there is every Friday in summer. Little children in their pajamas tried to get past the guard so they could race out on the runway and grab

at their daddies before their mothers did. Terry didn't see Sidney
at first. He was expecting the grubby look, her shrouded in rags
standing at the back of the crowd—or even sitting in the car. But
she was right in the front in a straw hat, dark glasses, and a white
linen pants suit. He started to walk past her.

"Hey."

"Oh, my God, Sidney. I thought you were Barbara Walters."

"You did not. You would never have walked past Barbara without saying hello. Anyway, she isn't here this year."

They walked back to the car.

"Well, how *are* you? Don't be silly, I'll carry that," Terry said
when Sidney tried to take his briefcase.

"Are you tired?" she said. "You look tired."

"No, I'm not tired. I'm fine."

"Really?"

"Of course, really. Well, you look better."

"Better than what?" Sidney demanded.

"Better than the last time I saw you. Hey, where are we going?"

Sidney made the wrong turn leaving the airport. "Oh, didn't I
tell you? The Winklers are having a head-of-the-department clambake and dinner dance, for Davey. I hope you don't mind."

"I don't mind." Terry frowned.

"You don't have to go pee-pee or something?" Sidney looked at
him and caught the frown. "Your plane got in so late, we don't really have time to go home first."

"Pee-pee?"

"Well, I know there isn't any place on those Beechcrafts and
you do have one, don't you?"

"At last check."

"I'm glad to see you." Sidney took her hand off the knob of the
gear shift and held it out to him. He squeezed it briefly and put it
back. "I really am," she insisted.

"Well, I'm glad to see you," Terry said.

"You don't mind going to the Winklers', do you? I sort of had
to say I'd come. They've been very nice and it's their first big one
of the season. She's so excited about Davey and everything. . . ."
Sidney didn't add that Laney had heard from Elsa that Sidney
and Hank had gone to the Kafe in Edgartown one night a week

before and Laney had been nagging her about it ever since. Taking Terry there for dinner would put a stop to that.

"Oh, Terry Hammer," Laney shrieked when she saw him. "How gorgeous. Sidney told me she was bringing a mystery guest, and I couldn't make her tell me who. I thought it was *Barrett*, but I'm so glad it's you. You don't mind, darling?" Laney said to Sidney. She took Terry by the arm and led him to a clot of people standing around the bar they had set up.

The Winklers' house was on a grassy hill in Chilmark. Sidney went outside with her bloody mary to see if there had been a hole dug in the lawn for the clams to bake in. She found a skinny young man with a mustache building a tower-like structure out of what looked like wooden shelves with holes in them. There was a mountain of seaweed, lobsters, clams, and corn. They discussed the methodology of clambaking in back yards while he built the tower. The things that took the longest to cook were already steaming away on the bottom.

People began to spill out of the house by twos. Two people from Harvard. Two novelists. Two television news people from different networks, Henry Meadows and Walter Cronkite. Sidney waved. She went to say hello to Walter, whom she had adored ever since she met him while doing an article on workaholics several years before. She had asked him how he managed to stay away from the office for two months every summer. He laughed, and she never got an answer. She liked him because he wasn't self-important and didn't know how to be rude. The summer before he and Betsy had come to dinner and brought a reporter who was doing a story on him for another magazine. The reporter was supposed to be quietly following him around to get the flavor of his life style. But he never stopped talking. Throughout the meal, every time Walter or anyone else opened his mouth, the reporter interrupted. He told about the time he went to China with Nixon (Walter had been there too), the time he was in Europe during the war (Walter had been a correspondent there, too), and all about this great little restaurant in Marrakech they had to get to someday. Barrett sat there clenching and unclenching his fists and making rude remarks whenever possible, but Walter was not so easily annoyed. "Some of your friends say you should run for President, Walter. What do you say about that?" the reporter asked at one point when they were attempting to talk politics. "You'd get at least two votes. Yours and"—he turned to Betsy—"you'd vote for him, wouldn't you, Betsy?"

"Oh, I don't know. It depends on who was on the other side," Betsy said. Everyone else laughed but it didn't shut him up for a minute.

Kisses all around and small talk while they waited almost an hour for the lobsters. A small speech from the humorist in the group and finally they all sat down at plywood tables set with checkered tablecloths and plastic utensils. Sidney sat at the table with the two novelists, a public relations lady and the client with whom she was spending the weekend, whose name Sidney never got, Henry Meadows, and another man who didn't say a word throughout the entire meal.

The novelists were having an argument about going to China. The lady novelist had gone with a group organized for and by writers. She was talking about how marvelous it had been. How stunning and fabulous. She was writing a novel about it, she said.

"I could have gone," the male novelist said. "I was invited."

"Of course you were. How could a writer of your stature not be invited?"

"I was invited, but I couldn't go."

"Oh, were you teaching?"

"No, I just wouldn't be with a group like that—full of hacks. I couldn't have my name on a list like that."

"It's good lobster, isn't it?" Hank said into Sidney's ear.

"What are you talking about, 'hacks'? Well, I suppose Johnny isn't the most intellectual writer. But he's a wonderful guy," she said.

"That crap he writes. It makes me sick the money he's minting. Not that I'm jealous," he said, "I could have gone."

"You should have. Do you know him? He's wonderful. He doesn't pretend to be a genius. I'm writing a book about it, did I tell you?"

"I couldn't compromise my principles. Just think of what everyone would think, seeing my name on a list like that. No, I couldn't have done it."

"Sidney, why are you avoiding me?" Hank said, leaning close to her. "You didn't even say hello to me tonight. Did I do something?"

"No, of course you didn't. I've been writing a book, did I tell you? I always get absorbed when I write. Do you want me to do that for you?"

Hank relinquished the claw to the cracker Sidney held out.

"Sidney, you look very nice tonight. Did I tell you that? I have to go home on Sunday night. I don't know when I'll be back. You can't be busy all weekend. I want to see you before I leave."

"I told you Barrett's lawyer is here for the weekend."

"Terry is staying with you? In your house?"

"Yes, why?"

"In your house? I can't believe it. Sidney, is he—"

"Of course he isn't. Here." Sidney handed him the freed lobster meat. *I'm getting pretty good at this, she thought. Every time she looked at Hank she wanted to take her clothes off. He was so sweet, so appreciative—just take her clothes off and come out into the ring like a bullfighter, to great roars and applause, and then go back to her dressing room before the fight started.*

"I really like you," she said. She leaned closer to him and kissed him on the cheek. Under the table he grabbed for her thigh.

As she looked up, she caught Terry watching her from another table. She waved with one finger, but he turned his face to the redhead sitting next to him without acknowledging it.

"Do you want to have a drink before going to bed?" Sidney asked when Terry opened the front door with his own key and let them in. He had been very quiet on the way home.

"I'm tired," he said, "I started early this morning."

"Did you hate that very much, you look depressed. Come and have a drink, and talk to me for a minute. What do you want?"

"Ah, scotch, I guess. A small one." Terry sat down on the couch and put his head back. He *was* a little depressed. He was depressed about Morvan's not being able to write, and about Sidney. What was she doing getting dressed up and going to parties like that when all previous behavioral data on her indicated that she should be falling apart. She had certainly never willingly gone to a party before.

Sidney handed him his scotch and sat down next to him. Both

of them put their feet up on the coffee table though it was against Barrett's rule.

"Did I tell you I was glad to see you?"

"Yes, you did say something like that at the airport."

"What did you do today, you look so grim."

"Do I? I guess I'm just tired. I went to see Morvan, and that's always kind of depressing. He gave me a short story or something, all he's done in years. I've never seen him so defeated. He looked old."

"I guess you wanted to stay the weekend and get the first couple of chapters started."

Terry smiled for the first time since he arrived. "How did you know?"

"You're not all that difficult to read. You get this unfinished business look on your face. The last time you were here, you had that look about me. Got to tidy Sidney up."

"That's not true. I don't think of you like that."

"Well, you do want to tidy me up," Sidney said.

"We've been friends for a long time. I don't like to see you unhappy."

"I'm not unhappy. Barrett always told me I'd be miserable alone. But I'm not."

"Barrett is."

"But you're not. You're alone and you're not unhappy. Why do I have to have someone hanging over me all the time telling me what to do? I know what to do. Marriage is a repressive institution, you know that."

"I don't think it has to be," Terry said somewhat cautiously.

"Well, you're not a very good advertisement for it." Sidney stretched and took her jacket off. "You know what I discovered?"

"What? Is it something I want to know?" Terry frowned.

"I discovered that I don't need Barrett. If you came here on his behalf, you can go back and tell him that."

"I didn't come on his behalf. I came to cheer you up because you're my friend."

"Oh, Terry." Sidney sat closer to him on the sofa, put her head on his shoulder, and took one of his hands. "That's what I like about you. You're completely untouched by the sexual revolution. All everybody else can think of is getting it in."

"Sidney, don't say that."

"No, I mean it, Terry. You wouldn't believe how crude men can be. There isn't any kissing any more, or anything. It's just like business, you know. Or washing your hands. I like your hands, Terry. They aren't too soft. I didn't realize how bad this scar is. My God. It looks like you cut your hand in half."

"I had a fight with a scythe. The scythe won." Terry was looking at the ceiling, trying to count the number of boards in the ceiling. Sidney must have washed her hair that afternoon. Maybe that was why she didn't answer the phone. Her leg was pressed against his leg from thigh to ankle and it was distracting. He didn't put his arm around her but left it hanging limply between them, bent forward because she was examining his hand.

"You remember the time I got drunk at my birthday party and you had to hold my head."

"How could I forget?"

"I still don't believe you did that. Nobody ever held my head. How many bathroom floors have you picked me up off of?"

"Only one."

"Yes, but there was that time. . . ."

"That doesn't count. I didn't have to pick you up that time."

"You must have thought I was very neurotic."

"Noooo, I didn't think that."

"Terry, why can't more people be friends like we are? Really good friends without anything spoiling it. You know, Terry, other men don't know about friendship the way you do. Maybe it's the sexual revolution that's ruined everything, made everybody forget about love. There isn't even any pretense any more. I didn't realize it before, how mechanical everything's become, Terry."

"Mmm."

"Terry, are you in a coma?" Sidney demanded.

"Uh-uh. I'm listening to you. You didn't realize it before, how mechanical everything's become . . ." Should he tell her he didn't want to know. That Henry Meadows, the way he kissed her good-bye. God, she was squeezing his fingers one by one. Terry crossed his legs first one way and then the other. Did she do it with Meadows? With Garth? God, he'd never realized how appealing she was.

"Terry."

"What?"

"Are you all right?"

"Of course I'm all right. Why do you ask?"

"You're so rigid all of a sudden. Am I upsetting you?"

Terry crossed his legs the other way. "No, I"—he swallowed—"I guess I just keep thinking of Barrett."

Sidney sat up. "I was just holding your hand. The most rigid hand I ever held. I wasn't going to do anything else. My God. Does friendship stop at kissing hello? As a matter of fact, you didn't even kiss me hello."

"The last time I tried—"

"Never mind. I understand what kind of friend you are."

"What kind?" Terry was alarmed. "I didn't mean—"

"Yes, you did."

"Sidney, I'm sorry." What could he say? He was guilty.

"I am too. I guess it doesn't work either way, does it?" Sidney got up and adjusted the creases in her trousers. "Don't worry, I'm not upset."

"Ah." What did that mean? "Sidney," Terry said. She was leaving and he was still sitting there. But he didn't want to go after her, unless he was sure that was what she wanted. And it didn't seem to be what she wanted, or did it. God, what was all that about friendship supposed to mean if not that she wanted a safe shoulder.

"Good night, Terry."

"Good night, Sidney."

Terry picked up the glass of scotch he hadn't touched before. It felt as if his heart was beating in his neck and his stomach at the same time. He tried to visualize it, the way his heart would look in a biology book, a sack like a bellows with lots of tubes attached, going in and out. He closed his eyes to see it better and remembered instead how it felt when Sidney held his hand and then squeezed his fingers one by one. There, it happened again, the sudden tightness in his chest. Funny way, wasn't it, for a body to react to pain. He opened his eyes and held the glass up to the light. There was a small pattern cut into it in several places and if he held it up to the light and twisted it first to the left a little, and then to the right a little, it looked like diamonds.

CHAPTER 26

Since she awoke, Sidney had been trying to think of a way to apologize to Terry for getting angry at him, but he had a way of acting more normal than normal sometimes. He just looked so healthy and unconcerned—and, well, empty. He could chomp down three eggs and a half a pound of bacon no matter what. By nine o'clock when she got up he had already been out to get the paper, had already made the coffee and was squeezing oranges for juice. He said good morning just the way he said good night.

Sidney didn't know what was worse, Barrett who didn't like to be touched because he couldn't stand having good feelings, Henry who couldn't be touched because it made him an animal, or Terry who didn't like to be touched by a girl. Poor Terry.

Not poor Terry, poor her. He gave her the creeps, padding around barefoot in her kitchen with the dishes as though he were a female roommate. Worse than a girl. A girl you could always hug from time to time. Sidney put on her old bathing suit and her beach robe, and her straw hat, and went outside to the beach with a book. She knew she was being unreasonable, for Terry's preferences certainly weren't his fault and he had tried not to offend her. But he had offended her; that was the truth. Sidney knew more than one girl who had a way of falling in love with homosexuals over and over. Such exquisite pain it was for them. Week after week they would go out, have these romantic evenings together—give each other presents, for homosexuals can be as attentive (even more attentive often) as anybody else—and nothing would happen. Each time nothing happened, the girl would make excuses. Nothing, nothing would convince her that nothing would ever happen. Sometimes the affliction was so serious that eventually what the girl hoped was that he would do it for her just once. So she could say he was bisexual, which would make it all right. It would be strange how a woman could love like that, if it weren't that homosexuals were so attractive, so much nicer than men.

It was too hot to stay out there for long without falling asleep. Sidney closed her eyes, thinking about how clean homosexuals always were. You never saw a homosexual picking his nose.

When she opened her eyes sometime later, Terry was lying on his back in the sand a few feet away from her. He had his bathing suit on and was sleeping. She had thought she was alone and was surprised to wake up and find him there. For a long time she watched him from under her hat, waited for his mouth to fall open and the snores to come out. His lips were parted, but he wasn't, apparently, a heavy breather.

Terry was a large handsome man of the type that Sidney most despised. Unlike Barrett, who was skinny and had a chest that was narrow and flat, Terry was well developed and covered with curly hair that was now lighter than his skin. His waist was a good deal smaller than his chest (or else he would have been heavy), and his legs were straight and padded in such a way that the cords showed whenever he moved. His was the sort of body that was used as a model in anatomical drawings. It was also the sort of body a heterosexual would hesitate to take to a steam bath. Sidney examined him as though he were dead. She was looking for the place where the alcohol had lodged. Probably in his brain, the only place where it wouldn't show. She imagined having him carted away by the Vineyard garbage service. She hunched inside her terry cloth robe, clutching her knees and burying her feet in the sand with her toes.

He'd have to go home this afternoon. That was all. She'd tell him something. Christ, where did he get that thing he was wearing? It was practically a bikini. His hipbones showed, and his belly button. He didn't have much of anything down there, did he. Maybe it was the sort of thing that shrank with disuse. As Sidney looked she noticed that Terry had a small mole on the inside of his right thigh. She thought that was odd. He wasn't a moley person. In fact, as she looked him over, she couldn't find a single other mole anywhere. So he had a mole.

She sat with her knees up, completely covered, and with her hat on. She looked at the water, at Terry's sleeping face, at the mole on the inside of his thigh. It seemed wrong, somehow. And it seemed to change as she watched it. I really am certifiable, she thought. Yet she was sure the mole was growing. She looked away and then back. It was the same. She looked away for a longer time, tried to count sailboats, clouds, anything to keep her mind off that growing mole. She looked back at it again and, this time, she was sure that it was fatter and darker even than it had been before.

"Excuse me, Terry, but you seem to have this thing growing on your leg." Sidney couldn't wake him up like that. She would be admitting that she had been looking at him. The state of his inner thigh was certainly no business of hers. Sidney began to feel very nervous. Maybe there really was something wrong with him, and he was dying from a rapidly growing mole. With the cancer problem they were having these days, anything was possible. One couldn't really dispose of a body via the Vineyard garbage truck. She leaned over to get a closer look and gasped. It had legs. It wasn't a mole; it was a tick—the biggest, most blood-gorged tick she had ever seen.

Terry opened his eyes at the gasp. "What's the matter?"

Sidney held her mouth with one hand and pointed at his leg with the other. She couldn't speak.

He sat up and brushed at his leg while she made little horrified noises. The thing was firmly embedded in his leg. It wouldn't brush off. He began to bleed a little where it was hooked on and he had pulled at it.

"It's nothing," he told Sidney. "It's all right. It'll be gone in a minute."

She had her fist in her mouth and was whimpering as though the tick were bleeding her and not him. She had had ticks on herself and not been this disturbed. He told her not to look, and pulled at it while she begged him not to. In a second or two there was a thin trickle of blood leaking out of where the tick had been, but the tick itself was gone.

Sidney took off her robe and mopped the blood up with it.

"You're not supposed to pull," she said. "The head stays in."

She leaned over him to examine his wound. "Now you're going to die of undulating fever."

"I've had a lot of experience with ticks in my youth," Terry said. He looked down her bathing suit that fell away from her breasts as she leaned forward. "It's all right. I'm sure the head is gone."

He put his hand on her arm to pull her away, but Sidney insisted that he sit still. She probed and pinched the spot on his leg. It was red but seemed all right. It was then that Sidney realized that there was something wrong with his bathing suit too. It seemed to be swollen all of a sudden. She felt as though she had been hit with a hammer, as though she had stolen something, and if she looked up just then her eyes would meet those of the only one who knew it. So she looked away from him. She wondered if homosexuals got erections if probed in their erogenous zones by women, and if so if they felt any worse than the ones they got from men. She lay down on the sand and closed her eyes. He had to go, right after lunch.

"Sidney." Terry leaned over.

She leaped up, hitting him in the eye with her elbow.

"It's undulant fever, not undulating fever," he said.

"Yeah? Well, you got blood on my robe." She picked it up and marched toward the house with it.

Barrett used to say—and it always made Terry extremely uncomfortable—that Sidney was the perfect woman: she was never aggressive, but never said no when he wanted her. To Terry, it meant that Sidney never really wanted to; he didn't like the idea of Barrett's making her. But now he didn't like the idea that she wouldn't do it for him. What was wrong with him, anyway. Terry trudged back to the house. This wasn't the Sidney he knew at all. Maybe he'd go home. But if he went home it would reinforce this paranoid fantasy she seemed to have that men only cared about sex. If he only cared about sex, he would have—well, he wouldn't go into that.

"What do you want for lunch?" Sidney said churlishly.

"Sidney, if you talk to me in that tone one more time, you're going to rupture my eardrums."

"What the fuck do you want for lunch?"

"What's the matter with you? Do you want me to go home?"

"Yes."

"You do? Why?" Terry looked surprised. "I haven't done anything. What have I done?"

"You're making me nervous."

"I won't do anything."

"I know."

"Then why are you nervous, sweetheart?"

"Don't sweetheart me, you—I don't *know* what." Sidney had been standing on the kitchen side of the counters, now she came into the living room and collapsed on the couch. "I'm sorry, Terry. I just feel so—I don't know. I just—all those *women*. It's so much easier, you know, when you know for sure beforehand. I never know *what* to say to them."

"What are you talking about?"

"Those women, the ones who call you up."

"Oh, they don't mean anything to me, Sidney." Oh, that was it. Terry came closer.

"But they don't understand you—you make it so hard for everybody. Nobody cares any more, you could . . . You know."

"What are you talking about?" Terry sat down facing her.

"Terry."

"Well, I don't understand what you're trying to say."

"Why can't you admit it? It's not a crime any more," Sidney demanded.

"What, for pity's sake, will you tell me, are you talking about?" Terry said, getting very annoyed. He couldn't imagine what she was getting at.

"Your problem. You know, the closet."

"Oh, oh, oh, oh. *No.*" Terry got up again and turned his back on her.

"I'm sorry. I didn't mean to call it a problem . . . Terry."

Terry was on the other side of the room making a drink.

"Terry."

Terry shook his head. "You, the most repressed person on the East Coast, the only person I've ever met who admits to having *no bodily functions at all.* And you have to tell me I have a problem."

"I said I was sorry."

"Sorry. You've been thinking all this time I'm a God damned flit. For Christ *sake*, Sidney." Terry drank some scotch and put some more in his glass. "Look at you, buttoned up to the eyeballs. What are you afraid of anyway?"

"Terry, you son of a bitch."

"Well, take off that tent, and we'll see how gay I am."

"My God, *Terry*. Don't talk to me that way. I'm sorry I didn't know. But you never, you were so . . . and last night when I—I guess I made a mistake, huh?" she finished lamely. "I guess I'll go perform some bodily functions." She went past Terry (who was pacing furiously back and forth) into the bathroom to cry, to wash her face, and then cry some more so that her face had to be washed again. It was terrible to be yelled at. After a while she got out her nail scissors and started cutting up the black and red striped caftan she had put on when she came into the house. Finally she took it off and cut it and ripped at it and cried, and cried some more. God damn Barrett. Damn him. Damn him. After some time there was a tap at the door.

Sidney said, "Who is it?"

"It's me," Terry said.

"What do you want?"

"I want to come in."

"You can't come in."

He opened the door and came in. She was sitting on the toilet cutting her caftan into little pieces. There were bits of red and black Indian cotton all over the bathroom. "I never liked that thing anyway. Here." He held out some dripping ice cubes for her eyes. This was a scene they had played before. She took the ice cubes and turned away. She was sitting cross-legged on the toilet, braless and puffy-eyed. She crossed her arms over her chest. It was a habit, she couldn't help it.

"Terry."

"Come on, let's go have some lunch."

"I'm not hungry," Sidney muttered.

"Well, then. Let's take a walk. Come on, get up."

"I . . ."

"Come on, it's all right."

"Terry, I know you don't find me appealing."

"Sidney, I don't think 'appealing' is a strong enough word for the way I feel about you. Now come on, get up."

"Don't shout at me."

"I didn't raise my voice." Terry, who never got angry, never raised his voice, was now shouting with exasperation. She was impossible.

She got up. "There. I got up. See." She started to cry again.

Terry put his arm around her and led her out of the bathroom. His hand dropped to the pink satin bikini panties she wore, traveled up her side and under her arm to her bosom, which seemed to be the source of her tears. He didn't squeeze the one he could reach, or nuzzle it, just put his hand there and held it. Then he turned her around and hugged her as tight as he could the way one hugs someone who has just been rescued. Now if he could just get her into the bedroom it would be all right.

CHAPTER 27

Friday was the day scheduled for the winner of the competition to be announced. All week Barrett wondered how Garth was going to handle it. He knew that Garth simply couldn't allow anyone else to win. It was his magazine; it was going to have to be his name as well. Barrett could feel Garth's decision in his bones and it tickled him. Now that everything was beginning to fall into place at last and his days at the magazine were numbered, Barrett felt almost detached from *Inside Track*. He felt almost mellow about it, as though it were an old girl friend whose parents had moved away just in time.

Barrett did have several bad moments during the week. The first was when he finally reached Adams on Tuesday morning. Adams said he had another offer that he was considering and wanted to know what Barrett's intentions were.

"Who is it?" Barrett wanted to know.

"Well, I really like you better, Barrett. But this is beginning to look like a better deal."

"How better?" Barrett asked. Could it be Garth, or was he just bluffing.

"I've been offered more money, that is an incentive, but I don't like the guy, and that means something to me, too."

"Who is it?" If he didn't like the guy, it could be Garth.

"Well, you know. . . ."

"I don't know," said Barrett, getting annoyed.

"I didn't mean you knew. I meant, you know, it's something that's confidential, man."

"Oh," Barrett muttered. He was bluffing.

"Have you got the money?" Adams asked.

"This other offer," Barrett began. Then he stopped. There was some sort of blowing sound going on at the other end of the wire. Adams, Barrett thought, was either sniffing coke or smoking grass. The idea disturbed him. This was no way to buy or sell a business. Surely this wasn't how it was done at Lehman Brothers.

"Well, are you in or out?" Adams had stopped blowing into the phone.

"I'm certainly interested. . . . And I am exploring the financial aspects."

"Uh-huh," Adams said. "Well, I'll just go ahead and have my lawyers draw up the papers then."

"Uh. You haven't sent me the reports you promised, and my lawyer has a lot of work to do on it yet."

"Listen, let's get on this thing. I've got to get it settled by the end of the month."

Okay, Barrett had said. Okay, he would get on it right away, as soon as he got his financial picture all worked out and he'd seen his lawyer. By the beginning of the following week, say, he'd be ready to sit down and work on the papers.

Adams argued that they should draw up the papers first, but Barrett was adamant. He wasn't even sure what the papers should say, but he knew that Terry had to be there. And he wasn't going to sign a thing until he was sure he could pay.

On Wednesday he had his second bad moment when Mr. Poupont called. Betty was away from her desk and Barrett had to answer the phone himself.

"I just wanted to say hello to Sidney," Mr. Poupont said. "I haven't heard from her in so long, I just wanted to have a little chat for a minute."

"Oh, I'm sorry you missed her," Barrett said. "She's gone out of town on an assignment. . . ." He was afraid that Poupont was going to ask for her number and began to perspire. He had forgotten that Poupont had no reason for suspicion. As long as he made the check out to the right person, he was quite in the clear.

"That's too bad. Now about this, ah, sum."

"Oh yes, I know all about it," Barrett said heartily. "Are there any problems?"

"Problems? No, no, as I said, I just wanted to say hello. I'm a great fan of Sidney's, you know. Known her since she was a little girl. I haven't seen her in years."

Barrett could tell he was dying to ask a few questions, he must be about a hundred years old by now, if he knew Sidney when she was a little girl. Sidney was never a little girl. "Well, she's fine, Mr. Poupont, fine." It wasn't any of his business where the money went and Barrett wasn't going to tell.

"Well then, I'll just go ahead and issue this check. You want a cashier's check for the entire amount, is that correct?"

"Yes, thank you," Barrett said.

"It's going to take a day or two, but I'll send it Special Delivery."

After he hung up Barrett felt he should perhaps be feeling guilty for doing this without Sidney's permission. But he was full of such elation, such excitement at doing something, for once, just purely for himself, he couldn't feel guilt. He was sure in his bones that Sidney would forgive him. He was certain he would earn it back; he would even put it back in the same account, if Sidney wanted him to.

Barrett watched the hair issue come together. For the first time that he could remember he felt no pain at the many petty crises the putting together of each issue engendered. At the last minute Garth decided that no hair issue could be complete without a special report on hair in California. A lot of copies of *Inside Track* were sold in California. Hardly a week went by when there wasn't a California story. Sometimes there were several. Garth had always been unwilling to set up offices in key cities with a tiny staff and a telex machine. He didn't care if his coverage of national news was not all it could be. *Life* when it died had a national editorial staff of 170. *Inside Track* relied for the most part on free-lance writers. A really important issue with lots of national items and extra pages might have been put together by a total of thirty-five people, no more. Garth believed that only by keeping the expenses low could they continue to make money. So each week—since so many of the stories were assigned and written at the last moment—there was a panic when stories did not arrive when they were expected. For legal reasons it was always better to have a manuscript, he felt. But sometimes one of the girls had to sit at a typewriter with the phone in her ear and type while a writer in Detroit or Houston read his story.

There was going to be a great improvement in the quality of his life, Barrett felt, when he could concentrate on local matters. *New Journal* would be much easier to run. There wouldn't be people all over the place he had to keep track of and make decisions about. Nearly all of his material would come from New York, the stories would be New York-oriented. The sales and advertising would be much easier to oversee. When he ran his magazine, there was not going to be a weekly panic as there was at *IT*. And he was not going to have people all jumbled together so that no one had a moment's privacy in a ten-hour day and the decibel level was comparable to that of a blasting site. This many rats in a cage would begin to eat each other.

"You didn't use one of my ideas," Muriel said in Barrett's ear after the magazine had closed on Thursday while he was chuckling to himself far away from the problems of hair. He jumped, knocking Muriel off balance.

"Muriel, for heaven's sake."

"I'm sorry, Barrett, but you promised and you did not keep your promise."

"I most certainly did. I read your headlines and your captions" —it caused Barrett some pain to say this—"and I thought they were very good indeed. Very original. However, I'm sure you realize that Blake and Seth and Alden and Molly all have autonomy in their departments. We do not run a competition for headlines every week. Thank God. There's enough disorder around here without that."

"It isn't true. Lespedeza has done captions, and headlines."

"She has? When?" Barrett asked. He was surprised.

"Sometimes she just has them set and puts them in the pages. But I wouldn't do that without your permission."

"Quite right too, Mur. You're a rare jewel. Now don't make me angry. You know I have nothing to do with all of this. Ask Garth if you want to do more."

"Barrett, what's going on around here? I feel that things are changing, you know. It isn't the same family it used to be." Muriel sat down in Barrett's guest chair.

"Sure it is. It's just going to be a bigger family, that's all. Don't worry about it, Muriel. Just think that, with the new magazine and more copy and responsibility, you may just come into your own."

"I don't think I can work on a sex magazine," Muriel said doubtfully. "I might have to resign."

"Don't be silly. It's going to be a family magazine." Barrett found that he could talk to her almost normally. Only a month, he was thinking, maybe less, and he would never have to see her again. "Think of it like that, as a guide to happier family life."

Barrett had the list of finalists in the name-giving competition in front of him. Muriel strained to see if her name was on it. "Tomorrow, Mur. You'll have to wait for tomorrow like everyone else."

He told her that he had to get back to work now—and she bristled. "You don't talk that way to Lespedeza," she complained. "Why are you always so specially nice to her?" She didn't wait for an answer; she had to go to the ladies' room, and besides, she didn't want to get Barrett angry at her after being so nice for a change.

Barrett examined the list. He had written the finalists down in the order of his preference: *Lovelife, Love Today, Lovers' Digest, Making It,* and Garth's favorite, *Pairs.* He wondered how Garth was going to resolve the problem of awarding himself his own prize. One resolution would be for Garth not to appear in the office and then never mention the subject again. Barrett dialed Terry's number at the office, then at home. He couldn't reach him. He wanted Terry to work on *New Journal* next week. He wanted to know what Terry was doing for the weekend. Not that it mattered, though, since Lespedeza had said she wasn't doing anything special and would stay with him on Friday night.

Muffin, who still hadn't found anything useful to do, was hanging over Lespedeza's desk. She wore a peasant blouse with strings around the neck that had come undone. Her blouse yawned open

177

over an expanse of brown, braless chest. Muffin had gone all pink in the face and Lespedeza was grinning at his discomfort. Watching this, Barrett felt a familiar rage bubble up, but then Lespedeza caught his eye and winked. Somehow, in spite of the small betrayal he felt at her exposed flesh, he had a peculiar sense of victory.

CHAPTER 28

Sidney walked up and down the beach as she waited for Terry to get up. She had left him sprawled face down across her bed half covered, and once again breathing so quietly he could almost be dead. He never got up afterward, just fell asleep with his head burrowed into her shoulder. For a long time Sidney lay there trying to fall asleep too. Barrett always moved away from her right away, and now she found she couldn't relax with Terry holding her hand in his sleep. It felt heavy and hot in the places where they touched. She thought if she pulled away he would wake up, and became stiffer and stiffer with the effort of staying still.

Terry didn't wake up, though, and hours passed. At first Sidney thought of how tired he must be. She was pleased that he trusted her enough to fall asleep so easily with his arms around her in that sweet way. She washed the kitchen, the kitchen floor. She read last week's *Newsweek* and the parts of *Esquire* she hadn't already studied. Ever since leaving there Sidney couldn't read *Time*. Now she knew it would happen with *Inside Track* too. How could a person fall asleep like that in the middle of the day when there was someone waiting. Several times Sidney went into her room to see if he was up. She couldn't make the bed with him in it, she told herself. Each time she went in there she checked to see if he had changed his position, but he hadn't.

Then Sidney began to think of it as symbolic of the way her life had been going ever since she had had the misfortune to grow up. It was the same thing as the job, as Barrett, the same as everything else. No matter how nice anything seemed at first there was nothing in it really. And the longer she waited for Terry to wake up the more cynical she felt about him. She could feel the loss of him already, even before there were any substantial losses to be had. Nothing ever changes. Barrett would stay at *Inside Track* forever; her leaving ultimately would make no difference to his life. And Terry, too, would continue on for the next twenty years as he had for the last fifteen. They would go out and drink together, he and Barrett, and talk and talk and talk about the same things they always talked about. If she did anything to get their attention, they would talk about her, then dismiss her like a bad movie they had once seen. Only she would have changed.

She went to the kitchen again and began chopping up the eggs she had boiled earlier. She chopped up some olives and celery and threw in some capers. She was hungry all of a sudden, looked up at the clock, and saw that it was already two. There was no mayonnaise in the refrigerator. Sidney began to make some by hand because she was bored. She was always waiting around. It seemed as though she had been waiting all her life—for her mother, who left her places and then forgot to come back on time. In the beginning of her column, Garth had been so skeptical about her ability to do it, he wouldn't allow it to be set until he read it. Sidney waited for days every week for a moment when he could sit down, read it, and make suggestions. Sometimes he jumped up in the middle and didn't come back until the next day. And Barrett could never sit still. She was always waiting somewhere for Barrett. Here or in New York, it didn't matter. She was always waiting, if not for his very presence, then for a shift in his mood. Waiting for one of Barrett's good moods was like being in a ship long becalmed. It was the same now.

As if on cue, Terry arrived when the mayonnaise was finished. Sidney had no idea of the anxiety she felt over what he would say when he saw her again. Whatever it was, it wouldn't be the right thing. As soon as she saw him, Sidney was overcome with anger. He had put his blue jeans on but no shirt, his face had a sleepy unfocused look about it, and his hair stood up in all directions.

"Hullo" was what he said, and that somewhat hesitantly. "I'm sorry I fell asleep that way."

If he had advanced into the kitchen and put his arms around

her, she would have been disgusted. His not doing it only confirmed every unhappy-making fact she knew about men. People simply did not renew each other the way they did their pets. He hovered around the table just out of reach, where two places were set for lunch.

"Have you been waiting a long time?" Terry asked. "I'm sorry. I don't usually fall asleep like that."

"So you said. What do you usually do?"

"I mean, I'm sorry I didn't make it plainer, that I must be very tired. I didn't sleep well last night."

"It's all right. I don't care." The time she had been waiting, Sidney had sculpted radishes, made cucumber and carrot slices into flowers, added artichoke hearts and pimento and sardines. In short, she had garnished the egg salad to death.

"It's very pretty," Terry said.

"I guess it looks kind of disgusting. I'm sorry."

"Don't say you're sorry. I said I liked it. I'm going to eat it right now." Terry sat down. Then he stood up and held Sidney's chair.

But she got up again in less than a second. "Would you like a beer or white wine?"

"I'll have a beer. Thanks." He wanted to get it himself, but she looked like she'd knock him over if he moved. The other women in his life often had a way of clutching at Terry and mooning at him with what he always felt was a kind of perverse possessiveness that had little to do with him. Women who had been there for little more than an hour began cleaning up his apartment in their underwear. They examined his clothes, his possessions, his drawers. "Oh, what a beautiful shirt—from Italy (France, England)?" They were like mice. Once they had been there, they wanted to stay on.

"Here." Sidney put the beer down so hard that it sloshed over the sides of the glass.

Yes, it was clear Sidney was very different. She had been faking it. She didn't really like him at all. "Mmmm," Terry said, contemplating the egg salad.

Sidney giggled nervously. "I guess you could say I'm a *Redbook* mama *manqué*. I don't know why everybody's so eager to go out to offices, I just want to stay home and make cookies."

"I like your cookies, Sidney," Terry said seriously. He didn't know whether he was going to be able to eat that egg salad, though. He wiped up the beer.

"Every Christmas I go out and buy *McCall's* and go through the recipes for candy and cookies. Do you know that those women's magazines alone are killing off one quarter of America? One person in four is going to get diabetes and they never give a recipe without at least one cup of sugar. . . .

"I should know better, but I still believe in those stupid magazines." Sidney shook her head. She wondered how long he planned to stay. Would he stay the afternoon, the night. He really didn't think anything of it, did he. Well, if he wasn't going to, she wasn't going to either.

"So I quit, just like that," she said. "There he was banging on the door, and I said, 'Garth, you're going to have to fire me.'" She laughed. "It was easy, like falling off a mountain."

Terry was shocked. "He really did that."

Sidney paused; the old feeling of loyalty was still very strong. "He didn't mean it, though. I don't think he meant it. I think he just came all this way and he expected it, you know, and when I said no—well, he just got mad. I don't think he would have gotten mad if we had been in New York. Anyway he apologized a hundred times."

"He called me up on Thursday of last week. He wanted an assurance that you wouldn't write anything about him. He's afraid you're up here doing a book or something about him."

"What did you say?"

"What could I say? I didn't know. I also got a few calls from other magazines."

"Really, Terry. Why didn't you tell me?"

"Well, it happened on Thursday. They were really sort of fishing expeditions—wanted to know if you had quit the magazine. I said you were on vacation. They said they had heard there was some trouble brewing and if you'd like to write the story they'd like to have it. That sort of thing."

"Oh, no job offer."

"I thought you wanted to stay home and bake cookies." Terry smiled.

"I do, I just—well, an offer would have been nice."

"Sidney, you haven't even let it be known you're available."

Sidney took some egg salad finally. "I would never do an article like that."

"I'm glad," Terry said. "A book would be much better."

"Terry, I wouldn't do anything about it," Sidney said. "It wouldn't be fair. He runs a magazine. I happen to think it's a tough job. If he's autocratic and difficult, it comes with the territory. You know perfectly well that the magazines run by committee are not nearly as interesting as the ones run by one quirky personality."

Sidney took a bite. "It's good, take some. Every really successful magazine is run by one iron-willed person. Why pretend that Garth is some unusual monster? He isn't. Anyway he thinks I'm beautiful."

"I agree. But I'm surprised at your attitude. He'd certainly do anything he could to screw *you*."

"Well, I think if a few people had said no to him from time to time he wouldn't think of it as his right."

"I meant the other kind."

"I know, but I don't care. Don't you want any of this?"

"Sure I do. I'm just stunned at your reactionary point of view. I would have thought you'd be dying to tell."

"Why did Garth call you? I wonder."

"I represent you."

"Do you?"

"I always have. I don't have to, of course, if you don't want me to any more. I can see that there might be advantages—"

"Have you been making money off me, Terry?" Lawyers were such slimy creatures. Imagine, he practically lived with them. It never occurred to Sidney that Terry might be charging them for his services.

"No, as a matter of fact, you're the only one I do for nothing."

"Do me for nothing. Is that what it is?"

"Well, I love *you* Sidney, you know that." There, he had said it. Now Terry could eat his egg salad. That was what he wanted to say and he said it.

But as he said it, Sidney realized for the first time why Terry never brought his girl friends around. He didn't have girl friends. He was too busy taking care of his clients. It was a most upsetting thought, Terry's adding her to his list after years of accepting Barrett's friendship. Well, that takes care of old Sidney. . . .

Sidney didn't say anything for a long time. She had a glass of white wine in front of her and kept taking sips out of it. He was worse, he was really worse than Garth. With Terry there were no rules at all. No wonder he made those girls so desperate.

"I don't have to come all the way up here for someone I don't love, you know," Terry said defensively. "There are plenty of people I don't love right in Manhattan."

"I'm sure there are," Sidney said, sip.

"What do you mean by that?" So she really thought he was a jerk. That's what she thought all along, that he was some kind of gay jerk.

"I just agreed with you, you don't have to get defensive." Sidney raised her voice. "I agreed. I'm sure there are tons of people dying for you."

"Don't talk to me that way, Sidney," Terry said very softly.

"Don't call me Sidney," Sidney snapped.

"Why not?"

"I hate the name."

"What should I call you then? . . . I'll call you love." He smiled.

"Oh, drop dead. Do you think I'm an idiot?"

"You know something, Sidney. When two people have an affair the beginning is supposed to be pleasant. Didn't anybody ever tell you that?"

"Usually when two people have an affair they don't know each other. That's why they're nice. I have had a long time to become familiar with all your faults. I don't have to be nice. Eat your egg salad."

"I know why you're doing this. I won't get mad." He got up from the table. He felt suddenly vulnerable with Sidney shouting at his bare chest. He went to get a shirt.

"Terry." Sidney followed him.

"I understand that you have to make up for being so submissive to Barrett, but you don't have to shout at me. I don't shout."

"You're shouting now."

"Well, you're very difficult, Sidney." He had gotten to his room and was looking around for a shirt.

"Does this mean you're going home?" Sidney asked.

"Is that what you want? If that's what you want, I'll go."

"Well, what do you want? Don't you have any feelings in the matter? Don't you know what you want?" Sidney was sitting on his bed. She'd never sat down in that room before. It was not a favorite room of hers. Like her own, it had Barrett's choice of brown plaid sheets. On the dresser were the only things that made it different from one of Bloomingdale's hotel modern model rooms. There, Sidney had arranged her collection of "things found on the beach," black stones with white circles bisecting them, a whole bleached crab the size of a fingernail, some tiny orange shells they called angel nails, sea glass, a turtle shell with the legs still attached, and various ordinary shells.

"Hell, I want to go back to bed." He sat next to her and took her hand. "Does that sound terrible to you? Because that's what I really want."

"More than anyone else?"

Terry nodded.

Who could resist that, even if it was a lie.

Sidney sat on his lap on the edge of the bed. He didn't have to do anything; she was excited just looking at him, just touching the back of his neck with her fingers. She didn't even want to make love, but rather sit there for a long time as they were, with their arms around each other and their foreheads touching. She had never had a pleasant affair. She had had unpleasant affairs, one or two that she could call stirring. And Barrett, of course. But pleasant she couldn't imagine. She didn't want to be pleasant for Terry. Even ghastly was better than pleasant. Terry was certainly very practiced. He had her shirt unbuttoned before she was even aware he was working on it, and knew without any experimentation that bras don't hook in the back any more. He seemed to know a lot of things.

Knowing that he knew those things both enraged and thrilled Sidney. She had heard Terry say many times that an afternoon or an evening had been a pleasant one. For Sidney a pleasant afternoon was one in which nothing happened. Was the world so perverse these days that love-making had become nothing more than a way of passing time. Did Terry find it pleasant to hear someone sighing and groaning as though near death, to see and feel all the flaws of someone once known as dignified and intact. Did everybody just forget it and go home. She meant to ask him. She meant to ask him about Barrett, too. Barrett had a schedule for venting his sperm. Sometimes she wondered what he was doing about that. Terry's kisses were the kind that interrupted thoughts. They started unremarkably enough but then went on and on. They seemed to have a life of their own that forbade any other reality. Sidney had a lot of things she wanted to say, but in the middle of a very early kiss she forgot them all.

CHAPTER 29

It wasn't until they had gotten to the airport on Sunday afternoon that Terry raised any of the important questions. They were sitting in the car in Sidney's favorite no-parking place, just opposite to where the plane would park when it came in. Even though the other passengers were already checking in and going through the metal detector, Sidney and Terry were not eager to get out of the car.

"What are you going to do, Sidney?" Terry asked after they had been sitting in silence for some time.

"I'm going to throw out all the furniture and make the whole place look like a boudoir. I've always wanted a boudoir with flowered wallpaper and embroidery on the sheets."

"I mean it. I want to talk about it before I go."

"I'm going to have my IUD taken out and have an illegitimate baby. Would you like to be the father?"

"Sidney, please."

"What's your favorite color, flowerwise, yellow, blue, or orange?"

"You don't want to talk about it." After two days of quite terrible ups and downs, Terry still wasn't sure if the weekend was a success or not.

"How did you guess? Terry, I'm thirty-four years old. I don't need anyone to tell me what to do, especially not you."

"I don't want to tell you what to do. I just have an interest, that's all. I want to know. Besides, you have a lot of things to do in the city, and it's not healthy to be here all isolated and alone."

"There. You just told me what to do."

"I didn't tell you, I gave you an opinion."

"I don't want to leave here. I'm not leaving here, and there's no place else to go anyway."

"I wasn't suggesting that you go back to Barrett, if that's what you think."

"If you won't be the father, I'll get someone else to do it. It would just be a temporary thing; you wouldn't have to hang around or anything."

"Please, Sidney, don't even joke about that. Promise me you won't do anything like that." Terry was really alarmed at this. When they got started on this they were genuinely crazy.

"Oh, Terry, you live your life through a rubber just like Barrett."

"Oh, God."

"It's my body. If I want to make something out of it, it should be my choice, and I want to. I could go and live with Garth. He made an offer. So did someone else who shall remain nameless."

"I know who that nameless person is. Christ, you're not sleeping with him, are you?"

"I suppose I could go back to the city and get my own apartment. A studio maybe. Would that be healthy?"

"Sidney, you're mad at me because I have to leave."

"Oh, come on. I was here before you got here. And since you wouldn't tell me who you sleep with I don't see how the identity of my other lovers could be of any interest to you."

"I didn't tell you because they're not of much interest to me—"

"Not of much interest to you—people you take clothes off of, people you lie in bed with. What kind of healthy life do you live?"

"If you want to shout, please roll up your window."

"You're very pompous."

"You have a very sharp tongue."

"It's a legacy."

"It's not any nicer in you than it is in him."

"I don't care what you think . . . I don't want to be any pleasant affair. I don't want to be any affair at all. I've never had a happy affair. I've never had a happy anything. I just want to be left alone. You can get out now, there's no point in both of our waiting." Sidney toyed with the car keys. If she could have done one violent thing—like kicking him in the shins or hitting him in the face—she would have.

"I'm very upset leaving you this way," Terry said.

"You're so patronizing. You're not leaving me like anything. I'm a big girl. I'm staying, I'm not being left."

"No," Terry said grimly. "I'm being a good friend who loves you and you are being incredibly selfish and small. Barrett is trying to buy that magazine; you owe it to him to go back there and talk to him. If you're planning to get a divorce, you should tell him. You should tell him and move out properly. This limbo you're both in is ridiculous. One way or the other you'll have to make a decision. . . . Sidney, I know this is all very hard for you to think about, but sooner or later you're going to have to. And it would be so much better for everybody—"

"He's really doing it, Terry? How can he do it?" This was the first time all weekend that Terry had volunteered any information about Barrett.

"I don't know. I had a fight with him a week ago, and I haven't spoken to him since."

"About what? About me?"

"No, something silly. It doesn't seem very important now. Anyway, he went to see someone at your bank about a loan. They wanted him to put in some of his own capital. I don't think he wanted to."

"Terry, I think Barrett put all the book money in his name. I'm not certain, of course, but I do know he always bought stocks and things in his name. I think the house is in his name too. But the mortgage is in mine. That's funny, isn't it."

"You must be joking." Terry chewed on his finger. It was times like this that he wished he hadn't given up smoking, that he carried a pocket flask.

Sidney had calmed down enough by now to look at him. She was sorry she yelled. "Don't look at me as though I were an idiot.

I know it sounds terrible, but you know what kind of a fuss Barrett always made about things. He yelled at me and said that I didn't trust him, and I wished him dead so I could have all the money. He said if I didn't trust him he might as well be dead. There's not too much one can say when accused every time one asks a question of wishing someone dead. Anyway, I've decided not to fight about the money. He can have it."

"Now you really are sounding crazy. What would you live on?"

"I'll take some money from George." As soon as she said it, Sidney knew that this was what she would do.

"Who's George? I'm confused," Terry said. They didn't know any George.

"George was my father."

"Oh, Sidney . . . I didn't know your father left you anything."

"It's always been a sore point."

"How much is it?"

"Well, it isn't enough to retire to the Ritz in Paris for the duration. But—I don't know, what's the interest on $250,000? I think that's about how much it is."

"Jesus."

"Now I suppose you'll charge me for your services," Sidney said. She was surprised that he didn't know. She thought Barrett told him everything.

"Jesus," Terry said again. No wonder Barrett thought he could do it.

"It's in trust, of course."

"Oh, it is. That's good." Terry found another finger and started chewing on that. "You don't know what a relief that is."

"Oh well, my father didn't trust men, you know. I guess he thought someone jerky would try to marry me for my money or something. Or I'd just let it go. It's wonderful the way fathers have such a high opinion of the female character. I would never let it go."

"Sidney. I still think you ought to come into the city and straighten everything out. I think you should take the first plane you can get on and come back. This is serious, you know. It isn't just the furniture that's involved."

"Oh, I don't care if he wants to use the book money to buy a failing magazine. Let him. In fact it'll give him something to do."

"Oh, come on, Sidney. You know you'd bail him out if he got into trouble. Anyway I'm not sure he should have all of the book money."

"Well, I want the house."

"The house isn't even paid for. The least you could do is choose something that counts."

"It makes sense to me, Terry, and I'm the one who counts. How can you sit there arguing with me over possessions anyway, it's terrible."

There was the great roar overhead. The plane came in and parked at the gate. They watched the few people lucky enough to arrive on Sunday get out.

"Sidney, it's serious. Tell me you'll come in this week."

"I'm not ready yet."

"You can stay with me. I want you to—and I never let anyone stay with me."

"That's very generous of you. But I wouldn't want you to break policy for *me*. . . . What color are your sheets?"

"Maybe they're too military for you, some are khaki and some are navy."

"Well, that settles it. I could never sleep on khaki sheets."

"If you loved me you could."

"If you loved me you'd buy some new ones."

"Would that constitute solid evidence to you?"

"Everybody's getting on, you better go."

"You didn't answer."

They watched people getting on the plane. It took about seven minutes for the plane to load and take off. Five already were gone.

"What's the right answer?" Sidney said. Maybe she could stall him long enough to miss his plane.

"You know it, but you won't say it." He reached for the door handle. They had been sitting there for a long time. His legs were stiff. He was angry. Sidney sat there hunched over the wheel like a racing driver eager to begin. She was difficult. Difficult and mean, and for some reason, probably a perverse one, the most appealing woman he knew. She was sitting there scowling and he knew that if he bent over to kiss her she'd snap at him like a mean little terrier. "Aren't you going to say good-bye, Sidney?"

"Gubye, Terry." Sidney didn't look up.

"I'm going to miss you."

"You could call," she said.

"I will call, but I'll miss you anyway."

Sidney didn't wait to see him get on the plane. She didn't want to see the plane take off, for that matter. Like Terry himself, she didn't believe in whatever principle it was that kept flying things in the air.

CHAPTER 30

Esta Peare's writing about food was like no one else's in the world. Every two weeks she had a page in the magazine and that page was so beautifully photographed, so lubricious and stimulating, that even if she did a story on something hardly anyone liked like kidney beans (with two kidney bean recipes), people would make the recipes and eat the results. People had faith in Esta Peare. She had a way with words; she made food seem better than any other thing that life had to offer. She was interested in gnocchi, veal shanks, watercress soup; and although she did sometimes give a recipe for a plain cake or a plain *pot de crème*, these delicacies never contained a single speck of sugar. She believed in small amounts of molasses, in honey, but never gave any advice on any kind of food that specifically called for sugar. It was something of a joke around the magazine because Esta, a writer whose raptures were many, had a face like a small pitted prune and a tiny underfed body. She abhorred sugar and, since she ate everything else in large quantities and still was not nourished, it seemed as though sugar must be the vital nutrient she lacked.

She sat at the very front of the editorial department at a desk that Garth had long ago reserved for free-lance writers on assignment. Esta, of course, was supposed to do her work at home. Certainly there was no reason for her to have a desk at the magazine and come in every working day for a page that required two recipes (that had to be perfected at home anyway) and five hundred stunning words she could do in her sleep. Esta also had a hot plate up front which frequently blew out all the lights. She had this so that the results of her experiments, which she brought in nearly every day, did not have to be served cold. Once when she blew the fuse on an early wintry evening she ran out for candles and checkered handkerchiefs. Along with several bottles of wine that had been sent from a wine advertiser to celebrate one thing or another, she served what was meant to be a hot mussel, shrimp, and rice dish cold. It was a sensation. The party in candlelight was described at length in her column and the recipe altered so that the dish was featured as a cold one. Nearly everyone at the magazine found Esta a pain in the neck. Aside from Barrett, she was the only one who kept files to which it was actually possible to refer. She had every article of hers meticulously planned months ahead of time. Since she only did twenty-five pieces a year, she had plenty of time to waste forcing food upon reluctant members of the staff and disrupting things in general.

Muriel, who was her best friend in part because Muriel never turned down anything that was offered, told her that Sidney had quit her job. Also that she, Esta, was the only one who could fill it. Muriel wanted Esta's job. She set about encouraging and harassing Esta, who soon decided that she wanted Sidney's. Between the two of them, they decided that Esta should approach Garth first.

On the day the competition was over, there was to be a lunch and the announcement. Esta slunk into Garth's office with her request. Garth was not guarded at that moment by either Jenny or Anne. He was alone with his feet up on the desk. He was staring at the ceiling, unsure for the moment why he had found it necessary to be sitting there at ten o'clock on a Friday morning when he could be somewhere else. On Fridays in summer he rarely came into the office, and never before noon when he did. Garth and Barrett had chosen five names from the forty offered. Everyone except Barrett had entered the contest. Barrett said he couldn't enter because he was a judge. But Garth knew he really had no idea.

The list was in front of him. He looked at it every way. Rearranged it with a different name at the top each time. *Pairs*, he knew, would never do. He liked it because it made him think of

Noah's Ark. He'd always liked Noah's Ark and tried to offer as an alternative *Two by Two*. Barrett had sneered over *Two by Two*, though. The naming of a magazine was a crucial operation. It wasn't a thing to be taken lightly. That was why Garth was sitting in his office so early on a Friday morning in summer. The problem was, he decided, that all the good names were already taken. Used up and gone. *Lovers' Journal*, yech. *Lovers' Digest*. What did those idiots think they were trying to sell, anyway. There was only one name that would do at all. Only one and Garth circled it with a pencil, then sat there staring at the ceiling.

"Garth," Esta whispered as though he were asleep. "Can I come in?" The fact that she was in already, in front of his desk firmly planted, did not correspond at all well with her tiny terrified voice.

"You're going to have to get rid of that hot plate, Est. I've been getting a lot more more complaints about it lately, and this time, I'm afraid it's going to have to go. There's just no other way."

She opened her mouth but no sound came out.

"And no, you can't have a stove, or an icebox or any other damn thing. If you want a kitchen, go home, or go to *McCall's* for Christ's sake. They'd be happy to give you a kitchen." Garth raised his name list to his face one more time. He looked at the five names. The same one still seemed the right one. When he lowered the paper, Esta was still standing there.

"What now?" Garth said, although he knew just by the way she was standing there, her toes pointed painfully inward. She wanted a raise. He frowned. Didn't she know that they were going to have to tighten their belts in this year of new trials, conserve whatever resources they had.

"Garth, I was wondering what you were going to do about 'Eye,'" Esta said. When she got going she could be quite firm, and now her face solidified like one of her famous unsugared fruit-flavored gelatines.

"What about it?" Oh, there it was, Garth's second worry of the week. They always came in twos. Here it was Friday and Sidney still had not called. It was very clear what that meant.

At first Garth was extremely upset at the possibility of Sidney's abdication. He was terribly remorseful and wanted to do something very special for her. But he had discovered after years of ex-

perimentation that the doing of special things only worked for ex-
—or present—lovers. Sidney would prove quite invulnerable to a
case of champagne or a bracelet or anything like that, so why
waste the money. It was not a subject he wanted to discuss with
Barrett either. For Barrett, too, seemed grief-stricken and ashamed
(at least that was how Garth explained Barrett's increasingly peculiar behavior). But Garth didn't think Barrett could help anyway since Barrett undoubtedly was the cause of it all. As the days
passed and Sidney did not return, the patterns of Garth's thoughts
on the subject subtly shifted. By Friday he was fairly certain that
revenge was the appropriate action to take.

"Well," Esta was saying. "I know that my area of expertise here
has always been food, but I did do a radio spot once on person-
alities in the news . . . it was pretty good. And I feel I could
bring fresh insight—"

"What?" Garth put his list down and sat up for the first time.

"Well, I thought I could start out with a few food people so no
one would be really startled. And I could do a couple of hard
news stories and then move right into the job. Garth, you just
couldn't have a better person to do it than me. I'm right here already, and you wouldn't have to pay me a nickel more for a long
time." Esta's fists were clenched at her sides with the effort of facing him. She spoke very rapidly to a point in the middle of
Garth's forehead.

"Esta," Garth said pleasantly, "I'm so pleased you came to see
me about this. I wanted to tell you how happy I've been lately
with your page. I thought it was getting kind of drab there for a
while. And uninspired. I was becoming alarmed at the number of
stories on bones and beans, if you know what I mean. And it
looked like you were just slowing down altogether. That's why I'm
so pleased at the way you've perked up recently. Were you kind of
depressed or something?"

Esta opened her mouth to answer, but Garth raised his hand.
"Never mind. You don't have to say a thing if you don't want to.
Let's just forget it happened." Garth looked down at his list once
more, but Esta didn't go.

"What about 'Eye'?" she said.

"Oh, I wanted to tell you about that," Garth said grimly. In
two minutes, if that female didn't get out of his office he was

going to throw her out on that wizened little fanny of hers so hard she wouldn't be able to sit for a month.

He put on a funereal voice. Actually he was kind of glad it was Esta. Esta had total recall and broadcast range that was better than that of WINS. "As you know, I haven't been at all satisfied with the column for some time," he said.

"Really? I didn't know that." Esta sat down.

"Well, Sidney's a good writer, of course. But she isn't a great writer. And lately she's had these ideas of things she wanted to write that were, well—you know, not at all appropriate for us. This is strictly between us, you understand, Esta. I wouldn't want any of this to get around."

"You can rely on me, Garth. I won't tell anyone."

"And that along with her delusions of grandeur. I guess it was that book that really unhinged her. She wanted a lot more money than this poor little operation had to give. You know, this is a tough time for us. We have to tighten our belts, cut the fat out. . . ."

"I agree with you about the fat," Esta said.

"The personality problems of course were the final difficulty. It hurt me, but we couldn't go on that way."

"Oh, Garth, I'm so sorry."

"Well, let's not talk about it any more."

"What about Barrett?"

"Well, Barrett is very noble. He understands. Now, Esta, let's get back to our own duties, shall we."

"But what about 'Eye'?" she wailed for the third time.

"I'm going to be 'Eye.'" Garth had to put a stop to this once and for all. "I am going to be the column. There won't be any by-line. If you or anyone else on the staff has a contribution you'd like to make, you're more than welcome to submit it."

Garth rubbed his hands back and forth. That, of course, was the only solution. There would be no identifiable Eye. That was how the column began and that was how it would be from now on. Garth called Anne into his office to check on the food for the lunch. She said it was being delivered now.

An hour later all the food was prettily arranged on the art department table—a cold Italianate feast complete with squid salad and gallon jugs of chianti. Garth called everyone together and they stood some forty deep (half were sitting or squatting on desks because there was not enough room for everyone to get in any other way). They nudged each other in anticipation and eyed the food.

Garth made a short speech about the importance of a name and the general high quality of the offerings. He made a few jokes about the rate of literacy in the advertising and subscription departments, but how otherwise he was well pleased with the efforts of his staff. There was much laughter and several boos and cheers because they all knew the names were rotten and Garth knew it too. These were the times that made everyone think that *Inside Track* was the very center of the universe. Never mind that the room was hot, too crowded, and covered with a film of grease that had not been tackled in a dozen years. This place was home, and these people jammed together, who would in less than five minutes fight for first crack at the food, were family.

"And now," Garth said from the door of his office where he alone had some uncluttered air space of his own, "I would like our beloved executive editor and my co-judge, Mr. Barrett Martin, to announce our winner."

There were some cheers and some boos (the boos came mostly from those in the editorial department).

"Barrett, Barrett, where the hell are you?"

Everyone laughed.

Barrett, who had been at the very back of the crowd near the door in fact, in case fire was declared and he had to get out fast, was stunned. He, announce the winner. Garth hadn't even bothered to tell him who the winner was. He struggled through the crowd to Garth's office. Why him, he wondered. Why wouldn't Garth make the announcement himself. Unless, of course, Garth himself was the winner.

He made it to the front of the crowd, faced it, and as if it had been planned that way, he held up his hand. "May I have the envelope, please."

Everyone laughed, but Anne placed an *Inside Track* letterhead envelope into his hand. He opened it very slowly, savoring his audience's excitement.

"The winner is—" He looked around in amusement. What would they do when they heard . . .

Barrett looked down at the slip of paper in his hand. He opened it and read out the name Garth picked. "*Making It.*" There was dead silence in the room while everyone thought about it. *Making It.* Well.

Barrett called out, "Alden. Alden is the winner." And everybody cheered, while hunching closer to the food. So Alden was the winner. That's what came of being a governor's son. Several people rushed on Alden to say how great it was, would he buy them a drink, and Seth punched him in the arm. But most people had already switched their focus to the food. Barrett turned to say something friendly to Garth, but he had already left for the weekend.

CHAPTER 31

Monday morning Barrett leaped out of bed at the usual time and went into the bathroom. He took a quick shower and washed his hair, after which he cursed Sidney again for taking the small hair dryer. In recent weeks, each time he passed a drugstore with them displayed in the window he had been tempted to buy another dryer. But even though he hated to rub his head with a towel—he was convinced that with every rub fistfuls of the precious protein would come out in the nubs—he did not go into the store and make the purchase. Now as he rubbed, he had the terrible feeling that the terry cloth was acting like Velcro. Barrett had very curly, one might almost call it kinky, hair. In spite of its texture, which he abhorred, Barrett was nonetheless loath to lose a single one. He rubbed his head gingerly and then put his head out the door to see if Lespedeza was still sleeping. She was.

The first time he had slapped Lespedeza on the behind to get her going (he wanted to train her to get up and get his coffee ready the way Sidney always did) she bit him on the shoulder hard enough to make him scream and deep enough to leave little red marks that now were yellow. Then she had turned over and gone back to sleep. The second time he decided a little talk with her would do the trick. He told her that if she wanted to sleep in his nice clean apartment, with its spectacular view down Third Avenue and across the East River with all the bridges included, and be taken out to dinner and everything, the least she could do was get up and make the coffee he needed to face the day. Lespedeza regarded him with icy eyes and the closest thing to genuine contempt he had experienced since growing up.

"For Christ's sake," he said, "it's not as though I'm asking you to clean the stove or change the sheets or anything. You would have some too, you know."

Lespedeza didn't care. He could tell she didn't care a fig whether he was able to face the day or not. There she was, hogging three of the four seventy-five-dollar down pillows and making no concessions at all to his upset. In fact Lespedeza wouldn't say a thing to him at all. He walked away and came back later, but she still wouldn't talk to him. Eventually he begged for forgiveness.

"It's all right, Barrett, " Lespedeza mumbled. "I forgive you."

Barrett was quite certain he hated her. On Saturday morning he had awakened with a really sick feeling in his stomach because Lespedeza was sleeping where Sidney should be. And even with her body on her side of the bed where it should be, she still managed to be in his territory. A clump of her hair, like a pale paintbrush, lay there only an inch from his mouth. He had a strong urge to get up and flee, and leave her right there. He lay there for a while and considered his escape. He knew he could go to the retreat of any one of a thousand friends, who would be more than happy to have him. It was still very early. He could get away. But even as he thought about this, he knew he was too depressed to go anywhere. He was depressed at making the deal next week, though he wasn't exactly sure why. He thought perhaps getting away from IT was almost as bad as staying. What if he didn't like it; he could never go back—and it hadn't been so bad. And what if he was being cheated. What if there wasn't a chance in the world for success.

He was also terribly upset that his mother had begun calling him again in that hysterical way she had. That was perhaps the most upsetting thing of all, getting those shrill, screaming phone calls at every hour on the half hour from two-thirty in the morning until five-thirty. The first time she had done it was when they moved into this apartment. She had wanted to move into Manhattan, wanted Barrett to get one of those sprawling apartments on Park Avenue, so big they could all live together and wouldn't have to run into each other except at dinner. Barrett had said at the time that he'd rather go blind. But actually he suffered over it a great deal. And his mother had begun calling in the middle of the night complaining at his bad treatment of her. She demanded money and got a weekly payment.

And now she was calling again. She wanted to know why he and Sidney never came to dinner any more. She wanted to know why two months had passed since she last received an invitation to come into the city. She offered to come now. She had a nose for trouble; it was her only comfort in life. Unerringly she focused on Sidney as the trouble.

"Let me talk to my daughter," she screamed at Barrett. She only had two voices. One was contained in a scream, the other in a shriek. "*She* loves me."

Barrett reminded her that Sidney was not her daughter.

"She's more a daughter to me than you're a son."

He'd asked for it, of course.

She talked about sending the Vice Squad. Somehow she seemed to feel there was a Vice Squad in a precinct somewhere just to protect neglected and unloved mothers. Barrett was afraid to be alone with the telephone. He wanted Lespedeza there to answer the phone and talk Puerto Rican to her to confuse her. Lespedeza couldn't really speak Puerto Rican, but nobody except maybe another Puerto Rican would ever guess that from her Puerto Rican dialogues.

Every day he spent with Lespedeza Barrett resolved would be his last. At first he couldn't understand why, after being so reluctant to have anything to do with him, she was now so unwilling to go. He asked her sometime during the week when she started hanging around waiting for him to leave the office at night. "Why this change of heart, Clover?"

She said, "I don't like it when people threaten me." She didn't say that since she was threatened she felt safer on his side than

Muriel's or that she now felt sure Sidney wasn't coming back. She added, "Anyway I like you," which was sort of true.

On Monday Barrett stood in the doorway of his bedroom in his silk dressing gown and debated what to do. For the two days that they had stayed in the apartment, Barrett made the morning coffee. He had even gone up the street for the croissants, something Sidney used to do while he shaved. Lespedeza had lolled in bed—wearing nothing, which both irked and excited him. He offered her a pajama top to sleep in. He had rummaged through Sidney's collection of nightwear and chosen a rather old lime-green satin nightgown which he offered her. She turned her nose up at it and said she couldn't live all trussed up like that. He thought perhaps she was asking for a new one.

For two days Barrett had deposited the breakfast tray on the bed and Lespedeza had roused herself sufficiently to eat and drink whatever she found on it. But this morning was not a weekend, and Barrett felt that it was her turn to reach out the front door for the newspaper and boil the damn water for the coffee. On weekdays, it should be her responsibility. Finally he decided that he would wake her and gently make the suggestion. He advanced into the bedroom just as the phone began to ring. He grabbed for the phone. He took it around to Lespedeza's side of the bed and put the bell part against her ear.

"Okay, okay," she said. She picked up the phone and a torrent of undecipherable words and phrases that sounded very like Spanish poured forth from her babyish mouth. It was a remarkable and seemingly effortless display. She ended with, "Fuck you, okay," and hung up. This had happened several times during the last few days, and each time it happened, Barrett felt a thrill nearly equal to the thrill he experienced on Monday mornings when he saw his name in the accustomed place, second on the masthead.

So far the Vice Squad had not appeared at midnight with coshes to beat his brains in for being unkind to his mother, nor had his mother herself appeared with a shopping bag filled with her best crystal relish dishes that she thought he and Sidney should have now that she was on her way to the grave and would no longer need them—because her only son refused to talk with her when she called on the phone. Barrett had sent her a check for five hundred dollars on Friday morning before Lespedeza arrived with her knapsack. He knew that she would be afraid to get really nasty until she could deposit the check on Monday morning.

"Clover, honey, that was wonderful," Barrett said. "How about some coffee?" He leaned over to help her up.

Lespedeza looked all of eleven and three quarters. She rolled over in bed as though falling into a deep coma.

"Coffee?" she murmured. "Okay."

"Why don't you get it?" Barrett said. He restrained himself only with an effort from slapping her little bottom that was as browned as the rest of her.

Lespedeza sighed but did not answer.

"It's your turn," Barrett whined.

Still she did not respond.

Barrett stamped back to the bathroom but made no noise because of the thickness of the gunmetal-gray carpet. Barrett thought it very chic to have mahogany Swedish modern coupled with the gunmetal lacquered walls and a very thick carpet. It was a rather military-looking room and small because a large part of it had been made into closets and floor-to-ceiling mahogany doors. He decided that he would have to punish Lespedeza by not making any coffee himself. She would have to go to the office unfed and that would teach her a lesson.

He slapped more water on his face, and soaped up for a second time. He washed the soap off, and as he reached for a towel he caught sight of the clock. It had a large second hand and every day Barrett timed each part of his bathroom routine. He was proud of being able to shave in three and a half minutes. He was much later than usual. He tried to calculate where the time had gone this morning to make him so late. And as he tried to figure out where his minutes had gone, he was overtaken with the same uneasy feelings that had been slowly accelerating ever since Sidney left. There was something wrong. Several things in fact were extremely wrong. For the last week since Fire Island the most pressing one—aside from Muffin, whom he hated on principle, and *New Journal* and Sidney—was the absence of Terry.

Barrett dried his face, sat on the toilet, and dialed Terry's number on the wall phone he had installed right next to the toilet paper dispenser. He waited for eight rings and then finally gave up. Terry clearly had already left for the day. He certainly did not have guile enough to let a phone ring when he was physically able to answer it. Barrett remained on the toilet and played with the fringes of his dressing gown. He knew he was wasting more time, but now that twenty minutes were already lost, he thought that a few more really wouldn't matter. He considered trying to think while shaving, but thinking while shaving was something he had never been able to do very well. The toilet, however, was a very good place for thinking—even better when the top with its disguising furry little pad was down.

From time to time over the last eighteen years, their friendship had cooled enough to allow a week or so to pass without Barrett and Terry communicating. In the early years it was not unusual for a month or so to pass without their having a lunch or dinner together. But that was when Terry tried living in the Village and Barrett had a tiny apartment on the upper West Side. For the last five years when they had lived in the same building, they had seen each other almost daily. They shared friends. Barrett sent Terry a lot of business. If one went out of town the other knew about it. If one had a week filled with business lunches from which the other was excluded, they made up for it by drinking together, playing pool in Terry's apartment, and then going upstairs for dinner with Sidney.

Barrett was used to discussing everything with Terry. There wasn't a thing that happened at *IT* that Terry didn't know about. That was what made him so good in negotiating contracts for writers with Garth and other publishers. He knew how they thought. Barrett would have told Terry all about Muffin, had Terry been available. And Terry would have told him what it meant since Garth wouldn't. Barrett simply didn't know if Garth was easing him out. Even before he told him he had decided to go. Barrett didn't like the idea of Garth doing that. After all his years of loyal service, he shouldn't be allowed to go so easily, Barrett thought. Garth shouldn't threaten him, hire someone new, and plan to make his life miserable forever after. Rather, he should reason with him, offer him a better position in specific terms.

He was nervous about going to the office and looking at the

masthead. He had seen the page last week, okayed it, and sent it to the printer. Most of the time there weren't any changes from the week before anyway. And Garth had called him "executive editor" on Friday in front of everyone. But still, Barrett had the tiniest apprehension that when he looked for his name on the masthead today he wouldn't find it there.

Once before Garth had been unable to inform someone he was about to make a masthead change. It took him weeks to decide to make the change and then, as he said, he "forgot" to tell one of the persons involved. The person lowered, who happened to be a woman editor, had her new position pointed out to her by her assistant, a girl who read the masthead religiously every week in the hope that she would be promoted without being told. This senior of senior editors quit as soon as the art director and a few other people could locate some ammonia with which to revive her. As the next part of the story went, Garth followed her home and made a few successful mercy passes at her. Anyway they knew he followed her home. After some time had passed they both came back to the office grinning happily and the masthead remained the way Garth had changed it. Barrett figured that she had been lowered on the masthead because she was a woman. Garth always felt sure he could mollify any woman. He didn't, however, have the same compulsion about appeasing men. If Muffin got Barrett's place, one thing was certain. Garth wouldn't follow him home and make a mercy pass.

And he could have talked with Terry about Lespedeza, too. Barrett tied the fringes of his belt into neat little knots and then untied them. He should have said something to Terry about Lespedeza on the way back from Fire Island. Why hadn't he, he wondered. It would have been so easy. But Terry had seemed very quiet then, almost hostile. Barrett had thought it was simple paranoia his interpreting Terry that way, but even so he couldn't say anything. Terry drove and Barrett kept sneaking looks at him. Lespedeza was sleeping in the back seat. He could have said something then. But Terry didn't seem to want to talk. He had a feeling that Terry had been interested in Lespedeza himself and that was the reason he was avoiding him. It made Barrett angry as he thought about it. Christ, if Terry had wanted Lespedeza why didn't he do something about it years ago. He certainly didn't have the right to threaten their friendship over stupid rivalry. Terry had to see that, didn't he. Barrett untied the last row of knots with some decision. He would go over to Terry's office right now and have it out with him, make him see how silly he was being. And then he would ask him to negotiate with Adams for *New Journal*.

Barrett shaved in four minutes and fifty-five seconds, but was not upset. It was not a good thing to hurry too much with a razor when one was in a state of mental torment. As he rinsed his face for the last time, he cursed all ethnic minorities and Lespedeza for not making him his coffee. He went into the bedroom to choose a suit and found her all dressed with her knapsack hanging over her arm, combing her baby hair with her free hand.

"Hi," she said.

She finished combing her hair while Barrett stood watching, trying to formulate the words for "How about some coffee since I'm so miserable and late and all my needs are ignored?"

"Not dressed yet?" she said sweetly. Then, "I'm off, see ya."

She didn't hesitate for a second, but trotted off through the bedroom door and then out the front door the same way she had the first time: as though it had all been something of a bore, not to be repeated or mentioned. She left without a second look.

In spite of his certainty that it had to end soon, he was afraid her leaving that way meant she had decided now was the time, and she would never come back.

Barrett balled up his silk dressing gown and threw it on the floor. It wasn't her leaving that made him angry, he told himself. He wouldn't have left her in the apartment alone, or walked into the magazine with her anyway. It was that she didn't even bother to make the bed, that she didn't wash her face or anything. Unless she had used the powder room. Barrett put on a shirt and a pair of shorts, and while he was buttoning up, he walked out into the powder room. He felt the sink to see if it was wet. It was, and Lespedeza had managed to soak through all four of the guest hand towels.

CHAPTER 32

Barrett finished dressing and then dialed Terry's number at the office. Marion, Terry's secretary, put him through right away without even ringing Terry first.

"How are you, Barrett? I haven't seen you in ages," Terry said eagerly. He had meant to call the night before when he got home from the Vineyard. He had even considered ringing Barrett's bell when he came up in the elevator. He had never felt guilty before about sleeping with anyone's ex. But even though he had rehearsed what he would say—certainly not anything personal about Sidney—he found that he was unable to face Barrett. He only wanted to talk about business, to save Barrett from disaster, he thought. But there was more to it than that. He and Barrett had always been so careful about not competing in anything. The only thing that they had competed in was skipping stones on the flat water of the Sound, and Barrett always won. Even when they played Scrabble it wasn't competing. Sidney knew more about words than either of them.

"Well, you haven't been around," Barrett complained.

"I've been busy," Terry said. "One can't afford to neglect the paying customers for too long, you know. What's happening?"

"I don't know. A lot of things. Have you had breakfast? I'm still at home . . . I thought we might meet somewhere."

"Well, I had planned to tackle a few things here. That's why I came in so early. How about lunch? I have a meeting at eleven and then one at three. How about twelve-thirty somewhere?"

"Terry, I'd like to talk to you now."

Terry hesitated for a minute. Barrett was always very melodramatic about everything, but still it made him nervous. Suppose someone from the clambake had called him. If he had been anything other than a lawyer he might have confessed right them. Or attacked first. But he knew better than to put something in Barrett's mind that might not be there yet. When he went to see Sidney on the Vineyard, he hadn't exactly known what would happen. He wasn't sure then that Barrett and Sidney wouldn't get back together again eventually. But when he got there he knew. Sidney wasn't the same as when she left.

That was the problem. That was where Terry was guilty. He didn't help guide Sidney back home the way he should have. He didn't show her how facing Barrett with her complaints would have been the better course for both her and Barrett. He had certainly done that kind of thing for other people often enough. Usually it worked in the short run. Sometimes it worked in the long run and sometimes it didn't. Terry agreed to meet Barrett in the coffee shop downstairs in twenty minutes. The only time he had ever been confronted by a suspicious husband, the couple had been divorced for two years. Even then Terry had denied it. He put on his jacket, which had been hanging over the back of his chair, but didn't get up.

For years Terry had been aware of feeling a greater attraction for other people's wives than the single women who wanted to become his. He knew all the psychological reasons for this phenomenon. He knew why perfectly acceptable nice women made him want to scream—but in fact turned him into a zombie for whom no amount of tears or entreaties or home-cooked meals could make the slightest difference. You can't spend very much time in shrink city without getting your neuroses down pretty well even without a single session. He also knew that if the married women he admired so much suddenly became available, he would almost as suddenly find a good many things wrong with them he hadn't noticed before. Hell, he didn't want to be anybody's second husband. This instant dissatisfaction he felt with any woman who tried to get close to him disturbed Terry not so much because he wanted to be married, though he did sometimes, but rather because he didn't want to be neurotic. He wanted to think of his singularity as a matter of personal preference and not what it was. When he examined all the other cases of arrested development around him, however, his did not seem the worst kind one could have. He had decided long before that if he had to be hung up about something it was far better that it not involve the suffering of someone else.

Sidney was one of the two women who had mattered to him without provoking any feeling on his part that immediate plans for defense were necessary. The other one was a female partner in his firm who was a not well preserved woman of fifty-five with four grown children. He always thought that if she had been young and beautiful she would have been the one. That he and Sidney had never been completely comfortable with each other, Terry blamed on Sidney's extreme shyness with men and fear of all things sexual. This was also the reason he thought he would never want to go to bed with her. To him, it would be like tackling someone who had been a nun since birth. Immoral as well as unsatisfying.

And, of course, if it had been anyone else, Terry would have said straight out, "Look, your husband is fooling around, you'd better decide one way or the other how you want to handle it." Discussing how it would be handled usually gave Terry some peculiar pleasure (because once again neither one of the pained parties was he). He didn't want to tell Sidney right away because he felt such information might make Sidney feel inadequate as a woman.

Ha-ha.

Then when she started teasing him—Terry looked at his watch. He should be leaving. But he was excited just thinking about Sidney teasing him. He wanted to finish the thought. But the thought didn't end pleasantly; it ended with how she must have been laughing her head off at him all these years. He didn't tell her then because he thought she might go back to Barrett. That was the other thing wives could do to make a single man feel safe.

He was guilty. He didn't want them to get back together again. He hadn't said one thing to make Sidney even consider it might be the right thing to do. Terry looked at his watch. He was late. He roused himself and went downstairs to the coffee shop.

Barrett was sitting alone in the deserted restaurant. He had an empty coffee cup in front of him.

"I'm sorry, Barrett," Terry said. "I guess I got involved." He sat down, flipped open the menu (the disloyal friend), and then ordered his second breakfast of the day, the same thing he had eaten the first time. "Aren't you eating?"

206

"Oh hell, I have so many things on my mind I may never eat again," Barrett said.

"Tell me." Terry burned his tongue on the coffee. It wasn't going to be a good day for him, he could tell.

"Well, first. About this Lespedeza thing," Barrett said. "Look, you can have her."

"What?"

"I know that's what's been bothering you, Terry. Do you think you can hide something like that from me, your closest friend? Hell, I know that's why you avoided me all last week."

"I haven't been avoiding you," Terry protested.

"Well, you have, and you don't have to be ashamed in front of me. I've been thinking about it, and I want you to have her."

"Barrett, a woman isn't a possession that you can pass back and forth. Don't be ridiculous."

"She's very easygoing, Terry. I'm sure that after a few—"

"For Christ's sake. What makes you think I even want her?"

"Don't get all exercised. I can tell by the way you're acting. You can't fool me about something like this."

Terry's breakfast came, and Barrett ordered another cup of coffee. He took a piece of Terry's toast.

"All right, why are you so excited if you're not jealous of me?"

"Listen, I have one or two things of my own on my mind. Not every thought I have relates to you, you know."

"Jesus."

"I don't want the girl. You keep her. I don't give a damn, believe me."

"I don't want her either," Barrett said.

Terry shrugged. "That's not my problem, thank God."

"Well, I really *don't* want her. I mean I don't. If you asked her out right now, I wouldn't mind a bit."

"That warms my heart, Barrett. But I haven't ever asked her out before, and I'm not going to now just to get you out of a jam."

"I'm not in a jam. I was just being generous."

"Thanks. I appreciate it. It doesn't please me, but thanks anyway. Now let's forget it, okay?"

Barrett slid one of Terry's poached eggs onto his butter plate and asked the waiter for a fork.

"You could have ordered your own, you know," Terry said.

"Are you kidding? I wouldn't order eggs. Don't you know eggs are bad for you? I'm just eating this one for your own good."

Terry pushed over his plate with disgust. "Here, have the whole thing. I'm not hungry anyway."

"Oh, come on, Terry." Barrett pushed the plate back.

Terry left it where it was halfway between them. He wanted to say something about Sidney, and settling things, but Barrett seemed to be in one of his obsessive moods. He was now rearranging all the flatware on the table to his side because now he was the only one eating. Terry looked at the clock. The place was empty and it gave him a sort of eerie, out-of-work feeling. They had been sitting there for twenty minutes.

"Terry." Barrett finished both of the poached eggs and all of the toast, and then pushed the two plates aside.

"Yes, Barrett."

"I need your help," Barrett said woefully.

"Okay, you know I'll do whatever I can."

"Well, I know that. But I really need your help and I want you to promise me you'll do what I ask before I tell you what it is."

Terry frowned. This was the kind of thing about Barrett that always seemed so amusing when things were going well. It was the way a schoolboy handled his problems. Everything required a promise of some sort, either to tell or not to tell or do something without knowing what it was. Everything was always in the strictest of confidence and, whatever it was, Barrett never told the whole story.

"Well, you don't trust me."

"I haven't said anything yet," Terry snapped. He didn't feel quite so tolerant about Barrett any more.

"Well then, what do you say?"

"No."

"Terry, please," Barrett whined.

"For God's sake, Barrett, you know I can't do that. What's the matter with you? Suppose you asked me to kill somebody, or steal something."

"I wouldn't *ask* you to do something like that. How about an English muffin or something? You didn't eat a thing."

"You ate it."

"Well, a cup of coffee then."

"I'm not hungry. You know perfectly well that when you ask me to promise something beforehand it's because you know it's something I won't want to do. It doesn't help a thing. Just ask. You know I'll do anything I can."

"Were you aware," Barrett said, "that every time you open your mouth a qualification comes out? You can't say one simple thing without qualifying it ten times. Did you know that? Just yes or no is all I asked for and you have to go on and on about—"

"Barrett, I said no. Now ask the question, will you? I've got to go."

"Okay." Barrett raised his hand and asked the waiter to take away the dirty plates. He arranged what was left of the flatware.

"I've decided to go head with this deal," Barrett said finally.

Terry let his breath out with a whoosh. Until then he hadn't realized he was holding it.

"Adams and his lawyers are drawing up the papers. How long is something like that supposed to take?"

"It can take weeks, or it can take months," Terry said. "It depends on how complicated the terms are, and how close in agreement the principals are in each aspect of the contract. Each clause has to be gone over very carefully, as you well know. Quite often the principals think they're in accord all through the preliminary talks and then when they see it all written down in a contract they find they meant two very different things. Everything breaks down for a while and then they have to start all over again, parrying back and forth until they get it straight. Language is a funny thing, it hardly helps in communication at all." All the time Terry was talking he was trying to work out what Barrett had done, how committed he was. "Have you signed anything yet?" he asked.

"No, of course not. I wouldn't sign anything without a lawyer."

Terry looked at the clock again. He had to go in a minute. "Did you get the money?" he asked finally.

"Of course I did. Do you think I would go through with this kind of thing if I didn't have the money?"

"Did you borrow it?" Terry was trying to be casual, but he was nervous.

"I didn't have to." Barrett smiled.

Terry didn't like the smile. "Barrett," he said, "I have a very serious question for you. Did you speak to Sidney about this?"

"You know I didn't," Barrett muttered.

"No, I don't know for sure that you didn't. But you can't do another thing until you do."

"Now look here, Terry. She left me and she's going to have to come back to me. We agreed on that a long time ago."

"Don't shout. We never agreed on that. I thought you were crazy from the beginning. It's a terrible way to handle anyone, and particularly someone you love."

"Don't tell me about love. You're no expert on that subject."

"I'm so tired of hearing that." Terry gritted his teeth. "You can't imagine how tired I am of hearing that. I do know that if you love someone you should at least offer help when it's needed, even if it costs you something to do it."

"I've always helped Sidney. God knows I've—"

"There's a big difference between offering help when you think it's needed and offering it when she thinks she needs it."

"You're crazy, you know that. Sidney's a professional, she's not the mad housewife. You don't know a thing about it. I'm sure it's better this way. She'll come back when she's ready. Even if it takes a few more weeks. In fact I'm certain that a few weeks on her own was just what she needed."

"Barrett, you can't go ahead and make this deal, or any kind of a deal, without talking to Sidney. Do you understand me?"

"Of course I can. Husbands make deals every hour of every working day without consulting their wives. I don't have to consult Sidney about anything. That's absurd."

"Did you use any of Sidney's money? If you used even a dollar of her money, you have to get her permission to use it."

"Our money is both of ours. I don't even know any more what's whose. We just put it together. I'm sure some of it *is* Sidney's, but I've always managed our finances and she's never objected to any of my investments yet. It would be a breach of our normal working procedure to ask her opinion on this."

"Barrett, listen. Will you try really hard?" Terry was as tough and persuasive as he could make himself without using his fists. "Sidney does not want any part of this magazine. You know it and I know it, so don't pretend she won't mind when she finds out. It's one of the reasons she went up there—that was a silly thing to do, we both agree on that, because now Sidney doesn't have anyone to protect her interests. It may not be illegal for you to take money out of a joint account without Sidney's permission. But it is certainly unethical. Don't kid yourself about that."

"This is how friendships break up," Barrett said very quietly. "Do you want that to happen?" He was so angry he had to speak slowly to make sure his mouth would make the words.

"I'm sorry, Barrett, but you've got your head screwed on all wrong about this. You don't want me to lie to you."

"Since when are you more concerned with Sidney's interests than mine?"

"I don't want you to make a mistake, I'm not against you. If Sidney agrees, I'm all for your going ahead. I'll help you in any way I can. How about that?" Terry got up to go. "Will you please promise me you won't be crazy about this? Will you call Sidney? Will you call me later?"

"I'm going to get another lawyer," Barrett threatened. He was furious that Terry was leaving.

"That's your right." For the first time in eighteen years, Terry did not offer to pay the bill.

"Terry . . ."

"I'm sorry, Barrett, I've got someone waiting in my office. Call me later, will you?" Terry stopped one more time. "Please don't do anything stupid."

Barrett sat there for a few minutes waiting for various parts of his body to unclench. How could such a trusted old friend turn out to be such a schmuck. Why did he say all those things about Sidney. Terry had to know it would be insane of him to call Sidney now. Well, there was only one thing to do, call another lawyer. Damn Terry; damn him. Barrett put a five-dollar bill down on the table and walked out. It was then that he realized he had forgotten to ask Terry if he meant to take Lespedeza out.

CHAPTER 33

All day Muriel made advances on Barrett. She looked as though she wanted to talk about something serious. It made Barrett twitchy every time he turned and saw her eyes fixed on him. God, here it was starting all over again. Lespedeza was cutting herself off from everything. She sat bent over her galleys all day. Whatever they were, they couldn't be that compelling, and Garth called to say he wasn't coming in. He wanted Barrett to continue working on the summer enclave series, two issues beginning that week on the most glamorous summering places in America. It was a series Barrett particularly liked to do. He also liked working on the winter versions. It was always a source of both satisfaction and frustration to him that some people actually set aside times for real escape. He hardly ever left the magazine for longer than two or three days at a time. It just seemed impossible that it could come out without him. He hoped his leaving would halt it completely.

"Barrett, can I talk to you?" Muriel sidled up to his desk chair as though it were a moving target.

"Not now." Barrett refused to look up lest she be encouraged. He buried himself under a pile of summer-house and summer-resident photographs.

Twice he saved himself by getting the author of the summer series, who was spending the week in the office, to sit with him and go over the copy. It was easy copy, though, and after discussing it twice there wasn't much Barrett could think of to change. Reluctantly he let him go. Every time he reached for the phone to call this other lawyer he knew, Barrett looked around and found Muriel staring at him. He knew that stare. Barrett couldn't dial the phone until Muriel went out to get her sandwich. Luckily the lawyer was in, but he said he was too busy to meet with Barrett until late the next day. Barrett agreed to meet him at his office and hung up with relief.

He had lunch with Seth and Alden. It was almost impossible to have lunch with one and not the other. In spite of all their fighting, they were inseparable. After lunch, because he saw Muriel hovering around his desk, Barrett spent some time visiting around in other departments. He returned to his desk once and then left again because she got up from hers. It became like a game. He just wasn't going to let her corner him. He went into the men's room hoping that she would have gone away by the time he came back. He read all the graffiti on the walls, looked out of the window, combed his hair, washed his hands, and finally emerged trying to look as though he had needed to be in there. Then he actually did look relieved because he found Peter Marshall sitting in his guest chair and Muriel once again back at her own desk with her glasses and her plastic arm guards back on. He had won.

"Hey, Peter, how great to see you. Do you want to go out for a drink?" Barrett asked Peter. Peter nodded though he had just finished lunch himself. They left almost immediately, Barrett at a trot.

Muriel, however, got him in the end. Barrett was just congratulating himself on making it through the whole day without having to talk to Muriel when she came up to his desk and stood there with an unusual look of determination. Barrett simply did not have the energy to find an instant excuse for sending her away.

"I want to talk to you," Muriel said belligerently.

"Of course, of course, Muriel, any time." Barrett flipped his perpetual calendar over to Friday. "Friday looks kind of cramped to me. How about Monday morning first thing?" Barrett looked at her with as much cordiality as he could muster, considering the vision he was beginning to have every time he saw her. She looked to him like a chicken with a scrawny neck and a scrawny body that scratched around the office like a hen in a barnyard. His fingers twitched. He somehow imagined them tightened around Muriel's feathery neck. He was shocked at both the twitch and the image.

Muriel flinched at the grimace he made but held her ground.

"How about now?" she said. She sat down in his guest chair. She was going to talk now and there was nothing he could do about it.

"Sure, I only have"—Barrett checked his watch—"about five minutes. I have to go to the dentist because of this terrible ingrown tooth I've developed."

"It's six-thirty. No dentist in the world is open at six-thirty. I want to talk to you about the copy department," Muriel said. "It's very important. In fact it's urgent. We have a situation that can't go on any longer."

"I think the copy department has been functioning splendidly," Barrett said, suddenly relieved. "What seems to be bothering you about it?"

"Splendidly?" Muriel sputtered. "Well, for one thing. No one uses my marking pens. I still don't know who is responsible for mistakes."

"Well, it was a try, Muriel. You know how difficult it is to regiment people here. That's one of the beauties of the place." Barrett sat back. For God's sake, why had he been afraid of her. She couldn't do a thing.

"Well, if you think that my having to stay here every night checking and rechecking copy because some people are slacking off, going home early, and taking three-hour lunches is fair, then I suppose all the beauty of the place is only for *some* people to enjoy. . . . Now I have a list of all typos, sloppy editing, and misspellings and who let each one by before I caught them. They are gross and would have caused considerable embarrassment to the magazine if any had gotten through. Some people can't even count lines."

"We're grateful for your diligence, Muriel," Barrett said and started to put his files in order to demonstrate that the day, at least for him, was over. "You're an expert in your field. A pearl of unusual quality. Also a person of intelligence. I mean it."

"And," Muriel went on, "I have a list of all the time off every person in the department has been taking. Lunch hours. Time in and time out. The number of personal telephone calls and the time. It's all here."

"That's very conscientious of you."

Muriel shoved the notebook across the desk at him. "I'm sure you'll be very interested to know just how little a few people are doing for their salaries."

"Thank you, Muriel. I appreciate your loyalty to the magazine." Barrett had put his last paper away. His pencils were in their holder; his desk was clear. He took a paper towel out from the bottom drawer and dusted the desk quickly. He looked up as though surprised that she was still sitting there, still holding out the book.

"Well, aren't you going to look at it?" Muriel said anxiously.

"What exactly do you want me to do with this, Muriel? I'm not sure I understand what's on your mind."

"I expect you to act like the motivating executive editor you are, Barrett. Punish the offenders." She said it as though it were a patriotic slogan.

"All right, you tell me who the offenders are and I will talk to them." She was disgusting, but all the same Barrett got a warm glow hearing himself referred to as a motivating executive editor. It was true that he could work miracles with the most slovenly staff.

"Just look in the book. Just a short look; it's all documented."

"All right," Barrett said, although he disapproved of Muriel in general and therefore could find little tolerance for any suggestions she might have. This wasn't a work camp after all. He picked up the book with distaste. He saw that the two copy girls in the department took an hour and a half each for lunch, had an average of 2.5 personal calls a day, and usually left at six-thirty. He saw that Lespedeza took three hours for lunch more often than not, had an average of 5.7 calls a day, and left at six exactly. He didn't turn the page to see what else Muriel had documented. "I'll take care of it," Barrett said. He handed the notebook back. He kept his face impassive as Terry did when he was angry, but he was so angry that if he could have found a way to touch Muriel without vomiting he surely would have wrung her neck.

"Are you as appalled as I was?" Muriel asked, raking his face for any signs of disgust or disillusion.

"I'm going to have a little talk with everyone and tell them they must pitch in and do a better job."

"What about Lespedeza?"

"What about her?" Barrett raised his eyebrows.

"I don't think she's doing her job. I think she's lost her efficiency."

"I said I would talk to her," Barrett said. He got up. "I think you're going too far, Muriel. The copy department, as I said before, is functioning splendidly. Thanks to you and to the rest of the staff. There are times when we all slack off, and I will see about it. But I will not have this office become a vipers' nest of listening and bugging and spying. Do you hear me? That's what makes governments fall, and I won't have it here." Barrett had what is known as a sallow complexion, but he had turned quite pale with anger.

"You take that notebook of yours and get rid of it. In fact, I'll get rid of it." He snatched it from Muriel's hand and threw it into the wastebasket where it landed on the remains of someone's half-eaten egg salad sandwich.

"The next time you have a beef, you come to me right away. I won't have this place turned into a vipers' nest." He reached for his jacket and added, "Now you just forget about all this spying and do what you're good at doing."

Muriel stared at him with what he thought was a fairly harmless expression of soon-to-pass malice. All right, so she hated him. What could she do, he was leaving anyway. He knew it was her way of getting back at Lespedeza—even her way of getting back at him because she could always go to Garth and complain about both of them. But Garth would never fire him because of anything Muriel could find to say about him. Barrett thought about it as he put his jacket on. So she might be able to get Lespedeza fired. Well, he shrugged his jacket into place on his shoulders, Lespedeza would just have to find something else to do.

CHAPTER 34

It was not entirely because the money she had brought with her was gone that Sidney decided to call Mr. Poupont in Providence. She did need some money, of course, and hadn't brought any of the checks from her New York bank. But also she wanted to see if it would work after all those years. The money was in trust like the knowledge that any woman could have a child if she really wanted to and did all the right things. The money was in trust like the letters one sends to a psychiatrist.

Sidney once had a friend who wrote a diary for her psychiatrist. Every day she told a little more of her life story and what she thought were the causes of her troubles. About a year after she stopped going she asked the psychiatrist for the letters back. The psychiatrist claimed they were gone, all destroyed. The friend felt as though her own life had been destroyed because she could not remember what she said on all those pages she had given away. The friend wrote letter after letter asking why such a thing had been done without her permission; she only lived a block away, she could have come to get them. She had always been confident that the letters were there for her in trust waiting for the time when she could read them again. The psychiatrist had had the woman as a patient for years, but never saw fit to answer any of her letters.

Barrett had said, what could anyone expect from someone in that cannibalistic profession. But Sidney and Terry were appalled. Terry wanted to sue. He wrote several letters. His, of course, were answered. But in the end there was no case, no evidence that the letters had been used for something else as he suspected, for psychiatrists are the last people to throw away documented illness. Her life was there in some graduate student's thesis on something or other. Or in trust for the psychiatrist herself in case she ever wanted to write a book on the pathology of women. If he ever found it, Terry would move. Sidney was upset because it was a woman. Betrayal from a doctor who was also a woman was the worst thing of all.

It seemed a good punishment for trust. And so, too, would not being able to have a baby even though *Life* magazine had proved without a doubt years ago that the process worked. A good punishment for merely trusting that something was there, and not making sure before it was too late.

Somehow, Sidney could just hear Mr. Poupont's regretful voice saying, "But we thought you didn't want it. We gave it away of course. Didn't you know there's a statute of limitation on unclaimed money?" Well, she certainly knew there was a statute of limitation on unclaimed love.

Sidney called Mr. Poupont at nine o'clock on Monday morning. All Sunday night after Terry left, she had a feeling that everything was gone. Her life was defined by pieces of paper on which certain information was written. Proof of possession, proof of marriage, proof of employment. Fifty-one stories a year at eight hundred dollars a story. Her allowance from Barrett was about twelve hundred dollars a month. She had never asked him why he chose that amount as the appropriate one for her personal expenses. She always supposed he just needed to, because she knew he made less than she did. She also assumed that, since he had managed and nurtured it, whatever talent she had was his. That was his view, too, of course.

She figured she could afford to do it if it made him happy, though it didn't. Nothing, she now knew, could have made Barrett happy. Some people are just born to brood forever, no matter how well life turns out for them.

Mr. Poupont was not in.

Sidney explained who she was and what she wanted, and Mr. Poupont's assistant assured her that five thousand dollars was easy enough to get. Sidney said she needed it right away—which was sort of true. She wanted it right away, which amounted to the same thing. She wanted to be sure that one thing in the system was still working as it should.

And she was assured that a check would be issued before noon and sent by special delivery. Four times Sidney repeated where she was. Martha's Vineyard, not New York. If the money was sent to New York, she'd never see it. Martha's Vineyard, she said.

The secretary said, "Oh, I thought—Mr. Poupont thought you were in New York."

"Well, I was," Sidney said, exasperated because she had just said that she wasn't and the girl still wasn't sure. Did she think that all long-distance calls had to come from the same place. "But I'm here now, do you understand? Will you make sure to send it here."

"Yes, I will, don't worry about it," the girl said.

Already Sidney was worried about it. She was just about to hang up when the secretary said, "Oh, I'll have the check issued and sent. But will you send me a confirmation with your signature? I know it's you, but we have to be very careful."

"Of course. I'll do it right away."

It was ridiculous how careful one had to be about those pieces of paper. They were always having lawsuits at the magazine, and each time there were fits over the pieces of paper. Once, Sidney remembered, there was a libel suit in which the author claimed the defamatory piece of information was not in the original manuscript and had been added on later in the office, by someone other than himself. He claimed he never saw it that way. There was an uproar at the office when everyone tried to find the original manuscript, and all the galleys and page proofs. Of course it was months after the fact and no one remembered any more where any of it had been put. The story, as it turned out, had been set and reset. Sometimes it was too long and sometimes too short, and nobody would admit to having worked on it. They found six versions in galleys and pages, but no original manuscript. Nothing could be proved about anything. Since no one would admit to working on it, no malice could be proved, and neither could the complainant prove that he wasn't a public figure and that the statement (whatever it was) wasn't true. The suit was dropped. They always were. What was the point of them anyway if both sides played with the pieces of paper. Garth was a fanatic about keeping the pieces of paper, but Sidney suspected that he tore them up whenever they were needed but proved damaging to his side. She didn't know that for sure, though.

Sidney wrote a note requesting the money and signed it, then went into town to mail it. She wondered how long she could live up there on five thousand dollars. She wondered how long she could live there alone. Ever since she left New York, Sidney had been feeling that life was terribly fragile. Every day she thought she might die without ever having taken charge of herself. Driving back home the day before, she had seen what had to be Terry's plane flying over her on the way back to New York. It seemed, too, that Terry's life might end at any moment. Who knew. And then none of the pieces of paper would matter as much as her not having said a proper good-bye.

Although she was pretty sure Hank had already gone home, she drove over to his house to say good-bye. The house was boarded up and the car gone. She drove back to town and had lunch in a restaurant. She didn't want to think about being alone. It was Monday. There was a whole week to go and not even then was there any hope for company over the weekend. She'd as much as told Terry to drop dead. He wouldn't come back twice anyway. Anyway she couldn't take the chance, could she. As she had lunch in the little Frenchish restaurant off the main street of Vineyard Haven, she wondered if she ought to go to Europe. She stayed out all afternoon, went to State Beach where *Jaws* was filmed and read for a while. She drove to Edgartown and walked around. She was waiting to see if her money would come, and aware as she waited that even if it did come it wouldn't make any difference.

She waited until three on Tuesday to go into town for the mail. She knew if she waited too long she wouldn't be able to deposit the check in the bank. But that would give her an excuse to come back in the morning. To pass the time she went clamming in the morning. Then she had lunch, washed her hair, and got dressed for town. She put on an old blue work shirt and a blue-jean skirt from several years before. Rope shoes. She had two handbags that she used on the Vineyard. One was tiny and was the one she usually took to town. It was just big enough for a wallet, a comb, the house keys, and her driver's license. For some reason that day she took the other one with her credit cards and the other junk. She locked the house and then went back and locked the screen porches and the back door where the garbage cans were. Sometimes she did all this for a half-hour trip to town and sometimes she didn't. She didn't know why she did it this time except that she was nervous and it gave her something else to do before getting into the car and driving to town.

She couldn't believe that the letter had gotten there so quickly. She turned the envelope over and examined both sides. It was about the amount of the income for that whole first year. She had finally taken it. Sidney stood in the post office with the letter in her hand. She felt so emotional about it she thought she was going to cry. So she went and sat in the car before attempting to open it. Lots of women couldn't ever leave because they didn't have what she held in her hand. What she had was freedom from everybody. She had had it all along and had to make herself a slave to a man anyway. Sidney shrugged inwardly. Oh well, she thought as she always had, how could anyone complain about eight years in which one had grown and prospered. Barrett might have had a slave for eight years, but she couldn't have paid for the education she got. Ha-ha. Her father always said it was stupid for a woman to marry a man, but her mother said there was no other joy in life. Even alive, they had seemed like a chorus from Gilbert and Sullivan. She said one thing and he stood behind her winking and shaking his head.

At last she opened the letter. There was the check all right, and a letter from faithful old Mr. Poupont. He must be a hundred by now.

> Dear Sidney:
> So sorry to have missed you yet another time. Mr. Martin told me you were out of town, but he said you wanted the check for $50,000 sent directly to you in New York. Enclosed is the additional $5,000 you requested. I hope everything is in order. Please let me know if there is anything else I can do.

Mr. Poupont closed with kindest regards and a postscript to the effect that he had tried to reach her several times the day before but there had been no answer at the house.

Because Barrett had long ago explained it to her, Sidney knew instantly why the trust hadn't protected her against such a large withdrawal. She also knew with what kind of rationalization Barrett must have done this. There were two pay phones across the street but Sidney didn't see them. She kept thinking that it was after three. It was too late to reach Poupont. She didn't know when the checks had been issued anyway. It might be too late to cancel the check. What could she do.

Sidney was parked in front of the post office. She looked wildly around as though there were someone who might be able to help. It was a summer town, though, calm and quiet in the afternoon sun. Sidney thought she'd call the police; her hands were shaking. The police station was a little house not a block away. Sidney had never been inside. The crime had been committed in New York, or was it Providence. Up here they wouldn't even understand what the crime was. She had to go to New York. She fumbled with the car keys, almost flooded the engine trying to get the car started. She put it in forward instead of reverse. She would have crashed into the post office if there hadn't been such a high curb. By then she was so nervous she couldn't remember which pedal was which. All she knew was that she had to get to New York, right away. A telephone call to anybody wouldn't do. She had to get to Barrett herself.

Driving to the airport, she pictured herself having it out with Barrett. This time she would face him and win. God, she hadn't believed Barrett could do such a thing. Sidney always said that driving a shift car would never be like breathing to her. She would always have to stop and think every time she had to slow down. Each time she had to make a turn, she was afraid the car would stall. She had to keep track of which foot was on which pedal every minute. By now she wasn't paying any attention. She was so busy winning her own back from Barrett, she wasn't even aware of what road she was on.

She was so angry she left the keys in the car at the airport; so angry she tried to pay for her ticket with the five-thousand-dollar check from Poupont. She was so agitated and upset she didn't even think twice about being right on time for the four-thirty flight to New York. She went back and got the keys out of the car. Last year they had been going to buy a new one. But after going shopping for one and seeing what a new car costs these days, Barrett decided against it. Sidney didn't like the car, but she didn't want it stolen either. She was on the plane halfway to New York before she realized what had happened.

Barrett had actually stolen her money. After all she had done for him, the only thing he could think of to do when she left was steal whatever part of her money he didn't already have. What punishment could be bad enough for him. Sidney thought of that all the way home and also that she was wearing the worst clothes her wardrobe had to offer. For this kind of confrontation she should be wearing something grand.

It was Tuesday afternoon, maybe there wouldn't be much traffic, she thought. If she could just get into the city by six-fifteen, six-thirty even, she would still have time to change before Barrett got home. She kept looking at her wrist and then cursing herself for always forgetting her watch. God, Barrett was a slimy creature. How could she have overlooked that when she left. It took an hour to get from Martha's Vineyard to the Marine Air Terminal right across the highway from La Guardia. Since it was a weekday and clear, the plane landed on time. After she got off it, Sidney could not have told what kind of plane it was.

She got a taxi easily and settled back for the ride into Manhattan. After two minutes in the taxi, she snatched the mirror out of her bag and examined her face, then looked in the bag to see if the check and the letter were still there. In her wallet was $13.50. Well, at least she had enough to pay for the taxi. God, she looked awful.

"Mrs. Martin," the doorman said nervously when she arrived at their building. "How good to see you." He was a twitchy man. He twitched now, followed her to the door and revolved it around. He followed her inside. "How are you?" He hovered. Robert, as he was called, was a very warty man. Sidney always thanked him, but rarely looked him in the face. "I'm fine, thank you. Is Mr. Martin in?"

"No, he hasn't come in yet." Robert twitched. It was the kind of information he didn't like to give, even to the tenants. "Would you like to wait for him here?"

"No, thanks." Sidney made an effort and looked Robert in the face. "When he comes in, would you not tell him I'm here. I want to surprise him." She smiled in what she hoped was a friendly fashion.

"He'll be surprised all right," Robert muttered after the elevator door had closed.

Sidney didn't think it was strange that the doorman of her own building had suggested that she wait downstairs for her husband. Not at all. Doormen are the strangest people in the world. There's no accounting for the things they do. One set of doormen in a perfectly decent Madison Avenue building let two young white men and one young black one dismantle an entire apartment while the owner was out for a Saturday afternoon walk. Why did the two doormen open the door for three strangers with a rented van? Because they said they were friends of the apartment's owner and were helping him move.

Sidney opened the door of her apartment. It had the hush of an empty place. Somehow she expected the living room to look different. But it didn't. It was still the same spare, modern—suitable for photographing at any time—model room it always had been. Only now it had the empty cave hush about it. There was a stack of mail on the lacquered bar. Sidney wondered who had brought it in. The maid came on Monday, not Tuesday. She left the mail without touching it and went into her office. That room, too, looked the same. Barrett hadn't even changed the margins on her typewriter.

She thought she'd better change her clothes and walked back toward her bedroom. The door was half closed and inside the room it was dark. Sidney slid her hand to the light switch and was about to turn it on, but something about the way the door was closed and the blinds were drawn (both things were very unlike Barrett, who always liked all doors and windows open and uncovered) stopped her. There was somebody inside, she was sure. She backed away from the door. Sidney considered running. If she slammed the front door, she might frighten the intruder into coming out. She stood outside the bedroom door holding her breath. There was no sound from inside the room. I'm just being crazy and nervous, she thought. She was surprised that she felt so guilty sneaking into her own house.

Sidney approached the door a second time, then pushed it with the flat of her hand. The door made no sound as it swung open. The blinds were drawn; the bedclothes were in a heap on the bed. It didn't look like there was anyone in there. She hesitated for a second and then took one step into the room. On the floor, half hidden by the corner of the bed, there was a pile of clothes that didn't look like either hers or Barrett's. Once more she looked at the bed. This time she could see that the heap on the bed wasn't just sheets and blankets. It was a girl curled up like a baby, covered up to her forehead with only a long twist of pale hair hanging out. Sidney knew that hair. She knew it almost as well as she knew her own. There was only one piece of it showing, but it gleamed in the dark as vividly as a neon sign. For a minute it confused her, she couldn't figure out what it was doing there. And then all she wanted was to be somewhere else before she was caught.

She had this terrible feeling of being caught. It was inconceivable that she could get out of the front door intact without someone hitting or abusing her. She backed into the hall, tears she didn't even make leaking out of her eyes. Once again nothing worked properly. Any second Barrett would be there, but all four of her limbs wouldn't get together and move her toward the door. She had to get out of there right away. But she didn't know where she could go. She had only six or seven dollars left. She couldn't even go back where she came from.

Where was her bag. Sidney started to gasp with terror. She looked at the front door certain that Barrett was standing behind it. If she stayed where she was Lespedeza would wake up. Sometimes the most peculiar things take on awesome proportions. Right then the apartment seemed like a mine field, the girl in her bed was an enemy soldier waiting for just the right moment to sit up and spray her with machine gun fire. Sidney couldn't find her bag. Where did she put it. She couldn't think, couldn't breathe. She opened the shelf drawer under the mirror where the gloves were kept and pushed them aside as though somehow she could have put her bag in there. She was looking for something but she couldn't remember what. Her hand touched the key to Terry's apartment that Barrett kept there. Yes, it had the same old piece of surgical tape wrapped around the top, and Terry's initials in faded ink. She grabbed the key. It gave her a feeling of safety like the magic charm in a fairy story. She felt calmer just holding it. She forced the gloves back into the drawer—or almost—and went to find her purse. She found it where she had left it, hanging from her desk chair in her office. She found she could walk back to the front door and open it. There was nobody on the other side. In fact, from one long end to the other, the hall was completely empty.

CHAPTER 35

Sidney sat on the bottom step of the back stairs, on the floor half-way between theirs and Terry's. She couldn't go either up or down, but sat there thinking about Barrett and Lespedeza. She couldn't get them out of her mind. So often in the past he had made jokes about her. They used to invite her for the single men they knew, and she would arrive looking like a gypsy, with a scarf around her head and enough jewelry to make her jingle at the slightest movement. She even jingled when only her lips were moving.

Midway through the evening she always took her scarf off and her fine hair, until then pinned up somehow, would tumble down her back. In the ladies' room she bragged to Sidney about her conquests. She claimed there was no such thing as a faithful man and compared Sidney's relative bondage to her freedom. It was a frequent theme of hers, her freedom; and Sidney tolerated, even encouraged, the confidences she offered because it was true that Lespedeza, unlike herself, had no fear of the future and not the slightest respect for the intelligence of men.

"I've seen a glimmer or two in Barrett," she said every now and then. "You think he's such a paragon . . ."

Not true, she never thought of Barrett as a paragon of anything.

Sidney would never give Lespedeza the reaction she wanted, and Lespedeza always said, "But you're my best friend. I would never do it to you."

It was Barrett, however, who ultimately banned Lespedeza from the social side of their life. Instead of settling down with the years, she became more of a character. Things she did that were endearing in a young girl were not so funny when one was approaching thirty-five. That was what Barrett said. He had strong views about the impropriety of eccentricity in the unfamous. Lespedeza took up more attention than her status allowed. He also said he felt (without having any proof of course) that she did not bathe as often as she could. And anyone could see that her clothes anyway were untidy, unrepaired when damaged, and often unclean as well. Yet it was not beyond belief that Lespedeza could be a temptation.

Sidney sat there with her handbag on the step beside her. What had she thought would happen when she got here anyway. Did she really think Barrett would dissolve with remorse just because she hated him. He had never dissolved with remorse before. When threatened, he attacked. She opened her hand and looked at Terry's key. It was an old one, dirty and with a heavy metal smell. She closed it up in her hand again.

She always thought the back stairs were the most dangerous place in the building. Anyone could prowl those stairs looking for a girl to rape and strangle. Sidney wouldn't go into the basement either, to the laundry room. Anyone could close the door there, too, and rape and strangle. She was always very careful. On the streets she wore cloth coats, black or brown. No jewelry that could be seen. If Barrett had offered her a mink coat, she wouldn't have taken it. She didn't want to be a target, had half believed all those years that a victim had no cause for complaint. After all, what was a decent girl doing on the back stairs alone (a bar, the streets, the basement, her own apartment) if not looking for trouble. It didn't matter how much she made every week or how nice an apartment she lived in, inside Sidney knew that she was still about six; and Garth and Barrett and Terry even (no matter how much they protested belief in feminism and equality) acted each in his own way exactly like a father. If Barrett had really taken her seriously he would not have done many things. But mostly, he wouldn't have dared to take her money.

The reason she was so afraid of being raped was, more than anything else, the fear of not being able to react. Inside, she suspected that even if her life was at stake, she could not strike back. It would be far easier to be raped, maimed, even strangled than to lift her knee in protest. Her own magazine, and all the others, said that this was a female thing that came from a thousand years of careful training. Neither could Sidney ever have told Barrett that he was stultifyingly boring in bed. No magazine had to tell her why that was. He wouldn't have listened, for one thing. But she also knew from seeing it happen to other people that, once one starts finding fault in small ways, one can no longer believe a person is competent in any area. The same thing is true with an employer, doctor, dentist, lawyer. Liberation, whatever the kind, is like a mold on old cheese: once it starts, there's no way to get rid of it without the cheese going too.

But recently Sidney had been feeling that she could fight back. She had been dreaming of being sent to prison for stabbing an attacker in the Fourteenth Street subway station. It was a peculiar dream because the knife was the mugger's own weapon turned

227

against himself. And Sidney never took the subway. She had also told Garth that she'd rather starve on the streets than go to bed with him to save her job. She didn't know whether she would or not if starvation were really the alternative—but it wasn't for anyone else either and she at least had said it.

Well, so what if there was someone in Terry's apartment along with or exclusive of himself. She had a right to life too. Right?

Sidney had left her watch at home. She didn't know what time it was or how long she had been sitting there. Her knees were stiff and in spite of everything she was hungry. It occurred to her that she could just ring Terry's bell and wait for him to answer the door. She didn't have to sneak in like a burglar. But if she rang the bell and he answered the door, she would not be able to catch him in bed with a show girl in garters. And that was what she needed to make the day complete.

It was an extremely dishonorable thing to do, Sidney knew, but she turned the key in his lock anyway and went in as quietly as she could. Whew. There was no one in the living room to see her sliding through the front door like a ghost in a comic strip.

The entrance hall, such as it was, in no way blocked the view of the living room. Two steps in and she could see his dining room with the pool table on one side and the door to his bedroom on the other. There was no cavelike hush here. The television (or rather Walter Cronkite) was blasting the news from the bedroom, and all the lights were on. Sidney walked across the hall and looked in his room. She was almost disappointed to see his clothes, but no girl, strewn across his bed. His bathroom door was open and, over the Sominex commercial, she could hear the shower running. Just before she stepped into the bathroom she noticed there was no bedspread on the bed and he really did have khaki sheets.

Terry had a see-through shower curtain with large black circles on it. He had his back to her and was rinsing shampoo out of his hair. Sidney took one of the black and white towels off the rack by the tub. In a second with his back still toward her he reached for the towel and she put it into his hand.

He screamed.

It wasn't the choking sound of a person caught off guard. It was more like the scream of a person falling five stories. Pure terror. It scared Sidney and she turned around to see if there was someone else behind her.

When she turned around again he had recovered enough to turn off the water and get out of the tub. Still dripping, he caught her in a great bearlike hug. "Sidney, my God. Don't *ever* do that again." He put his wet face into her hair. "Didn't you see *Psycho?*"

"Let go, Terry, you're getting me all wet." There it was in one second, that stupid ache in the stomach that made humans no more advanced than the lowest form of life. Here she was more wretched and scraggly and angry than she could ever remember being and still those ovaries charged around battling for the last word.

"I thought you were my friend," she snapped. Just because he was parading around in a towel didn't mean he could make her forget why she had come.

"Where have you been? I've been trying to reach you for two days." Terry went into the bedroom and turned off the television. She hadn't been there for five minutes and already it seemed like he had been beaten with a stick. Why was she always accusing him of not being her friend. Who had ever been a better one.

She followed him into the other room and watched him get dressed. He was squeaky clean and clear proof of the existence of God. No mere accident could have produced such cruel revenge on women.

"You betrayed me," she said bitterly. "You came to my house when I was lonely and miserable and you seduced me without telling me the truth about anything."

"What are you talking about?"

"Where did you get that purple mark on your neck?"

Terry looked in the mirror. There was indeed a purple mark on his neck. "You put it there," he said.

"I did not. Mine was on the other side."

"Sidney, you always had a poor sense of direction," he said wearily. He put on a shirt and buttoned it all the way up to the top. Then as if it had just occurred to him he added, "For God's sake, you didn't come all this way to examine me for hickeys, did you?"

"Oh, Terry." Sidney began to cry. "You didn't help me at all there's somebody in my bed and all the money is gone and you should have known you should have done something and I don't even know what to do but what does it matter anyway when they fish my body out of the river it won't matter I'll be dead and the trust and she's probably been wearing my clothes and you didn't even tell me." Sidney said all of this while blubbering into a piece of Kleenex which early on she fished out of her handbag. Now, in case he hadn't heard her (which he hadn't), she raised her head and said very clearly, "I'm going to kill myself."

Terry made a move to comfort her, but she backed way. "Don't you touch me, you pervert, you crummy opportunist. You *rat*—where the fuck do you think you're going? I just said I was going to kill myself."

Terry stalked into the living room where he kept a few bottles and glasses on a tray table. Sidney followed him sobbing and rummaging through her bag for another tissue.

"Oh, you *lush*. You can't even have a talk with a person without getting drunk. You can't face anything."

"Sidney, if you don't shut up, I'm going to smack you one. This isn't for me, it's for you. You're hysterical and I can't understand a word of what you're saying." He advanced on her holding out the glass. "Here."

"Oh, so you beat women, too. Go ahead, hit me. I'm just the right size for you. Go ahead anywhere you want. I won't hit back." Sidney stuck out her chin.

"Here, drink a little of this. It'll make you feel better. . . . For Christ's sake will you stop that, you're making me crazy."

Sidney was tapping her jaw, inviting him to sock her one.

He held out the glass for her but she wouldn't take it. After a few seconds more of her carrying on her hitting pantomime, he drank it himself. He sort of thought he should tap her one to calm her down. But even if he had had a guarantee that she was the kind of person on whom such methods work, he couldn't have done it. He refilled the glass and started back across the room with it.

"I'm going to put this down right here," Terry said, "and then I'm going to sit down over there. And you're going to take a little drink and tell me what happened."

"I hate you," Sidney said. "I really do." He couldn't even get the drink right. It was scotch. She hated scotch. If she drank even the tiniest sip of it she would choke. She might even drown. She went over and took a big swallow of the scotch. She choked. It was horrible and burned, and it didn't even make her feel better.

"See," Terry said encouragingly. "Now you feel better, don't you?"

She was so upset she couldn't even tell him what had happened. She handed him the letter and the check.

"I thought you said the money was in trust," he said sharply.

Sidney began to cry again. "You don't have to talk to me like that. You didn't think of it either." She raked through the contents of her bag and came up with another used tissue. She wept into it, holding her face as though it might fall apart if she let go. "You're all so mean and cruel."

"I'm sorry. I was just surprised. You told me the money was safe." Terry moved uneasily from one chair to another. He couldn't stand to see Sidney crying like that. He never could stand it. She got so small when she cried. She wasn't like other women, who sobbed loudly while dabbing at their eyes in an attempt to save their make-up, peeking through their fingers, and then reaching for the closest man (him) for support. But when Sidney, who worked so hard all the time to control herself, let go she was like a lost child. There were no other words for it. She cried as though there were no comfort anywhere. In some cases disappointment acts like a cement block that holds down a drowning person. Terry didn't want that to happen to Sidney. He wanted her to complain and cry, just not at him.

He wanted to feel her hot tears on his neck. He wanted to taste them. He could hardly sit still for wanting to hold her. "Sidney?" Should he go to her or wait for her to come to him. If he waited it might take hours.

"What?"

"I'm going to send Mr. Poupont a telegram."

"My whole life is over and all you can think of is money."

"Sidney."

"What?" She wouldn't look up.

"Why do you talk to me like that?"

"It's my disaster. I should handle it my way." Sidney sat up in her chair, tried another sip of scotch, and coughed again. "Ugh, this is horrible. Don't you have anything else?" She looked over at the tray and the bottles. One of the crystal decanters had a lavalier around its neck with "Sherry" written on it in script. The lavalier really depressed her, also the ferns in the elephant feet that clearly hadn't been watered in several months.

"I feel so awful," she said, looking away from him. "I don't know why, I just can't seem to find the bottom. I feel like I'm falling into the Grand Canyon in slow motion and can't find anything to grab onto." She put her face back in her hands.

"When George and Marion died I thought there was a big hole where my innards should be. I kept looking in the mirror to make sure everything was still there. I couldn't believe it didn't show. But I didn't really *feel* anything. I feel worse about them now than I did then."

She was quiet for some time.

Then she said, "It isn't the money, you know."

"I know it isn't."

"I trusted you and you lied to me. How could I love someone who lied to me. Everybody lies to me."

"Sidney, you make me so unhappy I don't know what to do."

"I do?" Sidney looked up at him as though this were an altogether new idea to her.

"Of course you do. How do you think I feel when you come barging in here scaring me to death and then start screaming about what a rat I am and how bad a friend I am and that I drink too much. I can't stand it."

"Well, you do drink too much," she said, looking at his glass. He was all she had; what if his liver was shot and he was slowly dying.

"I don't drink that much." He had gotten himself a small glass and still hadn't finished it. If he really drank, he would have had two or three by now.

"Yes, you're always drinking."

"Sidney, what are you trying to do to me?" Terry groaned.

"You didn't tell me about that girl in my bed wearing my clothes."

"Oh, for God's sake."

"You didn't tell me." Why didn't he do something to save her. Why was he just sitting there as though this kind of thing happened every day. Did he love her or didn't he.

"No, I didn't."

"Why didn't you? Don't you think it's the sort of thing I should know?"

Terry took a sip of his drink. Sidney made a face, so he put the glass down. "I told you to come back, didn't I? I told you there were things to settle. I told you to move out properly. Didn't I say all that?"

"But you didn't tell me about her."

"I didn't tell him about you either. Should I have told him that too?"

"What do you mean about me? What about you?"

"Sidney, you make me so tired. I have a headache. I'm not perfect. I was very upset when I saw you up there, and I'm very upset now."

Terry did look very upset. Now he was the one who had his face in his hands, and for a minute it looked as if he, too, might cry. Oh, God, what would she do if he cried. She couldn't stand it if he cried. "Okay," she said quickly.

"Do you want some aspirin? I'll get you some." She stood up. She started to go into the bedroom and then she stopped. "Will I find anything upsetting in your medicine cabinet?"

"Not unless you faint at the sight of Gelusil." He smiled. It must have been a reflex she had, that trick of hers of saying something so wonderful just at the moment he thought couldn't stand to have her around for one more minute.

She came back with a glass of water and two white tablets. "I looked, but I couldn't find anything."

"Sidney, I'm not as efficient when I'm emotionally involved. Do you understand that? But there isn't anything else now." He took the aspirin. It was ridiculous. She found Lespedeza in her bed and he had the headache.

"Do you have anything to eat, Terry?"

"I don't think so, let's go out."

"Go out? I can't go out. I don't have anything to wear, and suppose we met Barrett?"

"If we met Barrett, then Barrett would meet us. Besides, I've tried for years but I've never met you in the elevator."

"Well, you've never tried to avoid me either."

"Does that mean you're going to stay the night?" Terry knew as he said it that it was the wrong thing to say, but he couldn't help it.

"I'll stay in the guest room," Sidney said huffily. "I forgot my pajamas."

"I'd lend you some, but I don't use them. I'll go make the bed." He got up.

"Wait," Sidney said. He really was going to make the bed. "What about dinner?"

"I'll call up for something. What do you want, pizza, Chinese, or Mexican?"

"Jesus, is that how you live?"

"A person can't go out every night, and it's better than shopping."

"I thought you liked to shop," Sidney said.

"Only when you go with me." Terry smiled oddly. "I guess we've done a lot of things together, haven't we?"

"Does it feel funny to have me here?" Sidney asked. She was sitting on one of his antler chairs. She had the uncomfortable feeling that any minute one of the horns would move over and goose her.

"I don't know yet. I could tell after a week," he said seriously. He tried picking up his glass again and this time took a sip; Sidney was looking the other way.

"I didn't mean it that way. I'm leaving tomorrow."

"What?"

"I just came to settle with Barrett," she said indignantly. "You didn't think I expected to move in with you, did you?"

"Why not? You can't do it in one day."

She nodded.

"You think you can do it in one day?" He shook his head. "How can you do it in one day? If what you said is true you can't even go back to the house. It's his house. What are you going to do about that?"

"Terry, I know a wife can't testify against her husband, and I know he could take anything of mine out of a joint account and launder it. But what he did in Providence is forgery. Once you call Mr. Poupont and tell him that—and whoever it is in the bank here—it won't have anything to do with me. I wouldn't have to say a word. Shown the light of truth, I think Barrett will agree

234

to give me the house, the Providence money, go to the Dominican Republic for the weekend, or the moon if it came to that."

"I don't think it's a good idea. In the first place, the minute you call him, he could transfer the money."

"It wouldn't alter the case against him. He'd still have to go to jail."

"But first you want to make sure to get the money back."

"Chinese."

"What?"

"You asked me what kind of food. I chose Chinese."

"Oh, I'm sorry. I'm a lousy host."

"I'm hungry."

"If it were any faster, I'd go out myself. But they're very fast. Is there anything special you want or should I order?" He started into the bedroom to call.

"I don't care, anything." While he called, Sidney went into the kitchen and looked around. He had the same cupboard space as she did, but there was nothing in his. He had a minimum of crummy pots and pans, and very few provisions. A lot of club soda and tonic. It was sad, somehow.

"Terry, if you send the telegram first, you can't back down later. I don't want Barrett to go to jail," Sidney said after they had finished a surprisingly good dinner from a place around the corner that Sidney knew didn't usually deliver. She was drinking the green tea she had made from the little tea bags that came with the food.

"We could just ask him to stop payment on the check."

"I think it's too late for that. I think he'd deposit it right away," Sidney said.

"It wouldn't hurt."

"I don't know." Sidney shook her head. She was tired, and the more she thought about it the harder it was to decide where to sleep.

"I know what you're thinking." Terry smiled. "You begin to lose your top lip when you start thinking that. You think, No, I won't. Not for anybody I won't, I won't, I won't. And your top lip gets narrower and narrower and narrower until it's gone completely."

235

"Oh, shut up. Nobody can know what anybody is thinking," Sidney said.

"If you don't believe me, hold that face and go look in the mirror in the bedroom . . . no, don't say anything, just keep your face just like that and go take a look."

Sidney made a face and laughed.

"Go on, it's still there."

Sidney shrugged. It was silly. She got up and went into the bedroom. It was a nice bedroom; he probably wanted her to look at it, so she did. He had two antique wicker and bamboo dressers, with a large bamboo-framed mirror hanging over them. In one corner was a fancy campaign-like chair with a table beside it. There were bamboo shades on the windows and gauzy white curtains over them, that fluttered with the breeze from the air conditioner. Sidney looked in the mirror for her top lip. Over her shoulder she caught sight of his bed. It had blue sheets on it now, covered with enormous pink peonies.

CHAPTER 36

Since seven o'clock when the television automatically came on with the "Today" show Sidney and Terry had been arguing about whether or not she should stay the rest of the week. Sidney said she couldn't stay in any apartment whose owner watched television from the moment he woke up.

"Don't be funny. I'm trying to be serious about this. How can you make a decision about me based on one night? The least you could do is give me a week. How about it? Just stay here until the end of the week and then we'll go someplace for the weekend. And then if you want to go back to the Vineyard forever, I won't argue."

"I hate putting on the same dirty clothes, don't you?" Sidney said. She was wearing one of his T-shirts. "Don't you have anything in my size?" she complained. She didn't like the way anything was done around there. He brushed his teeth in public and now he was standing there in his shorts shaving in public. Didn't he know that bathroom doors were there to be shut. Sidney went into the kitchen to make coffee. There was a Bloomingdale's $250 model espresso machine, but though she looked everywhere she could think of, she couldn't find any coffee. She stayed in the kitchen for a long time anyway in case there was anything else he didn't mind doing in public. On the counter was one bag of green tea left over from the night before. She boiled some water and made that. She looked, but there was no paper outside the front door.

This was what happened when single people went out to dinner, of course. One of them ended up in a strange apartment the next day with no clean clothes, no newspaper, and no coffee. And no place to sit in the kitchen. Sidney went and sat in the living room with her tea and stared at the pool table with disgust. There was no place to sit in the dining room either. This was really unpleasant. If it had been any place but Terry's she would have been out of her skin with distress. Terry wandered in buttoning his shirt. He seemed to be dawdling.

"There's no coffee," Sidney said.

"I'm sorry. I usually go out. I'll get some later." He stood there. He wanted her to say she'd be there later to drink it.

"I suppose you're used to this," Sidney said. She could tell he was so used to it he didn't know what she was talking about.

"Used to what?" he said.

"You know, waking up with some strange person, then going off to work as though it were nothing. Then doing it with some other strange person the next day, or a few days later."

"How many times do you want to go over this same ground?" Terry said. Maybe it would be better if she left. How could a person put up with this constant criticism. After a week of it, he'd probably be dead anyway. She wasn't worth it. He wished she'd put her clothes on.

"I'm not jealous. I know that's what you think, but that's not it," Sidney said glumly. "I'm not jealous."

"There's nothing to be jealous *of*."

"I know, that's the problem."

"Oh, God. I don't understand." Terry went back to his room

for his trousers. He tried to concentrate on his schedule for the day, which was what he did every morning while dressing, but he was too worried about what would happen if Sidney weren't there when he got home. He went back to the living room carrying his socks and shoes. Maybe if she just stayed a day or two longer, he'd be glad to see her go. Usually, it didn't even take this long.

"What are you going to do about the money?" he asked.

"Oh, the money." Sidney watched him put on his socks, one at a time. "I don't know. It doesn't seem so important today."

"Sidney, you're making me crazy, you know that. Yesterday you spent half the night convincing me not to send any telegrams because you were going to take care of it today. And today you say it isn't important any more. I don't know what to do."

"You're always saying that. Don't do anything. It's my problem."

"You want me to turn my back on this whole mess—"

Sidney nodded.

"Well, I can't. It's my problem too."

"If you start in on my incompetence one more time, I'm going to scream," Sidney said. "You want to hear me scream? I have a good scream."

"I *never* said you were incompetent. *Never*. I just said—"

"I know what you said. You said it was all too complicated and difficult and I need someone to represent me and handle me and fix all the little pieces of paper. Don't you understand that I have to do it myself? I'm not trading him for you or him for anybody . . . oh, you're all the same the way you think you're God." Sidney turned away with disgust.

"If you were a man I'd say the same thing. It has nothing to do with—"

"I'm tired of this conversation."

"You make it very difficult for me." Terry completed his shoe-tying task and went back into the bedroom for a tie. He had thirty ties. They were all variations of red and blue stripes, stars, and medallions. He stood there trying to choose one. For some reason none of them looked as if they went with the gray summer suit he was wearing. He couldn't even keep coffee in the house; how could she think he thought he was God.

She followed him in and pointed at one, almost completely hidden under all the others. It was purple with green and red fishes on it, had been given to him by some girl whose name he didn't even remember any more. They always did that, chose things no man in his right mind would wear. He took out a striped tie that was almost identical to the one he had worn the day before.

"You see," she said triumphantly. "*That's* why I have to go home tonight." She pointed at the tie.

"It was a horrible tie, Sidney. I couldn't have worn it."

"It was a perfectly nice tie. And it's proof that a woman always has to adjust to a man. I'm telling you, and I know a lot more about ties than you do."

That was so crazy Terry couldn't think of an appropriate reply. He deliberately put on the tie he had chosen. It suddenly occurred to him that nothing he could do would please Sidney. Taking her to bed seemed to please her, but they couldn't stay in bed all the time. She was just like all his clients when they made a decision, he could slit his wrists, but it wouldn't make any difference. Sidney just didn't want to stay. He reached for his watch, his wallet, his jacket.

"Do you want to go out for some breakfast?" he asked. He knew she would say no.

"No, thank you," she said.

"I'm going to go then." He walked out of the bedroom. He knew if he asked her to have lunch she'd say no. He walked very slowly to give her time to change her mind about breakfast. He debated about mentioning dinner. Could he ask her what she was doing that day.

She followed him to the door but didn't say anything.

"I'm going to go then."

"Good-bye. Thank you."

"How are you going to get Barrett to see you without scaring him to death?" He paused at the door. He didn't really want to leave, but he knew he had to. He couldn't sit there all morning arguing with her. He was a busy man; he had things to do. She looked very cute in his T-shirt; she was going to lose her money. Those two things kept going through his mind. She was going to go back to Martha's Vineyard where God knew what would happen to her, and there wasn't a thing he could do. Christ, he was getting another headache.

"What would you think if I said I was going back?"

"Back, back where?"

"Back to Barrett. Think about that."

CHAPTER 37

Sidney closed the door on him with a satisfying click. He was so dumb he thought telling Barrett she was coming back made it the truth. Boy, he was dumb. He also had no faith in her, none at all. Sidney shook him out of her mind. There were a lot of things she had to do. First, she called the only rent-a-car place she knew of that rented station wagons. Then she got dressed and went to the bank that was around the corner. She didn't know why she was so certain that the money would still be there in their joint account. But she was sure it was. She had been afraid to go home to get one of her own checks because it was only nine o'clock and she couldn't be sure they were not still there. When she thought about them she got angry all over again.

It took a few minutes to realize that she didn't need a check. Sidney made a display of her identification cards for the man at the first of the four desks. He was the one who knew her best. He smiled uncomfortably and told her that wasn't necessary. She said a person couldn't be too careful these days and asked for the balance in her account. While he went to get it, she was so nervous she couldn't stand up. She sat down and jiggled her foot.

"$53,326.30," he read out with some satisfaction. It was nice to have such solid clients.

"I want to close the account," Sidney said.

See, she could manage things herself. The man kept asking her if she was unsatisfied with the bank. Was there anything he could do. He seemed very unhappy.

"I love the bank," she said. "You've been swell. But I'm moving out of town." Twice she made him assure her that, once an account was closed, it was closed. She worded it several ways. But he made it clear that as soon as he gave her the check any other check (mistakenly of course) drawn on the account by her husband would bounce. She walked out of the bank twenty minutes later with two checks in her bag that amounted to almost sixty-thousand dollars. She did not feel any better.

It was a crummy thing to do to tell Terry that, in just that way, so that he didn't know whether she meant to go back to Barrett or not, or go to the Vineyard, or what. It was also crummy to say she didn't care about the money. But whatever she said he believed. He thought she was a fool, an idiot who was capable of anything. She wanted to tell him she got the stupid money.

All the way over to the rent-a-car place, she raged at him for thinking she was so accommodating and dumb that after living with one man for eight years she could move in with another—just for a week or so to see how he liked it. She picked up the car and drove it back to the building. By then it was after ten and she figured it was safe to go upstairs.

After she let herself into the apartment, the first thing she did even before looking around was to make an appointment to have her hair done. Then she looked around. She found the bed unmade and a pile of unwashed glasses and cups in the sink. There were no particular signs of Lespedeza and the only thing that was unusual was a sodden mound of mildewing guest towels in the powder room. Aside from a certain untidyness, the place looked pretty much the same as it always did.

Sidney went into the bedroom and opened her side of the closet. As far as she could tell, nothing was out of place there either. She pulled down the complete set of Louis Vuitton luggage that Barrett had bought over the years for her birthdays, though she said she didn't like it, and started cramming things into the suitcases. She did not examine her clothes with a critical eye as she would have done if she were merely moving. She had resolved that she wouldn't leave anything of hers behind. She found that, aside from the typewriter, her clothes, and a few books, there wasn't much. Barrett did not believe in clutter and systematically weeded out almost as soon as they were acquired all of the things people usually keep as mementos. There were no framed photographs, old theater playbills, newspaper clippings, or vacation souvenirs, and the only knickknacks around the place were functional. He had spent a fortune on making the apartment as austere and junkless as possible.

Sidney went on a tour of the house to see what she could take away with her. She had taken her cosmetics with her the first time. The large hair dryer she didn't want. The linens were all shades of brown. The living room contained not one thing she had chosen on her own. Only in the kitchen was there a profusion of things that seemed her own. Sidney stopped and looked at all the expensive glassware they had collected. Barrett liked glassware because he liked to drink. The dishes and silverware were hers, chosen after months of indecision. She had worried about how curry would look on the intricate patterns she liked but thought food looked unappetizing on the cobalt-colored Swedish plates Barrett was so fond of. Why did everything have to be so bare and modern—why indeed, his mother had chunky crystal and plates with ladies in evening gowns. Eventually they had bought two sets of dishes, one set to satisfy each of them, and silver from Buccellati. She took the silver and left the dishes.

There was a large pegboard on one wall that held her pots and pans and an enormous assortment of those French gadgets that look so good but are too complicated to be useful. The pegboard held her attention for a long time. She sat on the high stool at her workbench where she had spent so many hours poring over cookbooks as though they contained the secret of life, and even more hours chopping and paring and patting different ingredients into shape. The workbench had nothing on it now but a bottle of orange pills that the label proclaimed as papaya enzymes. It was very clear whose those were. They looked kind of vulgar in her kitchen, Sidney thought, but that was probably because of their source. She debated about throwing them out as a gesture but decided against it. She glanced at the clock, saw that it was getting late, and for some reason snatched the garlic press off the pegboard and put it in her pocket as she left. Before opening the kitchen door, she took one last look at the shelf of cookbooks. She was tempted to take them just because they seemed part of her; they were all marked and dog-eared. But she had another set on the Vineyard.

It took her less than two hours to pack up everything she felt was indisputably hers. She gave the doorman five dollars to help her pack her dress bags, her suitcases, two boxes of books, three cartons of files, and the typewriter into the car. Since the car wasn't completely full and she thought it would be bad luck to leave them, she went back for her desk chair and typewriter table. Then she took a bath, put on her favorite summer dress, hat, and shoes, parked the car in the building's garage because she was afraid to leave it on the street, and went to Elizabeth Arden.

When she left Elizabeth Arden three and a half hours later, she did not look like the shaggy-headed, brown-haired person in the faded shirt and blue-jean skirt who'd left Martha's Vineyard the day before. Now she wore a watered silk jersey dress of impeccable cut from Italy and a picture hat that wasn't too big for the city and didn't completely hide the new golden color of her hair that had been carefully cut to dip provocatively at the sides and curl under in the back. She had been right, gold was best. All of those lessons had not been in vain. It was perfectly possible with ashy hair to dye a string here and dye a string there and make the whole thing come out looking kind of yellow and shiny.

Sidney sat there fidgeting while her fingernails were painted pink. Then when she saw her pink fingernails, she wanted her toes to match. Why not, she could certainly afford it.

While she has having herself painted and dyed and styled, Sidney was aware of the waste. She was going to get in the car in her best dress with her stupid money in another stupid Gucci handbag and she was going to drive for five hours to Woods Hole. In a funny way it was like committing suicide. She was playing the New York game to the bitter end. She couldn't even say good-bye without style. Hell no. Three and a half hours of hair dyeing, leg waxing, fingernail painting, and eyebrow plucking just so two stupid male persons would swoon and be sorry.

Even though it was only six blocks away, Sidney took a taxi to Terry's office. She didn't want one hair to be out of place when he saw her. All the way there, she told herself she was not going to tell him what a disappointment he was, what a jerk he was, or anything like that. She was just going to tell him she got the money, and thanks for everything. That was all, and that very sweetly. Maybe she'd kiss him good-bye and let him have a whiff of that hundred-dollar-an-ounce stuff they had sprayed all over her.

She told the receptionist in Terry's office not to announce her because he knew she was coming. Sidney did not, however, feel as confident as she looked when she swept down the hall and confronted Terry's elderly secretary, who had blue hair and was called Marion and whose only fun in life seemed to come from thwarting, as rudely as possible, anyone who wanted to see Terry.

"Hi," Sidney said in a friendly manner.

"He isn't here." Marion was the sort of person who wore hats. She contemplated Sidney's.

"Where is he?" Sidney asked. She had not expected him to be out of the office and was stunned at the news.

"Hasn't come back from lunch yet." Marion glared at her. "You're not in his book," she said.

"Well, put me in it. I'll wait inside." Sidney marched into Terry's office and arranged herself decoratively on the window sill. It was extremely cold in his office and the leaves on his plants fluttered even though they were on the other side of the room from the air conditioning vents. Sidney shivered for twelve minutes while trying to take an interest in the traffic on Park Avenue. It was almost four o'clock. What kind of lunch could take until four o'clock.

Sidney knew all too well what kind of lunch. What a shit he was. He couldn't even wait until she left. She was going to go out and ask Marion who was in Terry's book. Then she decided she'd just leave. Terry's not being there really depressed her. She knew it was unreasonable, but she couldn't help it. She also knew that when she was depressed her face fell about a foot. The lights were red. When they turned green she would leave. In a second, they turned green. She decided to wait until they went red again. By the time they had changed three more times, she was completely absorbed. If she had had a watch she would have timed them. It looked like they were red longer than they were green.

The office was carpeted and there was a steady whoosh from the air vents that sounded like the flapping of many tiny wings. Terry came into the office without her even hearing him. Marion had not been sitting at her desk when he arrived and there was no warning note. He hesitated at the sight of a dress he'd never seen

244

before, a hat he'd never seen before, and some yellow hair he was sure he didn't know. The part of one leg that showed didn't look familiar either. He was standing there on one foot undecided about advancing or retreating when Sidney turned around.

"Oh, God," he said. It was true. Nothing else could have been such clear proof of Sidney's return to Barrett as her dressing up like a Kewpie doll.

"What's the matter?" Sidney said, alarmed.

"Nothing, I just—well, I'm surprised."

"I'm sorry I didn't call first, but I always assume people are in their offices in the daytime." This Sidney said in a huffy tone, for he did not look at all glad to see her. She was sorry she had come and looked around Terry's office for a clock. There were three swiveling armchairs, a tweedy sofa with a tiny bar and icebox on one side that didn't look like a bar, a tree, several bushy plants that were watered regularly, and a coffee table. But no clock. It was more like a living room than an office, and Terry's desk had only two small drawers and a glass top.

Terry shut the door, then he sat down at his desk. All day he had been so miserable he hardly knew what he was doing. He didn't know what was worse, Sidney doing God-knows-what where he couldn't even reach her, or Sidney popping up when he didn't expect her looking either like death or Doris Day. This was the very thing he had tried to avoid during all those years of concentrating on other people's problems. Some big wrenching change that would magnify what he called his small dissatisfactions until they were so large they overpowered everything he felt was good about life.

"I got the money," Sidney said. "Do you want to see it?"

So, she got the money. Why didn't he care all of a sudden.

"I told you I could. Don't you want to see it?"

"I don't care about the money," Terry said.

"You're just saying that because I did it myself. If you had done it you would have considered it a triumph."

"I'm glad you got the money, Sidney," Terry said. He watched her get off the window sill and debate about which of the three swiveling armchairs she should sit in. She wouldn't sit in the middle one (that was the one most often picked by widows and actors), the one closest to the door was for divorce cases and writers. He was right; she sat in the one closest to the window.

"I wanted you to know I'm competent," Sidney said. She swiveled one way and then the other. How could anyone do any work in an office like this. She wondered if he ever locked the door and did anything on the sofa. She was annoyed with herself for always letting thoughts like that intrude. She was always stopping in the middle of thinking something else to wonder if he thought she was pretty—how pretty. As pretty as Caroline, Lespedeza. Catherine Deneuve. When she was in his kitchen she wondered who else had been there; and was there coffee then. And even with his brand-new Bloomingdale's sheets purchased just for her, she could hardly lie down in his bed for worrying who else had been there first. On a scale of one to ten, how good was she. Better than a five. A seven.

Was she the best.

Sidney fiddled with the top button on her dress. He hadn't swooned yet. She couldn't leave without a swoon.

He was saying, "I know you're competent. May God make me a pygmy if I ever thought you weren't."

She didn't laugh. He had stolen that line from somebody and she wasn't going to laugh for a stolen line. Only a short person would think of shortness as a curse.

"Want to see my money?" she said.

"Why are you so concerned about the money all of a sudden?" Terry said. "I thought you didn't care about it."

"It's symbolic. You don't even know a symbol when you see one."

"I see that you dyed your hair. What is that a symbol of?"

"I did *not* dye my hair. At least half of it is just the same as it was. The other half was dipped in a little lemon juice to bring out its true golden hue." Sidney took off her hat and swiveled her chair around so he could see it better.

He raised his eyebrows.

"What does that mean?" Sidney demanded.

"What does what mean?"

Why did he always repeat what she said. He knew perfectly well what she meant. "That twitch."

Terry crossed his legs as casually as he could. It had never occured to him before that there might be drawbacks to having a glass desk. Sidney was a tease. How could such a thing have escaped his notice so long. Even if she did go back to Barrett what difference could one more time make. On the other hand, maybe he could do something special, impress her enough to give him some more time. Maybe he could lock the door and draw the curtains. They could stay there until it got dark and then go some place wonderful for dinner. He could feel his heart pounding in his throat. He was thinking of all those times they had stood side by side in the supermarket arguing over whether or not some product contained red dye number 2 when he hadn't thought of touching her. All the chances he'd missed of kissing her in corners when no one was looking. Maybe that was the reason she was so angry at him now. God, it was awful. He wished she had left Barrett for him, he really did. He took a deep breath.

"Sidney, *why* are you going back to that jerk?"

"I'm not going back to him."

"But you said—"

"I said I was going to tell him that. I was just mad at you for thinking I'm so stupid I'd do anything. How good a lawyer can you be if you believe everything a person says . . . you even believed I slept with Garth."

Sidney put her hat back on. To hell with the swoon. What did it matter if she couldn't even talk to him. She wasn't stupid. He was stupid. They were having such a good time and he didn't even know enough to keep his mouth shut.

"Sidney, I'm sorry. I'll never believe a single thing you say again. Where are you going?"

"It's none of your business. You didn't even say you like my dress."

"I like your dress. Will you go out to dinner with me?"

"No." Sidney stood up.

"Sit down. What are you so mad about now?" If she didn't sit down in one second, he was going over there and smack her one. She was asking for it, that was the truth.

"You're so shallow and insensitive. There are a thousand other women you could take to dinner. Why bother me? What do you think I am anyway, an emotional yoyo? You think you can just invite me in for a week to see how you like it, to see how I do.

What would you say at the end of a week, 'Well, tough luck, Sidney. You were fine until five on Friday, but after that—' "

"Don't shout, Sidney, you're in a law firm."

Sidney laughed in spite of herself. That had to be an original line. He had probably used it on hysterical females before. But still, it was funny. It made her ashamed. She swiveled in the chair, first one way and then the other. Well, she had to go. Going was what she had come for.

"Well, I've got to go now," Sidney said. "Do you want to smell my hair before I leave?"

"Why do you keep talking about going? Where do you think you're going? I've been waiting for you all day; you can't leave now."

"That's a lie. You weren't even here when I got here."

"I waited until three for lunch."

"What did you have for lunch?"

"Sidney, let's go."

Sidney shook her head. "I don't think I'm pleasant enough for you."

"But I love you; that makes a difference."

"It's a cultural thing, you can't fix your brain."

Terry swiveled in his desk chair. From all the way across the room he noticed that the sofa needed reupholstering. He could tell by the buttons on his phone that people were calling. He just wanted to go home and go back to bed. He wanted Sidney to go with him. Finally he said, "Sidney, do you want me to say I'll marry you?"

"If you were put in solitary confinement, Terry, and given nothing but cockroaches to eat and your only hope for release was to answer this one question, you would never work out why that was the worst thing you ever thought or said in your whole life."

Sidney counted the lights of the floors as the elevator went down. From 39 to 10. After 10 there were no more lights. It was interesting that she could make somebody else as miserable as she was herself. In the old days she used to kill them off in plane crashes, Barrett and Terry. Or they were shot by muggers on the way home from a bar. Occasionally, while she was making their lunch on the Vineyard, they would drown in the Sound. Always she was polite and friendly and always somebody else would kill them dead. Sidney went through the revolving doors and was hit by a blast of hot summer air. It seemed funny to her now that never once in all that time had it ever occurred to her that she could do it herself.

She looked around for a cab. She didn't want to stay out in that heat and sweat in her dress. Everything felt broken. Several taxis passed her by, but she didn't have the energy to raise her hand. She thought maybe she should go back upstairs and say she was sorry for being so strident. What if he really hurt.

What if he wasn't hurt but just hated her.

She couldn't stand it if he hated her. Sidney stood outside of his office building. She had forgotten to give him his key back. She could use that as an excuse for going up there again. But she couldn't go up there again, it was a law firm. Sidney turned slowly toward uptown and began walking. It was too hot to take a taxi after all.

CHAPTER 38

Barrett did not like public displays of affection. Usually he could avoid them. But since he had not seen Sidney for such a long time, and she was clearly making a large concession by coming back, he felt that perhaps the occasion demanded something special. He spent a good deal of time in the afternoon wondering whether he ought to kiss her when they met in the Sign of the Dove at six-fifteen, take her hand, or what. As soon as she had hung up he wanted to go home and prepare himself spiritually for the meeting, but right away it occurred to him that his home was not exclusively his any more. There was no way to be sure she wasn't there. Barrett tried to remember if there was any incriminating evidence in the apartment. He couldn't think of anything but that, of course, was no guarantee. The complications of Sidney's return began to weigh almost immediately.

He was there at exactly six-fifteen. Sidney was not. He sat at a small table in the corner, furious that she had picked Sign of the Dove where she knew they removed the outside walls in summer so that everyone inside was exposed to the stares of people on the street. He ordered a drink, adjusted his collar, which was not too tight, chewed on his drink stick, and made angry faces as the minutes passed. Sidney, even the name seemed suddenly peculiar. The vacation from her had begun to seem permanent. It was amazing how fast a wife could seem superfluous. It had been ghastly, of course, Barrett reminded himself. Every lonely, miserable minute. Ghastly. But it was also strange to cut a piece out of one's married life and then sew up the gap as though nothing had happened. Barrett ordered another drink. Perhaps they could make it up by talking to each other a lot, he thought.

Sidney came in like a summer breeze from the ocean. She streamed in all silk and straw and pale colors. She had the ability to look as though she was never too warm and hadn't a working pore anywhere. Dramatic was how she looked, and people turned for a better view of her. Barrett raised his hand, and Sidney approached. He noted the golden hair, now a little longer, the perfect pink fingernails, the blue eye shadow, and what had to be the most expensive pair of sandals in the city. Barrett did not remember the shoes. He was still debating about kissing her when she sat down with some help from the waiter. She did not attempt to kiss or touch him. Barrett wished he had gone home and changed his clothes.

"Well," Sidney said. The waiter hovered until she ordered a drink.

"You look marvelous," Barrett said. "Welcome home." It felt a bit odd to say the words, but he thought he should, especially since she had gone to so much trouble. He was mad; he couldn't help it.

"Thank you." She sat for a moment and looked at him.

Barrett had the feeling that she didn't remember what he looked like either. He also had the feeling that she had been hiding somewhere all this time while he waited, watching him be nervous. It was not like Sidney to get done up like that without being told to. He didn't know what to think of it. She seemed to be finished looking at him and started speaking as soon as the waiter brought her a drink and went away. Barrett didn't even have time to ask her what the Vineyard looked like, or what she had done for the last nearly four weeks now. Or who was there, or anything. Although these things occurred to him later.

"First of all, Barrett," Sidney said, "as you may have guessed, I want a divorce."

Barrett laughed nervously. "You didn't get all dressed up to tell me that, did you?" He smiled, tried to be a lizard but failed. Sidney had this peculiar, almost hateful look on her face. "I mean you really look nice."

She took a sip of her drink and looked around. Barrett felt that he was being given a cue of some sort but didn't know what it was. He remembered the day she bought that dress—in the middle of winter, to cheer her up, she said. He even remembered the price. Thinking of that day made him feel that it would be all right. She had tried it on for him, pleased that she had been able to choose something herself. And afterward they started fooling around, pretended they were in a resort somewhere and had just met. They were half undressed when Terry arrived to take them out to dinner.

"I like that dress," Barrett said finally. He began to feel excited at the prospect of taking it off.

"Naturally, I'd like to do it as soon as possible," Sidney said.

"Let's go home," Barrett said.

"For once you're going to take me seriously, Barrett."

"I'm taking you very seriously." He looked around quickly, then said, "Let's go home. We can talk about it later."

"Barrett, I'm not going home with you. I just wanted to tell you what we're going to do. We're going to make a trade."

"Sidney," Barrett said quickly. "I forgive you for leaving me like that, and embarrassing me in front of everybody. I know that Garth forgives you too. Now don't say anything you'll be sorry about. Let's forget it, okay . . . no, let's not forget it. Let's talk it out and then let's forget it. But let's not do it in public, all right?"

"I'll leave the apartment without taking a thing. I've taken what was in the household account, but I'll let you have the rest of the money. I want the house, of course. But you can have the furniture in it. That's all I want, just the house. Since it isn't even paid for, I don't see how you could object."

"Sidney, I won't listen to you talk that way, not even as a joke. It's not funny," Barrett whined.

"Barrett, I remember more than once you thought it extremely amusing to throw me out and divide the property. I must say I am being more fair than you were. And I am not joking."

"Yes, you are. You're joking. You're just overreacting to this whole situation."

"Why didn't you call me when I left? You didn't even call me after eight years of marriage to see if I was all right. You never asked me to come back. Not a phone call, Barrett. And you think I'm coming back. You must be crazy."

"Shh, Sidney." Barrett looked around again. It was getting crowded, and the people made him nervous. "I'm sorry I didn't call you, but I knew you were all right. Terry told me."

"He did, did he? Well, I think it was pretty low of you to send him. What kind of man sends his lawyer after his wife? You're less afraid of flying than he is."

"For Christ's sake, Sidney. Will you stop this. I'm sorry it all happened, but you're the one who left me. How do you think I felt about it?"

Sidney leaned over the table. "I'm not going to listen to your miserable-and-abused act, Barrett. I'm through with hearing how hard your life has been, how you struggled and suffered against overwhelming odds—"

"Sidney, please."

"I've decided I'm not going to make a fuss. I just want the house and a divorce. If you agree to that, I won't make any trouble for you. You can't buy any magazine. Get that straight in your head right off. But if you do what I tell you, you can stay at IT with your precious life style intact."

Barrett's jaw tightened with fury. For a moment he forgot where he was. "Who do you think you are, threatening me like that after everything I've done for you?" Barrett shook his head. "God, my own wife a viper. That's the worst. My house, my wife, my job even. You don't leave much, do you?" She had taken off her hat and was fanning herself with it gently. She looked to him as though she were enjoying herself, and that infuriated him. "Everything you are you owe to me," he said.

"I'm glad I can't say the same thing about you," Sidney said.

She stood up and leaned over the table so that he could see the tiny pink bow on her bra. "In a few days you'll get some papers to sign, and a ticket to the fastest divorce on the market. Did you think I wouldn't find out about what you did in Providence, Barrett? Did you really think your wife was so stupid she wouldn't care? Let me tell you, Barrett, that's forgery. They send people to jail for that. I swear to God, if you don't do everything I tell you, I won't hesitate to send you to jail."

"Now, Sidney. Damn it, you sit down. You're not being fair. Christ."

Sidney had replaced her hat and was now threading her way past the tables toward the door. Barrett wanted to yell at her to stop, but he couldn't. "Shit," he said. He sat for one minute muttering to himself and then pulled his money out. Shit, he didn't have anything smaller than a ten. Shit, he realized that he didn't know where to reach her. He left the ten on the table, deciding that it was more important not to let her get away. She might do anything, even call a lawyer.

CHAPTER 39

Barrett got outside of the restaurant and looked up and down the street. The Sign of the Dove is on a corner; their building was on the other side of the street. The entrance of their building was not on the avenue but on the side street part way down the block. Barrett stood on the corner of Third Avenue in despair. He didn't see her going down or going up. He was poised to run, to get her before she got away, but she got away. Then as he turned once more toward their building he thought he saw the edge of Sidney's dress going round in the revolving door.

He made a little hop for joy. He knew she couldn't do it. He just knew she couldn't. He walked slowly across the street. Yes, she had gone home; she had to, there was no place else to go, after all. He slowly went around the revolving door. He didn't want to catch Sidney waiting for the elevator. He didn't want to catch Sidney with her key in the door. He wanted her to be waiting for him inside the apartment, at home where she belonged.

Even though he saw her, he wasn't exactly sure it was she. He was nervous. He thought perhaps he might go and have a drink somewhere before facing her again, but he knew he couldn't do that. He had to see her now, right now. He got in the elevator and went to their floor. He turned the key in the lock, went into the apartment calling her name. No answer. He walked around looking for her, knowing even as he looked in the kitchen, in the bedroom, in the bathroom even, that she wasn't there. He didn't ring the doorman to ask if she had come in though he considered it for a moment. He knew it was futile. If she had come in, she would be there. God, Sidney was a bitch. God, he couldn't believe what a bitch he had married. Christ, what could he do. She had him over a barrel; how could he explain.

Barrett sat on the bed in an agony of indecision. Should he go up to the Vineyard and talk to her. Should he just ignore the outburst (how could he ignore it). Barrett looked at the phone. He thought of calling Terry. He couldn't call Terry because Terry was no longer a friend. Barrett was still debating about calling Terry when he was distracted by the door of one of Sidney's closets that was partly open. He went over to close it and saw that it was empty, that in fact all of them were empty. She had taken his luggage, he thought. "My God." She really meant it.

Quickly he went to the phone and dialed Lespedeza's number. He didn't even know he had made a decision until it was already made. When she answered, he told her to come over right away.

"Do you want to make a chili omelette?" Lespedeza asked. "Do you have any eggs? I'll bring the chilis. I just bought some today. Of course I have to do contrology first. I'll be over about eight, okay?"

"Come now," Barrett yelled. "I have to talk to you."

"All right. All right. You don't have to shout. I hear very well on regular speaking. Do you want me to bring the chilis or not bring the chilis?"

"I don't care about the fucking chilis. Just take a taxi."

It took Lespedeza fifteen minutes to get there. During that time Barrett cursed everything he could think of. He examined every closet, every cupboard in the apartment. He couldn't believe she had taken the silver. He paced and swore and put his face into the pillows. There was no harm done, he kept telling himself. She was already gone, he didn't even have to adjust to that. There was nothing she could do (she wouldn't do it); it would all be the same as before. Please let it be the same as before. He didn't want any dumb magazine anyway. He made faces into the mirror. Finally he took a shower and by the time Lespedeza arrived he felt better. He was going to divorce her, that's what. He was going to be free.

"Clover, my precious Clover," he said, leading Lespedeza into the living room. "I'm glad you could make it."

"What's the matter, Barrett, something's wrong."

"Well, yes and no." Barrett got halfway into the living room and embraced Lespedeza. Over her shoulder he noticed that the glove drawer in the hall was open and there was one glove hanging halfway out. He released her and went to replace the glove in the drawer and close it. It amused him that Sidney had opened the drawer and then forgotten to take her gloves. Sidney was usually so careful and organized. He brought Lespedeza a Pernod and himself a scotch. She was still standing there, so he hugged her again.

"I think it's time for growth and development, Clov," Barrett said. "You've been a researcher too long. That's what I've been thinking about today. It's time for you to stop carrying that knapsack around and sitting with the untitled. You've got to grow and advance."

"Yech! What is this?" Lespedeza had tasted her Pernod.

"That's what I mean. We have to try new things, be open to change. That's Pernod. P-e-r-n-o-d, anise liqueur. Very good, isn't it?"

"I happen to like checking facts," Lespedeza said somewhat testily.

"Yes, but it would be better for you to collect them and arrange them and let somebody else check them, wouldn't it? Now, Clover, you have watched copy made and remade. Nobody knows better than you how it's done. Now is the time to start doing it yourself. Advance yourself out of the copy department and maybe —just maybe—you could become a star.

"Look, I've seen your memos. I know you've been doing head-lines and captions and things. Look, I know how you think. You're a natural. It's my judgment that you absolutely have the ability."

"I don't really think I like this." Lespedeza put her drink down.

"Take one more sip. It's an acquired taste."

"I don't see you drinking it. Look at how cloudy it is."

"Just because I never acquired the taste doesn't mean it isn't a worth-while taste to have. Now about your first assignment. . . ."

"I don't want to, Barrett. I really don't. I'd do it if I could. But—"

Barrett was sitting on the tufted leather sofa. He was thinking that he would have to tell Lespedeza about Sidney. How he was going to have to divorce Sidney. Poor Sidney, he thought, what was she going to do without him to look after her.

Lespedeza was sitting on the floor in front of him. She was tell-ing him about how bad it was when a person started having ambi-tion. "It ruins you for life," she said. "I just want to be free, you know, and happy like I am now."

"Would you be happy if you didn't work at IT?" Barrett asked.

"Of course not. I—"

"Well, then you're going to have to try writing. You see, Muriel has made up some kind of work record for everyone in her depart-ment. She's very mad. And I'm afraid she's being very unpleasant. She seems to have something against you. Now, if you don't leave her department, I don't know how much longer I can defend you. Muriel is perfectly capable of going over my head to Garth. And you know what a terrible stink it all would make."

Lespedeza got up and deposited herself in Barrett's lap. She tried to hide in his shoulder. Barrett found it very appealing; it made him feel optimistic after all.

"Please, Barrett, I can't start looking for another job now. I can't. Please, Barrett, I don't want to go; I like it the way it is. Can't you do something?"

"I have a very easy assignment for you. I'll help you with the questions and the writing and everything. Come on, sweetheart. I know you can do it."

"Do I have to, Barrett; do I really have to?" Lespedeza was whining like a ten-year-old.

Barrett thought he even detected a tear. His shoulder was warm and, he thought, wet. He kissed her on the neck, twisted his fingers in her long pale hair. "I'm afraid it's the only way, my love." She wore a short skirt and her bare legs dangled over his. He stroked her thighs.

Lespedeza wanted to stay right there and lie on the floor in what was left of the afternoon sun. She pulled his shirt out of his trousers and tried to get him to come down on the floor with her. But Barrett was afraid that even that high up someone might see them. He led her into the bedroom. As they went through the hall, Barrett looked down and noticed another of Sidney's gloves that must have been kicked out of sight. As he leaned over to pick it up he thought that Lespedeza was right about one thing. Ambition could ruin a person's judgment. Why hadn't he seen before that *Inside Track* was a far, far better place to be than a dumb little local paper whose time was clearly past.